DEADLY CARGO

STEVEN J TAYLOR

SEVERED PRESS
HOBART TASMANIA

DEADLY CARGO

WWW.SEVEREDPRESS.COM

ISBN: 978-1-922551-22-1

For Patrick and Thomas

1

The Grand International Hotel was famed for having one of, if not the very best, breakfast buffets of any of the five-star hotels in not only Jakarta, but perhaps the whole of Indonesia itself. Top chefs plied their trade passionately in the kitchen over scalding hot fry pans and bubbling pots. Spices scented the air colourfully as they were delicately applied to the various hand-crafted dishes that adorned the tables of the main dining area. All the traditional Indonesian breakfast dishes were here, from Bubur Ayam to Katupat Kandangan, any Indonesian plate you could imagine was served here with the highest quality ingredients and prepared by the region's leading chefs. And Matt Sanders wanted nothing of it, despite the hunger that crawled in his stomach.

"I'm a fish out of water" he mumbled quietly to himself as he rubbed his unshaven cheek with an open hand and surveyed the platters before him. Rices of various colour, skewers of what appeared to be fish covered in a green sauce, orange shredded chicken, fried eggs in coconut milk and who knew what else sat beautifully presented on plates and serving trays across the various tables on the buffet.

"Can't a man just get some simple eggs on toast?" Sanders grumbled.

But it was not just the food that made Sanders feel out of place, it was the clientele as well. All around businessmen, both local and international, fluttered in groups between the tables and the buffet, making observations about how this or that would affect the market price of whatever local product they were trading in. They all wore suits with crisply ironed shirts, perfectly knotted neckties and shiny black shoes. They all seemed to walk with an air of arrogance as if born to it, and those who bothered to even acknowledge Sanders' existence did little to hide the condescension in their eyes.

"A stranger in a strange land," Sanders muttered again as he looked down at his own clothes. He had been told to dress formally, but it was hard to dress to a code that you owned no clothes for. He had chosen his best polo shirt for the occasion. Plain navy blue, though the colour was starting to fade a little. When it came to pants, he had had to make the tough decision of jeans or shorts. He chose shorts, and the sight of his tanned, hairy legs drew more than one derisive look from a passer-by as though this sight of his bare legs was a blight on the ambiance of the room. He had chosen boots to match his attire, but the only ones he had on hand were scuffed around the edges.

"You look a little lost," a female voice said beside him, interrupting his thoughts.

He turned, drawn by the warm tone and familiar accent to see a beautiful, slim blonde woman standing beside him. Her blue eyes and half smile bore both warmth and humour, and he found himself immediately attracted to her. Her hair was straight, parted in the middle with not a single hair out of place. She wore a silk shirt and tight skirt, and despite wearing heels, she only stood as high as his shoulder. Not surprising, as he was quite tall and broad.

"Yeah," he said in reply, "you could say that."

"Ah, a fellow Australian. I thought as much. Did you know you've been staring at the food for five minutes now? Aren't you hungry?"

Sanders reddened. "I'm bloody starving, but I have no idea what any of this food is. I could kill for a simple plate of Vegemite on toast right now."

The blonde snorted a small laugh. "Me too, actually. There's none of that, but there is a continental breakfast section over there where you could get toast and jam and scrambled eggs with bacon."

"Are you serious?"

"Absolutely," she said, nodding her head towards another section of the buffet area. "Come, I'll show you."

Sanders followed her, resisting the temptation to slide his eyes down and check out her rear end, as she wove her way through the suited men. When Sanders saw the continental buffet, it was like an oasis in the desert. Scrambled eggs, fried eggs, poached eggs and omelettes. Sides of fried bacon, mushrooms, hash browns, small pork sausages and boiled spinach. White bread, wholemeal bread, sourdough, rye and more. Danishes, donuts, muffins and cinnamon rolls. It was a treasure trove of breakfast delights.

At the urging of his aching stomach, Sanders strode forward and began filling a plate high with fried foods before filling a mug with coffee. It was only as he turned to find a seat did he realise the gorgeous blond had disappeared and he had not even so much as thanked her. Quietly, he cursed himself, not just for failing to thank her but also for letting her get away.

But with a quick look over the seated area he spotted her at a small two-seater table near the window. He wound his way between the tables and placed his plate and coffee on the table in the place opposite her and sat down. She looked up and smiled.

"I wanted to catch you to say thanks," he said. "You may very well have saved my life back there."

"Oh, I highly doubt your situation was that desperate."

"Near enough," he said. He picked up a hash brown with his hands and bit in in half. She watched him eat, a bemused look on her face. He swallowed and put the rest of the hash brown in his mouth, suddenly realising how awkward the scene was. As self-awareness dawned on him, he looked out the window at the sprawling mass of the city below him. The city stretched as far as he could see, disappearing into a dense haze. Sanders had rarely travelled, and big cities made him uncomfortable. The noise of bustling and angry traffic, the dirty air wickedly smelly from the stench of vehicle exhaust fumes, the claustrophobia from having so many people about him, the rubbish that nobody picked up and the overall unnaturalness of the walls of glass, steel and concrete everywhere. He was a country boy by heart, and nature is where he belonged.

He swallowed the potato mashed in his mouth and turned to see she was still watching him. He smiled. "Nice view from here," he said, internally admonishing himself for such a lame line.

She nodded her head. "If you like that sort of thing." She reached a hand across the table. "My name's Jess O'Mara, by the way."

Sanders stared at her hand, momentarily dumbfounded. "Shit, sorry," he said, wiping his hand on his pants to clean it, before taking her hand and shaking it. "I'm Matt Sanders." Her skin was soft, but her hand had strength and her handshake steady and business like. He withdrew his hand and scooped up a forkful of scrambled eggs.

"If you don't mind me saying this, Matt, you are more than a little bit out of place here."

"You can say that again," Sanders remarked, his mouth full of food. "I'm certainly not one of these hoity-toity business types."

"Then I hope you won't mind me asking why it is you are here?"

Sanders swallowed the eggs, stabbed his fork into a sausage and took a bite from the end of it. "To be honest," he said, again with a mouth full of food, "I don't really know. I'm here for a job. Some rich fella waved some cash my way and here I am."

Her smile froze and her eyes narrowed. "What job?"

He swallowed his mouthful of sausage and took another bite before continuing. "Don't really know to be honest. I was told everything would be explained when I got here, though looking at this crowd in here, I'm starting to think that this isn't the kind of job I would want."

At the sound of a throat being cleared, Sanders looked up to see a man standing over him with two mugs in his hands. He was a medium height man with grey tinged hair. He was reasonably slim, but had a small pot belly. His skin was pale, and he had the look of an academic who spent too much time in the library and not enough in the great outdoors. He was dressed in a simple brown suit. The knot of his tie was ungainly, and there were creases in his shirt. There was also a hint of hostility in his brown eyes.

"Simon, I'm glad you're back. Simon, this is Matt Sanders. Matt, this is Simon Dower. Matt was just telling me an interesting story."

Dower placed one mug down in front of her and she blew the steam away gently. Dower then turned back to Sanders with one eyebrow raised.

"Interesting? How so?" he asked. Sanders noted from the accent that Dower was also Australian.

"He's come here for a job he knows nothing about."

Dower's eyes flicked to hers and she gave a subtle nod of her head. His mouth tightened and he placed his own mug on the table before retrieving a seat from another table to join them.

"That is interesting," Dower agreed. "What is it you do for a living, Mr Sanders?"

Sanders stopped chewing and eyed them both. He was not used to dealing with people in the business world, but surely this was not their normal behaviour. He swallowed the food in his mouth.

"I'm a ranger. I work at Kakadu National Park."

Dower sat back in his chair and crossed his arms. He looked past Sanders to the view of the city and beyond.

"Is there a particular duty you are in charge of at Kakadu?" O'Mara asked.

"Mostly I monitor crocodile movements to ensure they stay away from the tourist hotspots, and if any do happen to stray that way, it's my job to move them back." Sanders put his fork down on his plate and cleared his throat. "Look, I feel like you two are in on something here. You mind telling me what's up?"

"What's up?" Dower parroted, pulling his eyes away from the cityscape and again focusing them on Sanders. "What's up is we've been called to Jakarta for a mystery job, just like you."

Sanders shifted in his seat, suddenly feeling uncomfortable.

"Is that so? Well, what is it that you two do?"

They again exchanged a quick glance.

"Well," Dower continued, "Jess here is a vet, and I'm a lecturer at the University of Western Australia. I teach natural sciences."

"Okay," Sanders said, eyes passing from one to the other of them, "do you think all of our mystery jobs might be related?"

"Could be," Dower answered, his voice drifting off as his eyes once again turned to study the view.

Sanders watched him a moment then turned to O'Mara. Her eyes had also taken a distant, and somewhat worried, hue as she stared at the steaming mug before her. Sanders frowned, confused at how a job could require a ranger, a vet and a university lecturer when he noticed an Asian man approach their table and clap his hands together loudly.

"Ah, here you all are. I take it you have all met then?"

The man now before them was short, with a round face and a small pencil moustache adorning his top lip. He had a crooked mouth, which made his smile seem lopsided and appearing somewhat like a sneer. His nails, moustache and hair were well manicured, and he was suited neat and clean. He wore bright colours, his jacket gleaming like gold while underneath he had a pressed bright pink shirt with an extra-large winged collar and a black tie. To Sanders, he appeared like a clown, but for any young person who frequented the local hotspots and hottest bars, he was wearing the height of modern fashion.

Dower turned and spoke for the group.

"We have. And you are?"

"Mr Cheong. I am here as your organiser and your local liaison. Come, I have the boardroom over there booked and we are just about to speak with our employer via video link."

"Hold on," Sanders said, "can we get an explanation of what's happening first?"

"Everything will be explained in time, Mr Sanders. But first, you must all please come this way for the video call."

Dower and O'Mara stood up and followed Mr Cheong's directions. Sanders looked down at his plate before him, still piled high with fried food. His stomach growled hungrily. "I haven't finished eating yet."

Mr Cheong blinked slowly and appeared to be fighting the urge to roll his eyes. He licked his lips and then sighed audibly. "I suppose you could bring your plate along with you then."

"Beaut," Sanders said. He stood, scooping up his plate in one hand and his coffee in the other. He followed Cheong past the other diners, who looked up at the odd pairing with quizzical looks as they walked by, and down a passage to a small boardroom. As they arrived, Sanders saw Dower and O'Mara standing, mouths agape, just beyond the doorway. As he entered, Sanders turned to see what had surprised the others so. As he turned, his face lit up. The face projected on the wall was one he recognised instantly.

"Strewth," Sanders exclaimed. "Would you look at that? It's Connie! Our employer is Connie."

Dower and O'Mara turned to Sanders with their mouths still agape. Dower clenched his eyes shut and shook his head.

"Wait a minute," Dower said, re-opening his eyes to focus on Sanders. "Do you know Conrad Higson?"

"Well, yeah. Sort of."

"Sort of?" Dower's brow crinkled and he shared a look with O'Mara before turning back. "Do you know who Conrad Higson is? What he does?"

"Not really," Sanders replied, feeling suddenly self-conscious.

"Then how do you know him?" O'Mara asked.

"I gave him a guided tour of Kakadu one time. Good bloke. Generous tipper. Though a bit funny, you know?"

"A bit funny how?"

"Oh, he just kept asking about bunyips and stuff." Sanders smiled, then snorted and rolled his eyes. "Bunyips, bunyips, bunyips. As if we'd find one swimming around the waterholes of Kakadu. Bunyips," he said again and laughed.

Dower and O'Mara shared another glance and then sat at the table. Dower pursed his lips and drummed his fingers on the table, he eyes shifting from Sanders to the image of Conrad Higson, and back again.

Behind Sanders, Mr Cheong quietly squeezed past and approached a laptop sitting at the head of the table.

Sanders studied everyone's faces and his smile suddenly dropped.

"What happened? Why has everyone suddenly become so serious?"

"This man you know as 'Connie'," Dower began, "is Conrad Higson. He's *the* Higson of Higson Mining."

Sanders glanced around the room, sensing he was missing something important. He could not place what it was though.

"And?"

Dower's look was bordering on exasperation. "And he's a mining mogul. He's one of the richest men in Australia. Sanders, this guy is a billionaire."

Sanders turned to look up at the image of Higson projected on the wall. He had suspected the man had some wealth behind him when they had previously met. Connie had expensive tastes, and Sanders had been impressed at how easily and freely Conrad had spent his money. He even remembered drinking at a bar with Conrad afterwards, when Conrad shared a bottle of Scotch Whiskey that cost more per glass than Sanders earned in a week. But a billionaire? Sanders had long thought meeting people that rich was well beyond his reach.

Sanders watched as Dower started doing his 'stare in the distance at nothing' thing again. Sanders picked up his fork and shovelled scrambled eggs into his mouth. He was still missing something here and he knew it.

"Ok," Sanders said, spitting a wad of scrambled egg onto the middle of the table as he spoke, "so he's rich. That's why he's flown us to Indonesia and lodged us in this fancy pants hotel. That surely can't be a surprise to you all, can it?"

"No," Dower answered distantly, "it's not that."

Sanders swallowed the egg and stared at Dower, waiting for him to elaborate. But when Dower only continued to stare blankly at the wall, Sanders turned to O'Mara and raised a questioning eyebrow. She glanced quickly at Dower, before leaning forward conspiratorially.

"The thing is," she started cautiously, "Higson is also famous for one other thing. He has an obsession with cryptids."

Sanders frowned. "Cryptids? What is that? A type of flower?"

"It could be," Dower cut in, suddenly back in the room and focusing on the present. "Cryptids are a type of creature whose existence is claimed, but not scientifically proven. Think Bigfoot, the Loch Ness Monster, that sort of thing,"

"And bunyips," Sanders added.

"And bunyips," O'Mara agreed.

Sanders shovelled more eggs into his mouth. Events were starting to become clearer by the moment.

"Higson recently bought an extensive piece of land just south of Perth," Dower continued. "The rumour doing the rounds is he plans to build a zoo there. When questioned by the press about why Perth needs another zoo, do you know what his answer was?"

Sanders opened his mouth to answer, but then closed it as it occurred to him that Dower may have been asking a rhetorical question.

"He said," Dower continued, "and I quote, 'this will be a different kind of zoo'. Now what do you suppose he meant by that?"

Sanders stabbed another sausage with his fork and bit off a hunk to chew. He expected it was another rhetorical question but as Dower stared at him questioningly, he realised it was not.

"We're here to catch one of those crypt-things for his zoo, aren't we?" Sanders asked.

"Very good," boomed a deep voice across the room. Sanders jumped, then turned to see the image of Conrad Higson on the wall was no longer a static image, but a live feed from a camera. Mr Cheong dashed forward and started tapping on the computer, and a smaller bar on screen appeared showing the volume of the feed was being decreased.

"Connie, you never told me you were a billionaire, you sly old bugger," remarked Sanders.

Mr Cheong looked up from the computer to give Sanders a sharp look, but behind him Higson only laughed. Higson was one of those men whose age was difficult to guess based purely on appearance. While on one hand his face bore the signs of aging, from the deep crow's feet to the sides of his eyes, skin that was marked by years of exposure to the sun, eyes that bore a deep wisdom and hair that was peppered with greys, all suggesting he was quite senior in his years. But on the other hand, his very being was spritely and energetic, curious and adventurous, anything but a man who was past his best years.

"Matt, it's good to see you again. How is little Ravager going?"

"He's good, mate, though he still wants to tackle crocs on his own. Had to leave him at a mate's place to come here just to keep him out of trouble."

As Higson laughed again, Sanders became aware of the stares in the room directed his way. He turned and shrugged. "Ravager is my dog. Don't worry, he's not as vicious as he sounds. Unless you're a croc, that is."

"Ah, and I see we have Professor Dower and Doctor O'Mara in the room. How are you both? I trust the trip and hotel have been comfortable for you both?"

Both Dower and O'Mara nodded. Sanders glanced their way curiously. They both seemed shellshocked.

"Very good. Well, I did want to start proceedings today with an apology as unfortunately I was not able to come in person to Jakarta myself. It seems our friends in the Indonesian government may have caught wind of my plans here and are denying me entry into the country. But never you mind that, just leave all the legal wrangling to me and my team and you worry about your job over there.

"Now, as you have all correctly deduced, I have pulled you together for the specific purpose of capturing a cryptid on the island of Java. You will, of course, be getting help from a number of locals in the area, which will be arranged through Kenny here," Mr Cheong gave a short, half smile, "but for all practical purposes, you three will provide the leadership and take control of the mission.

"Matt Sanders, you may know, is a ranger at Kakadu National Park and is one of the bravest and most extraordinary people you are likely to meet. I had him take me on a tour to some of the deepest parts of the park, well beyond where tourists are usually allowed to dwell. It was a dangerous and wild part of Kakadu. It was there I watched with sheer disbelief as Matt jumped into crocodile infested waters to pull Ravager to safety. The boldness of the rescue, the instinct and reading of the crocodile behaviour around him, plus his ability to anticipate their moves, was truly something to behold. He is exactly the type of man we need to guide a capture like this.

"And Professor Dower. I have read many of your papers hypothesizing the biology of cryptids and their genetic history. I have read many papers by many authors in the field, but I find yours by far the most convincing and enjoyable. I trust you to be the expert on the creature when you do find it.

"And finally Doctor Jess O'Mara. Your reputation as a vet is nothing but impeccable. I have high expectations of you to work alongside Matt and Professor Dower here to ensure the diet and the health of this cryptid, when we do have it, is maintained at the highest level."

O'Mara nodded and gave a half smile in return. Higson was momentarily distracted as his mobile phone buzzed. He picked it up and studied it a moment before looking back at the screen.

"Sorry, where was I?"

"I think, Mr Higson, you were about to tell us what the cryptid you want us to catch is," Mr Cheong said.

"Ah yes, thanks, Kenny. The cryptid I want you to capture is the Sipatahunan Cave Horse Serpent. I take it you know of this creature, Professor Dower?"

Dower cleared his throat and straightened in his chair. He glanced about the room and turned to the screen.

"Yes, I know a little of it. Located in the Bogor region, which is not far from here. The Horse Serpent looks exactly like the name suggests. It has the head and body of a horse, but one crossed with a serpent."

"Sounds like a dragon, but without the wings," Sanders added.

"A bit. Cynics have speculated that it is probably just an extraordinarily large monitor lizard, while those with more fanciful ideals have suggested the existence of a dinosaur."

Sanders scoffed, but as all eyes turned, he reddened slightly before motioning for Dower to continue.

"The dinosaur that best resembles the descriptions is the Iguanodon, a dinosaur that was supposedly extinct some ninety-four million years ago. You are right to scoff, Sanders, the idea that one lone dinosaur has somehow survived that long past extinction is more than fantastical. But let's not forget that the Loch Ness Monster in almost every picture and every account resembles a plesiosaur, another dinosaur thought long extinct."

Sanders glanced at the screen then looked down at his plate. He scooped up another forkful of scrambled eggs into his mouth and turned it over slowly. Dower continued.

"An expedition to find the Serpent Horse was launched many years ago, but the group returned with no evidence other than the claimed sighting of footprints in the cave."

"Sorry," Higson interrupted, "but I may have to correct you a little there, Professor Dower. The official story was, as you say, that the team returned having seen signs only, but abandoned their efforts fearing the cave was about to be flooded. But my researchers have dug deep on this one, and there is another story doing the rounds.

"The supposed true story was that the team never came out alive. They were never seen again. A while later, the cave did flood, and when it did, the remains of the team were washed out and found by local villagers. The bodies were broken, torn and partially devoured. The official release was invented to stop local panic and to keep curious foreigners like me out of the country."

"Well, that kills the Iguanodon theory then."

"Why's that?" asked Sanders.

"Iguanodons were herbivores."

"This mission," O'Mara cut in, speaking for the first time, "it sounds a little dangerous."

"It may well be," Higson answered, conceding the point, "but Kenny here is consulting with the best in local helpers. Your safety is a top priority here and Kenny has assured me your safety is as close to guaranteed as we can make it. Are you having doubts about proceeding, Doctor O'Mara?"

"I…" she stammered, before glancing at Dower.

Sensing her look, he turned to her. "I'm definitely going. If this thing is for real, it would make headlines all over the world. This is far too exciting to miss."

"Me too," Sanders added, though she took no notice of him.

"Doctor O'Mara, if you're having doubts and want to pull out, we need to know now so Kenny can make some quick, alternative arrangements," Higson said.

O'Mara and Dower stared at each other a moment and he gave her a slight nod. She frowned slightly, before turning back to the image of Higson on the wall.

"No," she began, "it's ok. I'll join the expedition."

"Good, good," Higson said, seemingly pleased. "Now I am afraid at this point I will have to leave you as I have a meeting with some of my lawyers. I will leave you in the capable hands of Kenny here for now. He has organised transport south to Bogor and with luck it won't be long before I am in the country to greet you all properly. Thanks, everyone."

Everyone thanked and farewelled Higson, but Mr Cheong killed the link before they had properly said goodbye.

"Ok," he said, closing the laptop in front of him. "I have organised two trucks to take us to Bogor. They are waiting downstairs for us now. You will need to go back to your rooms and pack before meeting me in the lobby. I have documentation for you all to read on the way and I'd like to get going soon. Any questions?"

Sanders raised his hand. Cheong looked at him and his eyes narrowed.

"Yes, Mr Sanders?"

"Do I have time to go back for seconds, Kenny?"

Cheong's eyes narrowed even further.

"Only if you hurry; I want to leave in the next half hour and I won't wait around if you are late. And please, it's Mr Cheong to you. Only the boss calls me Kenny. Understood?"

Sanders studied Cheong a minute, his own eyes narrowing as he did.

"Sure thing, Kenny," he answered.

2

Despite Cheong's low expectations for him, it was Sanders who appeared first in the lobby.

"Heya, Kenny," Sanders yelled, much to Cheong's chagrin, and his voice echoed throughout the marble lined entrance. Cheong was still dressed immaculately in his suit. Sanders picked up his bag from the porter's trolly and walked over to greet him. Cheong rolled his eyes and directed Sanders to the front desk to check out of the room while he tipped the dumbfounded porter, before guiding Sanders outside.

The two trucks were parked on the opposite side of the street and were causing chaos on the road behind them as traffic merged amid a torrent of honking and shouting. The two trucks were green in colour, consisting of a large cab and tray covered by a cloth draped over raised rails.

"Are those ex-military cargo trucks?" Sanders asked over the din.

"Yes, decommissioned some time back, but still serviceable enough to get us and our equipment to where we need to go."

Sanders stared at the trucks, wondering what equipment Cheong had deemed necessary for the job ahead. When catching and moving crocodiles, Sanders did not need two truckloads of equipment, just a strong dinghy and some rope. Two trucks did feel like overkill.

"Ah, here are the others now," Cheong said and Sanders turned to look.

Jess O'Mara had taken the opportunity to change in the short break since the meeting. Gone was the iron shirt, skirt and heels to be replaced by a loose-fitting apricot coloured t-shirt with tan shorts and sneakers.

"Damn," Sanders remarked, "she looks great dressed casually as well."

Cheong turned and looked at him with one eyebrow raised, but said nothing. As they greeted each other once more, Sanders offered to carry O'Mara's bag for her.

"No need," she said, turning to tip the porter before raising a handle from the top of her suitcase, "mine has wheels."

As they crossed the road, Sanders had to fight the urge to cover his ears to block out the cacophony of noise from the angry traffic. He turned to comment as much to Dower, and noticed that Dower was already producing pronounced sweat stains under the arms on his shirt.

"Not used to dealing with the heat, mate?" Sanders asked.

"It's not the heat that bothers me," Dower replied, "it's the humidity. It must be at least eighty percent here."

"Bah," Sanders said, waving him away, "humidity I can deal with. I'm used to that from back home. It's the noise and pollution in the air that bothers me."

"Never been much of a city person?"

"I guess you could say that. I don't see the appeal of it personally. I mean, look at this place. It's all steel and concrete and glass, and it's completely crowded. Who'd want to live here?"

"Sometimes it's not a matter of want, but rather need." At the confused look from Sanders, Dower decided to elaborate. "In countries like this, big cities are where the wealth and the jobs are. People are forced to leave their rural backgrounds and come to cities like this just to find work. It's why cities grow at a much higher rate than small towns."

"Right," Sanders said in response, though with little conviction behind it.

On the opposite side of the road, Sanders spotted the two drivers smoking and chatting up a local girl. Cheong yelled something in Indonesian to them and, judging from the hostile looks he received in return, the words were far from polite. They stamped out their cigarettes on the ground and mounted the cabs. The girl walked on. She seemed to be relieved to be freed from their attentions.

"Please, if you could all place your bags in the back of the truck and get inside the cabs we will be on our way."

At the rear of the second truck, Sanders got a glimpse under the tarpaulin for the first time. The truck held some sort of large cage. The frame was heavily reinforced on all sides, and glinted with a steel polish. The bars were thick and black, and they looked strong enough to hold a four-hundred-pound gorilla.

Sanders hurled his pack in the back and turned to offer his help to O'Mara. This time she assented, much to his pleasure. He hefted her bag up over the tail gate and into the back and was about to turn and follow her when his attention was drawn by Dower.

"Do you mind?" Dower asked, red faced as he pushed his bag forward.

"Sure," Sanders muttered, lifting Dower's bag and tossing it in with little care. Pushing past Dower, Sanders skipped ahead to reach the truck before O'Mara and opened the cab door for her.

"Why thank you," she said, and set about climbing up. He watched her climb, his eyes drifting down to her round but tight rear end. He resisted the urge to reach out and help her by putting his hand there and pushing.

"Thanks," Dower said as he passed by Sanders and climbed into the cab behind her. Sanders grimaced. Dower's rear was far less appealing to his eye so he looked away, only to find Cheong grinning at him.

Once Dower was safely in the cab, Sanders slammed the door and walked to the first truck. Cheong had already seated himself in the centre of the cab next to the driver as Sanders hauled himself up.

"Looks like it's me and you for the trip, Kenny," he said, slapping Cheong on the shoulder before closing the door.

"As I said before," Cheong said as he looked disdainfully at the spot where Sanders had slapped him as though he had left a handful of germs where he had touched, "you call me Mr Cheong."

"I hear you barking, big dog," Sanders said, drawing yet another frown from Cheong.

"You do know, Mr Sanders, that Mr Dower and Miss O'Mara are a couple, don't you? Or hadn't you noticed?"

Sanders looked at Cheong, tilting his head slightly to the side as he tried to read him.

"Bullshit," Sanders said at last. "She's at least ten years younger than him and way out of his league. No chance they're a couple."

Cheong gave a derisive snort. Sanders leaned forward to get a view of the truck behind them in the side mirror. He could not see much, only half of Dower's head.

"Nah, it couldn't be," Sanders asserted, before turning back to Cheong. "How would you know, anyway?"

"I booked the hotel rooms, Mr Sanders. One for you. One for both of them."

"Really?"

"Yes, really."

"Well, I'll be blown. Good for him. She's at least a mile out of his league."

The truck sputtered to life as Sanders again leaned forward to try to view the truck behind them, but the mirror vibrated and shook too much for Sanders to see anything. He sat back as the truck lurched away from the curb to a torrent of horns and shouts.

The truck rattled and bumped as it rolled along the road, causing the men in the cab to bump shoulders regularly as they travelled. Jakarta was quite unlike anywhere Sanders had been before. But then again, Darwin was the previous biggest city Sanders had ever visited, and that only had a population of just over a hundred and fifty thousand people. Jakarta, on the other hand, was just so big. Roads that stretched across as far as four lanes wide. Towers that reached up to the clouds. Cars and motorbikes everywhere. And the traffic was chaos, everyone ducking and diving between lanes to claim any gap in the road ahead. At more than one point Sanders found himself holding his breath as motorbike riders squeezed through a gap it should never have tried for. Yet somehow, there was never an accident.

"Do you know who you remind me of, Mr Sanders?" Cheong asked, breaking Sanders out of his reverie of staring out of the window.

"What?"

"I asked, do you know who you remind me of?"

"No. No idea."

"Crocodile Dundee."

A smile broke out on Sanders' face. "Really? I love that movie."

"I hated it. Stupid movie."

The smile disappeared from Sanders' face as he regarded Cheong. Cheong ignored him, and began giving directions to the driver and pointing ahead. After a short dialogue, Cheong turned back to Sanders once more.

"Tell me, do you know how to read, Mr Sanders?"

"Of course I can bloody read, Kenny."

"Good. Then read this," Cheong replied and dumped a folder in Sanders' lap. "I have calls to make and you need to study up on this monster we're catching before meeting it face to face."

Without waiting for Sanders' retort, Cheong pulled a satellite phone from his jacket pocket and began dialling a number in. Within seconds he was speaking in a flurry of language Sanders could not understand.

Sanders turned his attention to the folder Cheong had passed him. He opened it and was greeted by a plain white sheet of paper bearing the name 'Sipatahunan Cave Horse Serpent' in plain black lettering. The first few pages bore artists' renditions of the beast based on first-hand accounts of those who had seen it. Sanders had been correct with his conclusion based on the description Dower had provided. It looked remarkably like a wingless dragon in most pictures. He flicked back and forth between the pictures, noting the definition of the legs and the angles they bent at. 'Horse' felt like a loose description that only applied to the head. The body was squatter, and the legs broader and more muscular than that of a horse.

The next pages covered the reports of the team that had previously set out to find the Horse Serpent. First was the original report, where the group had claimed they had heard and seen signs of the beast but left the caves for fear of flooding from the river that ran through the caves, and the heavy rain falling outside. The second was the supposed 'secret true' take on the exploration, detailing the grisly remains of the tunnel explorers. This was of most interest to Sanders, and he read over the section a couple of times, deep in thought. Crocodiles were known to hide food away under mangroves or in burrows under the water, and Sanders wondered if he was seeing a familiar pattern of behaviour here.

Sanders flicked through the pages and found the deeper he got into the folder, the more fantastical the stories and accounts of encounters with the beast became. He started to wish he had ridden with Dower just to get his opinion on some of the material presented here.

At one point during his reading, Sanders noticed Cheong shift noticeably to one side. He thought nothing of it, but then a pungent stench assailed his nostrils, almost making him wretch.

"Jesus, Kenny, did you just lift a cheek and fart?"

Cheong was still talking on the phone, but evidently heard the remark and turned to give Sanders a dark look. Sanders pretended to dry retch before turning to open the window to get some fresher air in the cabin.

Sanders returned to the documents and tried to sort the fact from the myth in the various tales of Horse Serpent sightings. There were a lot of inconsistencies across a number of documents. First it was long, then it was short. Mostly it had a long tail, but sometimes it did not. One report had it attacking and killing a wild pig, whereas another had it eating leaves from a tree. He decided he needed to put a line through that account, having already concluded that the Horse Serpent was a meat eater.

"Can I have a pen?" he asked.

"Eh? Eh?" answered Cheong.

"A pen," Sanders asked, miming writing on his hand.

"I know what a pen is," Cheong admonished.

"Can I have one then?"

Cheong rolled his eyes and pulled a pen from his inner jacket pocket and passed it across in between bursts of yammering into the phone. Sanders took the pen and read the writing along the side. The Grand International Hotel. He smirked and shook his head.

Pulling a blank page free, Sanders began collating facts about the beast that appeared consistently through the various witness accounts, together with his own deductions and theories on the meaning. After collating this data, he turned back to the various sketches at the front of the folder. Based on some of the data he collected, he could quickly dismiss a number of pictures that did not align to the descriptions. Eventually he settled on one picture, the one that seemed the most closely aligned to everything he knew, and set about updating the picture to how he believed it would look.

It was as he finished this work the trucks pulled into a stop and Cheong finally got off the phone. Sanders looked up to see they had stopped in a small town. It was quite a shift from Jakarta; the roads were cracked and dusty, the cars were less vibrantly coloured and bore dents and rust, the motorcycles were traded down to bicycles and children ran shoeless through the streets. This place felt far more homely to Sanders.

"We get out here and have a break."

"Break? We haven't been travelling that long."

"Break for those of us who've been working instead of drawing pretty pictures when they should be reading."

Sanders' lips tightened and he slammed the folder closed. "Righto, Kenny, we get out and have a break, just like you say."

"You call me Mr Cheong."

Sanders lowered himself out of the cab with his folder. He was tempted to turn around and slam the door in Cheong's face, but changed his mind at the first sight of O'Mara's beautiful long legs emerging from the cab of the second truck. Dower waved a greeting and approached Sanders.

"How was your trip?" Dower asked.

"Oh, it was fine except for Kenny's toxic farts."

"That was the truck driver," Cheong called, having overheard as he dismounted the truck.

"Get your hand off it, Kenny. I saw you cock your leg."

"I have my hand on nothing. It was the truck driver. And you call me Mr Cheong."

"You two are getting along well it seems," Dower said sarcastically as Cheong walked past them and around the corner.

"He talks to me like I'm a caveman. I know I'm not as educated as you lot are, but that's no reason to treat me like an idiot."

Dower gave him a humourless smile. "No, you're right, it isn't an excuse. But do you think it's wise to keep needling him like that?"

Sanders rubbed the stubble on his chin and turned to the corner that Cheong had just disappeared behind. "Well," he began thoughtfully, "either I needle him or I knock his block off. Which do you think is better?"

"Probably needling. Just be aware there's a line. Listen, why don't the three of us sit over in that café over there and compare thoughts on the notes Mr Cheong gave us?"

They walked to the café and ordered some cold drinks. O'Mara and Sanders went with water, while Dower asked for a soft drink. Sanders let the two scholars talk first, but as they spoke, he found their conclusions just as jumbled and contradictory as the accounts in the folders.

"No, no, no," he said at last, "it's not like that at all."

They both turned with their eyebrows raised, surprised to have their views challenged.

"Well, what did you make of all the reports then?" O'Mara asked.

Sanders pushed their folders aside and opened his to the pages he had been working on; the picture and the table summarising the key traits of the beast. He explained his workings, and how he had diluted the data down to get a clear description of the beast, then used that description to correct the drawing.

"This is exceptional work," Dower muttered as he examined the picture closely. "I'm really impressed."

"This creature sounds quite dangerous," O'Mara added as she ran down a list of key attributes. "It's fast, agile and has large front claws with which it kills its prey. It doesn't sound the tiniest bit like a horse. Plus, these conclusions you have made about the scales on its hide. Impenetrable?"

"Near enough to impenetrable, but yeah, close to. When I did this, I put the name to the side and drew my own conclusions lest the name distort my perceptions," Sanders said. "The horse part of the name may be true for the shape of the head, the neck and the size of the beast, but in terms of body shape the descriptor felt wrong. The habitat is thick rainforest. Horses roam open plains and can't turn the way this thing can. If anything, this moves like an African big cat. Read over the third, fourth and sixth accounts of sightings with that in mind and you'll see what I mean."

"Fascinating," Dower said as he pored over the notes. For a long moment both he and O'Mara lost themselves in the notes. Sanders let them be and leaned back in his chair and looked out the window. The truck drivers were smoking again, only this time they had not found a local woman to harass and instead sat on the curb and played a game of cards. Not far from them a barefoot boy kicked a ball against a wall. Outside of that, the street was quiet and still.

Suddenly, the two drivers stood up, hastily packing the cards away and stamping their half-finished cigarettes out in the dirt. They rushed to the rear of the first truck to open the tailgate of the vehicle. Just then, a group of soldiers appeared, marching in lines from behind the corner that Cheong disappeared behind. They were dressed in mostly black, and carried AK-47 automatic rifles over their shoulders and small packs on their backs. They were mostly young men, and the expressions on their faces were hard and serious.

"Who the hell are these guys?" Sanders muttered, drawing the attention of his companions to the newcomers outside.

Just then, Cheong appeared alongside the men, shouting directions and pointing to the trucks. As the soldiers mounted the rear of the first truck, Cheong crossed the street to enter the café.

"We are going now," he announced as he reached the table.

"Who are those men?" Dower asked.

"They are soldiers. They are going to help us catch the Horse Serpent."

"Are they Indonesian Army?"

Cheong licked his lips, glancing at the men climbing into the trucks before returning his gaze to Dower. "It doesn't matter who they are. They are here to help us and that's all you need to know. Now come back to the trucks. It's time to go."

Not waiting for any more questions, Cheong promptly turned and left the café. Dower watched him leave through narrowed eyes.

"I have to say, this does make me slightly uncomfortable," Dower said.

"You and me both," added O'Mara.

"Who do you think they are?" asked Sanders.

Dower bit his lip. "I'm not sure I want to think about it. Listen, I think I need more time with your work here, Sanders. Do you think I could take it to read over on the next leg of the journey?"

"Yeah, no problem."

Dower nodded, stood and began pulling the papers together on the table and filing them into his own folder on the Horse Serpent.

"If you can," Dower continued, "in the next leg of the trip, try and ask Cheong about those soldiers. Their presence here worries me."

"What are you thinking?" O'Mara asked.

"That what we're doing here, this operation, goes a bit beyond just Higson's visa not getting the approval of the Indonesian government."

There was a pause then, and Sanders noticed O'Mara glance at the truck and suddenly appear nervous.

"Listen, about the next leg," Sanders cut in, "I was hoping that one of you might be able to swap seats with me." Preferably Dower, he thought to himself.

"You mentioned something about toxic farts earlier?" Dower asked.

"Yes, the worst. I felt my nose hairs burning."

"Then the answer is no. Besides, Jess and I should travel together so we can go over your notes."

Sanders frowned. It was a good excuse. He could not argue with that.

"Great," Sanders replied without emotion, wishing he had a peg for his nose for the journey ahead.

3

If talking with Cheong for the next leg of the truck ride was Sanders' intention, his plan was quickly scuttled when Cheong jammed two cordless earbuds into his ears and started playing music loudly through them. The whining melodies could clearly be heard over the cranking noise of the truck engine, which combined created a horrible din that caused even the driver to grumble in annoyance. After a short while, the gentle rocking of the truck got the better of Cheong, and his neck started to take on a jelly-like strength as his head lolled from side to side. His eyes fought hard, but the heaviness of Cheong's eyelids was too much and soon Cheong was snoring with his head resting against Sanders' shoulder.

Sanders scowled as he regarded the small form of Cheong. The only positive Sanders could see in it was at least the little man's poisonous mouth was shut. He doubted he could take much more of the runt's condescension.

Sanders tried to strike up a conversation with the driver, but the two failed to pass more than a word of comprehension between each other and he quickly gave up on the idea. With his notes and folder with Dower and O'Mara in the second truck, Sanders had little else to do than stare out the window at the passing landscape.

Once they had passed beyond the limits of the town, Sanders felt himself enjoying the view of the landscape that rolled out before him. Lush, green hills undulated on either side of the road, their sides dotted with trees and farms of varying kinds. There were rice paddies, orchards of lined trees with fruits Sanders did not even recognise, and fields of plump cattle. The roads were fast and well maintained, but they curved like a boiled noodle around the hills and mountains so much a weaker stomached individual would have had motion sickness.

At one point in the trip, Cheong farted audibly and the wretched stench soon assailed Sanders' senses once more. The driver rolled down his window with a splash of colourful language. He turned to Sanders, pointing at Cheong before waving his hand vigorously in front of his nose. Sanders laughed, enjoying the brief moment of contact and shared experience with the driver before returning to the solitude of his window view.

Sometime later in the day, as Sanders' stomach started to grumble with hunger, the trucks turned off the main highway onto a narrow road that quickly degraded from asphalt to a rough dirt track. The truck shuddered and bounced, waking Cheong and causing him to lose one earbud onto the floor. He cursed and fished around the floor for it, but it somehow eluded his grasp as it jumped like popping corn on the convulsing floor. Eventually he sat back up, though Sanders was not sure if he had retrieved the lost earbud or not.

"How long to go?" Sanders asked over the noise of the vibrating truck.

"One more hour."

"And then?"

"And then we arrive at a small town near the cave where we will stay the night."

Cheong fished into his jacket pocket and checked the satellite phone. He flicked through a couple of screens and read and responded to a text message he had received. Sanders watched over his shoulder, but the messages were in another language. Cheong tucked the phone away after finishing the message and cast a glance at Sanders.

"So…" Sanders began, "who are those guys in the back?"

"Like I said earlier, they are here to help us catch the Horse Serpent."

"Yes, but where are they from?"

"Where they are from is not of your concern. All you need to know is they are here to catch the monster."

"With rifles and guns?"

"Please, no more questions about the men in the back."

"But why are they…"

"Uh," Cheong interrupted, waggling a finger at Sanders like a teacher admonishing a misbehaving student, "no more questions on the men."

"Right" said Sanders, crossing his arms and frowning. "What should we talk about then, Kenny? Do you have a girlfriend? Any pets? That sort of thing."

"I'm not interested in telling you about myself either."

"Fine. What about a game of 'I Spy' then?"

"What about we just finish the ride in quiet?"

"Fine, I can deal with that, just so long as you don't drop any more of those toxic farts of yours."

The rest of the bouncing, shuddering ride across the bumpy dirt road was carried out in silence. If the air in the cab was thick with tension, the driver did nothing to acknowledge it. The undergrowth grew thicker and denser around the road, and Sanders started to wonder just how frequented this path was. At times Sanders spotted movement in the trees and on the ground, but whatever creature was there moved away too quickly to be seen clearly.

The road eventually led to a small village where the trucks pulled to a stop. Cheong ordered Sanders to dismount, and after exiting himself, Cheong slammed the door and slapped it twice. With the heavy crunch of shifting gears, the truck continued down the road away from them.

"Where are they going?" Sanders asked.

"The soldiers are staying elsewhere. Now come, this is where you will stay."

Sanders glanced around the small town. The unsealed roads were dirty and rough. The buildings were ramshackle and bore the signs of amateur patchwork to the damaged exteriors. Old women sat in chairs and watched them silently with dark eyes. Two stray dogs humped in the street while a group of young boys watched on, giggling. It was a strange, beaten down town that felt as every bit as remote from civilisation that it was.

Cheong directed them to a dirty old bar where they would spend the night in the rooms above. To say it was a step down from the Grand International Hotel would be the grandest of understatements you could make. Paint peeled from the walls and the mattresses sagged with age. The curtains were discoloured with age and spiders roamed carefree on the cornices. The lights flickered and the windows were grubby. But it was still the best accommodation this town had to offer.

After dumping his bag on the bed, Sanders quickly returned downstairs and ordered a bottle of beer from the bar. The woman behind the bar did not speak a word of English, but pointing vigorously soon got the message across. He was joined shortly afterwards by Dower and O'Mara who came bearing the folders and paperwork.

"How did you go with it?" Sanders asked as they sat and indicated for two more beers to be brought to the table.

"Your work was flawless," Dower remarked, "I'm really impressed."

Sanders tried not to blush. It was not often he was praised like this by a professor.

"It's really useful too," O'Mara added. "I've been able to make a number of assumptions on the dosage levels and food requirements we need to keep it alive and docile."

"That's great," Sanders said taking a swig from his beer.

"Have you thought about how we might catch it?" O'Mara asked.

Sanders placed his beer back on the table and started scratching at the label with his thumbnail. "It's a different kind of animal than what I'm used to," he began ponderously, "but I think it might have a softer underbelly where we might get a sleep dart into. Failing that, I'd try taking out the front legs first. Those are its chief offensive attack weapons. If we disable them, it could quickly be on the defensive."

Dower nodded and exchanged a glance with O'Mara before quickly glancing about the empty bar. Leaning in, he spoke in a much lower volume.

"What about the soldiers? What did you find out about them?"

"Nothing. Cheong snored through half the ride and refused to talk for the rest of it. He farts in his sleep too, just so you know."

Dower and O'Mara again exchanged a glance.

"We have to confront him about it," O'Mara said. "We need to know who they are."

"Leave it with me," said Dower.

Just in that moment, Cheong entered the bar from one of the back rooms. He was again talking on the phone, but he cut the call off after seeing them and approached the table. He frowned at the sight of the open beers.

"Lunch is arranged and will be served shortly," he announced.

"That's great," Dower said. "Listen, we wanted to ask a few questions about the plan here, if we could."

"Plan is simple; we stay here tonight. Tomorrow morning, we go to the cave and catch monster, then we drive back to Jakarta. From Jakarta, we load the Horse Serpent onto a ship and make our way to Singapore. Any questions?"

"The men on the truck..."

"Are here to help us catch it."

"Yes, okay. But who are they really?"

Cheong crossed his arms and glanced sharply at Sanders. "Again with the men on the truck. What is with all the questions about the men on the truck?"

"Well," Dower began, sharing a glance with each of his comrades before continuing, "we've already surmised they aren't Indonesian Army. The thing is... we just want to know we're not working with extremists here."

Cheong's eye twitched and he drew a deep breath in, letting it out audibly. "And if they were, would you feel more comfortable or less comfortable knowing that fact?"

Dower cleared his throat and glanced nervously about him. "Are they terrorists?"

Cheong frowned, and looked out the window at something distant. Then he refocused on the group, pulling a seat to sit at the table with them.

"Look, if you must know, this mission, this whole operation, is going ahead without the approval of the Indonesian government. Mr Higson intended for them to be involved, but he has sat on this plan for over a year now waiting for their approval and they haven't budged. He's tired of waiting on bureaucrats. So, he's taken matters into his own hands."

"So, this isn't just a bait a catch job, this is a smuggling operation."

"Yes, which is why we have to work with people we would not normally choose to associate with."

"Hang on" Sanders interrupted, "are you saying what we're doing here is illegal? If we get caught, we could all go to jail."

"There is a small possibility of it, yes."

"Why weren't we told about this earlier?" O'Mara demanded, jamming her finger on the table.

"It didn't seem necessary to do so just yet."

"Didn't seem necessary?" O'Mara parroted, her voice rising in pitch and volume. "I'm in a foreign country and I'm breaking their laws and you don't think it was necessary to tell me?"

Cheong regarded her hysterics calmly. "Right now, nobody is breaking any laws. You're just three tourists travelling through a quaint rural town in the Bogor region of Indonesia. You also happen to be experts who have been asked to give an opinion by a local businessman; me. Unless you actively help in the capture or smuggling of the Horse Serpent, then you have broken no laws."

O'Mara clucked her tongue and looked out the window. Dower glanced her way, then turned to Cheong.

"Just say we decide we don't want any part of this," Dower said.

"Then you stay at the hotel. It makes no difference to me. I am confident I can catch this animal without you."

Sanders snorted and shook his head.

"What, Mr Sanders? You think because I wear a suit, that I can't catch this monster? You think it's only a job for big Aussie apes like you?"

Sanders clenched his fists and his voice hardened. "No, Kenny, it has nothing to do with the suit. It's that you have a truckload of kids with guns walking into a rainforest to catch a beast you nothing about."

"I know plenty; didn't you read the folder?"

"Oh, I read the folder, Kenny. The question is, did you? Because whoever put that folder together doesn't know a thing about what he is doing."

Cheong stood up suddenly, causing the seat to tumble over behind him and crash to the floor loudly.

"I don't need any more of this bullshit. You don't question me. I can catch the monster alone. You're only here because Mr Higson insisted on it. An uneducated oaf like you has no place in this mission. Now for the last time, you call me Mr Cheong."

Cheong was panting heavily and his hair had fallen out of place. He stared at Sanders, who wore a bemused look, before glancing at the others and then to the woman behind the bar. Realising he was causing a scene, Cheong straightened his jacket, fixed his hair and cleared his throat.

"Now, I must go. I have business to attend to and you won't see me for the rest of the day. The expedition to the monster's lair leaves here tomorrow at eight sharp. If you don't want to join us for fear of breaking any laws, that is fine. I will notify Mr Higson and we will arrange for your trip back to Australia. After we catch it, you can then decide if you want to continue with the smuggling part of the mission or not. Now, as I said, I have business to attend to, so if you have the balls for it, I'll see you all in the morning. Good day."

Without waiting for a response, Cheong stormed from the room and out onto the street before disappearing from view.

"Well, that was dramatic," O'Mara said.

"I don't get it," Sanders mused as he stared at the doorway through which Cheong had disappeared. "Why does he hate me calling him Kenny so much when he was fine with Connie doing it?"

"It's cultural, I'd say," Dower put in. "We're not that formal in Australia, but in his culture, I imagine you have to use suffixes as a show of respect. Higson can get away with it because he's Cheong's boss, but you doing it is a show of disrespect."

"Okay, seems I'm doing it right then. There's no way I can respect that little weasel."

Dower sighed. "Even so, it's a big part of his culture and you calling him Kenny like that is a massive insult. You are giving him no respect."

"Well, in my culture, respect is earned and not freely given. And you don't earn someone's respect by looking down your nose at them."

Dower opened his mouth to reply but was stopped short when O'Mara laid a hand on his. He closed his mouth and turned to her.

"Perhaps let's leave that for now," O'Mara said. "We should really talk about if we think we should continue with this quest or not. Where's your head at with this, Matt? Or should I call you Mr Sanders?"

Sanders smiled. The joke was a nice touch.

"Matt is fine. Look, I'll be honest, I highly suspect that if I don't go, Cheong and his mates will get torn up out there by a wild beast and the world would probably be a better place for it. But if I'm really, really honest about it, I can't in good conscience let that happen. They could be the biggest pricks in the universe, but it's not in my nature to let people die like that. So as much as I'd like to say stuff them, I'm still in."

"What about you, dear?"

Dower pursed his lips and turned to her. "You already know my answer on this. I've studied cryptids all my life. I've challenged theories, written papers, been to conferences… I just can't come this close to proving one real and walk away from it. Even if we walk a thin line with the law here, I just can't."

"I know, and I wouldn't ask you to, either. I'm in too. This is bigger than any of us. This creature, if it's real… this would be a massive discovery. And if it isn't real or we can't find it, we've lost nothing and broken no laws. No, I can't walk away from it either."

"It could be dangerous," Sanders suggested.

"Oh, please. I'm a vet. I've handled snakes, I've had pit bulls take a run at me and I've been kicked by a horse. I think I can handle this Horse Serpent."

"So, it's settled then. We're all in. All for one and one for all, or whatever it was the three musketeers used to say," said Dower

"As long as we're the three musketeers and not the three stooges, I'm definitely in," added O'Mara.

"Right, well we should probably talk tactics then. Higson employed us as his experts, so we better have some strong views on how to go about this tomorrow."

"Agreed," said Sanders. "But first, what happened to the lunch Kenny said he had ordered?"

4

The trio of hired experts spent the remainder of the day in the bar sharing thoughts and plans about the monster they were brought here to catch. As the day grew older and the line of empty beer bottles grew longer, the conversation began to turn away from the grim realities of their situation and task ahead to jokes and personal stories of their lives.

Sanders learnt, as he had expected, that Dower was many years senior to O'Mara. They had met at university, with Dower a lecturer and O'Mara the student at the time. Despite warming to each other and forming a bond quite quickly, it was not until after O'Mara had completed her course, and a chance meeting at a bakery one day, did the two reunite and become romantically involved. As they retold the story of their first awkward dates, Sanders found himself re-evaluating his view of their relationship. There was a lot more to them beyond a simple physical attraction. There was a certain kindred-spirit type connection going, and on a mental level they had a great alignment. But deep in the back of his mind, Sanders still thought Dower was punching above his weight class with a hottie like her.

They retired not long into the evening, with both Dower and O'Mara more than a little tipsy from all the alcohol they had consumed.

Sanders was the first to arrive in the bar the next morning. Partly from the restless night he had spent tossing and turning on the uncomfortable bed, but mostly because he wanted a full breakfast without interruptions this morning. O'Mara was next to arrive, white faced and clutching a bottle of water in one hand, shortly followed there after by the grim-faced Dower. Sanders did his best to hide it, but their looks told him they were less than happy that he found their states amusing.

The truck loaded with soldiers appeared two minutes before eight o'clock, and then right on the hour Cheong emerged from the back room to greet them. His smile was less than warm, more a showing of teeth than something with any great feeling behind it, as he greeted them. He was again dressed head to foot in a sharply pressed business suit with a bright yellow shirt and navy-blue tie, with his hair slicked back and his pencil moustache neatly trimmed.

"Are you planning to catch the Horse Serpent dressed like that?" Sanders scoffed as Cheong approached the table.

"Some of us like to take pride in our appearance when we go out and not look like we have just rolled out of a ditch," Cheong responded.

"Now, I take it from you all being here that you have all decided to join this expedition?"

They all nodded one by one.

"Okay then. Well, chop chop, time to get in the trucks."

To Sanders' dismay, he found himself again sharing a cab with Cheong. Cheong suggested this time Sanders should take the middle, but Sanders insisted on taking the window seat just in case he needed the fresh air.

The trucks left the small town in a plume of exhaust fumes and turned down a narrow, single lane dirt road. The road they took was much rougher than the one they had taken yesterday to arrive here, and the trucks often slowed to walking pace as they traversed through gullies and over large rocks. The plant life was thicker here too, often breaching the boundaries of the road to thwack loudly against the windscreen or mirrors of the truck.

At one point, through a narrow clearing of trees, Sanders spotted a large grey shape on trunk like legs grazing in the undergrowth. The beast faced away from him, but he could clearly see the thick, knobbly hide and small, whip-like tail before the view of the beast was obscured. Quickly he turned to Cheong and described the beast.

"Ah, that sounds like a Javan rhinoceros. You are very lucky to spot one, Mr Sanders, they are an endangered species. Seeing one in the wild is a rare treat indeed."

Sanders leaned forward to look into the side mirror, hoping to get one more glance at the beast.

"Why is that? How did their numbers get so low? Is the Horse Serpent responsible?"

Cheong scoffed. "No, Mr Sanders, we are responsible."

"We are?"

"'We' as in the royal 'we'. People. Humans. We hunt them and destroy their habitats for our own needs."

Sanders frowned and his eyes took on a saddened look. "It's a story I've heard all too often," he said sadly.

"Don't feel sad for them, Mr Sanders. Life is a competition, and in a competition, there are winners and there are losers. They are the losers."

"You can't think of endangered animals like that," Sanders objected.

"I can't? Mr Sanders, I'm a businessman, and in the high-stake world of business, that is the only way I can afford to think. If you're not winning at business, you are losing."

"That's a very narrow view of the world. Animal species are not like businesses, Kenny."

"Perhaps not. But progress is only made by moving forwards and adapting, and if you can't, then you become extinct. It's a fact of life."

Sanders was about to object when the driver interrupted. A quick conversation ensued and the truck pulled to a stop.

"We are here," Cheong announced.

Sanders dropped down from the cab and waved a quick greeting to the others. His brow was furrowed, still annoyed from Cheong's cold view of the world as he surveyed the rainforest around him. The trees towered high above, their broad, thick leaves blotting out the sunlight leaving the forest floor in a dark, gloomy light. The air was thick with moisture, with droplets of water forming and falling from the leaves around them. Small lizards skittered through the light undergrowth, and insects buzzed through the air noisily.

Cheong dropped down from the cab beside him, his features tight and business-like. He walked briskly to the rear of the second truck to start ordering the soldiers out. To Sanders' annoyance, they all still carried their AK-47 rifles on their shoulders. Only one soldier held a different gun; a rifle with what Sanders assumed was tranquilizer charges on his belt. They also carried light catch poles, aluminium poles with a plastic covered wire cable loop at the end to catch animals around the neck, and heaved out great hessian sacks from the rear of the trucks before marching down a narrow track that passed through the trees. Cheong followed, shouting orders all the while.

"I guess we had better follow," Dower suggested, sweat patches already forming under the armpits of his t-shirt.

"This is all wrong," Sanders complained, leaping into the rear of the truck. There was little he could see of use, so he grabbed a couple of coils of rope and a Bowie knife before jumping back down and leading Dower and O'Mara forward to follow Cheong and the soldiers.

Cheong, remarkably, kept his suit jacket on and buttoned at the front, despite the heat and humidity around him. Often, he would stop and draw a handkerchief from his jacket pocket to pat his brow, after which he would check the knot on his tie was still tight before continuing on. Sanders shook his head. Cheong's dress sense was as out of place here as his views were. Now it was Cheong who was the stranger in a strange land.

The narrow path slowly became rockier and Sanders became aware of the sound of flowing water. A hill began rising to their left, while the path descended towards a slow-moving stream below them. The vegetation gave way to rock the closer they came to the stream, and within a few yards it became a sheer rock face.

Cheong started shouting and the soldiers broke ranks and started opening the hessian sacks to draw out large, rope bound nets.

Sanders walked past the soldiers to get his first view of Sipatahunan Cave. The entrance was large, reaching well above Sanders' head, and semi-circular in shape. The stream, not more than ankle deep, flowed into what Sanders expected was quite an extensive subterranean cave system. He glanced along the stream, measuring the waterline visually, and could see that with a heavy rain, the caves could get flooded to quite dangerous levels.

Cheong continued to issue orders noisily, and sent two men traipsing through the thick forest with a series of sharp words.

"What's the plan here, Cheong?" Sanders asked. "I see no torches or caving equipment on the men here."

"We are not going into the cave. We will draw it out."

The soldiers unfolded a great net and laid it out across the stream, sinking it down to hide it amongst the bubbling waters. The soldiers then moved back, each holding a rope connected to the net while secluding themselves between the trees and shrubs along the shoreline of the creek. Sanders rubbed his temples, a bemused look on his face. The two soldiers who had been sent away returned shortly thereafter with a small, wild pig which they tied to a stake that they hammered into the creek bed in the middle of the net. They then secluded themselves, leaving Sanders alone in the open, shaking his head.

"Mr Sanders, you need to come and hide behind cover now," Cheong called.

Sanders turned and gestured to the creek and net. "This is your plan, Kenny? There is no chance this will work."

"Of course it will work. Don't be an imbecile."

"Kenny, that net won't hold anything like that."

"Of course it will. When the horse steps on the net, we pull it up and tangle its legs. The more it panics, the more it gets entangled. Then we slip across and use the tranquilisers on it."

"It's not a horse, Kenny."

"Stop calling me Kenny," Cheong shouted suddenly. "It's Mr Cheong to you." The outburst was loud, and all eyes turned to Cheong; he visibly reddened. He cleared his throat, checked his tie and jacket, before speaking once more. "Please, Mr Sanders, this is my plan. Mr Higson put me in charge and this is how the Horse Serpent will be caught. You are only here because Mr Higson insisted upon it, but in reality, you are not needed. At all. So, no more questions, no more criticisms and no more Kennys. This is my task and my plan, and any more nonsense out of you and I'll have my men tie up and cage you with it."

Sanders help up his hands in a placating gesture. "Okay, Kenny, I hear you. I'll be quiet and I'll wait on the sidelines just over there and, if you're lucky, I'll join the action just in time to save your arse. Okay?"

Cheong responded with a hate filled stare and what may have been a gurgle, but sounded more like a growl, as Sanders walked up the bank to join Dower and O'Mara.

"You really shouldn't be riling him up like that," Dower said.

"I'm not doing or saying anything to him he doesn't deserve."

Time slowly ticked by as eyes fixed on the cave entrance for any sign of movement from within. The pig grunted as it chewed and pulled at its restraint. Bird calls echoed and insects buzzed, but apart from the sound of the occasional slapping of skin on skin as one of the watchers tried to kill an annoying insect, the group of humans who had invaded the forest were silent.

Sanders slowly paced back and forth between trees, his eyes flicking about the landscape. Between the hasty mopping of his brow and checking his satellite phone, Cheong spared little in the way of dark glares. There was a thick tension in the air, and not just the one that existed between Cheong and Sanders either. The soldiers stared at the cave with aggravated intensity, their faces slick with sweat and jaws working silently as they ground their teeth. Dower, whose t-shirt was now more wet than dry, whispered assurances to O'Mara, though the tension in his face suggested he did this more for himself than for her. O'Mara, for her part, stood as still as a statue, her arms crossed and lips pursed.

Sanders stopped pacing a moment and started unwinding the ropes he had brought from the truck. He looped one around a nearby tree before tying it off and leaving the slack resting on the ground. The remaining ropes he started tying into a series of knots and nooses. At one point he stopped, looked up and studied the pig a moment, then returned to his work with greater haste.

His work did not go unnoticed, having drawn a scowl from Cheong. O'Mara edged close to him and leaned forward to whisper.

"What are you doing?"

"The Horse Serpent is coming. I'm getting ready to catch it."

"How do you know it's coming?"

But rather than answer, Sanders placed a forefinger to his lips and pointed to the small pig in the stream. As if on cue, the pig began pulling hard at its restraint, squeals escaping its mouth. Realising it was stuck fast, the pig's actions became more and more panicked. It began to thrash and splash about, desperate to move away.

Cheong must have noticed this too, as he beckoned a nearby soldier to him. They exchanged a quick, whispered dialogue and Cheong pointed to the pig. The soldier nodded, and started edging down the bank towards the pig.

"Psssst," Sanders hissed. When Cheong turned, Sanders pointed to the soldier and waved an admonishing finger. Cheong mouthed a reply.

"What's he saying?" Sanders asked in a low whisper to O'Mara.

"I think he said the pig is getting loose," she replied.

"Shit," Sanders cursed, pointing at the soldier again before sliding his finger across his neck in a throat slitting gesture. Cheong waved him away. Sanders scowled and redoubled his rope knotting efforts.

"I hope you have a strong stomach for blood, Doc," Sanders whispered.

"I've operated on animals before. I can deal with blood."

"It's not the animals I'm worried about."

The soldier reached the edge of the stream and stopped to peer nervously into the cave. The thick canopy of leaves from the treetops high above drowned out the light, and the cave interior loomed as dark and as black as an abyss.

Cheong rolled his eyes and snapped his fingers to draw the attention of the soldier. When the soldier looked back, Cheong gestured aggressively at the pig. The soldier nodded, and gulped.

Turning back to the cave, the soldier slid the AK-47 from his shoulder and pointed it at the black mouth of the cave. He stepped slowly into the creek, his eyes wide as they stared into the abyss. He edged towards the pig, not taking his eyes away from the cave. He reached the pig and stopped. He stood a moment, watching the cave, before slinging the AK-47 back over his shoulder and crouching down to check the bonds that held the pig.

The birds and the insects in the area suddenly went silent. Sanders looked across at the soldier, closed his eyes for a second then turned back to his rope work, cutting lengths with the Bowie knife and fixing nooses and loops.

The soldier crouched in the water felt around the pig's leg and pulled the rope tight. Cheong was right, it had begun to loosen. He then felt around the stake to make sure it was firmly imbedded in the ground, when he heard a low growl coming from the cave.

His heart rate immediately climbed and his hands began to shake. He slowly twisted his body to turn back to the cave. Two yellow eyes with slit pupils glowed malevolently in the dark. The growling continued as the soldier slowly slipped the AK-47 from over his shoulder. The soldiers hiding among the trees did the same, aiming their rifles at the cave entrance.

The beast suddenly roared, a sound that reverberated through the tunnel and out of the entrance. The soldier in the stream panicked, dropping his rifle as he jumped to his feet and tried to flee from the stream. The creature leapt from the cave, launching its attack against the fleeing target and coming into view for the first time.

The creature was as large as a horse and had wet, glistening, emerald-coloured scales. Despite bearing distinct similarities to both horse and snake, the Horse Serpent's body was more shaped like that of a tiger, but with a longer neck and horse shaped head. Its legs were thick and muscular, each ending with large, scaled claws big enough to fit around a man's chest. It had a long flexible neck which twisted with the agility of a snake. The horse-like head bore a mouth brimming with razor-like teeth, and instead of ears, two horns stuck up from the skull. A long tail trailed behind it, whipping the air with an audible whoosh. The beast roared ferociously as it arced down on its prey.

"It looks just like your picture," O'Mara said breathlessly to Sanders.

The creature landed on the unfortunate soldier's back, its claws piercing skin as it gripped him in its great claws. The man screamed as he fell forwards and was crushed beneath its bulky weight. The creature bent its head forwards and latched its jaws over the side of his neck. There was a horrible, wet crunch as the beast flexed its muscles and tore away the skin and muscle from the right side of the soldier's neck. Blood spurted and pooled around the soldier's corpse as the Horse Serpent gulped down the fresh meat.

The air was lit up by a sudden burst of AK-47 fire as one of the soldiers hiding behind the trees, panicked by the sudden and merciless slaughter of his friend, opened up with automatic fire. Dirt erupted into the air as the bullets impacted the earth around the Horse Serpent, but before he could adjust his aim it was upon him. His ribs cracked under the force as the Horse Serpent punched him in the chest as it pounced on him. The soldier was thrown onto his back, and had time only to look up and see the Horse Serpent's mouth bear down around his face before the beast's powerful jaw flexed and crushed his head like a grape.

"My God," O'Mara gasped, watching from the opposite bank of the stream, "it moves like and is as agile as a cat."

Panic spread quickly and more gunfire exploded as the gloomy rainforest was lit up by the flashing muzzles. Vegetation erupted like fireworks and fell like confetti as the soldiers blazed at the forest. The Horse Serpent, camouflaged with its green scales, slipped in and out of view, ducking around trees and through bushes as the panicked gunfire spattered the air. It was an experienced hunter, and the soldiers were in disarray. Cheong and the fellow soldiers that shared the opposite side of the bank could only watch in horror as the Horse Serpent slashed its way through the ranks.

Here, a man shooting into a thick clump of foliage where the second soldier had fallen was suddenly attacked from the side and had his chest raked open by the monster's massive claws. There, another soldier was struck viciously in the side of the head by the thick, whipping tail of the beast, only to fall down with his neck bent at an unnatural angle. And there, two men bowled over and torn apart by tooth and claw. And finally, there, a soldier run down in the stream as he tried to flee to the other side for help, the creature holding his head under the water with one heavily clawed foot as its head tore chunks of flesh from his arms and shoulders and gobbled it down greedily.

The ten men who stood on the opposite bank had been torn apart in mere minutes.

As the stream water became stained red with blood and the last pained cries of the dying soldiers on the far bank ceased, the Horse Serpent looked up and focused its eyes on the remaining men hidden among the trees watching it. Its face was wet with crimson blood, but its hunger for the kill had not yet abated.

Cheong shouted an order and the men started running back through the forest towards the trucks. Dower turned to run before realising O'Mara was not with him. He turned to see her standing, frozen to the spot, staring at the Horse Serpent.

"Let's go, Jess," he called.

"I can't. It's staring straight at me."

"Jess, the soldiers are leaving."

"I'm not sure they'd be much help anyway."

"Damn it, Jess," Dower cursed, glancing at the backs of the fleeing soldiers then turning back to his partner. He bit his lip, coming to a decision, then ran after the soldiers.

The Horse Serpent slowly stepped forward out of the stream and onto the bank. Blood dripped from its maw as it regarded O'Mara curiously. O'Mara shivered. There was a calculated calmness to the creature and the way it moved. While it would be easy to view the carnage that had preceded this moment as frenzied slaughter, O'Mara could see now there was nothing crazed about this beast's actions. It had not acted out of blind rage. It had measured, stalked and killed each solider with calm assurance. It was a cold-blooded killer, and right now it was focused on O'Mara.

She took a slight step backwards and her gaze faltered away from the beast. A moment ago, she had thought Sanders had been standing next to her, but as she glanced there now her eyes met only empty space. She took another step back and the beast took two more forward. She glanced quickly to where she had heard Dower's voice come from, but he too had gone. Had the men all been so cowardly as to leave her alone with this monster? So much for all for one and one for all. Not even her boyfriend had it in him to stay by her side.

She inwardly cursed as she took another step backwards. The beast took three more forwards and lowered to a crouch. She swallowed, wishing she had a knife or a gun or anything to defend herself with. She glanced at the ground and spotted a stick the size of her arm that was sharp and splintered at one end. She lowered herself into a crouch, keeping her eyes on the Horse Serpent, and felt around for the stick. It would be no use as a club against this monster, but maybe if she held it point out as the beast pounced, she might have a chance of impaling and killing it by piercing its soft underbelly. Any notion of catching the creature had long passed, it was only self-preservation now, and pitted one on one with the monster, she knew only one of them could live.

Behind her, she could hear the shouts of men and the coughing of the truck engines, but that noise faded into the distance as the Horse Serpent started to growl.

O'Mara's hand found the stick and she raised herself back up, wielding the stick before her with two hands like a broadsword. She moved her feet apart, setting her stance for the final confrontation. She nodded at the beast. She was ready for it.

The Horse Serpent kicked powerfully forward and settled into an assured gallop straight towards her. Despite its bouncing run, the Horse Serpent's head remained perfectly still and its eyes focused on its prey. The creature moved easily, its bulky body seeming to glide across the ground as its muscular legs pumped athletically.

O'Mara drew in a shaky breath. This was it. The moment of truth.

The Horse Serpent closed and entered the tree line. As it started to ready for the pounce, one of the ropes Sanders had tied to a tree suddenly snapped taut right as the beast passed it. Too late to react, the beast was tripped and it crashed forwards into the dirt with a tumbling, ungainly roll.

"Get out of there, O'Mara," Sanders called, having just appeared seemingly from nowhere.

O'Mara glanced down to see the Horse Serpent scrambling to its feet. She took a couple of steps away, still holding her stick at the ready, but the beast no longer had eyes for her. It had a new quarry to concern itself with.

Sanders backed towards the tree, picking up a second rope he'd laid on the ground. This one had also been tied to the tree, and this one ended in a noose.

"You see me now, don't you girl?" he said to the Horse Serpent as it rose and turned to focus its yellow, slitted eyes onto him. "Come on then. Come at me."

The Horse Serpent growled and launched into her stride straight at him. Sanders started twirling his rope like a lasso as he crouched with the tree forward and to his left. He opened his lips slightly, revealing gritted teeth underneath. He knew he had only one chance at this.

The Horse Serpent pounced. Instinctively, Sanders threw the lasso and leapt forward and to his left. He hit the ground and rolled forward, the beast's tail smashing the trunk of the tree next to him and showering him in broken bark. Sanders used the momentum of his roll to push back onto his feet and spin just in time to see the Horse Serpent leaping at him again. He staggered back, putting his hands up to uselessly defend himself when the beast was jerked backwards to land on the dirt with a whump. Sanders' throw had been accurate, landing over the monster's head. The opposite end had been tied to the tree, and it had tightened the noose when it leaped at him.

But the battle was far from over yet. The Horse Serpent would eventually break free and the man with the tranquilizer gun had long fled.

Sanders had two more ropes ready. He picked one of these up now. He had been busy and he was prepared, but the situation was still up in the air.

The Horse Serpent pumped its feet as it twisted its long neck around to bite at the restraint that held it. Teeth clashed with a resounding snap, and Sanders knew one bite would slice through the rope with ease. He threw the lasso along the ground and under the front to claws which pumped up and down madly. He picked his moment and pulled, catching both legs. The loop tightened and he ran around behind the beast and pulled. The Horse Serpent crashed forward, landing on its chest and forcing its claws to be held under its stomach. The beast's tail whipped frantically, kicking up dirt and scattering debris as it whooshed through the air in wild swipes. Sanders had seen what happened when the tail had impacted the soldier's head, but he pushed the memory aside. He did not need that vision invading his thoughts right now. He needed to mount the beast, and the only way he was doing that was from behind, while he had it lying on its chest and its claws tucked underneath it.

Sanders watched the tail swipe left and right a few scant seconds before leaping forwards. The beast seemed to sense the slack on the rope and tried to squirm its front paws from underneath. Sanders' weight slammed onto the back of the Horse Serpent, momentarily winding it. He leaped forwards again, this time onto the neck to push his forearm down on the point where the back of the neck met the skull. He pushed down hard as the beast squirmed under him, lying forwards with his hips over its shoulders. He held fast, knowing for now, while its front paws were stuck under its body and its tail was out of range, that mouth was the biggest threat to him.

As he struggled, he knew in that moment if he had wanted to, he could have killed the Horse Serpent right then and there. All he had to do was get the Bowie knife from his belt and drive it into the creature's skull. But Sanders could never do that. Despite the carnage around him, the numerous soldiers who were mercilessly killed and the danger this monster still held for him, Sanders could never kill an animal in return for doing what its natural instincts told it to do. He never killed crocodiles who killed people. He caught them and moved them. Never killed. Not before and not now.

"O'Mara," he called, "you still here?"

There was a moment of silence before Sanders heard a meek 'yes'.

"Good. I need you to bring me that last rope I prepared. Do you see the X I scratched into the ground?"

"Yes."

"Then about a foot from it you should see a short, looped rope. I need you to bring it here and help me place it over the Horse Serpent's mouth."

"Are you serious?"

"Not always. But right now, absolutely."

He heard her shaky footsteps as she moved to collect the rope, then with trepidation approach Sanders and the monster. She held it out and dangled it in front of his face.

"Here," she said.

The beast tried to buck and Sanders pushed hard down on its head to prevent it from escaping.

"Oh no. My hands are full right now, you are the one who is going to loop it over her nose."

"Me?" she said meekly.

"That's right. Now kneel down and get in close. That's it. That's it. You can do it. Now hold the loop in front of her face. Yes, like that. Tighten it a little. Good. Now, here's what's going to happen. I'm going to let the Horse Serpent lift its head a little. When I do, I need you to get that rope underneath and pull that noose tight. You got it?"

Silence.

"You got it?" he repeated.

"Yes."

"Good. Okay, count of three. One… Two…"

The beast thrashed with its tail and kicked with its back legs, renting long divots in the ground in an attempt to get him off.

"Three."

Sanders eased his grip and the beast raised its head. Sanders' muscles burned as he allowed it to lift its head a small way but not shake it free. He could sense it again trying to pull its front legs clear so he squeezed into its flanks with his thighs. O'Mara slipped the loop over the mouth. The beast opened its mouth, not in time to stop the rope, but enough for O'Mara to drop the rope and flinch away. Sanders pushed down on the head with renewed effort and forced it back on the ground.

"The rope. Tighten the rope."

Sanders watched as O'Mara reached forwards with shaky hands and pulled the noose tight. He then explained to her how to tie the rope to prevent slippage.

"Good. Now, there is one more thing I need to do."

"What's that?"

"Stop those damn idiots in the trucks before they leave us here."

***

When Dower caught up with the soldiers, they had already hustled the drivers away from their cigarettes and into their cabs to crank the engines. One truck came sputtering to life as the soldiers piled into the back.

Dower looked around for Cheong and Sanders. With a loud crunching of gears, the first truck started inching forward into a turn, while the second spat and sputtered before belching black smoke from its tailpipe. Dower looked up at the cab of the second truck and saw Cheong sitting in front, so he ran around the front to wave to the driver to let him in before they moved on. Cheong frowned at Dower as he rounded the truck and opened the door to climb in.

"Wait," he said as he mounted the stairs, "we have to see if Jess or Sanders make it out."

Cheong stared at him wide eyed as though Dower had just suggested the most stupid thing he had ever heard.

"No chance," Cheong rebutted. "If they aren't out now, then they are probably already dead."

"We have to wait. Just give it a minute."

"No waiting. You saw what that monster can do. We need to get out of here, get more men and bigger guns and come back."

The first truck completed its turn and edged past them to return to the town from whence they came. Cheong immediately urged the driver to turn their own vehicle around.

"We have to give them a chance to get back," Dower said feebly, clasping his hands tightly together and looking back towards the stream and cave. Cheong pretended not to notice and pestered the driver to turn the vehicle. With a crunch of gears the vehicle was slammed in reverse as the driver put the truck through a three-point turn.

"Come on, Jess, make it please," Dower said in a murmur as he turned to keep an eye on the spot where he hoped at any moment O'Mara would appear from. But nobody came, and with another crunching of gears the truck lurched forward to turn for home.

"Please, Mr Cheong, can't we wait a few seconds more?"

Cheong turned and for a brief moment Dower was sure he could see sorrow in his eyes.

"I'm sorry, Mr Dower, but I don't plan to join the dead today. That monster was on a killing rampage and we need to get out of its way before we are next. I can let you out here to wait, but this truck and I are leaving."

Dower gave the best beseeching look he could muster, but Cheong's eyes only hardened with resolve. Dower turned to look at the forest once more, willing O'Mara to be there, but still there was nothing.

"Well, Mr Dower, what will it be?"

Dower dropped his head and closed his eyes to hold the tears in. He could not even bring himself to say the words, and feebly motioned with his hand for them to go. Cheong stared at him tight-lipped, before turning to the driver and nodding. The driver released the clutch and the truck rattled forwards.

A few seconds passed and Dower lifted his head to wipe his cheeks with the palms of his hands. He turned his face away from Cheong and the driver, ashamed not of the tears but of himself. He leaned forward to look through the side mirror, still hopeful of a miracle. The mirror vibrated like a jackhammer, blurring the view into a collage of brown and green.

"I'm sorry, Jess," he whispered to the mirror.

Suddenly there was a flash of white amidst the blur of brown and green. For a second he frowned, wondering what the sudden change could be. Hope rose and he reached out with one hand and wound the window down. It screeched in protest but he wrenched at it with renewed hope and vigour.

He barely had the window down halfway when he thrust his head out to look behind. A branch brushed his head and he swore as he turned to see the star jumping figure on the road behind them.

"Stop!" he shouted as he pulled his head back into the cab. "Stop, Jess managed to get away."

Cheong stared at him a second as though he was half mad, then drew a long breath before talking to the driver. The brakes squealed as he applied pressure, drawing the old army truck to a stop.

Before it had fully come to a stop, Dower had already opened the door and leapt out. Cheong looked at the open door with cynicism before sliding across the truck seat to peer behind.

Dower's legs pumped beneath him as he ran with his arms outstretched towards her. She was shouting manically, and for a moment he was clutched with fear that the monster may have been chasing her somewhere out of sight. His feet faltered, but he pushed the doubt aside and ran on.

They closed and he went to hug her, but she stepped to the side to run around him. He tried stepping into her path, but she thrust out a hand to push him aside.

"No," she gasped. "Tranquilizers."

Before he could respond she was past him. He turned to see Cheong had dismounted and was walking cautiously towards them. She shouted and Cheong pointed to the back of the truck. With agility Dower had not seen from O'Mara before, she scaled the back of the truck and disappeared under the cover.

Dower started a slow jog towards the truck when O'Mara reappeared with a medical box in her hand and leapt from the tailgate, breaking once again into a run towards him.

"What is going on?" he shouted.

"Sanders… Horse Serpent… Hurry," was all he could make out between her blustered, panting breaths. Dower turned to see Cheong and the driver reach into the back of the truck and draw out two AK-47s before turning to follow in a slow jog.

Dower would have felt safer waiting for Cheong and the driver, but O'Mara was not waiting and he turned wistfully away from them to chase her.

She was moving like he had not seen before, and he was breathing hard and not getting any closer when she disappeared between the trees to the side of the road. He checked behind to ensure that Cheong and the driver were still in tow before diving through the trees himself. For a second he thought he had lost her, then he caught a flash of white ahead.

He heard the sound of the stream and followed it forward to come across a remarkable sight.

Dower slowed to a walk as he approached the scene. Jess knelt on the ground before the kit, measuring liquid visually as she filled a syringe. Behind her Sanders lay on his stomach, pinning the Horse Serpent to the ground. The Horse Serpent was more than twice his size, yet here he had it pinned like a wrestling world champion. Even Hulk Hogan would have given a nod of respect in this moment. The beast growled and shuddered, but held fast, his muscles bulging under glistening skin.

O'Mara leaned forward, finding a soft spot in the neck and inserting the syringe. Dower stumbled forwards with his mouth agape. The creature bucked again but already Dower could see from the eyes that it was weakening. Behind him, Dower heard the scuffing of feet and the exclaimed oaths as Cheong and the driver took in the scene before them.

Dower was transfixed, and he stumbled closer until he was standing over the mighty beast. Sanders was stroking its flank and mumbling softly to it as it drifted to sleep. O'Mara, too, reached out to touch the magnificent beast. Upon doing so, she looked up and smiled at Sanders. He returned the smile.

"She's a beauty, isn't she?" Sanders said.

Sanders released the beast and stood up, groaning and stretching. O'Mara stayed, stroking the beast a moment longer before standing up. Dower edged forward to stand between them, staring with a mixture of awe and fear at the sleeping beast, when O'Mara pushed past him to reach forward and hug Sanders.

Dower turned his eyes from the beast to his partner and watched sadly on as she shuddered in Sanders' arms and took comfort from his embrace.

5

The bottles clinked together for the third time in as many minutes to the shout of "cheers" and both Sanders and O'Mara leaned back to down their respective beers. Sanders emptied the bottle and slammed it onto the table with a whoop. He was still riding the high of the catch. Dower gave him a weak smile and replaced his bottle on the table, his drink barely touched.

Sanders and O'Mara had retold the story twice now, and as O'Mara settled her bottle down on the table again, she started recalling the moment she had thought she was alone when the beast charged her. Dower felt a tear forming in his eye and looked away. Sanders let out a raucous laugh and he and O'Mara joked about how the Horse Serpent had tumbled across the ground. The retelling was getting more exaggerated and more cartoonish with each telling, but Dower did not doubt the truth of it.

Cheong entered the room at that moment. While the others had sat at the bar, Cheong had gone into his room to change. Despite not having a speck of dirt on it, Cheong had insisted his previous suit was filthy and needed to be replaced.

Cheong had not exerted himself once nor engaged in any physical activity during the Horse Serpent capture other than to run away, jog back with a rifle and lay a handful of vicious kicks into the sleeping beast when he had the opportunity. He did not engage in what he deemed (in his own words) as 'grunt work', he was a leader and an order giver. He had lived up to his word, too, as he watched the others load the unconscious body of the Horse Serpent onto a canvas and drag it through the rainforest to the truck, where they struggled to lift it up and into the cage housed in the back of the truck. Sure, they could have used an extra pair of hands, but someone needed to tell them what to do, and the man for that job was Cheong. Yet somehow, despite all of that, his suit had somewhere become 'filthy'.

"Cheongy," yelled Sanders across the empty bar as he saw him. "Come over here, loosen that tie and have a celebratory beer with us, mate."

Cheong pursed his lips. Dower had to smirk as he wondered whether it was the decision of having a beer with them or not had him vexed, or whether it was deciding if being called 'Cheongy' was any better than 'Kenny'.

"No," Cheong said, approaching the table. "We must go. If we leave in the next ten minutes we can get back to Jakarta by dusk. I have a warehouse reserved in the docks where we can keep the Horse Serpent until a ship out of Indonesia is arranged. But we must hurry, so return to your rooms now and get your things."

"Righto, Chief," Sanders said, and stood up to give Cheong a mock salute. O'Mara giggled and stood beside him, and together they walked to the door that led to the staircase upstairs, joking and laughing. Neither had noticed Dower still sat at the table staring at them as they disappeared from view.

"Aren't you going too?" Cheong asked.

Dower sighed. "My things are already packed. I'll get my bag in a minute, I just want to finish this beer."

Cheong studied the beer with a raised eyebrow but said nothing. He turned to leave, but stopped and turned back to look at Dower once more.

"There was no shame in you running today, Mr Dower. Self-preservation is not cowardice. It's as Sun Tzu says, you do not engage in a battle you cannot win."

Dower tried giving Cheong a smile but instead nodded and watched Cheong leave. He turned back to the near full beer bottle. What had Cheong just said? Do not engage battles you cannot win? He pondered it, wondering if that was the correct quote. Then he pondered O'Mara and Sanders, and their newfound connection. He pushed the bottle away. He did not feel like drinking now anyway.

He stood up and made his way to the bar's bathroom. Inside he peed quickly and washed his hands before staring at himself in the mirror. He turned his head side to side, looking at the growing number of greys. He looked around his eyes at the growing crinkles of his skin. And finally, he looked down at his growing pot belly. He had always been slim and been able to eat lots without it showing. But now, as he lived through his forties, that was no longer a luxury he had. He sighed, wiping his hands on his pants to dry them before walking out the door.

Back in the bar area, he noticed his beer was gone and the table had been cleared. He shrugged. He had no real intention of drinking that beer anyway. He turned for the door that led to the stairs when he heard one of the trucks cough to life outside the bar. He approached the window to see the truck that carried the Horse Serpent edge forward in the direction of the soldiers that had escaped earlier. They were shouting in Indonesian and as Dower watched a new, third truck, identical to the one that just departed, pulled into the vacant spot. Dower kept his eye on the first truck, watching it move up the street and pull in behind a building further ahead. Seconds later, the driver reappeared and jogged back to the new truck.

Dower pulled away from the window, cautious not to be seen by the milling soldiers. Once out of view, he turned and ran for the door and dashed upstairs. He fumbled with his keys, banged on the door before finally composing himself enough to slot the key into the lock. The door opened to an empty room. Both his and O'Mara's bags were still on the bed.

He picked up the bags and dropped them in the hall at the top of the stairs. He turned to the door of Sanders' room. He sucked in a deep breath and stepped over to it. He banged on the door frantically. Sanders opened the door only slightly, blocking Dower from seeing into the room beyond.

"Everything okay, mate?" Sanders asked.

"We've been betrayed," Dower said frantically. "They've switched the trucks. They are going to steal the Horse Serpent from us."

"Who is?"

"The soldiers. They moved our truck up the street and hid it. There is an identical truck downstairs now. We'd never know it if I hadn't seen it."

Sanders stared at him a second before nodding. "Right. Does Cheong know?"

"I don't know what room he's in."

Sanders nodded, then turned back into his room and strode across to the bed to collect his bag. The door swung open to reveal O'Mara standing and watching the doorway. As her eyes met Dower's, she gave him a weak smile.

Sanders picked up his bag and approached the window to peer outside. He noted the two trucks waiting and the soldiers milling about. They carried their AK-47s on their shoulders and as Sanders watched, they moved about with restless energy.

"How far up is the real truck?" Sanders asked.

"Behind the building after the petrol station."

"Got it."

Sanders turned, his face tight lipped as he glanced from Dower to O'Mara, then back again.

"Okay," Sanders said at last, "here's the plan. Grab any possessions that can't be replaced, passports, wallets etc, out of your bag and keep them on you. You two go downstairs with my bag and wait on Cheong. Tell them I'm taking a crap or something and keep 'em waiting."

O'Mara stepped forward and placed a hand on his arm.

"But what are you doing?" she asked.

"I'll sneak out the back door and make my way over to the truck and hotwire it."

"You know how to hotwire a truck?"

Sanders shrugged. "What can I say? I was a wild child."

"Okay, so you start the truck," Dower said, "but what next? How do we get to you from under the noses of the gun toting terrorists?"

"The petrol station. Say you need to buy something for the trip. Gum or a chocolate bar or something. Get Cheong to come with you, then sneak behind and find me."

"Okay," Dower nodded, then shook his head. "My God. This is crazy."

"Just hold your nerve. We have to get that Horse Serpent back. There's no telling what those soldiers want it for, but I'd put a pineapple on it that their intentions aren't honourable."

Without waiting for further questions, Sanders vaulted down the stairs and out of sight. Dower watched him go, then turned back to his partner. O'Mara shrugged and walked over to pick up hers and Sanders' bags. Without a word, she started descending the stairs. Wistfully, Dower picked up his own bag and slowly followed.

***

The back door of the bar led out into a dirty alleyway. Bloated flies circled lazily over the overflowing bins and rats scurried between the shadows. There was an awful stench, and Sanders wondered how long the discarded food scraps had been left out here to rot in the sweltering heat.

Aside from the feeding vermin, however, the alley was clear of life.

Sanders crept forward to the corner and looked out to the street. Ahead there was an adjoining alley that would enable him to sneak closer to the truck undetected. To his right he could see the main street, and the front of the decoy truck. The driver leaned on the front bumper huffing on a cigarette. Sanders was wondering how he could sneak across to the next alley and remain unseen when someone called the driver and he turned and walked out of view. Sanders dashed to the next alley opposite him.

The second alley was equally dirty and its inhabitants equally fat and bloated, but they avoided him and he did likewise as he jogged up it. This alley ended in another side street, and as he looked to his right up it, he could see the petrol station.

Sanders approached the main road and carefully glanced back towards the bar and the trucks. The soldiers milled around with the same restless energy as before. One paced back and forth with his knuckles white where he clutched his rifle. Another kicked the tires of the truck. The driver was smoking like a chimney.

There was no cover on the street and no way for Sanders to cross without being seen. He pulled back behind the corner and thought. He was once told confidence is everything and if you have enough of it, you can get through anything. He had followed that philosophy a lot, both with women and with police during his wilder days. It had worked often. Not always, but regularly enough. He thought about that philosophy now as he considered just crossing the road in plain view of everyone.

And why not? The soldiers would not expect him to be there and had no reason to be suspicious. But then again, how often did this remote town in Indonesia have six-foot blonde Australian men crossing the road? Probably not that often. But in lieu of no plan at all, it seemed like the best thing right now.

So, he did it. He stepped out of the alley and walked across the street. He walked as nonchalantly as he could muster, being not too quick nor too slow. Sweat prickled his brow and he expected at any moment for them to shout to him or for a shot to ring out. The urge to glance their way was strong. He ached to see if any of them were looking his way, but resisted the urge. The crossing of the road seemed like an eternity, but in what had been less than ten seconds, he was stepping up onto the opposite curb and walking past the petrol station.

Sanders walked past the building and turned the corner to spy the truck. He immediately slowed, approaching the truck with caution. As he approached the back of the truck, he stopped and stooped down, looking under the truck for the feet of any soldiers that might have been left behind to guard it. There were none.

He approached the cab, carefully raising himself up on the step to peer inside, lest the guard be sitting there. But the cab, too, was empty. Sanders snorted, surprised at the soldiers' sloppiness as he opened the cab door to climb in.

He had completely missed the soldier sleeping in the back.

***

Dower glanced nervously at the soldiers as he exited the bar. He tried to look casual, act casual, but his legs felt like jelly and he was certain that if he stood still, his knees would knock together like castanets.

One soldier, who wore a dark cap, seemed to act as the leader. He regarded Dower and O'Mara through narrowed eyes, and was looking at more than O'Mara's legs, unlike the other soldiers. The one in the cap pointed to the bags and then the back of the truck. Dower nodded and stepped forward and threw the bags over the tailgate. If things went well, he would never see those bags again.

He stepped back and the soldier in the cap asked something of him. Dower smiled and shrugged. The soldier muttered something and gestured at him in frustration. A nearby soldier smirked at the remark. Dower found himself troubled by that smirk, knowing whatever was behind it could not be good.

The door of the bar opened behind him, and Dower turned to see Cheong joining them outside. The soldier in the cap stepped forward and spoke briskly to Cheong.

"They want to know where Sanders is," Cheong translated.

"He had to go to the toilet," O'Mara said. "He wasn't feeling good in the stomach. It might be the local water."

Cheong rolled his eyes. "Serves him right. Westerners and their mollycoddled stomachs. He should know better than to drink from the taps."

"I don't think he's ventured far overseas before," O'Mara said.

"No surprise there. I don't doubt he's never ventured far out of the primordial swamp that bore him," Cheong huffed and passed his bag to a soldier to put in the back.

The soldier put the bag in the back and, like the others around them, began to stare at Dower and O'Mara expectantly. The silence stretched, and began to feel more than uncomfortable. Dower looked at his shoes and began moving a pebble around in the dirt. The soldier in the cap muttered something.

"Do you think he will be much longer?" Cheong asked.

"Who can say?" replied O'Mara, moving closer to Dower.

"Perhaps I should go in and hurry him," Cheong said. "We need to get going."

Dower felt O'Mara nudge him. He opened his mouth to speak, but words failed him. His eyes could only focus on the guns slung over the soldiers before him and his brain refused to work.

"Uh, Cheong," O'Mara improvised, "I'm wondering if you could come across the road with me to that petrol station. I need to buy some aspirin and I need your help."

"Aspirin? I have some in my bag," Cheong said and stepped towards the truck.

"I also wanted to buy some snacks for the road," she quickly replied.

"Snacks?"

"I..." Dower croaked. He cleared his throat and tried again. "I would like to buy a drink as well. I was parched during that last road trip."

Cheong considered them a moment, before looking back at the bar. He exchanged a quick word with the man in the cap before turning back to them.

"Come," he said and started across the street.

Dower trotted behind, his legs again feeling like jelly.

"I suppose you want to put this on Higson's tab as well?" Cheong called over his shoulder as he stepped up on the curb.

"Uh, sure," Dower replied, turning and looking back to see the soldier in the cap watching them curiously.

As they moved out of the watching soldier's sight, Dower and O'Mara quickened their pace and directed Cheong away from the petrol station.

"What? Where are we going?" Cheong asked as they hooked their arms under his and moved him away.

"We've been double crossed by our associates," O'Mara murmured. "The real truck is over here, and Sanders is waiting for us with it."

"Sanders is where?" Cheong asked, flabbergasted.

As if in answer, Cheong heard the truck's engine crank and fire to life. They turned the corner to see the truck with Sanders sitting behind the wheel grinning like a proud child showing off his new toy to his friends. Before Cheong could say anything, he was hustled into the cab next to Sanders.

"You look surprised," Sanders commented.

"Hold up," O'Mara said, "have you checked the cargo?"

"Not yet. Do you want to have a quick look?"

She gave him the thumbs up and jogged to the back. She climbed up over the tailgate and ducked under the tarpaulin. The cage had a black cloth draped over it. She approached carefully and lifted one edge of the cloth to see the sleeping Horse Serpent underneath.

She stepped back to the tailgate where Dower stood waiting. He held out a hand to help her down.

"No," she said. "It'll be too squashy in the cab with the four of us. I'll ride in back and keep my eye on it."

"I'll ride in back with you then," Dower suggested.

"No," she said briskly. At his pained expression, she decided to elaborate. "I'd just… like to be alone for the moment if I could."

Dower dropped his head and nodded.

"Look, if I need anything I'll bang on the back of the cabin, okay?"

Dower nodded and trudged back to the cab and climbed aboard.

"Right, Cheongy, which way do we go to get out of here?" Sanders asked as he revved up the engine.

"There's only one way in or out of this town. Back past the soldiers."

"Right," said Sanders, drawing in a deep breath and shifting the gearstick into reverse. "You'd better hold onto your pocket square then."

***

Bonjole Mohede was not the most reliable soldier. He was not even a good Muslim. He had his vices and they controlled him. He carried the scars of flogging on his back for pursuing his vices, but even that could not make him stop. He was too weak willed to control his vices. Well, one vice in particular: alcohol.

The men around him had learned to tolerate Mohede and his sinful ways. How could they not? He was connected, by blood, to senior leaders who they could only hope to be recognised by. Not that Mohede abused those connections. It was just that his vices always got the better of him.

It was also the reason Mohede was given the lowest and easiest tasks within his unit. Ones he could not fail at, no matter how hard he tried. One such simple task was guarding a truck hidden in a side street that nobody knew about from three foreign civilians. Apparently, there was something important about the truck, though nobody told him what it was. It looked like a normal truck to Mohede. He suspected it may have been just another made up on the spot job to keep him out of everyone else's way.

Mohede hated that he had been designated this job and trudged back and forth along the side street with little enthusiasm. The sun was baking hot and he was feeling the worst effects of last night's vice indulgence when he decided he could take a quick nap in the back of the truck.

He climbed up over the tailgate and into the rear. There was some sort of big box or something covered with a black cloth in the back. It would provide the perfect cover for a quick kip. He skirted around the object and lay down, hidden and safe in the back. He relaxed, knowing if someone came, he could claim he was just checking things over in the rear of the truck.

Mohede was awakened by the sound of the engine turning over and sputtering to life. For a moment he froze, realising he would at any moment be caught sleeping on the job. Again.

The back of the truck was dark, with most of the light obscured by the thick canopy and the big covered box in the middle of the truck. He felt around for his rifle, and was relieved to find it lying on his side where he left it. He started to sit up when he heard someone climb aboard the truck. He froze, unsure if at this point it was better to come out and admit he had fallen asleep on the job or to remain hidden, when he heard a woman start to talk. A male voice answered. The words were unfamiliar to him, and he frowned until it dawned upon him that she was speaking a foreign language.

He drew his legs up and moved his body into a crouch and raised himself up just enough to see over the crate. A white skinned, blonde woman took a seat on the bench seat and reached up to hold onto one of the struts.

The gears of the truck crunched and Mohede felt the truck moving backwards as it reversed out of the side street. He cursed, realising he had not only fallen asleep, but he had let the truck fall into the hands of the very people he was supposed to protect it against.

Mohede slowly stood up, switching the rifle off safe mode and into semi-automatic mode. He raised the gun and pointed it at her.

"Hey," he called.

***

The truck rattled and clattered as Sanders reversed it out of the side street. He turned the wheel wildly, and the truck swung to the side in a violent, tire screeching turn. He slammed the brakes and kicked the clutch down and punched the truck into first gear.

Ahead on the road the soldier's heads turned almost as one, drawn by the noise. The truck thundered forwards over the bumpy road. Sanders slammed the clutch back to the floor and punched it into second gear. The soldier in the black cap's eyes bulged as he saw the truck surging towards them. With a flurry of shouts, he ordered the soldiers around him to make a line against the road and aim at the oncoming truck.

"Everybody down," Sanders roared.

The muzzles of the soldiers' guns lit up like a New Year's Day fireworks celebration. The windscreen cracked then shattered under the hail of lead. Bullets whipped about them with noised fury and the sharp clang of metal on metal rang through the air as the storm of steel rained down upon them.

"Faster, you piece of crap," Sanders urged the truck as sparks lit up the bonnet in front of him. The door beside him rattled under the impact of a torrent of gunfire and for a brief moment he regretted cursing the sturdy old warhorse. It was holding up well against the deluge of rampant fire. Sanders crouched over the wheel, trying to keep as small as he could while Cheong and Dower ducked under the dashboard and held their hands over their heads. A stray bullet thumped into the headrest behind Sanders, forcing him to duck lower and for a few moments he was driving blind.

Then they were clear. The guns still clattered but bullets no longer hummed through the air about them like angry bees, but thudded into the side of the truck and shredded the tarpaulin canopy at the rear.

"Everybody ok?" Sanders shouted over the noise.

Both Cheong and Dower, faces white as a freshly hung sheet, checked themselves and slowly rose back to their sitting positions. Everyone in the cab was remarkably unhurt.

"Turn here," Cheong said.

Sanders wrenched at the wheel without braking and the truck slewed wildly as he wrestled it around the corner. Almost immediately the gunfire ceased. Shocked expressions turned to smiles, and smiles turned to laughter. Sanders let out a whoop of delight.

"Oh my God," Dower said, his eyes wide with elation, "we actually made it. Ha!" He shone a broad grin as Sanders reached an arm around Cheong and gave him a one-armed hug. Cheong broke into a smile; an expression Dower had not seen from him before. As Sanders released him, Cheong straightened his jacket and tie.

"Hey," Cheong said jokingly, "careful of the suit."

Sanders turned to Cheong and then they both burst out laughing. Dower raised an eyebrow and smiled at the sudden comradery the two had found. It was a pity it took a near death experience to bring it out of them.

Then the smile died on his face.

"Jess," he shrieked, "oh my God, Jess was in the back. We have to check on her."

The smiles dropped from the faces of Sanders and Cheong almost immediately. Sanders checked the side mirror and continued to drive.

"We have to stop and check on Jess," Dower repeated.

"Can't do that now. We have company," Sanders said.

In the shaky view of the cracked side mirror, Sanders had spotted a dark green shape closing in on them. It was one of the other trucks. The soldiers were in pursuit. In solemn silence, Sanders pushed the accelerator down. There was a slight ditch in the road and all three of them bounced in their seats as he ploughed through it.

Suddenly there was loud banging on the rear of the cabin. Cheong ducked down. Sanders checked the mirror and held out a hand.

"That isn't gunfire," he said.

"It's Jess. Thank God she's alive."

Dower thumped on the rear of the cabin to give an acknowledgement that they had heard her. But the banging did not stop. It continued, but at a quicker and louder pace.

"What is she trying to tell us?" Cheong asked.

Dower stared at the rear wall of the cab and his eyes widened.

"Oh my God," he said, "she's in trouble."

***

The blonde swivelled her head and her eyes bugged out as Mohede trained his gun on her. He let a sinister smile crawl across his features and carefully stepped forwards. Suddenly the truck was thrown into a wild turn. Mohede was caught off balance and fell into the canvas cover before bouncing back to fall into the hard, square object in the centre of the rear tray.

Mohede was momentarily dazed, and was only just pulling himself to his feet when the gunfire started. He quickly ducked back down.

The canvas above him became punctured with holes, looking like a black night sky suddenly burst to life with stars. Sunlight knifed through the holes to vividly light up the rear of the truck. Bullets rattled around him, bursting like popcorn at full heat. He covered his face with his hands, wishing he had the moral strength to be a better Muslim and hoped that Allah would look upon his trials sympathetically during the day of judgement.

And then it was over. The truck had swung wildly around a corner and the gunfire ceased. The silence was so sudden, that for a second Mohede thought he had died. But the truck engine rolled on.

Mohede pulled his hands away from his face and felt at his body. He could not believe he had made it through the torrent of gunfire unharmed. Allah must have smiled upon him this day.

Mohede pulled himself up and retrieved his rifle. He checked it over quickly as he looked about him. There was no sign of the woman. She must be hiding beyond the large cube. Out the rear, he could see another truck in pursuit. He drew strength from the sight. He turned, determined to find the blonde woman.

He stepped carefully around the covered cube to where he had seen her sitting earlier. There was no sign of her here, not even a drop of blood. Mohede turned back to face the cabin end of the vehicle. She must be hiding under this cloth or between it and the cab.

Mohede lowered to a crouch. He held the rifle tight to his shoulder with one hand and reached out to grasp a handful of cloth. Slowly he lifted the cloth. Underneath, he saw thick bars of reinforced steel. It was dark inside and he lifted the cloth higher still. Beyond the bars, a large baleful yellow eye glowered in the gloom at him.

Mohede dropped the cloth and fell backwards onto his rump. There was something alive in there. He shook his head. Whatever it was, it was not the blond woman.

Mohede picked himself up and steadied himself. He stepped forwards, edging around the cage and keeping as far from it as he conceivably could. A sharp scraping sound came from the cage. He eyed it nervously, considering whether it may be safer to leave the blond alone and stand clear of the cage when movement caught the corner of his eye.

The rifle was knocked from his hands and clattered away, over to the opposite side of the cage. He turned to the blond woman giving a half snarl, half smile at him, proud to have knocked his weapon away. She pointed a length of wood at him, threatening a second blow if he did not back away.

Mohede reached around his belt and pulled a Bowie knife from it. The steel blade glinted reassuringly from the various pinholes of light that shone through the canvas. Her eyes darted to the blade and now it was his turn to smile. He was going to gut her like an animal.

Mohede feinted to his left. As she made to block it, he stepped forward. He needed to get closer, get her inside his range. He feinted again, and this time she stepped back as he stepped forward. He grinned again. She was less confident now.

He feinted a third time and, seeing his opening, pushed forward to strike. Suddenly the floor kicked him into the air, bucking like a wild animal. Mohede flew uncontrolled forwards, their bodies colliding heavily and collapsing to the floor. Mohede was quickest to recover, and rolled his body on top of hers. He sat on her stomach and grabbed a handful of her hair and held her down by it. He made to drive the knife down into her throat but she thrust her two hands up to grab his wrist and push him away. He leaned hard on the knife, pushing it closer and closer to her delicate white skin, both their hands shaking with the effort. She started kicking wildly at the cab as they wrestled, making a loud banging racket. But it was no use. Mohede was winning the battle, and his hard knife was inching closer and closer to her soft throat by the second.

***

"One of us is going to have to climb back there and see what's happening," Sanders said as the banging continued behind them.

"Climb?" Dower asked in a soft voice. Sanders shot him a quick glance then pursed his lips.

"Cheongy, I need you to take the wheel."

"What?"

"Take the wheel and drive. I'm going outside."

"Are you mad?" Cheong scoffed.

Sanders gave him a sharp glance that suggested that yes, he may indeed be mad, but also, now was not the time for questions like that.

"Okay, but I don't know how to drive."

"You don't know how to drive?"

"No, I never learned."

"Aren't you a business school major or something?"

"I have a doctoral degree to be exact."

"And you don't know how to drive?"

"I've always had someone drive me."

"Jesus. Right, Prof, you need to slide past Cheongy and take the wheel for me."

Dower shifted and slid across the bench seat and under the smaller Cheong. He had barely squeezed under when he was stepping over the gearstick. Sanders opened the door and stepped out of the cab just as Dower slid into the driver seat. The truck slowed as Sanders pulled his foot from the accelerator, but it surged as Dower pressed it back down.

Sanders stood on the step to the cab, holding the door as he watched the dirt road blur past underneath him. The truck shuddered as they passed over a rough patch, and Sanders looked for a way to clamber into the back.

"This was a lot easier in my head," Sanders shouted as he eyed the rear of the truck, realising there was nothing much he could hold onto.

Sanders stepped cautiously onto a tank that sat just behind the cab and reached out to the canvas. He looked up to see the green cloth was dotted with holes.

"Ok," he said, reaching up to one and pulling on it vigorously. He nodded to himself and felt comfortable the canvas would hold his weight. He heaved his body up and reached out to get a foothold on the rim of the rear tray. It was narrow, a mere two inches of steel for him to stand on, so he stood on his toes. He stood for a second, breathing heavily before raising his second foot from the tank and onto the slight ledge.

The balls of his feet screamed with stress as he held himself to the truck and stood on the smallest of ledges on his toes. He scrambled for handholds where the bullets had punctured the canvas and started edging his way to the rear of the truck.

There was a woman's scream from inside the truck and it spurred Sanders on. He shuffled along the side of the tray, his toes already becoming numb from the pressure of holding his whole weight on such a narrow ledge, when the truck hit a bump and his feet slipped. For a second Sanders hung, nothing but open air and hard gravel flashing past beneath his boots. His shoulders ached, still tired from his wrestling match with the Horse Serpent, and he let himself hang a few seconds while he tried to recover his breath.

Sanders glanced at the truck behind and saw it was closing. It was close enough now he could see the black capped driver motioning for his passenger to pass him a rifle and take the wheel. Sanders grimaced. All bad things came in groups.

Sanders lifted his knees up and tried getting one foot back onto the narrow ledge. His first attempt missed, and his hands almost slipped from their hold. Sanders glanced at the chasing truck and saw the driver lean out the window with his AK-47.

Sanders tried again and this time hooked his left foot onto the ledge with enough leverage to pull himself back up from the brink. He had just placed his right foot up on the ledge when he heard the first report from the rifle. Something pulled his shirt and stung his arm. Sanders gritted his teeth and cursed. The rifle reported a second time.

Sanders pushed himself faster, edging delicately along the vehicle while the driver behind aimed single, targeted shots at him. They passed over another bump and Sanders was almost dislodged again, but through sheer grit he held firm. He reached the edge of the tray and swung himself in, just as a bullet whistled past his head.

There was no time to rest as Sanders heard a whimper and vaulted back towards the cabin.

***

O'Mara kicked and kicked and kicked. Why weren't they stopping the truck?

The bearded man was heavy on top of her, his rancid breath steaming from his mouth as he panted on her. She pushed back with all her might, but she was weakening and the evil blade was edging closer and closer to her throat. She had never imagined she would be in a situation like this. She never imagined herself fighting for her life and watching as death's cold embrace slowly closed in on her.

The man above must have sensed her weakening as he pushed down with renewed effort. The tip of the knife disappeared from her line of vision and O'Mara felt something cold and hard press against her throat.

O'Mara screamed and pushed back against her attacker. For a moment she appeared to be succeeding, and the pressure eased from her throat. But the man let go of the fistful of hair he held and pushed down with both hands.

A shot rang through the air. The man was momentarily distracted and she tried to wriggle aside. In doing so, though, her grip on his arm slipped and the knife speared down. She turned her head and pushed his hands away. The knife hit the floor of the truck bed beside her with a clang. She thought she had avoided the blow, but the warm liquid sensation on her neck told her otherwise.

The man on top of her cursed and tried to bring the knife down on her once more. A second shot rang out as she pushed against the arms of her attacker. But she was weakening. This time the attacker intended to pierce her chest. Her arms shook under the strain as he bore his weight down on her. The knife pressed into her chest just above her left breast. She whimpered as the blade pressed hard. This was it, she thought, this is how it ends, when suddenly the man went limp and collapsed over her.

Too weak to even push his bulk from her, O'Mara could only stare as Sanders rolled the unconscious body away from on top of her. In his hands, Sanders held the man's rifle, butt first. He looked over her with concerned eyes and mumbled a few words she could not make out. A shot rang out and he turned and cursed. He stepped out of view, flicking a switch on the side of the rifle as he did so.

O'Mara's vision blurred and she sensed herself passing out. The last think she could remember was the sound of automatic gunfire and Sanders' maniacal yells.

6

"And that was it?" O'Mara asked, her eyes wide and curious. "You just shot out their engine and we got away?"

"Pretty much," Sanders replied, acting as humble as he could in the most boastful way possible. "I just aimed and fired the gun at their engine, took out the truck chasing us, tied up our new friend and attended to your bleeding. It was a piece of piss."

O'Mara gave a short smile. It was definitely more boastful than modest. "I highly doubt it," she giggled, before looking at him more seriously. "How did know how to use the gun? Before I passed out, I saw you click something on it before shooting."

Sanders reddened. "Yeah, I switched it to automatic. I'm.... ex-army."

"You seem embarrassed to say that."

Sanders scratched his head and looked away. "Not embarrassed about being in the army. It's just... I don't usually talk about it because I was dishonourably discharged."

"Oh?"

"Yeah. Something about a lack of respect for authority."

O'Mara snorted. "Why am I not surprised?" She smiled a moment, but then it suddenly dropped and she looked about her. "What have you done with the man who attacked me in the truck? Where is he now?"

Sanders chewed his bottom lip a moment while he studied her, before nodding to the truck.

Her eyes followed his nod and widened as she stared at the truck and its ragged, torn tarpaulin cover. "Is he..." she said, but the words died away before she got them out.

"Alive?" Sanders asked. "Yes, but don't worry, he's tied up tighter than the Horse Serpent. I made sure of that."

"Do you know who he is? Who he works for?"

"We tried interrogating him, but he didn't give us much. His name is Mohede, but that's about all we learned unfortunately. Cheong might know who he works for. They are part of the same group he hired, after all, but Cheong ain't saying shit either."

She nodded and stared at him a moment in deep thought. He coughed and her eyes flicked away from Sanders to take in the large, open space she sat in. It was almost all concrete. Concrete floor, concrete walls and even a concrete roof. The windows had black bars across them, but she could not be sure they were not just painted concrete too. But aside from the barred windows, the cage that housed the Horse Serpent (still covered with the black cloth) and the truck parked by a roller door, the concrete building was clean and empty. There was an odd smell to the air, a mix of rubbish and pollution, but also a soft scent of the sea.

"Where are we?" she asked.

"In Cheong's warehouse, back in Jakarta. We're down by the Port of Tanjung Priok."

"Where are the others?"

"Cheong is out arranging for meat supplies and after that he was going to try and arrange a ship to Singapore for us."

"And Simon?"

"Dower went for a walk. He wanted some fresh air and exercise. He didn't talk much. He seemed to have a lot on his mind."

There was a slight scraping sound and her eyes were drawn to the cloth covered cage. She looked at Sanders questioningly.

"Oh yeah, and her. She's awake."

"Really? What time is it?"

"Just after eight pm."

"Eight pm? How long has she been awake?"

"Can't say. I think she woke in the truck. Why?"

"She should have been out until ten. She must have a fast metabolism. She's probably also starving."

"We figured that, which is why Cheong is out sorting meat. Do you want to look at her?"

O'Mara licked her lips. "Yes, absolutely."

Sanders stood up then stepped forward to lend her a hand. She was still weak from the struggle and her neck was painful despite all the strapping.

She followed Sanders to the cage and watched as he pulled the cloth away to reveal the majestic emerald scaled Horse Serpent underneath. Only it was not majestic. Her majesty had been removed by the thick ropes that tied her legs together and closed her muzzle. The slitted yellow eyes focused on O'Mara and the beast started to snort.

"Easy, girl," Sanders said, settling in behind her and stroking her neck. "Easy."

O'Mara approached the cage slowly, her eyes examining the beast from nose to tail. In all of the excitement of the capture, she never had a chance to examine it in detail and up close. She leaned forward for a better look.

"Is it safe to touch her?"

"She's tied up, so safe enough. Just stay away from the tail though."

O'Mara reached between the bars and felt the scaley hide of the creature. Strong muscles flexed and pulsed under the thick overlapping scales. The scales were thick and hard, and as she looked along the beast's body, she could barely see a single blemish on it.

"All that shooting and not a single wound," she mused.

"Those scales are tougher than they look."

O'Mara gave him a frowned look. "Are you suggesting the Horse Serpent's scales are bullet proof?"

"Not bullet proof. Bullet resistant."

"By which you mean…"

"By which I mean unless the bullet hits the scale at the right angle, it's more likely to slide off its hide than penetrate it. But look over here, you will see not all shots were glanced away."

O'Mara leaned closer to see where Sanders pointed and saw the dull metallic grey of a bullet wedged between two scales. The bullet was surrounded by a dark red smudge of clotted blood.

"Are there many bullets?"

"A few. But she's a toughie, and she gave out far more damage than she took."

O'Mara reached to feel the bullet and tried to dislodge it with her fingernail, but it was stuck fast.

"We should take these out. Did you happen to see what happened to the medical kit that I got the injection from?"

Sanders jerked a thumb behind him. "Still in the truck." There was a pause and O'Mara lifted her hand to the bandage on her neck. Sanders stared at the beast a moment longer before turning to O'Mara's expectant eyes. "Oh," he said, "did you want me to get it for you?"

"That would be a great help."

Sanders pushed himself up and jogged to the truck, vaulting into the back with ease. Within seconds he dropped back down with a leather bag in his hands.

As he placed it down, she quickly dug through for the items she wanted: a pair of latex gloves, a scalpel, small forceps, a roll of gauze and some sterile water. She reached into the cage and began to cut around one wedged bullet with the scalpel. The beast was remarkably still, allowing her to work freely at the task. Blood began to well around the bullet so she quickly splashed some water over the wound before grabbing the scalpel and working the bullet free.

"You're good at this," Sanders commented.

"Well, you got to show your skills out by the river, now it's time for me to show mine."

The bullet came free and she dropped it into a tray before packing some gauze into the wound. She identified another bullet and began the process over. As she removed the second bullet, she noticed the large yellow eyes of the Horse Serpent on her. O'Mara suddenly became self-conscious under the creature's stare, and lifted the bullet into its eyeline as if to show it to the beast.

"She's a good patient," Sanders said.

"Indeed," O'Mara mused. O'Mara studied the beast longer, and as she stared into those large slitted yellow eyes, she swore there was much more intelligence behind them than she could have imagined. Frowning, O'Mara put the bullet to the side and began working on the next one. The Horse Serpent watched two more bullets get withdrawn before laying its head down and relaxing.

As Jess worked on, she noticed Sanders start to become increasingly impatient. At first it was just a twitch of his mouth, but soon it become a drumming of his fingers, then he would look around and huff until finally he started cracking his knuckles and grunting.

"Is there something wrong?" she asked when his mannerisms became too much.

He drew a breath through his teeth. "I was hoping Dower would be back by now. I was hoping us three amigos could have a conversation before Cheong returned."

"Oh, what about?"

Sanders took one last look at the door before turning back to her. "It's about the mission. I've made up my mind. I've decided I'm going to see it through."

She paused, withdrawing her hands from the cage to look at him. "You mean help Cheong smuggle the Horse Serpent out of the country?"

"Yeah. Exactly."

"You'll be breaking the law. If you get caught, you're going straight to jail. And from what I've heard, jail here can be very rough on a Westerner."

Sanders ran a hand through his hair and gritted his teeth. "Yeah. I know. But it's just... well, I caught the Horse Serpent. That makes her my responsibility now. You know? She's out of her habitat and it's my job to get her safely to her new one."

"Like with the crocodiles in Kakadu?"

"Yes, exactly like that. As a ranger I'm responsible for all life in the park, not just the people. I'd never leave a croc in the lurch and dump it anywhere and I sure as hell won't do it to this beauty."

O'Mara put down her scalpel and peeled the latex gloves from her hands before placing her hand on his. "I understand, and I think it's very honourable." She paused, looking at her hand as it lay on his for a moment before glancing at the Horse Serpent. It had lifted its head to watch her again. She almost blushed under its gaze before turning away.

"You know what," she said at last, "I've made up my mind too. I can't speak for Simon, but I'm going on as well. It would be remiss of me not to continue to look after my patient. Besides, we both saw the way Cheong kicked her. There's no way I'm leaving her at his mercy."

"What about Dower?"

"What about him?" she asked, much sharper than she intended.

"Well…" he started, suddenly uncertain, "don't you want to discuss this with him first?"

She stared into Sanders' eyes for a moment before hers began to blur over. "I don't know," she said and leaned to rest her head against his shoulder. He lifted his arm up around her shoulders to comfort her.

***

But for the winking lights of the city and the distant hum of vehicles, Dower felt as alone as he could be sitting outside the warehouse where they stored the truck and the beast. He sat with his knees raised and his face resting in his hands muttering to himself. He had been in that same position for over an hour. Maybe even longer. He was not keeping track of time.

It was the sound of distant voices that caused him to finally look up. His red lined eyes scanned his surrounds for the source. The voices must have carried on the breezes, as but for the distant glowing orange circles of two lit cigarettes, there was nobody in sight.

Dower gulped. His mouth was dry and he wished he had thought to bring a bottle of water before fleeing the warehouse.

Yes, fleeing. He hated to admit it, but that's exactly what he had done the first sign of Jess regaining her consciousness. He cursed himself for running but he needed more time to think. Things between him and Jess were changing fast, and it was all his fault.

Voices came to him again and two men seemed to appear from nowhere just meters from where he sat. They were engaged in an animated conversion but the man on the right caught a glimpse of Dower and put his hand up to stop his comrade. Their voices hushed immediately and they spoke in a low volume while staring at him. After about a minute they turned and moved on.

Dower began to feel exposed sitting outside and alone at night like this. Dower stood, rubbing his rear end that had become numb from sitting on the hard ground in the same position for too long. He stretched, before studying the wall of the warehouse and sighing. With his head bowed, Dower scuffed his way to the door to the warehouse.

The door was slightly ajar and he eased it carefully open. He slowly pushed his head through the gap to peer inside. Not far from him, Jess and Sanders sat together in front of the uncovered cage with their backs to him. Sanders had his arm around Jess in a close embrace. Though he could not see clearly from this angle, Dower was certain that their faces were close to each other, if not touching.

Dower withdrew from the doorway and stepped away. He wiped his eyes with the backs of his hands before thrusting one hand into his pocket. He withdrew a small box covered with felt. He studied the box a moment while his bottom lip quivered. He then pulled his arm back, set as if to throw the small box as far as he could away from himself. His muscles tensed, but he paused and stood as still as a statue. Finally, he let his arm flop down to his side and dropped his head.

Suddenly, Dower found himself lit up by a pair of headlights. He froze, much like a deer in, well, the same position he was. The truck behind the lights thundered towards him, before turning sharply at the last second. The truck's brakes squealed as the truck was brought to a halt. The door was cracked open and a figure jumped from the cab.

Partially blinded from the headlight glare a moment earlier, Dower retreated a couple of steps until his back hit the wall of the warehouse. Realising he was trapped, Dower began to shiver as the figure approached. Dower raised his hands in surrender, but realised he still clutched the small box in his hand. Foolishly, he pulled his hands back down and quickly stuffed the box back in his pocket. But he knew the jig was up.

"Mr Dower, what on earth are you doing out here?"

"Is that you, Mr Cheong?"

Cheong stepped forward as the glare spots began clearing from Dower's eyes.

"Of course it's me, and you should be damn grateful for it. What on earth are you doing out here at this time?"

"I just needed some air."

"Needed some air? Do you know how stupid that decision is? These docks aren't even safe for locals at this time of night. There are plenty of shady characters hereabouts who'd have no qualms about sliding a blade between your ribs for a few coins and notes. Honestly, Mr Dower, you are a far dimmer man than I had first thought."

Cheong turned away and started directing the truck driver. A second man spilled from the cab to open the rolling door of the warehouse and the driver backed the truck in. Dower followed slowly behind.

Inside, Sanders and O'Mara waited and watched. Dower tried to catch her eye, but she seemed to be refusing to look at him. As the truck parked, Cheong called the three of them together for a meeting.

"I have arranged to have a meeting with a ship's captain in ten minutes, but I won't be able to meet him on my own." He pointed to Dower and O'Mara. "I need one of you to come along and play the part of a wealthy Westerner to help persuade the captain to ship our cargo and our cargo alone."

"Is that wise? Wouldn't the ship look less suspicious filled?" Dower asked.

"It might, but it's too risky. We're smuggling a rare creature here. The less people around to stumble onto it the better. Besides, this captain only just arrived in port and is yet to have a consignment of cargo. The arrangement is perfect if we can convince him."

"Ok, but wouldn't the person who goes with you tonight need to also be on the ship?"

Cheong cleared his throat and looked momentarily uncomfortable. "Yes, they would."

"Well in that case we can't go with you now, we haven't even decided if we are going to continue with this trip or not yet," Dower stated.

"Actually," O'Mara cut in, "we have decided. Both Matt and I are going with the Horse Serpent."

Dower's eyes went wide. "But Jess, going any further with this is breaking the law. We could go to jail if we're caught."

O'Mara held up a hand to tell him to stop. "I know the risks." She glanced up at Sanders who met her gaze. He nodded. "*We* know the risks," she continued, "but we both agree that we should stay with the Horse Serpent."

"You didn't think to discuss this with me first?"

"I don't think it would have mattered. My mind was made up already."

Dower swallowed as he glanced from O'Mara to Sanders and back again. His heart was hammering and he felt like he wanted to puke. In his pocket the small box pressed uncomfortably against his leg.

"Well," Cheong stated, "I guess it's settled then. I will take Miss O'Mara with me to meet the captain."

"Wait," Dower said urgently, then paused and closed his eyes for a long second. He opened them again and turned to Cheong. "I'll go with you. I don't know this captain, but I know the type. It'll be easier for him to respect and take orders from a man than a woman."

Cheong studied him a moment before glancing to O'Mara and back to Dower. "You may be right, Mr Dower. I take it then that you too have decided to break the law with us?"

"Indeed, I have."

Cheong looked them all over. His face showed no emotion, but his eyes betrayed a slight look of disappointment. "Very well then. My car will be here in five minutes. Let's go meet the captain."

"Wait," Dower said, "we have no change of clothes. Ours were lost back in the village."

Cheong looked Dower up and down and frowned. "I have a suit you may borrow," he said.

7

Captain Jeffray Arwadi was not a man easily taken for a fool, nor did he suffer fools lightly. As a hardy veteran who had spent most of his life in the shipping trade, he had seen and done just about everything legal and illegal one could do as a merchant across Southeast Asia. He had smuggled drugs, guns and all other manner of contraband one could think of. He had bribed officials, been victim of pirate attacks and even been ransomed back to his government after capture. He had hidden refugees on his ship and helped them escape from overbearing governments. And yes, he had made many legal trips across the seas as well, but that sort of trade was becoming harder and harder for owner operators like himself in the region against the competing bigger multinational shipping companies.

But despite all the weird and wonderful experiences and the maddening conglomeration of nefarious and righteous characters he met along the way, none of it prepared him for the odd couple that now sat before him in his cluttered dockside office.

On his right was a man of Chinese descent seemingly dressed to resemble a harlequin. His bright yellow suit glared despite the dull glow of the old globe hanging overhead, and contrasted heavily against the navy-blue shirt and white tie combo he wore under his jacket. He had gleaming white teeth and a ridiculous pencil moustache. But worst of all, he was a Chinese Indonesian, and to Captain Arwadi there was only one thing worse than a Chinese Indonesian, and that was a Chinese Indonesian who he had to associate with. But for the smell of money and the Westerner that came with him, Arwadi would never have invited Cheong into his office.

To his left sat that Westerner and so-called millionaire who was equally gaudily dressed. He was a pale skinned and thin man who looked like a bookish nerd who had not done a minute of heavy work in his life. His face was dour, in stark contrast to the brightly coloured ensemble he wore. He wore a purple jacket over a pink shirt and navy-blue tie, and his pants were tan. More striking was how ill-fitting his suit was, with the cuffs on his wrists and ankles too short, while the material seemed to stretch around his stomach. He did not look the slightest bit comfortable.

Arwadi regarded them both with cynicism. He leaned back in his chair, which squeaked as his weight shifted, and crossed his arms. His eyes narrowed and his expression was close to a sneer.

"So let me get this right," Arwadi said ponderously to Cheong. "Are you seriously trying to tell me this man here is some sort of obscenely rich man who wants a private journey by boat to Singapore to ship one measly container with him?"

"That is correct. Now if you don't mind, Captain Arwadi, could you please switch to English so my boss here can understand?"

Arwadi glanced at the purple suited man, who seemed to be staring into the distance and oblivious to him anyway.

"What's the catch?" Arwadi asked in his own tongue.

Cheong responded with an open palmed gesture. "No catch. He is just in a hurry and he wants to get his cargo to Singapore, that is all. Now English, please."

Arwadi raised an eyebrow before continuing in his own language. "Yet he wants my ship to carry his cargo and nothing else? I smell bullshit. What's the real story here?"

Cheong gave a crooked smile. "There's no story. Please, Captain Arwadi, he is in a great hurry and must leave tomorrow. We will pay extra to cover for you not being able to carry any other cargo."

Arwadi snorted. "He certainly will for that level of privilege." Arwadi glanced again at the man in the purple suit, who wore a morose and distant look to his face. Arwadi's mouth twitched. He turned back to Cheong. "What's the cargo?"

"Livestock."

"One container of livestock?"

"Yes, that's right."

Arwadi's eyes narrowed again. "My ship is a container ship. I don't do livestock."

Cheong's eyes narrowed and his mouth tightened. "Perhaps there is another way we can come to an agreement. How about this? I write a number on a piece of paper. You look at that number, and then you tell me again whether or not you carry livestock on your ship."

Cheong picked up the briefcase he had brought in with him and snapped open the locks to withdraw a gold trimmed pen and a small piece of paper. He scribbled briefly on the paper before placing it face down on the desk in front of Arwadi.

Arwadi looked at the paper but did not shift from his position. He pondered the two men a little longer before leaning forward to stand up. The chair squeaked again and he pushed it aside to walk to the window. Outside in the dark he could see into the docks where he spied the dark silhouette of his ship, the *Kekal*. He pursed his lips as he pondered her.

Despite what he had said, it would not be the first time he had carried livestock on his ship if he took this job on. But there was something not right about this. Or about them. The arrogant little Chinese looking man and the sad white man. Such a strange coupling. He knew he should send them packing, if ever there were warning signs on a person, these two had them. But yet, something about the pair of them aroused a deeper curiosity in Arwadi. He turned back to look at them once more.

"One container of livestock you say. I smell a rat."

"If you smell a rat, Captain, it's because you don't tidy this office. Believe me, this request is nothing but above board."

Arwadi had a good mind to turf them out then and there, but instead he sat back behind his desk. His chair protested once more.

"Hey you," Arwadi said to Dower, switching to English.

Dower jumped as if startled, before turning to the old sea dog. "Uh, yes?"

"What is the animal you want transporting to Singapore?"

"It's a horse..." Dower began before trailing off as he realised his error.

"A horse?" Arwadi asked.

"Yes," Cheong cut in, "a horse."

"What kind of horse?"

For a moment the two men stared at Arwadi with wide eyes. Arwadi decided he had heard enough and leaned forward to stand up. It was time to kick these two buffoons out of his office and find some real cargo for transport. His chair squeaked as he put his hands on the armrests to push himself up.

Cheong held out a hand to stop him. "Ok, you got us. We... haven't been entirely truthful with you here, Captain Arwadi. We should have known better than to try to trick a clever man such as yourself. We will let you in on it all if you hear us out."

Arwadi paused. His eyes glanced down to the paper Cheong had placed face down before flicking back to the two men. He relaxed his muscles and eased himself back into his chair.

"Then speak."

Dower opened his mouth to speak but Cheong raised a hand to silence him. "Let me explain it," he said, before licking his lips and looking back to the captain. "Ok, Arwadi, it's like this. There's a major horse race in Singapore in two days. Mr Dower here is a horse trainer, and he has one of his horses in the main race. But there's a fix."

Arwadi leaned forward, his eyes alight with interest as Cheong spoke. Cheong looked around the room, as if to check there was no one else that could overhear them. He leaned closer to Arwadi and started speaking in a softer voice.

"The horse we have entered in the race is a renowned dud. Everyone knows it. We'd get more money by shipping it to the glue factory. But here's the thing. That horse is already in Singapore. This horse we have here in Jakarta is a dead ringer for it. And let me tell you, this horse we have here is the real deal."

"So, you plan to switch them before the race and claim the prize money when this other horse wins?"

"Oh, it's better than that." Cheong surreptitiously looked around the room again before leaning closer still. "The horse Dower entered in the race has fifty to one odds on winning. Fifty to one. Just think about that for a moment."

Arwadi found himself nodding. "You stand to win a lot of money."

"And so do you, Captain." Cheong tapped the piece of paper on the table. The one that he wrote the number on. "If you think that is a lot of money, think about what fifty times that value is."

Arwadi began stroking his chin. His eyes darted to the paper and he licked his lips. "And you are sure this other horse will win?"

"I've never seen anything run like it before," Dower cut in.

For the first time since they entered the room, Arwadi smiled. "You are going to be a rich man, hey?"

Dower gave a half-hearted nod. "Yeah, I guess so."

Arwadi laughed and slapped him on the shoulder. "You are being modest. Ha. You know what? I will take you and your horse to Singapore. And I will stay and bet on the race, just like you say."

"You're not even going to look at the number?" Cheong asked.

"No need, I am sure you put something big on there when you were trying to entice me. I will do it, and like you say, get fifty times the return when the horse wins."

With the matter decided, Arwadi and Cheong began to discuss the various details of the journey ahead. They would meet Captain Arwadi and his crew early the next morning to load the ship and be away. The trip would take around forty hours all up. The captain asked again if he could take other cargo with him but Cheong insisted that they travel alone. Arwadi raised his hands in mock surrender.

"Okay, okay, no extra cargo. Now tell me, as I will need to set aside some quarters, is it just you two that will be travelling with us?"

"No," Cheong replied, "there are three others coming. Mr Dower's wife, a horse handler and a jockey. We will need three rooms all up."

With business concluded for the evening, they all shook hands and soon Cheong and Dower had departed. Arwadi walked them to the door and closed it behind them. He turned quickly, his eyes zeroing in on the still unturned piece of paper on the desk. He approached the desk slowly and flipped the paper. He whistled. It was far more than he had expected.

Resuming his seat with a squeak, Arwadi leaned forward with his elbows on the desk and stared at the door through which Cheong and Dower had only just recently departed. He stared at it unmoving for a good five minutes before reaching for his jacket. Inside the inner pocket was a card. There was no name on the card, just a phone number, from the man who had approached him earlier in the day. He glanced back up at the door one more time, then reached for his phone.

***

"Are you sure we can trust him?" Dower asked when they were back in the car and well out of earshot.

"Of course. You saw how that greedy oaf ate up our story. I bet he's in there right now dreaming of what he's going to do with his race winnings." Cheong shook his head. "My God, that was close in there. You almost blew it. I thought for a second you were going to say Horse Serpent."

"I almost did," Dower admitted.

"Well, just as well I was quick enough to cover your error. You really ought to think more before opening your mouth."

Dower blinked slowly. He was starting to see how Sanders had taken such a quick disliking to Cheong now that he was on the wrong end of Cheong's sharp tongue. He turned to look away as the driver pulled the car away from Arwadi's office when a thought struck him.

"Mr Cheong, who else is coming on the boat with us?"

"What do you mean?"

"You said in there that there were three others coming with us. But aside from you and me, there is only Jess and Matt waiting back at the warehouse."

"No. There is another."

Dower frowned. "Who? The driver?"

"No, not him. The other one is Mohede."

"Wait, what? You plan to take the soldier we took prisoner with us?"

Cheong shrugged. "What else can we do with him? We can't let him go. Not with what he now knows. It's better if we keep him tied up in one of our cabins for the voyage to Singapore and let him loose there. By the time he works his way back to his mates in Indonesia, both us and the Horse Serpent will be long gone." Cheong paused, then leaned towards Dower and spoke in a hissed whisper. "Or would you prefer to slit his throat and sink him to the bottom of the harbour?"

Dower visibly paled. “You would do that?”

Cheong waved him away. “Of course not. I’d get someone to do it for me.”

Dower studied Cheong, unsure whether or not Cheong had just made a joke. He pushed the thought aside. “So, we’re adding kidnapping to our list of misdemeanours then. Great.”

“If you have another suggestion, Mr Dower, I’m happy to hear it.”

But Dower had nothing more to say and turned back to watch the passing buildings through his window, calculating the number of years he would end up in jail for this if they were caught.

8

Things had changed quite significantly at the warehouse since Dower and Cheong had left earlier. Sanders and O'Mara had wasted no time unpacking equipment from the new truck and setting everything up. Already three mattresses were laid out on the floor with unrolled sleeping bags on top of each of them. A fold out table had been set up and on top sat a humming laptop computer. Beyond that lay the great cage, and inside the Horse Serpent had been loosed from its rope bondage and was tearing greedily at a bloody animal carcass it had been provided.

Sitting on two fold out chairs with beers in their hands watching the Horse Serpent rend its meal to pieces were Sanders and O'Mara. They had appeared to be deep in conversation when Dower and Cheong had arrived, but their exchange stopped the moment Dower entered the room. Sanders rose and stretched before nodding a greeting and approaching them.

"We seem to be one bed short," he said without introduction.

Cheong glanced over to the three mattresses. His face was blank and he blinked slowly. "I don't know what you mean," he responded, "it looks to me like you have everything."

Sanders scratched his head and glanced at the three mattresses. "I may not have been the best maths student at school, but there are four of us and three beds here."

Cheong stared at him blankly a moment before snorting with laughter, "Oh, I get it. You thought I would be sleeping *here*? How quaint. No, I won't be sleeping here. But don't you worry, my lodging for the night is arranged. I can assure you that I will be comfortably lodged back in the Grand International Hotel. You didn't expect a man of my standing to just sleep on the floor, did you?"

Without waiting for a response, Cheong passed him to approach the computer and began reading from the screen. He began nodding as he scanned what had been written. "These are good notes, Miss O'Mara. Very concise and very helpful."

"What's that?" O'Mara said as she turned. "Oh, that. Those aren't mine. Those are Matt's notes."

Cheong turned with an eyebrow raised to Sanders. He pointed at the screen. "You wrote this, Mr Sanders?"

"Sure did, Kenny. You seem surprised."

"I am surprised. I've never seen a caveman operate a computer before. I'm sorry I missed it."

Sanders clenched a fist and stepped forward when a hand grabbed his arm. He turned to see Dower had reached for him, and as their eyes met, Dower shook his head. Sanders gritted his teeth and snorted, before nodding in assent.

"Mr Cheong," Dower cut in, "if you are leaving to stay in the hotel, why is it we are sleeping on the floor in the warehouse?"

Cheong gestured to the Horse Serpent. "To analyse the beast, of course. Mr Higson expects a full report on it before it's taken to Australia. He wants to know its dietary requirements, habitat, theories on how it has survived alone for so long without discovery and all that jargon. He's not just wanting to build a home in his zoo for it. He wants to be on the front page of the next issue of National Geographic with the beast too, so he needs to know everything he can and you lot are his supposed experts. So, get analysing."

Cheong turned to look at the Horse Serpent and repressed a shudder when he saw the beast's malevolent yellow eyes were on him. He quickly turned away from it and approached Dower and Sanders once more. He leaned in close to Dower and spoke in a hushed tone.

"This wasn't part of Mr Higson's brief, but I also want a report on how dangerous that thing is. You saw how easily it tore apart those soldiers at the Sipatahunan Cave. I need to know what would happen if that creature got loose in, say, a crowded city."

"Why do you need to know that?"

"So Mr Higson can see the potential dangers of meddling with such creatures."

"Of course," Dower agreed. "Of course."

Cheong took one last surreptitious glance over his shoulder to check if the Horse Serpent was still watching him before quickly moving away.

"I want you up early," he shouted as he walked towards the door. "I want to be on that ship and out of here as quickly as possible tomorrow."

And before anyone else could say another word, Cheong was through the door and gone.

Dower had watched Cheong go before turning around slowly. His eyes immediately searched for O'Mara, but she still had her back to him, eyes forward and watching the Horse Serpent. He turned to Sanders who offered a half smile.

"So, we have a ride out of here then?" Sanders asked.

"Of sorts. The captain thinks we're smuggling some amazing racehorse into Singapore in a racing fix, and the only reason he's agreeing is because he wants in on the action."

Sanders shrugged again. "No big deal. If we get caught, at least he has a legitimate story he believes. I'd rather not have innocent parties caught up in this. You know?"

"I agree. But listen, Cheong plans to take that solider Mohede with us on the boat too."

Sanders raised his hands in a stop gesture. "Hold on, we're taking that little terrorist along with us?"

Dower nodded.

"That's kidnapping," O'Mara said. "Smuggling a rare creature out of the country so it can finally be shown to the world is what I agreed with. I never signed on for kidnapping, bad guy or otherwise..."

Dower had not realised she had been listening until that moment. He felt somehow warmed that she had kept an ear on the conversation. "Cheong said it was the only way. We can't let him loose here in Indonesia, he'll alert his extremist mates and they'll be all over us again in no time. It's safer if we take him with us."

O'Mara pursed her lips and then turned back to the Horse Serpent. Whatever she thought, she was not willing to share it. Sanders gave him another half-smile and shrugged.

"I suppose I had better get to work then," Dower offered.

"I suppose you better," Sanders agreed.

***

The night had been a long and dull one. Dower busily clicked away at the keyboard, while occasionally Sanders came and took a look over his shoulder or offered some thoughts. The Horse Serpent paced its cell restlessly. It was a mere three steps each way, but it had pent up energy to burn.

At one point Sanders tried to feed Mohede some water and food. Mohede screamed the moment Sanders removed the gag from his mouth. A quick slug to his stomach told Mohede that Sanders had no patience for that, and after a few seconds of deliberation, Mohede had reconsidered the situation and let Sanders pour water into his mouth and give him some bites of a sandwich.

Not long after midnight, Dower shut down the computer and settled onto one mattress. Shortly after, O'Mara lay down in the bed furthest from him. Sanders paced the room before settling awkwardly between them.

Despite the cold, hostile nature of the sterile white concrete walls and the unforgiving steel beams that made up the warehouse interior, all three of the intrepid Horse Serpent catchers slept in relative comfort in their sleeping bags on the floor. Even the Horse Serpent seemed to settle easily despite restlessly pacing the lengths of its small cage earlier. That was, of course, until some overzealous ship captain let off four emphatic blasts of his horn that were loud enough to wake General Suharto from his grave. After that, there was no more sleeping for the trio or the caged predator.

Sanders was first to rise, mostly because his stomach demanded it of him, and began scratching around for something to eat. Cheong had only supplied meagre rations, and Sanders was not far off building a fire and roasting some of the meat they held for the Horse Serpent when Cheong arrived.

Despite his disliking for Cheong, when he finally arrived, Sanders could not help but smile and give a nod of respect Cheong's way. Cheong was resourceful when the situation required it, and it was clear he had been busy through the night. Cheong not only arrived with ample breakfast and a change of clothes for them all, but had somehow through the night sourced a racehorse trailer big enough to fit the Horse Serpent's cage inside. Sanders munched on his breakfast as he watched wide eyed as Cheong's driver hefted the covered Horse Serpent cage into the trailer with the forklift and slammed the door shut to complete the ruse.

Cheong, of course, was resplendent as always, today dressed in a sharp black suit lined with gold buttons and a crisp white shirt and yellow tie combination. He was quite the contrast to the group that spent the night in the warehouse, who had slept in their clothes and not had time to wash up or attend to their hair.

As foretold the night before, Cheong was on a tight schedule and he was very quickly bundling everyone into the 4x4 truck that pulled the horse trailer when Cheong suddenly remembered Mohede. He ordered Sanders to lift him out of the truck and stow him in the trailer with the Horse Serpent. After a grumble, Sanders set about his work and within minutes he joined the others back in the truck.

"Is he in?" Cheong asked.

"Sure is. Though I must say, right now he smells worse than the Horse Serpent."

"And he's safe?"

"Safe? Why are you suddenly so concerned about his health, Kenny?"

"I don't care," Cheong burst back, "but we told Captain Arwadi there was five of us so we need to keep him alive."

"Well don't worry, he's out of reach of the Horse Serpent and judging from his wide-eyed stare when I placed him down next to the cage, I doubt he'll be getting any closer to it either."

They pulled out of the warehouse with the trailer rattling behind them and after a short drive through the docks, they soon pulled up next to a container ship bearing the name *Kekal*. As the driver shut off the engine, Sanders leaned forward for a better view of it.

"Ah, Kenny, didn't you say we were renting this ship just for us?"

"Yes, we are. Why?"

"I don't know. Overkill much?" Sanders said as he ran his eyes the length of the ship. By his best estimate, Sanders reckoned it to be at least four hundred feet in length. Its shape was long and flat, but for the rear of the boat where a squat tower four storeys high sat. Atop the tower was the bridge, and below it on the various levels were the ship's quarters and galley. The length of the ship allowed three large cargo holds below deck, which when closed made room for more containers to be piled on top. The ship was a LoLo model, meaning it could lift on and lift off its own cargo, which was perfect for an independent operator such as Captain Arwadi as it enabled him to avoid the hefty wharfing fees associated with the gantry crane hire in bigger ports. There were two cranes built into the ship, one at the very front on the foredeck and one just in front of the squat tower. As they arrived, there were already three rows of containers loaded on the ship, and the cranes were busy lifting a fourth row aboard.

"What is this?" Cheong burst, his face already turning a deep tomato red. "There should be no other cargo than ours on this ship. Damn that treacherous captain."

The driver had barely pulled to a stop when Cheong had exited the cab to run and confront Arwadi. The captain was standing on the wharf with another man as they approached. The second man was dressed in a simple grey suit, no tie, and had a rather flat and plain face that bore no distinguishable features. He had the type of face that someone could try to describe later but come up with only blanks.

"What is the meaning of this?" Cheong burst out as he approached Arwadi. "We had an agreement. This ship is solely at my disposal."

Arwadi wagged a finger at Cheong. There was a hint of a smile at the corner of his mouth. "I agreed only to take your cargo. I never agreed to your terms that there would be no other cargo on my ship."

Cheong's mouth worked but no sound but a slight gargle came from it.

"I see you are upset," Arwadi continued. "I would not normally do this but Mr Sianturi is a good friend of mine in need. He also has some urgent business in Singapore and I felt obliged to help him."

Cheong swivelled his eyes to the plain faced man, who offered his hand forward.

"Pleased to make your acquaintance, Mr Cheong. My name is Azhar Levi Sianturi."

Cheong ignored Sianturi and returned his blazing gaze back to Arwadi. "We had a deal," Cheong said, finding his voice at last. "No one but us on the ship."

Arwadi gave his best disarming smile. "I'm sorry, Mr Cheong, but I have promised Mr Sianturi passage for his cargo and, as you can see, my men have almost finished loading his containers. If you are unhappy with these new conditions then you are welcome to make other arrangements."

Cheong's face darkened to the colour of a beetroot and his head wobbled. His upper lip quivered in a manner that made his moustache look like a crawling caterpillar and a small gurgle escaped his throat. For a moment it seemed as though Cheong might actually explode when he let out a deep breath.

"It seems you have won this round, Captain Arwadi. Fine then. You may take Mr Sianturi's cargo as well as ours, but I will have no delays on our voyage and want full privacy as you had promised."

"Very good," Arwadi said, careful not to gloat. "I have reserved the front hold for your cargo alone. I will have my men load your truck and listen, there will be no trouble on this voyage and your business will be kept quiet. It is only by coincidence that Mr Sianturi also needed an urgent shipment to Singapore."

Cheong again glanced at Sianturi but for a second time refused to greet him. He turned back to Arwadi with his mouth still twitching. "Very well. Have your men load my truck and trailer in your forward hold and have your first mate direct us to our quarters."

Without another word Cheong turned and began walking back to the truck.

"Certainly," Arwadi said, and then in a much lower voice, muttered "*tionghoa* scum."

Cheong stopped and his face began to redden once more. For a moment it looked like he would turn to confront Arwadi, but instead he sucked in a deep breath and walked on. Arwadi smirked and turned away.

A man from the ship soon approached the group and led them on board. He spoke no English, and Cheong was seemingly in no mood to translate for anybody. Both Cheong and Sanders were given their own cabins, while Dower and O'Mara were directed to share one. They did little more than drop their baggage before setting off to explore the ship.

The four-storey structure was all iron walls and fading paint. The stairs between floors were narrow and the bunks that occupied their quarters sagged in the middle and bore grimy old blankets and sweat stained pillows. O'Mara was glad it would just be the one night.

On one floor to itself was the galley and mess area. The ship's chef was already at work chopping vegetables and tossing them into a large fire-stained pot. The mess area was larger than it needed to be, and contained a chaotic variety of unmatched chairs and tables that it had gathered over time.

With the bridge locked off to them they next explored the long deck at the front. In all, eight containers had been loaded across the middle of the ship in four parallel lines. The containers were like walls dividing the deck into five sections, but there was room to go between or around each section. The very front of the ship was bare, allowing easy access to the cargo hold that held the truck and trailer with the Horse Serpent.

Within two hours of arrival the boat was fully loaded with all cargo stowed safely on board. Cheong had kept a close eye on proceedings to ensure nobody peeked a look inside the horse trailer or the coolers filled with meat for the beast. As the cranes were returned to a locked position and the crew turned to other duties, Cheong repeatedly glanced at his watch and drummed his fingers on the railing with impatience.

"Any word on when we are leaving?" Sanders asked as the group completed their loop of the ship's deck. Cheong turned and stared at him without saying a word.

Just then there was a call and they turned to see Sianturi approaching them. Sianturi was quick to introduce himself to everyone. Sianturi spoke excellent English that carried a hint of an American accent. Cheong still did not greet him but Sianturi paid him no heed.

"If you don't mind me asking, where are you all from?" Sianturi asked after getting their names.

"We're Aussies," Sanders said proudly. "These two are from Perth, while I'm based not far out of Darwin."

"Australians. Well, that is interesting. Tell me, what is it that brings three Australians onto a container ship here in Indonesia?"

"A racehorse," Dower cut in. "A really fine breed."

Sianturi raised an eyebrow. "We have many great breeds of horses here in Indonesia, descending from Chinese and Mongolian bloodlines. Tell me, what is the breed of horse that has most caught your eye here on Java?"

There was a moment of silence.

"It's the... Java breed," Sanders stuttered.

"Java breed? Well, that is a good horse." There seemed to be a twinkle in Sianturi's eyes. "Does your horse have a name? I might have to keep an eye out for it in Singapore."

"Yes," Sanders replied before he could help himself, "it's called… Phar Lap."

Sianturi nodded. "Very good. I'll make sure to remember that name. Well, it was good to meet you, no doubt we can do more catching up over lunch. I only came down here to pass on a message to Mr Cheong here from the captain."

"What?" barked Cheong, before straightening and turning to Sianturi.

"The captain only wants to know when your fifth man will get here. He is eager to get away and he's hoping he will be here soon."

"My fifth man? Tell the captain he is already on board and to set off immediately."

Sianturi looked about and frowned. "But where is he?"

"Down in the hold with the horse. Now tell the captain to get going."

Sianturi shook his head. "That won't do. He can't be down there when the ship gets underway."

"Is that so?" Cheong asked in a voice coming close to a growl.

Sianturi shrugged. "Captain's rules."

Cheong stared him down for a moment. Sianturi did not look away and for a long minute their eyes were locked.

"Very well," Cheong said at last. "Sanders, Dower, go fetch Mohede from his duties and take him to my cabin. He was busy most of the night and probably needs a nap anyway."

Sanders and Dower set off towards the front end of the boat. Sanders took great strides and Dower found himself occasionally having to break into a little jog just to keep pace.

"My God, Sanders, that was close. I thought you would blow it there. I almost fell over when you said Phar Lap," Dower panted.

A grin cracked the edges of Sanders' mouth. "It was the first thing that came to mind. Plus it sounds Asian."

"But Australia's most famous racehorse ever?"

"Well… that was almost a hundred years ago. Besides, Sianturi didn't react. I doubt he knows."

They were putting on a good pace and passed the third container. Dower was getting breathless, but he still wanted to talk.

"Mr Cheong doesn't seem to be in the mood for making new friends today," Dower remarked.

"Is he ever in that mood?" Sanders asked in reply.

"Ha," Dower said, before jogging a little to keep up. "Listen, I'm glad we are alone; I wanted to have a private word with you."

"Oh? What's on your mind?"

"I… I just wanted to say it's okay."

"What's okay?"

"You and Jess. I won't stand in your way if it's what you both want."

Sanders' face screwed up as though he had just smelled another of Cheong's farts. "She's your girlfriend, mate. Stop talking shit."

Dower was about to reply when they passed the fourth container where Sanders stopped. He stooped down to unlock and lift the hatch to the stairs that led down into the front hold. A frightening roar echoed from below.

"She's getting restless in the cage," Sanders commented. "It's not good to keep some creatures confined in such a small space this long. She's not used to it. Higson better have a nice safe space to let her out in, because she's going to go wild when she gets out."

The pair descended the steps slowly. It was dark in the deep hold, so they left the hatch open despite the noise. The Horse Serpent continued roaring restlessly.

"Perhaps she's hungry," Dower said as they arrived at the base of the stairs.

"Perhaps," Sanders said, and began approaching the trailer slowly. Despite knowing the beast was contained, Dower looked about nervously as the roars reverberated through the hold about him and echoed off the walls.

Sanders arrived at the trailer and opened it, only for Mohede to fall onto him. Mohede had been pushing against the trailer door to get as far away from the caged beast as possible. Sanders laid Mohede on the ground and retrieved a pole and a side of beef from the truck. He lifted the cloth draped over the cage carefully with the pole and threw the side of beef to the cage. It landed just in front of the cage. There was a strangled noise from Mohede and Sanders turned for a second. When he turned back, the side of beef was gone and the bars of the cage glistened. He sensed the Horse Serpent's eyes on him as he lowered the drape once more.

"Find a hat or something in the truck," Sanders said as he jumped down from the trailer.

"Why?"

"So we can cover Mohede's head. We can't take him back tied up. It'll raise too many questions. We'll walk him back. But I'm not going to risk taking the gag off, we need to cover it up."

While Dower searched the truck, Sanders hoisted Mohede onto his shoulder and carried him upstairs and out on the open deck. The deck was clear and the container blocked any view from the bridge and living quarters. Sanders pulled a Bowie knife from his belt and showed it to Mohede. Understanding the meaning, Mohede nodded and Sanders put it away. Dower returned with a wide woman's sunhat he had found.

Sanders frowned, but placed it on Mohede's head. He untied Mohede's feet and stood him up. He kept Mohede's hands tied behind his back.

"Okay," Sanders said, "you lead and I'll follow with Mohede. I'll keep his head bowed so nobody sees his face and my knife pressed against his back. If we run into anyone, you distract them so I can get past. Got it?"

Dower nodded and turned to lead. Sanders grabbed Mohede by the arm and led him forwards. He pushed his head down roughly, then gave Mohede another look at the knife to remind him of it. Mohede, for his part, seemed to understand and accept the situation passively.

The decks were clear of crew and their walk was untroubled. As they passed by the last container, Sanders gave a quick glance up at the bridge, wondering if they looked suspicious to anyone who was looking down.

They reached the accommodation block without any trouble and began mounting the stairs. As they reached the third floor, they found Cheong pacing.

"About time," he hissed, and led them to his cabin. Inside, Sanders re-tied Mohede's legs and tied him against an exposed pipe. Satisfied Mohede was not going anywhere, they left the cabin and locked it. The deck was clear and they left the area, satisfied they had successfully stowed Mohede in secrecy.

Not one of them noticed the door opposite Cheong's cabin was slightly ajar. It was almost closed, but open just enough to allow the person hiding behind it to see everything that had passed.

9

Time, it seemed to Sanders, passed more slowly at sea. There was nothing much to do on the ship and the scenery outside was much of the same every time he ventured on deck: blue water and the occasional island. He wandered the ship restlessly. He tried starting a conversation with off duty crew members, but very few spoke English. He ventured up to the bridge and was allowed to observe, but Captain Arwadi had little interest in explaining anything and soon tired of Sanders' questions and ushered him out. He looked for O'Mara and Dower, but O'Mara was secluded in her cabin and Dower was busy at the laptop working over his report for Higson. He did not seek out Cheong for company.

It was as Sanders was staring forwards at what looked like endless sea that Sianturi came to join him.

"It's the curve of the earth," Sianturi stated.

"What's that?" Sanders asked.

"It's the curve of the earth that prevents us from seeing the land ahead."

"Ah, of course."

"I have often wondered what the world would be like if it was flat, like some people believe. Just imagine. Right now, we would see the continent of Asia. We would see the rising towers of the great cities and mountains. We could view the undulating landscape all the way to the Himalayas. Wouldn't that be magnificent?"

"I've never really thought about it," Sanders conceded. He turned to Sianturi, suddenly finding himself curious about him.

"I often think about it when I travel," Sianturi said.

"Do you often travel with your cargo?"

"Not always. I do it when I can."

"And what is it you are travelling with? What do you have in these eight containers that couldn't wait to get to Singapore?"

There were a few seconds of pause before Sianturi spoke. "Medical supplies. There has been an outbreak of disease in Southern Thailand and I have the raw materials that can make up the antidote for it. From Singapore they will be taken across Malaysia and into Thailand by truck."

"And how is it you came to be on the same ship as us?"

"I was making enquiries at port to find out if any ships were leaving for Singapore that had space when Captain Arwadi filed his logs. It was a lucky coincidence."

Sanders bit his lip and stared out at the sparkling water. The story seemed solid enough, but there was a nagging doubt in Sanders' mind about Sianturi.

"I was wondering," Sianturi said, interrupting Sanders' thoughts, "if it was possible to see Phar Lap? I am quite the racing purist and I have attended many events but I don't think I have ever seen it run before."

"You wouldn't have. She's not raced yet. We bought her on potential."

"Ah, that would explain it then." Sianturi was staring at Sanders and he was doing his best to ignore him. "Would it though?"

"Would it what?"

"Would it be possible to see her?"

"Umm… I don't think so. She's become a little unsettled by the journey so now would not be a good time."

Sianturi nodded. "Of course."

Despite his eagerness for company in the hours preceding, Sanders now found himself suddenly wishing to be away from Sianturi. Sanders knew nothing about horses, and Sianturi was asking too many questions. Sanders was bound to slip up if the interrogation continued. Sanders glanced at his watch and made an 'o' with his mouth. He tapped his watch with his index finger.

"Listen," Sanders said, "I need to get back to the others. We have a meeting to go over… training schedules and stuff for the horse."

Sianturi bowed his head. "Of course, I wouldn't want to hold you up. But I did have one last quick question if I may?"

"Okay, sure."

"If your horse was bred in Indonesia as you say, why was it given a Thai name?"

Sanders shook his head, lost. "I have no idea," he said and quickly withdrew. As he walked away, he was certain he could feel Sianturi watching him leave.

***

After the meeting with Sianturi, Sanders decided to spend the afternoon confining himself to his cabin just to avoid running into him again. Sianturi's questions had made him uncomfortable and he wanted to avoid more questioning if he could.

Sanders could not have been more bored in his cabin if he tried. At first, he started inventing games to keep himself amused. He found a loose iron nut on the cabin floor and made a challenge for himself to try and throw it into his shoe from across the room. It got easy after a while so he started inventing trick shots, throwing it blindly over his shoulder at his shoe. It was as he reached the end of his ideas that a knock came at his door. It was O'Mara.

"They are serving dinner in the mess. Are you coming?"

Sanders did not need a second invitation and shortly after was seated next to O'Mara and opposite Dower and Cheong in the mess. The meal of the evening was some sort of black beef stew with rice and a boiled egg. Sanders turned over his thick, clotted rice with disdain before adding it to the stew. With a worried expression on his face, he shovelled the first spoonful in his mouth. It had a strong, nutty flavour and he was surprised to find it to his liking.

"Have you finished the report yet?" Cheong asked.

"Almost done," Dower answered. "I had a bit of trouble. That man Sianturi kept hanging around and asking questions about our 'race horse' all day."

"You too?" asked Sanders with a mouthful of food. "He was bugging me earlier as well. I hid in my cabin just to get away from him."

Cheong straightened in his chair and glanced at each of them sharply. "What exactly has he been asking?"

Sanders swallowed. "Horse related stuff. What breed is the horse? What's its name? Oh, by the way, it's named Phar Lap if he asks." Sanders scooped a large lump of his meat and began to chew.

"Same here. I found his questions were really honing in on niche details."

Cheong's eyes narrowed. "Do you think he suspects something?"

"He may. Or he's a real horse enthusiast. It's hard to say. Either way, we should avoid talking.... Ouch! Why did you just..." Dower's voice trailed off as he understood O'Mara's expression. She had kicked him under the table for a reason.

"Good evening, everyone" Sianturi said as he arrived at the table from behind Dower. "How are the avid horse trainers doing this evening?"

"We are fine," Cheong replied in barely concealed hostility.

"Good, good," Sianturi went on cheerfully. His eyes widened as he saw Sanders' plate. "Oh, how's the Nasi Rowan?"

"The what now?" Sanders asked.

"Your beef stew," Cheong growled.

"Um, good. I think. Is the flavour supposed to be this strong?"

"The stronger the better," Sianturi said before making his way across the mess to find his own plate.

"There's no need to be so hostile, Cheong," O'Mara said.

Cheong scowled. "He's spying on us."

"Yes, but don't you think..."

"Ah, shut your mouth. Women like you are better to look at than listen to," Cheong said.

O'Mara's mouth twisted and her eyes blazed. If her stare could produce heat, Cheong would have been burnt to a crisp in an instant.

Sanders glanced at Dower, who gaped at Cheong. Sanders swallowed his half-chewed meat and turned back to Cheong. "Listen, Cheong, that's no way to speak to a lady."

"Etiquette lessons from a caveman," Cheong scoffed, "that's a new one."

The scraping of Sanders' chair resonated through the room as he pushed it back and stood up. Dower stood with him, quickly placing a hand on Sanders' chest. "Easy there, mate. Let's not do this here."

All eyes in the mess were turned to the confrontation as Sanders stood over Cheong. Despite Sanders' overwhelming size, Cheong carried a confident smirk on his face. Sanders stared Cheong in the eye, and Cheong mirthfully refused to break contact. Tension in the room was as taut as a rubber band stretched beyond breaking point when a second chair scraped on the floor. Dower turned to see O'Mara leaving.

"Jess, where are you going?"

"To feed the horse," she said. O'Mara stepped away from the table, walked past Captain Arwadi, who had slipped in the mess unnoticed, and left the mess area.

"Ah, Captain," Dower blubbered, "we were just…"

"Oh, don't mind me," Arwadi interjected. "By all means continue. It's been a while since the men have seen a good fight between passengers and I always love seeing a *tionghoa* get a good beating."

Cheong broke his stare with Sanders to turn to the grinning captain. There were a few snickers around the room and Cheong reddened. His eyes swivelled back and forth across the seamen in the room and he scowled.

"We'll finish this later," Cheong said and stood. He stepped away from the table, adjusted his clothes and puffed his chest out and strutted past the captain and out of the mess area to a series of jeers.

Sanders exchanged a quick glance with Dower and shrugged. He began lowering himself back into his seat when Sianturi slid a plate on the table and settled into Cheong's seat. Sanders resisted the urge to groan.

"Not the best I've had," Sianturi said as he sampled the stew, "but still good for ship food, I must say."

Sanders nodded but said nothing. Dower stared at the empty chair O'Mara had only just abandoned. Sianturi chewed his food thoughtfully as his eyes darted from Sanders to Dower and back.

"Have you worked with him long?" Sianturi asked.

"Who?" Sanders asked.

"Cheong. Have you worked with him long?"

"No. Only recently."

Dower kicked Sanders' leg under the table.

"How did you meet him?" Sianturi asked.

Sanders glanced up at him sharply. "You ask a lot of questions, you know that?"

"I'm sorry, I didn't mean to pry. I'm just curious, that's all. Like I told you earlier, I'm a horse enthusiast. And just now I saw you almost come to blows. I am just curious as to how your working relationship came about."

"Speaking of coming to blows," Dower cut in, "what was it the captain said to Cheong just now? He called him a name."

"Yes," Sianturi said. "He called him *tionghoa*."

"And what does that mean?"

Sianturi licked his lips and glanced to where Arwadi was taking his seat with his men. "It's an old word that has only recently come back into use. Technically it means 'of Chinese descent', but said in the manner Captain Arwadi uses it, it can be seen as derogatory."

Sanders darkened. "So, it's a racist term?"

Sianturi's expression was pained. "It's hard to explain without going into a full history of Indonesian political and social history. Chinese Indonesians have been persecuted since the Dutch ruled in the seventeen hundreds…"

"I don't care about history or the Dutch, is it racist or not?" Sanders persisted.

"Listen, I am trying to explain to you that hostility towards the Chinese descendants has been deeply ingrained into our culture for hundreds of years, and is just as prevalent now as it ever was."

"Enough," Sanders said. "You can tell me it has been happening for a thousand years and that still would not make it right. Racism of any sort towards any people for whatever reason is wrong. Saying it is ingrained is making excuses for those who do it. Eventually someone has to stand up and say no. And right now, that's me."

Without another word, Sanders stood up and pushed away from the table. He was too quick for Dower this time and before Dower could stand, Sanders was already striding to where Captain Arwadi sat. Arwadi was sharing a joke with his crew when he looked up to see Sanders towering over him like a sculpted statue of Hercules. He raised an eye at the newcomer to his table.

"Can I help you?"

"Yeah, you can. You can cut the racist bullshit towards Cheong."

"Excuse me?"

"No, I won't. I know Cheong can be a rude little prick and there are times I've wanted to put his head through a wall, but that's no excuse for racist taunts. So, I'm giving you a warning, Arwadi. You can call Cheong out for being the turd that he is. You can call him a weasel. A rude little shit. Whatever you want. But if I ever hear you cross that line into racism, I'll punch your lights out. You don't cross that line. You got it?"

If one could appear both amused and confused at the same moment, his facial expression would match Captain Arwadi's in that very second. Arwadi opened his mouth to reply, before grinning then shortly thereafter, frowning. He pointed at Sanders.

"I think I understand. Tell me, what is your name?"

"Matt Sanders."

"On this ship, Matt Sanders, you address me as Captain. And as Captain, I am the highest form of law when this vessel is at sea. Now take a look around you. All these men serve me and will do as I say. So wise up, because next time you come over here with the intent to lecture over matters like this, I'll have you confined to your quarters, minus your own lights. You got it?"

Sanders pursed his lips and regarded Arwadi cynically. "You just watch your words," he said and returned to his table, oblivious to the stares behind him. Sianturi looked up as he sat.

"Can I give you some advice, Sanders? You might want to think more carefully before speaking to the captain that way again."

"I don't care. That sort of behaviour needs to be called out."

"Even so, the captain does deserve a level of respect."

"Respect is something you earn, not something that should be given so freely."

"I think I've seen this movie before," Dower said dryly. Both men cast him a glance before going back to their meals. Just then, Dower stood up. "I think I might go and find Jess. I think we need to talk."

Sanders nodded. "I think you need to too."

Dower stared at Sanders a moment, before leaving without another word. Sianturi watched him go before resuming his meal. As he chewed on his food, he stared off into the distance. Sanders did not mind. It was better than the endless stream of questions.

The noise in the room went quiet and Sanders felt someone at his shoulder. He looked up to see Cheong eyeing the room nervously.

"Mr Sanders, could I have a word?"

"Shoot."

"A private word," he said, nodding his head towards Sianturi.

Sianturi cleared his throat. "I'll get up. I am full anyway."

"Leave your bowl," Sanders said. "I'll finish it."

Cheong watched Sianturi like a predator as Sianturi awkwardly got up from the table and moved to another. He sat down with two other men, but sat in a position so that he still faced Sanders and Cheong. Cheong leaned down to speak softly into Sanders' ear.

"We have a problem."

"With the Horse Ser…"

"No. With Mohede."

"What about him?"

"I just went to my room and… well… he's escaped."

10

Sanders crouched over the roughly hewn fragments of rope on the floor of the cabin. He picked one up and held it close to his eye, before throwing it down in disgust.

"He didn't escape," Sanders said, "he was cut free. Someone broke in here and freed him."

Sanders stood and walked to the door to examine first the frame and then the door itself. He slid his hand along the side of the door, then crouched to look in the key hole.

"Are you sure you left the door locked?"

"Of course it was locked," Cheong burst out, "I'm not an idiot."

Sanders bit down a reply and kept examining the door. "Well, there's no scratches on the lock, so I doubt it was picked, and there's no damage on the door either. So, either you left it unlocked, or someone had a key."

Cheong said nothing but turned and bent down to pick up a cut segment of rope. He looked at the frayed end in confusion. "But who would do this? And why?"

Sanders stood sharply and shut the door, closing them both in the cabin.

"What is it?"

"Sianturi. He was coming down the corridor. Have you checked the room to see if anything else is missing?"

"Good idea. While I do that, you watch Sianturi through the peep hole in the door."

Sanders turned and found the peep hole quickly. He squinted through one eye, trying to make detail through the distorted view while behind him Cheong rattled through his possessions.

"Shit," Cheong swore.

"What?"

"My satellite phone is missing."

Sanders frowned and turned. Cheong was sitting on the bunk with an open briefcase in front of him. He was lifting the papers and checking the pockets inside. Sanders noted he kept re-checking the same pockets.

"Something else?"

"Shouldn't you be watching Sianturi?"

"He went into the cabin opposite this one."

Sanders watched as Cheong re-lifted papers and checked under them before opening the same pockets once more. He heaved a breath.

"Kenny," he said to grab Cheong's attention, "is there something specific you are looking for? What is it you are missing?"

Cheong looked up and his shoulders dropped. He bowed his head and rubbed his temples with his fingers.

"I… I usually keep a gun in here. A semi-automatic pistol to be exact."

"Jesus, Kenny, why?"

Cheong shrugged.

"Jesus," Sanders repeated, before running his fingers through his hair. "Alright, Kenny, time for you to fess up. Those soldiers you hired, who Mohede is one of, who are they?"

Cheong bit his lip and flipped over some more pages in his case in a half-hearted final search for the pistol. "They were from a group."

"What kind of group?"

"An extremist group."

"Don't edge around it. Were they terrorists?"

Kenny lowered his head and rubbed his temples. "I don't know. I decided not to look too deeply into it. They are a paramilitary group with extreme views. They became renown a while back when the police feared they could start violence in the protests against Ahok, but I thought the less I knew about them the better. They just seemed like someone I could hire who could do the job, take the money and not say a word to the authorities about what they saw."

Sanders stared, mouth agape, before shaking his head. "My God, Kenny, we may have an armed terrorist free on the boat somewhere with the means of calling his mates."

"What do we do?" Cheong said, his voice for the first time since Sanders met him not boiling with arrogance and disdain, but instead soft and pitiful.

"We have to warn the captain. He needs to lock the bridge and call for help before Mohede hijacks the ship."

Cheong nodded, slowly at first but the longer he did it the more rapid it became. "Okay, you go and warn him. I'll try to find O'Mara and Dower and tell them to run back to their cabins and lock the door."

Sanders nodded and swung open the door. He was halfway out when he grabbed the frame and pulled himself back.

"How many rounds?"

"What?"

"The pistol. How many rounds does it have?"

"Uh… thirteen. Why?"

"Because if it comes to it and he starts shooting, I'll count the shots to know when his gun is empty."

Then Sanders was gone. Cheong stared at the empty doorway a moment before slowly closing his briefcase.

Sanders paused in the hall as the lights around him flickered to life. He approached one of the west facing windows and looked out to glimpse the last rays of the sun as it descended into a dark orange haze at the edge of the horizon. Sanders cursed. The ship was too big to find someone quickly to begin with, they did not need the additional complication of the dark to help keep Mohede concealed. If that was Mohede's play, that is.

Sanders dashed up the stairs to the mess. Some off duty sailors had a game of cards going as a man in a grimy apron cleaned around them, but of the captain there was no sign. Sanders pushed away and tramped up another level and approached the bridge. The door to the bridge was open, and loud voices spilled out into the hall. Sanders slowed and listened. There was a high pitched, almost panicked tone to one voice. He only wished they were speaking English so he could understand. It occurred to him that Mohede might already be in there, waving his gun and demanding control of the ship. Sanders paused and looked about, but there were no loose items about he could use as a weapon. Captain Arwadi may have had an old ship, but he ensured it was kept tidy at sea.

Sanders crept up on the door and balled up his fists. The panicked chatter continued as he dared a peek around corner to see two men hunched over a screen. His view was partially obscured, but he could see the green screen with a line rotating like a dial that was instantly recognisable as radar. He appeared to be pointing at and discussing something towards the bottom of the monitor.

"Can I help you, Mr Sanders?"

Sanders jumped as the captain spoke. Sanders had been concentrating on the radar and had not noticed Arwadi turn and approach the doorway. He straightened sharply before relaxing and stepping from behind the doorway.

"Captain, we need to talk."

Arwadi raised an eyebrow. "Have you come to give me another lesson in morality?"

"No, nothing like that. I've come to warn you of a major problem."

Arwadi nodded towards the radar screen. "I am well aware of our problem already."

Sanders frowned and stared blankly at the two men pointing and chattering over the radar display. He gave the captain a quizzical look. "No, it's not that. Captain, what is going on?"

Arwadi stared searchingly at Sanders a moment before ushering him to the screen. The two men stepped aside to give Sanders his first unobscured view of the monitor. He watched the line turn the circumference of the circle, lighting up two blips near the bottom of the screen. He watched the line turn once more around, lighting the two blips once more. They appeared closer on the second pass. Sanders pointed to where they were.

"What are those two spots?"

"We believe they may be chaser boats."

"Chaser boats? Are they chasing us?"

"It would seem that way."

"Okay," Sanders said as he mulled this over. "So, tell me then. Who or what drives in a chaser boat?"

Arwadi glanced at the two nervous crew members behind Sanders. They continued to whisper to one another and had not taken their eyes off the screen. Their eyes were wide and their voices shaky. They were jumping to conclusions that Arwadi did not like but knew in his heart to be true. He closed his eyes a second to compose himself before turning back to Sanders.

"I believe," he began with a voice as steady as he could make it, "that we are being chased by pirates."

***

Dower leaned over the poop deck rail to look down at the water below him. He could feel the great thrumming of the ship's engine as the propellers somewhere underneath him cut through the warm tropical waters. A line of white water trailed the ship, fizzing like a soft drink, as the air churned up in the ship's wake bubbled to the surface. To his right, the sun burned a fiery red as it sunk behind the horizon. And behind him stood his long-time girlfriend Jess O'Mara, silently watching and waiting.

Dower turned to look at her. Wind whipped from behind her, blowing her hair forwards which she awkwardly tried to keep from her eyes. Despite the wild hair dancing about her face and the ever-decreasing light, he could still see her soft features and clear blue eyes. The very features that had attracted him so much since they had first met.

"Sorry," he stuttered, "I didn't realise it would be so windy back here."

"That's okay," she said as she clasped her hair into a pony tail, "I just wish I had a tie or something."

He gave her a nervous smile. It betrayed how he felt. Inwardly he felt ill, and he thought at any moment he might wretch. He resisted the urge to go back to the rail and lean over the edge. He swallowed uncomfortably. His mouth was dry.

"I think we need to talk," he said, the words having to be forced out.

"I agree," O'Mara said.

He looked into her eyes, wondering what she might have meant by the remark, but no clue was to be found. He cleared his throat. "I… this trip…" he stuttered. Damn, he thought, I had this whole damn speech in my head and now I've lost it. An itch prickled the back of his neck and he reached up to scratch it. He noticed his palms were wet, decided to dry them on his pants. As he wiped, he felt the lump of the small velvet in his pocket. He looked away from her a second as a tear blurred his eye.

"Jess, I've been thinking a lot about us lately. I've been thinking about our future, where we are going…"

"Stop," she said suddenly.

"Jess, I really need to say this…"

"Shoosh."

He turned to see her holding her palm face out to him and her head tilted slightly to the side. He looked about, but there was nobody near them.

"Is there something…"

"The engine. Did you hear it?" O'Mara asked.

He shook his head.

"They increased the power. We're speeding up. Something's wrong."

"It's probably just a manoeuvre of some sort. Listen, Jess, I really need to talk to you."

O'Mara glanced over her shoulder, up the tall structure of the ship where the bridge sat. She lowered her hand and talked to him.

"Sorry, you are right. It's probably just me being paranoid," she said. "You have my attention now. Go."

But now he had her focus again, he suddenly found himself lost for words. He cursed himself. He had been thinking what to say to her all day. He had sat in that mess hall sitting in front of the computer not seeing the screen in front of him while he thought and thought. He knew what he needed to do, but getting the words out and committing to the act was much harder than he could have imagined.

He cleared his throat and tried to start again. "Jess, I've been doing a lot of…"

"Wait," she said, again thrusting her hand up to stop him. She squinted, eyes focusing on something beyond his left shoulder. She took a couple of steps forward and pointed. "Do you see that too?"

He turned, looking out the rear of the ship to where she pointed. The light was low, and the first pinpricks of starlight began piercing the sky.

Out in the ocean there was little light, and the moon had not yet risen, and all he could see was dark murk. But then he noticed it. It was barely decipherable in the dark, but it was there. The spray of white water. A boat… no, more than one boat. Two. And they were coming fast.

"I see them," he said. "Do you think they are chasing us?"

"That's exactly what I think. The captain sped up for a reason." She turned and reached out to Dower, grabbing him by the shoulders and turning him to face her. "Babe, I agree with you. We need to talk about so many things. We need to talk about what happened in the forest, why you are acting so strange… everything. But now is not the time. Something is wrong. But I promise once we get past this, we'll sit down and talk everything through. Okay?"

"Sure," he said weakly.

She leaned forward and pecked him on the cheek. He gave a half-hearted smile.

"Now come on, let's go find out what is happening."

"I'll be right with you," he said, hanging back a moment. She turned and looked him in the eye. There seemed to be a sadness about the look. He bit his lip and she turned away, disappearing through a hatchway and up some stairs.

He turned and looked back out to the chasing boats, before dropping his head.

***

The two speed boats bounced and careened across the open water in hot pursuit of the dark, monolithic shape that was the *Kekal* ahead of them. Each boat held ten men with dark, swarthy eyes, and each man wore sharp, curved knives in their belts, a bandolier of magazines across their chest and an AK-47 slung over their shoulders.

In the lead boat was a thick bearded man with heavy eyebrows and scarred arms. His name was Leo Setiawan and he was the leader of the group. He was a career pirate, having spent most of his life performing raids along the Strait of Malacca. His target of choice was oil tankers, whose cargo was often worth millions and was so sought after that it was easy to find a buyer who did not ask too many questions. He had done container ships before, but his preference was tankers. It just made more economic sense. But this container ship was different. If his sources were correct, this container ship held something very special. Something Setiawan's backers could only dream of getting hold of.

Setiawan raised a pair of binoculars to his eyes and scanned the ship ahead. It had sped up, but they were closing. He rode the bumps of the speed boat as he scanned the ship, wary that something with such precious cargo would surely have some sort of security detail on board. But as he looked over the ship, Setiawan saw no sign of armaments, just a lone man standing on the poop deck with his head bowed. He allowed himself a smile. It was as the man on the phone said. There was no defence here. This ship would be an easy take.

Setiawan unclipped the radio at his belt and turned to signal to the other boat. A man on the second boat waved back, and Setiawan clicked on the radio.

"Surjanto, are you reading me?" Setiawan asked.

"Surjanto here," came the crackle back through the radio.

"I want you to go portside of the ship, and we'll take starboard. I have a man on board who says there is no defence. I see no signs of armed defenders either, but that doesn't mean they are not there, so be careful. Acknowledge."

"Acknowledged."

Setiawan stared out at the other boat as it peeled away to the left. His mouth twitched, and he lifted the radio to his mouth once more.

"And Surjanto, one more thing. No indiscriminate killings this time. We have two inside men on board. I need them alive. Kill only in self-defence. Acknowledge."

The radio crackled but there was no reply. Setiawan's brow furrowed and he stared at the other boat. He lifted the radio again.

"Surjanto, I said no indiscriminate killings. Acknowledge."

There were a few moments of silence before a flat voice came on the other end. "Acknowledged."

Setiawan put the radio down but continued to stare at the other boat. A snarl formed on his lips and he cursed the other man's name. He did not believe Surjanto one bit.

11

"We'll worry about your man Mohede later," Captain Arwadi said at the completion of Sanders' short tale. "A man can quite easily disappear on a ship like this and never be found. Plus right now, those pirates are a bigger concern."

Sanders nodded. He was not sure what reaction he expected from Arwadi, but dismissal was not one of them. Perhaps he was saving it for later, when they got out of this mess. If they got out of this mess, that is.

"Okay, I'll help. Where are the guns?"

Arwadi snorted and placed a hand on his mouth as though to hold down the laugh. "Guns?" he asked in a high-pitched voice. "We are merchants and seamen, not warriors."

"But how do you plan to defend the ship?"

Arwadi shook his head. "We can't. We can only hope to dissuade them. We can manoeuvre the boat on top of them when they approach. Maybe we can frighten them off or at the very least make it hard for them to board. Perhaps when they see how little cargo we have on board they will back off and decide it isn't worth the risk. That's the best outcome we can hope for right now."

"And if they don't?"

"You had better hide and hope they don't find you. Between your horse and Sianturi's eight crates, there isn't much on this ship of value other than its white passengers. So, for your sake and that of the others, hide. Because if they find you… Then all you have left is to hope your ransom bill is negotiated quickly."

Arwadi turned from Sanders and began barking orders to the men on the bridge. Two got up, picked up a radio each and clipped it to their belts and left the bridge. Arwadi approached the radio and studied it.

"Where did you send those men?"

"Out to get eyes on those pirates. I need to know where they are exactly. If we can turn into them at the right moment, we might be able to capsize their boats."

Sanders nodded. The captain switched languages and began chattering with the other men on the bridge. Sanders began pacing the length of the bridge, drawing a dark glare from Arwadi.

"You are not required here any further, Sanders," he said.

"I was thinking that. Your men, they are going down to the main deck, yes?"

Arwadi nodded.

"I'm going down there too then. If Mohede is working with the pirates, he may try to stop them."

Arwadi nodded again, though this time Sanders did not need his approval and was out the door in seconds. Sanders dashed down the stairs with his legs pumping like pistons. He reached the end and almost ran into O'Mara as she came to climb them.

"Matt," she gasped and stepped back to avoid being knocked down. "What's happening?"

"Mohede is loose and armed, and we are being chased down by pirates. We could be boarded at any minute. You should find somewhere and hide."

She felt her pocket when Captain Arwadi's voice blared through the ship's speakers mounted about the halls. He spoke no English, but his voice was filled with a sense of urgency. Crew members spilled from the mess area, dashing past them with feared expressions. One stopped and exclaimed something at them, before turning and running up the stairs to the bridge.

"I've lost my keys," O'Mara said suddenly as she felt at her pants pockets.

"Here," Sanders said, digging his hand into his pocket, "take the keys to my cabin and stay concealed."

"Where are you going?"

"Down to the main deck. Arwadi sent men down there and I'm worried Mohede might be there too."

"But didn't you just say he's armed?"

"Exactly," Sanders said and backed towards the stairs leading down. "That's why I need to go." Without a further word, Sanders turned and began descending the stairs.

***

Setiawan was contacting him by radio again. Surjanto scowled under his curled moustache at the speaker as he listened to the voice. One of the younger men picked up the handset and held it forwards to him. Surjanto snatched it from the boy's grasp.

"Surjanto here."

"Ease up on the side and see if you can hook the ladders on the rail."

"I know how to board a ship," Surjanto spat.

There was a pause, then Setiawan replied.

"Fine. Just remember, no shooting unless necessary. We have contacts on the ship and I don't want them accidentally killed. Acknowledge."

Surjanto rolled his eyes. "Acknowledged."

Scowling, Surjanto turned to the boy who passed him the radio and cuffed him around the ears. The boy scampered back with eyes filled with fear.

Surjanto was known as a man not to be messed with. He was big and ill-tempered, and his reputation for brutality was well known. Surjanto was instantly recognisable for his dark stare, gold tooth and the deep scar that lined his face that was almost as ugly as his personality. Prisoners who Surjanto ransomed rarely returned in one piece, bearing both physical and mental scars for life. But it was not just captives his cruelty extended to, and there was an infamous story doing the rounds of him gutting one of his own men, opening his stomach from chest to navel and tying the poor man's intestines to the rail before pushing him off the deck. Stories have a habit of growing with some exaggeration over time, but the reality of this particular case was that the story was one hundred percent true.

Surjanto threw the radio to the floor and turned back to the dark ship. They were drawing up close now, and the man he had seen earlier was still standing alone on the poop deck, watching them. Surjanto's scowl slid seamlessly into a grin as he studied the man. Carefully, Surjanto slid his AK-47 from his shoulder and clipped a magazine into place. He lined his sights onto the man, who remained stupidly standing there and staring.

Just as Surjanto pulled the trigger, the boat hit a wave and bounced into the air. Two shots rang out as he reached to steady himself from falling. Half turning, Surjanto cursed the driver before turning back to the ship. There was no sign of the man now, but whether the man fled or had been hit by one of the shots, Surjanto could only guess.

Surjanto's smile melted away and the scowl returned as he urged the man at the wheel to push on.

***

Dower crashed through the hatch door and stumbled forwards before falling to his knees. He was panting and his heat hammered at his ribs like a jackhammer. By God, that had been close. There he was, squinting out at those boats when a loud bang rang out followed by an explosion of sparks just a foot from where his hand held the railing. Not one to need a second invitation, Dower was out of there in a flash.

Dower stayed on hands and knees a moment longer to catch his breath. Over the ship's speakers the captain was shouting something incomprehensible.

Suddenly two hands dug under Dower's armpits and began pulling him to his feet. The grip was strong, and Dower assisted by pushing up with his knees. He was quickly back on his feet and turned to see much to his surprise that his helper was Azhar Levi Sianturi.

"Are you okay?" Sianturi asked.

"They shot at me," Dower exclaimed, before looking down at his body to check for injury.

Sianturi glanced back towards the open hatchway.

"They are pirates. They intend to take the ship. You should heed Captain Arwadi's message and lock yourself in your cabin."

Dower nodded and turned to the stairs when he noticed Sianturi remained where he was. "Aren't you going to do the same?"

"I will. Soon."

Dower nodded and watched as Sianturi continued to stare out the hatch. Dower turned to leave when Sianturi called again.

"Tell me, Mr Dower, is it really a racehorse you have stowed in that first hold?"

"Um, yes, of course. Why?"

Sianturi turned and regarded him sceptically. "Because I'm not a fool. Your horse trainer in Sanders told me you have a Java pony. A Java pony is a workhorse. They make terrible racehorses. So, either you have been taken for fools, or you are lying. And as my cargo is worth very little and we are being raided by pirates, I cannot help but feel there is something more important lying down there in the front cargo hold. Am I right?"

Dower said nothing and backed away from Sianturi. His back heel hit something and he turned to see the stairs were now behind him. He turned back to Sianturi, who studied him questioningly, before turning and running up the stairs.

Now on the second floor, Dower scampered to his cabin door and knocked quickly. He waited a few seconds before digging into his pockets for the keys. His shaky hands guided the key into the lock and he opened the cabin door quickly, rushing inside and slamming it closed behind him. He leaned back against the door and closed his eyes. Taking in deep breaths, Dower did his best to calm himself. He opened his eyes and scanned the room. He was alone.

For a brief moment he was relieved, before it dawned on him that O'Mara should be there. He pushed away from the door, crossing the room to where her bag lay on the bed. It lay open and the dirty clothes from the day before lay strewn over the pillow. Those were the only true clothes of hers, the rest were recent gifts from Cheong after their luggage was lost. He picked up the shirt and lifted it to his nose and sniffed. It was not clean, but it carried her scent. He lay it back down with shaking hands and turned to the door. He walked to it, breathing heavily the whole way, before stopping in front of it. The sound of gunfire and the blinding flash of sparks as the bullet clattered into the rail was still fresh in his mid. He slammed a fist against the door before dropping his head into his hands. He heaved another big breath and looked back up at the door.

"Not this time," he whispered to himself. "This time we don't run. This time we save Jess."

He reached out and clasped the door handle. It was cold to his touch. He paused, heaving another breath, before pushing the handle down and wrenching the door open and entering the hall once more.

***

Sanders scanned the main deck with the eyes of a hunting hawk. It was quite dark now, and the safety lighting was barely enough to see more than six feet in any direction clearly. He was certain Mohede would be here somewhere, ready to assist the pirates at any chance. Sanders was certain it was no mere coincidence the pirates appeared not long after Mohede's escape.

Sanders silently watched the two men Captain Arwadi had sent each rush to either side of the ship. Both were armed with radios and torches but little else. If Mohede made an appearance or the pirates got on decks, they would provide as much defence as a bullet proof vest made of paper.

Ahead of Sanders were Sianturi's containers, standing dark and silent and blocking his view to the front of the ship. Worse, combined with the minimal light, they provided plenty of cover for Mohede should he choose to hide there and wait. Sanders clucked his tongue. This was not a safe place to be.

Sanders decided it was useless standing where he was and waiting, so he followed the sailor who dashed left. He chased after him, his long legs easily covering the distance with little effort and soon he was beside the sailor. The sailor leaned over the railing and pulled back, quickly chattering over the radio. Sanders dared a peek, and saw the pirate boat close below. Two men stood on the bow, raising a ladder with curved ends above their heads, attempting to hook the railing with it. There was a clang as the ladder hit the side of the ship. Just a few more inches and it would be high enough to hook on. Sanders pulled back and looked up at the bridge, hoping Arwadi was ready.

***

Arwadi had watched from the bridge as the two men he sent below took position on the main deck. Each carried a handset to communicate back to the bridge. While he waited for the first message, he closed his eyes and took a deep breath to calm himself.

Suddenly one of the handsets crackled to life. Arwadi's eyes flicked open and he snatched the radio up and asked for a report. The first message came from the man portside of the boat. Men were raising a ladder in an attempt to board.

Acknowledging the message, he turned to the pilot at the wheel. "Let's show these pirates we are no easy take. Turn thirty degrees to port, now," he roared.

***

Surjanto watched as the two men on the bow deck raised the ladder above their heads. It was tricky balancing on the deck that bucked wildly with the rough seawater and lifting the ladder above you like that. Surjanto held his breath as the ladder was raised high. There was a clang as the curved ends of the ladder clattered against the side of the ship.

"Higher," he roared. "Come on, we're almost there."

The men redoubled their efforts and looked to lift it up enough when suddenly the container ship loomed over them. Surjanto looked up fearfully, almost feeling its tonnage bearing down on top of them like a landslide falling from a mountain.

"They're turning into us," Surjanto screamed to the driver. "Pull away, pull away."

The ship bumped against the boat roughly and the driver tore at the wheel to avoid the crushing weight of the ship. The two men at the front lost balance and the ladder slipped from their grips, clattering down onto the deck of the boat. The end dipped into the water and for a second Surjanto thought the ladder was lost when one of the men reached out and caught it before it fell into the depths.

"Idiots," Surjanto cursed. "Pick that thing up and try again."

Under the scathing eye of Surjanto, the two men recovered the ladder and raised it once more up above their heads.

Surjanto slipped the AK-47 from his shoulder and aimed it at the deck above. He scowled and looked through the sights to where the sailor above had previously poked his head out from.

"Again," he yelled. The speedboat's driver eased the boat close to the ship once more.

***

Sanders let out a roar of delight as the pirate boat veered away from the ship. He slapped the sailor on the back, but the man shrugged him off and continued to chatter through the radio.

Sanders turned away to look at the other man on the right-hand side of the ship. He could barely make any detail from here. He could not even see as much as a silhouette. He gritted his teeth, wondering if the man had already cut and run at the sight of the pirates below. Or worse, the pirates on the other side had already hooked their ladder and were climbing up in this very moment. Wiping the thought from his mind, Sanders turned to watch the sailor lean once more over the side to spy on their quarries.

Suddenly there was a muted bang, and something warm splashed on Sanders' face. Frowning, Sanders wiped the back of his hand across his forehead. Pulling his hand away, he saw it was smeared with a dark liquid. Movement caught his eye and he looked to see the sailor in front of him slump forward over the handrail. Sanders went to grab him, but then noticed the sailor's head had taken a mishappen shape, as though part of it was missing. There was another clatter of gunfire from below and Sanders released the body of the unfortunate sailor as divots of flesh exploded from his body and sparks kicked up from the railing.

Sanders backed away, knowing there was no stopping the pirates from boarding now. The corpse of the sailor slipped over the side of the rail and into the waters below. Sanders glanced to the opposite side of the ship and noted at least three or four figures there now. It was too late now. The pirates were aboard and the *Kekal* was lost.

Knowing discretion was the best part of valour, Sanders turned to leave when something small and hard pressed into his back just near his shoulder. Something was shouted in a language he did not understand, and instinctively he raised his hands above his head. As he did so, Sanders turned his head slightly to catch a glimpse at his would-be assailant. It was dark, but he made out the features easily enough. It was the grinning face of Mohede.

***

The radio handset tumbled end on end through the air before clattering into the wall with a crack. The impact shattered the hard plastic interior, splitting the radio in two before falling broken to the floor.

Captain Arwadi glared at the crumbled device. The ruptured casing, exposed wires and splintered shards caused by his throw did nothing to ease his temper. He screamed at the device but still his stress would not abate.

The crew on the bridge around him turned away, casting nervous glances amongst themselves. Arwadi stormed back to the window and pressed his head against it as he looked out. Pirates were already coming over the starboard side of the boat. There were numerus shadows already visible and more still were clambering onto his ship. Arwadi clenched a fist and hammered it against the window. He turned, noting how the crew turned away to avoid making eye contact with him, before storming over to a phone handset. He quickly punched a code and pulled the handset to his ear.

"This is the engineer," came a voice through the small speaker.

"This is Captain Arwadi."

"I'm sorry, Captain, the engines are running as fast as they can go. I can't push it any further."

"Forget that. It's already over. We have already been boarded by multiple hostiles." Arwadi paused a moment to let the information sink in. "I have a question. Is Darsani down there with you?"

"Darsani?"

"Yes, Darsani. Is he with you or not?" Arwadi burst out.

There was a pause. "Yes. He's here."

"Send him up to the bridge. I need him here pronto, before the pirates get here. I have an urgent mission for him."

"Yes sir."

Arwadi dropped the handset back in the cradle and stared at the phone. There was nothing to do now. His ship was lost. But if there was going to be one small consolation, he was going to take it. And that consolation was revenge on the man who did this to him and his ship. And in the mind of Arwadi, there was only one suspect over who was the root cause of this mess. The man that came to him late the previous night to hire his ship. A man he knew right from the start not to trust. It was that damned *tionghoa.*

***

O'Mara paced the small space of Sanders' cabin like a hungry caged lion, rolling her shoulders in a vain attempt to ease the stress out of them. She knew she should be hiding. She should be under the bed, or in the closet, or… there were no hiding spots in this room that were not plainly obvious. These cabins were so simple she could not even hide from a three-year-old child successfully here.

But it was not just the lack of a proven hiding space that stressed her. It was the not knowing and also, though she hated to admit it, it was that she was alone. If there was anyone on this ship to cower behind, it was Matt Sanders. He was strong and brave. He had single handedly captured the Horse Serpent with just rope at his disposal after it tore a number of armed men to shreds. It was also he who had clambered on the outside of a moving truck to save her from that extremist Mohede after he attacked her. He also claimed to be ex-army. Yes, if there was anyone to cower behind for protection it was Sanders. But damn it, Sanders just was not here.

Further, it pained her to admit, it was a mistake coming here. She should be with Simon. She stopped and pondered Dower for a moment. She felt bad that they did not have time to talk earlier. She had wanted to talk. She had so many questions. She only hoped that they would get the opportunity to have that conversation.

She stopped pacing and looked about the room. Sanders' bag lay on the floor wide open with clothing strewn haphazardly about it. A can of deodorant rolled into the corner. And on the bed was an old pair of stained white underwear. She stared at the underwear and shook her head.

"I shouldn't be here," she said and turned to the door. In the distance there was the muffled sound of gunshots. She clenched and unclenched her fists and stared at the door. "I need to go back to my cabin in case Simon is there. We can't be separated. He might go looking for me if I'm not there."

He might not either, a voice in her head said. Remember how he ran away and left you in the forest?

She cursed herself for thinking it and pushed the memory aside. She had to believe in him, because if she did not, then she would have nothing. And they were nothing.

O'Mara reached out and clutched the door handle. She stared at her hand, willing it to pull the handle. She closed her eyes and tried to recall the last words she had said to Dower. Whatever they were, they were inadequate. Too much had passed between them. If the worse came to the worst, then let it happen but only after they had the chance to talk.

O'Mara came to a decision. She gritted her teeth and opened the door.

In the hall there were panicked shouts all about her. A large dark-skinned man with a shaved head ran past and almost knocked her over. She shouted at him to watch where he was going. He did not even turn to acknowledge her. In the distance she heard more gunshots.

Recovering herself, she ran to the door of her cabin and twisted the handle vigorously. The door was still locked. In desperation she pounded on the door with her fists.

"Simon," she shouted at the top of her lungs. "Simon, are you in there?"

She kicked and thumped the door, but there was no answer.

"Miss O'Mara, what are you doing out here?"

She turned to the voice to see Sianturi approaching her along the passage. His eyes were wide with concern. "The pirates have successfully boarded. You need to hide." Sianturi turned and glanced about the hallway to ensure that they were alone.

O'Mara turned and slumped against the door. Her emotions were threatening to get the better of her.

Sianturi turned back to O'Mara and stepped closer to her. "Miss O'Mara, I must insist you hide. You cannot imagine what these men would do to a beautiful woman such as yourself if given the chance."

Sianturi reached out and clutched her wrist. She immediately pulled it away.

"No," she screamed at him. But as she turned back to his kindly face, she felt ashamed at the rashness of her action. "No," she repeated in a softer tone, "not until I find Simon."

"Mr Dower? I saw him earlier. He ran up the stairs and I assumed he was coming here."

"Well, he's not."

Sianturi continued to stare at O'Mara. "Well, I don't think he came back past me. Perhaps he continued to go up."

O'Mara turned and looked Sianturi in the eyes. After all of the questions Sianturi asked during the afternoon, she began to feel suspicious and distrustful of him. She searched his eyes for the truth, and there was nothing in those brown eyes that suggested he was saying otherwise. She turned and looked at the stairs leading up. It seemed obvious now, but if Dower did not find her in their cabin, he probably went up to the next level to search for her in the mess. She pushed away from the door and rushed towards the steps.

Sianturi paused, hovering on the spot for a moment before running to catch up with her.

"I think I had better keep you company."

"Do you?"

"I know my way around ships and this pirate attack isn't my first. You'll be safer with me."

O'Mara's eyes narrowed and she cast Sianturi a sideways glance. His words had been plain enough, but she said nothing. She found her earlier desire for company was beginning to evaporate. Her instincts told her not to trust him. She only hoped he was true to his word.

***

The movement and clatter of the ladder against the railing was only slight, but it was enough to catch Mohede's attention for a vital split second. The moment his eyes flicked to the right, Sanders burst into action. Sanders twisted his body at the hips, using his right arm to knock down the arm holding the gun to his back and using the turning motion of his shoulders to throw an overhand punch with his left fist. There was a sharp bang as the gun went off and Sanders felt a stinging pain on the outside of his thigh. Sanders' punch was not clean, but it connected with the side of Mohede's head with enough force to send him staggering backwards.

Seizing the moment, Sanders stepped forward, gritting his teeth through the pain in his leg, and planted his left foot to the ground, raising his right to push kick Mohede. The sole of Sanders' boot thumped into Mohede's chest and he staggered backwards into the container behind him. The shock of the blows was momentary, and Mohede pushed off the container to raise the gun at his assailant. But Sanders was quicker, lunging forward to clutch the gun hand just below the wrist and push it up and backwards to smash it into the container. One. Two. Three times he hit Mohede's hand into the container before Mohede's grip weakened and the pistol tumbled to the deck. Sanders looked down and kicked the weapon away.

Mohede growled and reached for Sanders' face with his free hand. He caught the skin of Sanders' cheek with a clawed hand that felt like a bird's talon. Sanders felt warm wetness on his cheek as Mohede's sharp nails scratched through his skin.

Mohede then planted one foot and side-kicked Sanders in the hip. Sanders grunted, then freed one hand to elbow Mohede in the head. The force of the blow rocked Mohede's head backwards where it slammed into the container behind him. The container boomed hollowly at the impact. Mohede's legs went to jelly and Sanders stepped back to let him collapse to the deck. Mohede was dazed, and Sanders took a quick moment to examine the wound on his leg. He had been lucky. His leg was bloodied and raw, but the bullet had only nicked him. There was no major damage.

A clang of metal to his left suddenly drew Sanders' attention sharply back to the pirates. They had successfully hooked the ladder onto the rail and would now be mounting the rungs. Sanders cursed and turned to look for the fallen pistol.

Mohede shook the dizziness from his head and pulled himself to his feet doggedly. Sanders now had his back to him and was looking about the deck for the lost gun. Mohede pushed away from the container and slowly approached Sanders from behind. Sanders was not aware of his presence until the arm wrapped around his neck and pulled tight. Mohede had wrapped one arm over Sanders' throat and held it by the wrist with his other hand and began tightening the choke hold on Sanders. Sanders clutched at Mohede's arm and tried to pull it away, but Mohede held firm.

The pressure on Sanders' neck increased and he was quickly finding it hard to breathe. He tried kicking backwards, but his foot only found empty air as Mohede leaned back and tightened his grip. Sanders' vision began to darken as Mohede increased his pressure on the hold. From the corner of his eyes, Sanders saw the head of the first pirate appear at the top of the ladder. Mohede said something. Sanders could not understand the words, but the mocking tone was clear enough. He was celebrating, and for Sanders this would all soon be over.

***

Despite the grimness of the situation and the fear that permeated his soul deep down, Captain Arwadi could not stop himself from smiling as the large shaven head engineer dressed in orange overalls appeared at the bridge door.

"Darsani," he cried with the elation of someone whose lucky lotto numbers had just come up, "thank you for coming." He slapped the man on the shoulder and invited him on the bridge.

Darsani looked about the bridge in wonderment. He had never been invited here before and it was a surprise to be welcomed in this moment. The crew on hand regarded him nervously.

"You look in good shape, Darsani. How was your last fight?" the captain asked as he opened a drawer and started rifling through it.

"Good. He was some out of towner who thought he could just roll in and take me on. He had a decent punch on him. Or so it was said. I don't know about that really, because I knocked him out in the first round."

Arwadi looked up and nodded with satisfaction. "Nice. I wish I had been there to put money on it."

"Some of the boys did. They cleaned up and shouted me beers all night. I woke up with a worse headache than I have when I get knocked out myself."

"Ha," said Arwadi. He pulled a key from the drawer and approached Darsani, placing the key in his hand. Darsani looked at the key with a dull expression before giving Arwadi a quizzical look.

"That key," Arwadi said, "is for cabin 2E. Inside 2E is that damned *tionghoa*. He is the one responsible for all of this. If it wasn't for him, we'd all be back in port loading this ship high with containers and you'd be out there earning money off another prize fight. I want you to go down to that cabin and sort him out."

"You want me to go down there and slug him around a bit?"

Arwadi glanced at the men on the bridge and leaned in closer to speak more quietly to Darsani. "Yes, but more than that. I want you to throw him off the ship."

Darsani's eyes widened. "But he'd drown."

"That's precisely the point. Listen, Darsani, you won't be at fault here, trust me on this. If we are ever asked, well, he went overboard when the pirates attacked. It must have been them who threw him over."

Darsani looked at Arwadi doubtfully.

"I am your captain, Darsani, and you have my word as your captain that you will not face any repercussions on this. Listen, we can't let that *tionghoa* get away with this. It's his fault we are in this mess and he should be punished."

Darsani chewed over the words a bit before nodding.

"Good, good," Arwadi said gleefully as he ushered Darsani to the door. "Be quick about it too. We already have pirates boarding. Best just drag him out back and throw him off the poop deck and hide. Now go, man, and be quick about it."

Darsani gave a nod and disappeared down the stairs. The captain returned to the bridge. Not one crewmember dared make eye contact with him.

"Okay," Arwadi called to get their attention, "it's time to seal the bridge. Someone lock this door, now. And turn on the main deck floodlights. I want to see what our raiders are up to."

***

Dower must have changed his mind at least ten times by now, and he still did not know what he was doing.

"This is stupid," he muttered to himself, but his feet kept moving and he roamed around the ship. Fear clouded his mind and he lost focus on what he was doing. He descended one flight of stairs after another and soon found himself in an area of the ship he had never seen before. All around him was exposed steel pipes, and sheet iron walls dripping with moisture. It was warmer here, and the sound of the engines was much louder than anywhere else he had been. He blinked slowly and looked about himself, lost momentarily before realising he had stumbled below decks.

As he wandered, he soon realised this area was filled with multiple nooks and crannies he could easily seclude himself in and not be found. It would probably be safer hiding here than in his cabin. He eyed one particular spot for some time, before pushing the temptation aside and moving on.

Dower turned, intent to return to the stairs and up to the main deck. As he turned, he realised he could have come from any of the corridors around him. He frowned, realising suddenly he had lost his bearings and had no idea which way to go from here.

If O'Mara was here, she would be laughing at him right now and reminding him of the time he had gotten lost in a mall car park. That had happened three years earlier. She had driven that day. He only needed to pick up something quickly, so she would wait in the car while he quickly rushed in to get what he needed. It was a Saturday and the mall was busier than normal. O'Mara parked underground on the west wing of the mall. It was an area Dower had not been to often. He found the shop easy enough, but in returning to the car park he got muddled up and lost. He had wandered the car park an hour that day and O'Mara had joked about his awful sense of direction ever since.

Dower huffed and ran his fingers through his hair. One corridor here looked much like the other and he was at pains to admit he was lost. It was the car park all over again. He sighed. At least O'Mara would not know about this one. Not unless she found him, that is.

The thought of O'Mara spurred him on and he knew he could not afford to dither. Dower chose a corridor at random and began following it. The corridor twisted right, then left again before ending in a short staircase. His eyes lit up and he jogged the last few feet, thinking he had found his way back, when he stopped at the foot of the stairs and looked up. The stairs led to a hatch.

Dower frowned. These were not the stairs he had come down. He turned and looked down the corridor he had just come from. In his mind he tried to recall the series of twists and turns that had led him here. He had never imagined that below decks this ship was such a labyrinth. All it needed was David Bowie and some goblins and the illusion would be complete.

Dower turned back to the stairs and looked up at the hatch. He sighed again. He had committed to this route far enough. He might as well see it through to the end. He mounted the first stair and began pushing himself up. The hatch was fortunately unlocked and fresh air wafted in as Dower pushed it open. Dower stepped up and realised he was on the main deck again. Ahead was the raised block that was the living quarters and behind the main deck stretched out to the bow.

As Dower climbed onto the main deck, his attention was drawn to the sounds of a struggle. He turned, squinting as his eyes adjusted to the darkness of the night. There seemed to be the wriggling shape of what appeared to be two men wrestling. He watched, yearning for his eyes to extricate some detail in the murk, when the shapes dropped to the floor. Suddenly the deck was lit up with bright, scalding light.

***

Sanders knew his time was running short, but he had one last desperate play.

He gave up trying to pull Mohede's arm away and instead reached around behind him. He felt Mohede's hip and leg, and followed his body until he found Mohede's crotch. Not wasting any time, Sanders clutched and squeezed. Mohede screeched and his grip immediately loosened. Sanders gasped at the air hungrily and increased the pressure in his hand.

"Let me go or I'll rip them off," Sanders wheezed. Mohede's grip loosened further and Sanders saw his opening. He twisted his body and tried to elbow Mohede in the head with his opposite arm. He made impact and immediately threw three more like it. Mohede's arms came away and the two fell to the deck in unison.

Sanders let go of Mohede and landed on his hands and knees. He coughed and spat as he hacked in large gulps of air into his burning lungs. Instinctively he reached up and felt his tender neck as he gasped at the air.

Mohede had hit the deck and rolled to the side, clutching at his groin in agony. He tried to push himself and get to his feet, but the agony was too much.

Suddenly the deck was lit up with a startling brightness. Sanders shaded his eyes and looked to the side. The pirate on the ladder was lifting his left leg over the rail but had paused in the dazzling bright light. He turned to Mohede, who was less affected and struggling to his feet. Mohede seemed to be staring at a single point ahead of him on the deck. Sanders followed his gaze and saw what he had his eye on. It was the lost pistol lying on the deck.

Sanders pushed himself up but Mohede was on his feet first. Mohede staggered towards the discarded gun. Sanders took up chase, one hand still clutched to his tender throat. Mohede led the race despite his awkward gait and was closing fast on the weapon. Sanders was gaining on his quarry, but it was clear Mohede would reach the gun first. Mohede slowed as he reached down for the pistol, but Sanders did not. He had another idea.

As Mohede bent down to grasp the gun, Sanders' foot flashed through, kicking both Mohede's hands and the gun in the process. The gun skittered across the deck and out of reach. But Sanders was not done. As Mohede straightened, Sanders turned and delivered a devastating right hook to the side of Mohede's head. Mohede staggered backwards and his back hit the handrail on the side of the deck. He blinked and looked behind himself to see open space and the rushing waters below.

Sanders closed in like a boxer on the hunt. He had his man on the ropes and he was looking for the knockout. He raised his fists and stepped forward. His throat and leg ached but he pushed the pain aside as he lined up his opponent.

Mohede raised his fists in defiance but leaned against the rail for support. Sanders went for the body first, ripping three right hooks just under Mohede's ribcage. Mohede grunted under the first blow and lurched forward to grapple Sanders. The second two blows landed but Sanders soon found himself entangled in a wrestle with Mohede. He tried to throw him off, but Mohede reached around to grab the back of Sanders' head. Sanders tried more punches to Mohede's body when Mohede's body spasmed with an attack. Simultaneously pulling down Sanders' head and lifting his knee, Mohede was going for a big knockout blow with a knee to the head. Sanders tried to push away but the knee hit him with a glancing blow. Mohede tried the move a second time. It missed and Sanders caught Mohede's leg.

Roaring a battle cry, Sanders lifted Mohede up. Mohede tried hopping on his one foot and getting his balance. He took a handful of Sanders' hair and pulled as Sanders pushed him back. He felt the cold hardness of the rail on his back. In a moment of panic, he realised Sanders was lifting him over it. Mohede moved from pulling Sanders' hair to raining punches at his head.

Sanders put his head down and pushed on through the blows, lifting Mohede higher on the handrail. At last, he got him above it and pushed forwards. Suddenly the weight of Mohede's body was pulling him forwards. Mohede desperately clutched at Sanders as he realised there was only open space and water below him. Sanders let go of Mohede's leg and started punching under Mohede's armpit. After the second blow Mohede's grip weakened and faltered. As Mohede fell away, his chin hit the rail and his body tumbled awkwardly into the water below and disappeared with a splash below the surface. Sanders leaned out and watched the spot as the ship moved on, but he did not see Mohede resurface.

"Sanders!" came a panicked yell from his left. He looked up and was surprised to see Dower standing there. He was about to greet him when he noticed that Dower was pointing over Sanders' opposite shoulder. His eyes were wide and panic stricken.

Sanders turned and saw a second pirate had climbed to the deck and was unslinging his AK-47 from his shoulder. Sanders looked about and saw an open hatch in the deck and turned for it.

"Run to the hatch," he yelled to Dower as he pushed off the rail. His leg ached through the first couple of steps as he gathered some momentum. He glanced to ensure Dower was running but as he turned, he saw Dower was bending over to pick up the gun he and Mohede had fought over.

"No!" he cried, skidding to a stop and immediately changing direction back to Dower.

Dower straightened with the gun in his hand. He looked up to see the pirate with the scarred face and gold tooth loading a magazine into his rifle. Dower raised the pistol and aimed it at the pirate. His hands were unsteady as he looked down the sights at his target. The magazine clicked into place and the scar-faced pirate raised the rifle. Dower pulled the trigger.

Click. Nothing happened.

"The safety!" Sanders roared, but he might as well have said nothing as Dower stared dazedly at the gun. Sanders saw the pirate raising the rifle and aiming at Dower. His legs pumped hard and thumped the steel deck below him as he crossed the floor quickly, but he knew he would not be quick enough. He leapt, intending to knock Dower down before his body was torn to pieces in a hail of AK-47 fire. But Sanders had made one horrible mistake. He did not see Dower was standing right next to the handrail.

Sanders hit Dower in the shoulder just as the gun from the pirate opened up. Bullets whizzed past as the momentum of Sanders' leap pushed both Sanders and Dower into the handrail. Dower was unbalanced and his feet lifted off the deck as he tumbled over the barrier. He clutched at the handrail but the weight and momentum of Sanders' leap was too great and his grip was instantly broken. With nothing but air on the other side of the handrail, Sanders and Dower tumbled over the side of the ship and down into the water. The last thing Dower heard before crashing into the hard water below was a woman's scream. As Dower plunged into the deep, dark water, there was just one thing on his mind.

There was only one woman on board the ship. His beloved girlfriend, Jess O'Mara.

12

Setiawan's men had been the first aboard the ship. Unaware of the struggles of Surjanto's men to hook the ladder on the opposite side of the ship, and oblivious to the brutal struggle between Sanders and Mohede on the deck, Setiawan sent his men to the main block tower of the ship to start capturing and herding prisoners to the mess. As his men trotted to work, Setiawan glanced across the open decks and frowned. He had hoped there would be more cargo to take, but there were barely any containers on this ship. He shrugged. Any additional cargo would have been surplus income anyway. They were here for one thing and one thing only, and that alone was worth taking the risk for.

Setiawan's men were quick and well drilled. They knew their way around ships like this and they were quick to take the first level. As they moved from cabin to cabin searching for crew and hostages, on the level above them the prize fighter Darsani pulled a struggling Cheong from his cabin and dragged him towards the rear of the ship. Moments later Setiawan's men claimed the second level, with Darsani and Cheong gone from the structure.

It was as O'Mara and Sianturi were leaving the mess in their search for Dower that the first of Setiawan's men breached the third level of the tower. His shout caught their attention from the opposite end of the hall.

"Run!" Sianturi shouted and urged O'Mara to the steps leading to the next level. She staggered and tripped but Sianturi caught her by the arm and pulled her back to her feet. The pirate behind them shouted again as Sianturi hustled O'Mara up the stairs.

They reached the top of the stairs only to see the door of the bridge slam shut in front of them. O'Mara reached the top of the stairs first and ran to the door and yanked on the handle. Sianturi paused, watching the stairs behind him as he walked slowly forwards.

O'Mara started pounding the door with her hands. "Open up and let me in," she yelled, "they are coming." There was no response on the other side of the door as she continued to pound. Sianturi joined her, hitting the door hard and shouting.

"Damn, it Arwadi, let us in, man. The pirates are almost here."

But despite their pleas, the door remained locked tight.

A sharp clang of metal on metal coming from the stairs told O'Mara and Sianturi that they were about to have company. Sianturi grabbed O'Mara by the arm and pulled her away from the door.

"Quick," he said as he forced her away from the door to the bridge, "we need to find somewhere to hide."

O'Mara cursed and was reluctant to move when another clang from the stairs gave her enough encouragement to move on. The two of them jogged down past the bridge before coming to two passages. Sianturi took the right and O'Mara followed; within seconds he pulled to a stop as the corridor ended in a small balcony overlooking the main deck. Sianturi had run them into a dead end.

Just then the floodlights flicked on across the main deck of the boat. O'Mara turned to leave when Sianturi touched her arm to draw her attention and pointed to the deck below.

She gasped as she saw Sanders and Mohede on the deck below on all fours. A pirate was climbing over the side. Just then both Sanders and Mohede got to their feet and started running. O'Mara leaned forward and saw as Sanders kicked the pistol away from Mohede and they engaged in a brutal life or death fight. Her eyes followed the pistol as it skittered across the deck to stop at the foot of another man.

"Simon," she whispered in shock as she recognised him.

Sanders threw Mohede overboard and made a break for it as a second pirate boarded the ship. For some reason Dower was not moving and O'Mara watched as he stupidly raised the gun. She was about to shout when she saw Sanders change direction and run towards Dower. The pirate fired and Sanders leapt. O'Mara screamed as Sanders and Dower disappeared over the edge of the ship and out of sight as they plunged into the waters below.

Sianturi pulled O'Mara back from the balcony and threw himself and her onto the floor. Suddenly the steelwork around them lit up with noise and sparks as bullets clattered about them. The onslaught only lasted a couple of seconds and was over in just a few short breaths.

"Are you okay?" Sianturi asked as he raised himself.

O'Mara turned to him with wide eyes and a quivering lip. "Simon and Matt.... They're gone?"

Sianturi bit his lip before talking. "I'm afraid so."

"Can we save them?"

Sianturi's throat bobbed as he swallowed. "The ship is moving too fast. They will already be well behind us in the ship's wake."

O'Mara's vision blurred as tears welled in her eyes. As one broke out and rolled down her cheek, Sianturi looked away.

"We have to hide," he said urgently.

"No, we have to do something. I can't leave Simon to..." the words caught in her throat. "It can't end like this," she sobbed.

Sianturi heaved a breath and looked about him. "Maybe there is one thing we can do. But we have to act now, or it will be too late."

Sianturi held out a hand. She took it quicky and he heaved her to her feet.

"Follow me," he said, and jogged back down the corridor from whence they came.

***

Surjanto lowered the gun and squinted up at the balcony.

"Did I hit them?" he asked.

The pirate next to him shrugged. "I couldn't see a damn thing with those bloody lights shining in my eyes."

Surjanto gave him a quick glance and then a smile trickled over his face. He turned and raised the rifle once more. One, two, three times he fired. Three floodlights over the bridge exploded with sparks as shattered glass rained onto the deck below.

"How about now? Can you see now?"

"Better," the other pirate muttered, "but I don't see any bodies."

"Bah," Surjanto said and waved him away. He leaned over the rail to see the men on the speedboat below looking up in wonderment. He glanced to the rear of the ship, but there was no sign of the two men that had spilled overboard. He supressed a grin. "Okay, you slackers, hurry up and get those useless butts of yours up on deck. We have a ship to take."

As he pulled away from the side of the boat, the radio on his belt crackled to life.

"Surjanto, this is Setiawan. Do you read me?"

Surjanto scowled as he unclipped the radio. "Surjanto here."

"I heard shots. What the hell is going on down there? I told you no unnecessary killing."

"It was self-defence."

"Self-defence? We haven't encountered a single hostile threat since boarding. Where are you right now?"

"Main deck."

"Is the threat still active?"

"No. The threat is done with."

"Good. No more shots then, got it? We have most of the crew rounded up. We are holding them on the third floor in the mess. If you find any more crew, take them captive. No kills. And send them up here. Acknowledge."

"Acknowledged." The words came out in a slow drawl.

"Good. Stick to the plan. Setiawan, out."

Surjanto looked at the radio a long time before clipping it back to his belt. He turned to watch the last few men mount the ladder to climb aboard. He signalled to the speedboat driver who pulled away from the ship to return to base. After the men had checked their gear, he sent three to search the main deck forward of their position, three more down the open hatch from which Dower had emerged, while he took the remaining two with him to explore the rear of the boat.

Surjanto followed the line of the safety rail around the accommodation block to the rear of the vessel. As he rounded the corner at the rear of the accommodation block the space opened up to the poop deck. His attention was immediately drawn to movement at the rear most point of the ship. Surjanto raised his rifle to his shoulder and advanced quickly. In the low light he saw two figures struggling. One man was much larger than the other and was dressed in orange overalls. He looked to be much stronger than his opponent and seemed to be getting the better of the struggle. Surjanto closed, stepping forwards with soft steps and keeping his rifle aimed on the fight. Just then, the man in the orange overalls stepped back and laid a vicious right hook to the second man. The fight seemed to be over then, and the man in the overalls pushed the second man against the rail before leaning down, picking up the legs of the second man and tipping him over the edge.

The man in the overalls watched the rushing water out the rear of the boat for a few seconds before turning. His brain barely registered the presence of the pirates before Surjanto quickly squeezed the trigger three times.

The man in the overalls staggered backwards and collapsed against the rail. Three distinct blood patches appeared and grew on his clothing. One was on his shoulder, one in his chest and the third in the stomach. Blood bubbled on the man's lips and he seemed to be struggling to breathe.

Surjanto advanced and peered over the back of the boat but saw nothing but churning, frothing white water and darkness.

"One of ours?" one of the pirates accompanying him asked.

Surjanto turned. "Can't say. I didn't get a look at him."

Surjanto then crouched down beside the man he had shot. Blood continued to bubble on his mouth and he was wheezing as he breathed. He looked at Surjanto with wide eyed fear as Surjanto tilted his head and examined his bald-headed victim. Surjanto's eyes narrowed.

"I know you," Surjanto said. "You're a boxer, aren't you?"

The man gave a short nod.

"Yes, I recognise you now. I had money on your last fight." Surjanto placed his rifle on the deck and drew his curved knife from his belt. He lifted the knife into the man's eyeline to show the glinting, sharp edge. "If I recall correctly, your name is Darsani, is it not?"

The man nodded again. Surjanto smiled innocently and began tracing the line of Darsani's face with the tip of his blade. "Yes, Darsani, you fought well that night. A first-round knockout and your opponent barely landed a punch. It wasn't much of a contest at all." Surjanto continued to trace Darsani's face with the knife before stopping just above Darsani's eye. Surjanto's smile hardened, then turned to a sneer. "That fight cost me two million rupiah, you piece of shit. So now it's time I… how does the saying go? I take an eye for an eye."

Before Darsani could react, Surjanto plunged his dagger down, piercing both eyelid and eyeball with his sharp blade. A bubbled scream burst from Darsani's throat as Surjanto pulled to the side and tore the pierced eyeball apart. Surjanto then stood and tucked his knife back into his belt and retrieved his rifle. He turned back and spat on Darsani, who was clutching at his ruined eye with blood streaming between his fingers. Surjanto turned away.

The radio again crackled to life with Setiawan's voice. Surjanto rolled his eyes.

"Surjanto here," he responded.

"Surjanto, I need you up on the bridge. The captain has barricaded himself in and no amount of threats will get him to open it. I need you to get up there and blow it open. Acknowledge."

"Acknowledged."

"Good. Now, I thought I heard more shots. I want no deaths here. Bring everyone you find to the mess. Over."

Surjanto clipped the radio back onto his belt and turned to his men. One was looking particularly pale faced as he stared at Darsani. Surjanto recognised him as the one who he had cuffed for passing the radio to him on the speedboat earlier. He pointed at him.

"You," he said, drawing the young pirate's attention. "You heard Setiawan's order. Take this prisoner up to the mess."

The young pirate looked at him wide eyed. "But…"

"But nothing. You heard the order. I need to go to the bridge. This man is your responsibility and if he's not in the mess when I get there, I'll have your eye next. Got it?"

The pirate nodded his head vigorously and Surjanto walked away, allowing himself a small smile of satisfaction.

***

"This way," Sianturi urged as he moved to the rear of the ship. "Quickly."

O'Mara paused, still unsure whether to trust Sianturi, when foreign voices behind her provided the impetus to move forward.

The top level of the ship's structure contained three major features. The first and most important was the bridge. Built high and facing the front of the ship, the bridge had a commanding view from the helm for the captain. On either side of the bridge were two balconies, otherwise known as the bridge wings. Behind the bridge sat the captain's office and the captain's quarters. If you took the walkway behind these two rooms, you would find a narrow stairway leading down to another otherwise unreachable platform that connected to a large steel frame. The frame was thick and heavy, tilting sharply downwards towards the waters aft of the boat. Inside the frame sat a large, orange vehicle that resembled a small submarine. It looked like a sort of wild carnival ride.

"What is it?" O'Mara asked as she shuffled down the narrow stairway to the small staging area.

"It's a freefall escape boat."

"Freefall?" O'Mara asked, before leaning over the edge to see the waters rushing by far below her. It would be the equivalent of launching from the top of a six-story building from here. She gulped nervously. "That's a long way down."

"It is. But you will be strapped in tight when I launch it. There will be a big bump when you hit the water but otherwise, you'll be fine."

"Me?"

"Well, yes. I thought that's what you wanted. I mean, a pretty woman like you in the hands of pirates… I think it would be better if you got away, if you catch my drift."

"But what about the Horse S…"

Sianturi turned sharply to her, cocked an eyebrow and waited. When it became apparent she would not say anything further, he spoke at last. "I don't care how fast this horse you have is, Miss O'Mara. No horse could be worth going through that. Especially not a Java pony."

"I suppose not," she said solemnly.

"Besides, those two men are a long way back. Someone will need to drive the boat and find them. It won't be easy in the dark. You will have to use torches and flares to light your way. And I'll be brutally honest. You are going to need a hell of a lot of luck as well."

"You sound like you aren't coming."

"I'm not. I need to stay here and try and negotiate with the pirates for my cargo. If this medical equipment doesn't go through, we are going to have a health crisis on our hands."

As nimble as a Borneo white-bearded gibbon, Sianturi reached up to grab the framework and swung across to the rear door of the safety boat. He opened the door and turned to O'Mara. "I'll check that there is food, flares and torches inside, but after that you're on your own."

"But how do you launch it?"

"It can be launched from inside, or by that lever on the panel in front of you. Better I launch it remotely for you."

Without another word, Sianturi swung down into the rescue boat with the door swinging shut behind him. O'Mara stared at the boat and shivered. She clutched her arms about herself and waited.

She turned and looked out the rear of the ship. The moon had now risen, casting a silvery glow over the sea around her. But it was dark, and there was a lot of water out there. It would need more than a lot of luck to find Dower and Sanders; it would need a miracle.

Suddenly the low sound of footsteps above her woke her from her reverie. O'Mara looked up and saw a shadow on the platform above. She pulled back, hiding under the cover of the stairs. She looked at the rescue boat. There were three windows down the side, and through them she could see a beam of torchlight flashing from left to right.

Above her the figure at the edge of the stairs leaned out to look at the boat. O'Mara pressed hard against the wall under the stairs and made rapid throat cutting gestures at the rescue boat. "Kill the light," she mouthed, praying that Sianturi would glance through the window and see her. But evidently he did not, and the beam of light continued to wave around like a child having a mock light-sabre duel.

The figure above her moved. She heard him start lightly padding down the staircase. O'Mara's gestures became more frantic. If that was a pirate above and he saw the light coming from the boat, then any chance of her getting on board and setting the lifeboat adrift would be lost. But then she stopped. Her eyes slid from the window of the rescue boat to the release lever on the panel. She stared at it a second then glanced quickly above her. There was a loud metallic click. O'Mara swallowed and took a deep breath. She closed her eyes and let the breath slowly and quietly out of her body. When her eyes opened, they focused solely on the release lever.

Taking another quick breath, O'Mara pushed off the wall and raced forward to the panel. She pushed on the lever but it would not move. She heard a shout from above her and turned to see a sharp faced man with a rifle pointed in her direction. She turned back, desperately shoving at the lever. But the lever seemed to be jammed.

"No!" she cried.

Behind her she heard the footsteps of the pirate coming down the stairs as quickly as he could. She hit the lever hard with her shoulder, using her whole bodyweight to move it, but still the lever would not budge.

The pirate shouted again. She turned her head to see he stood at the foot of the stairs on the platform with her now. He looked at her down the sights of his rifle aimed at her. She turned despairingly back to the boat. There was no torch beam from inside anymore. She sighed, looking down at the jammed lever when she noticed the small obstruction that stopped her from shifting it. The lever had a safety clip on it.

She could have slapped herself. Of course, it had a safety clip. The ship could not risk the lever getting knocked by accident and dropping the lifeboat in the water for nothing.

The pirate shouted something brusquely at her. She turned her body slightly, trying to seem relaxed while raising one hand. Her opposite hand slid across the panel towards the safety clip.

"It's okay," she said as her hand closed on the clip. "I give up."

The pirate shouted another order and indicated for her to move away from the panel. She undid the clip and pulled it away.

"I'm sorry," she said as innocently as she could muster, "but I don't understand."

The pirate yelled and stepped forward.

Suddenly O'Mara twisted with the speed of a released high-pressure spring. She swung at the hips and her raised arm slammed the lever forward. There was a hissing of gas and the rescue boat slid down the rail to crash into the water below. The pirate surged forwards as O'Mara let out a whoop of joy at the departing rescue boat. The whoop, however, was cut short as the butt of the pirate's rifle slammed into her head, instantly knocking her unconscious.

***

Captain Arwadi wiped the slick sweat from his brow with the back of his hand before replacing the cap back on his head. All eyes on the bridge were on him as he turned back to the door.

"No," he shouted, "I will not open this door. I will take you to whatever port you desire and you can take whatever cargo you want off this ship, but I will not open this door and let you take her over."

"Did you not hear what I just said?" a muffled voice called from the other side. "We have all of your crew as hostages. We are holding them in the mess right now. If you don't open this door, we will start executing them one by one. Is that what you want, Captain? Do you want all of your crew dead?"

"Please, Captain, open the door," a man on the bridge pleaded.

Captain Arwadi looked up with sad eyes. He looked about the bridge, taking it all in as if looking at it for the last time. Finally, his eyes settled on the man who had spoken. "I can't," he said softly. "This ship is my livelihood. I worked all my life to get here. Without this ship… I am nothing."

"But people are going to die, Captain. Their blood will be on your hands."

Arwadi nodded and bit his lip. He pushed away from the door and walked to the instrument panel. He walked along, running his hand across each screen, button and gauge. The crew watched silently as he wistfully stared out at the main deck and Sianturi's eight shipping containers. Suddenly his face screwed up in anger. His fist thumped down on the panel in front of him.

"What is all this for? Eight damn containers of medical supplies and a damn racehorse?"

"Captain, keep quiet, I hear something."

Arwadi turned, eyes ablaze with anger at the sudden insubordination on the bridge when he saw the culprit hunched over with his ear to the door. "What is it?" he asked.

The man at the door placed a finger to his lips to ask for silence. All in the bridge went quiet, their eyes staring with tension at the man at the door. Finally, he spoke.

"It sounds like a hissing. Or a fizzing. It's very soft," the man said.

Arwadi's brow crinkled, before his eyes went suddenly wide.

"Get away from the d…"

But Arwadi did not have time to finish the sentence before his voice was drowned by the roar of the explosion. The door blew inwards, smashing the man by the door. He was killed instantly from the blow and his corpse cartwheeled across the room to land in a broken mess across the control panel.

Smoke and dust filled the bridge as a bleary-eyed Captain Arwadi staggered to his feet. He pulled a man beside him to his feet as well and checked around for more survivors of the blast.

Through the open doorway a pirate strode in. He had a deep scar on his face and menace in his eyes. He studied the bridge door a moment, now hanging off one hinge at a strange angle. He turned back to Arwadi and grinned a sinister smile. A gold tooth glinted in his mouth.

"Hello, Captain," he said.

13

The sea swallowed Dower like a warm embracing cuddle from a loving grandparent. Only there was no love in this sea. All around Dower was unyielding blackness. It was the purest form of black Dower had ever seen.

Dower floated there a few seconds before swivelling his body and kicking back to the surface. For a moment he thought he may have dropped deeper than he first imagined as he kicked and kicked again only finding more water ahead of him. He had tumbled when he fell and started to wonder if he had gotten all turned about and was swimming the wrong way. He could not even be sure if he was closer or further to the surface than when he started. He stopped and tried to look about himself, suddenly unsure which direction the surface was in. He paused, waiting to see which direction he floated in, but in complete blackness of the water he could not even be sure he was floating up.

Dower felt rising panic and he spun on the spot looking for a vital directional clue. His lungs started to scream for air and he desperately wanted to open his mouth and breathe. The sound of Jess' scream as he fell from the boat still echoed in his ears and he could not think of anything more pitiful and pathetic than to have failed her for the second time in days only to stupidly drown because he simply did not know which way was up.

Sure now he was sinking, Dower fumbled for a prayer. Dower had never been religious, but in this moment it somehow seemed appropriate. But he did not pray for himself, but rather for Jess. He prayed she would find a new man to fall in love with her. Someone who could protect her where he had failed. Someone young, good looking, heroic and brave. Someone like Sanders, who was a man far more deserving of O'Mara's love than he was.

His prayer done and his head feeling like it was about to explode, Dower was just about to open his lungs to the sea when a hand grabbed him. Dower almost let his air out in fright, but held it to clutch onto the hand. He felt himself being pulled through the water and did not resist. He almost passed out when suddenly he was in open air and sucking down breaths. He never imagined the simple act of breathing could be this good.

"Damn, Dower, I thought I had lost you there," Sanders remarked.

"I couldn't see," Dower gasped. "I didn't know which way was up." Dower started to recover his breath and turned around. The moon had begun to rise, giving a unique sheen to the waves as they danced around him. He turned, seeing only dancing sea in every direction. He heard nothing but the sloshing of water. “Where is the ship?”

“At the speed it was travelling, it’s long gone,” Sanders said solemnly.

“Do you think someone saw us go over? Someone other than the pirates?”

“Probably. But I doubt they were in a position to do anything about it. They would have had their own concerns once those pirates came aboard.”

“So you don’t think anybody will be coming?”

The only answer Sanders had to this was solemn silence. Dower cursed and looked out into the distance. “I’m sorry, Sanders. This is all my fault we’re out here. I have no idea what I was thinking picking up the gun like that. I’ve never even held a gun before.”

“It showed,” Sanders said dryly.

“Are you angry at me?”

Sanders sighed. “I should be, but I’m not.”

Dower’s clothes began to feel heavy and he had to kick and paddle to keep afloat. Within minutes his muscles began to ache from the sustained effort to stay afloat and he found himself becoming overcome with despair.

“I should thank you for saving me,” Dower said, “but I feel it may be for nought.”

“Don’t talk like that.”

“I’m serious. I’m already tiring, and we’re stuck in the middle of the sea on a dark night. Even if someone knew we were out here, it might be some time before a boat or a plane came looking. Even assuming one came straight away, it’s hours until daylight and searching for us would still be like trying to find a needle in a hundred haystacks.”

“You have to try to stay positive. Focus on the things you can control and don’t worry about the things you can’t.”

Dower scoffed, but regretted it immediately. He bobbed on the water and swallowed a small amount of water. A coughing fit overtook him, expelling even more energy from his body.

“Are you okay?” Sanders asked when he had finished.

“Yes, but…”

“Try kicking off your shoes and removing your clothes if they are weighing you down. Also, you have to swim less and try to float.”

Dower nodded and kicked off his shoes. His jumper was heavy and he struggled to lift the heavy thing from him. He dipped underwater as he tried lifting it over his head before quickly deciding that was a bad tactic. Instead, he worked one arm out of its sleeve, then the other, before bunching the material and pulling it over his head in one quick move. He found it easier then.

Dower had never been a good swimmer and less so a good floater. But under some instruction he did manage to lay back and float for a few vital seconds of rest regularly.

"You know, when I was a kid, I never swam anywhere I couldn't touch the bottom," Dower said.

"Can I suggest you don't try touching the bottom here?" Sanders said trying to break Dower's negativity with humour.

Dower gave a wry smile, but with every passing moment he felt his energy draining away and knew he could not last long like this. He was only talking to keep his mind occupied and his thoughts distracted so he would not think about the yawning depths below him. Depths he had plunged into and could have sunk endlessly down through. Endlessly, that is, unless a deep-sea predator got to him first. Dower winced. Why did he think of that? He looked about again, despairingly considering their plight, the fathomless dark depths below him filled with hungry marine carnivores with mouths lined with sharp teeth and minds driven by primal hunger. He tried not to let his mind fall into gloomy thoughts of the many ways he could die out here, but he could not see anything in front of him to inspire any sort of hope. In his despondency, he thought of Jess again, and the need to clear the slate. He swivelled in the water to face Sanders.

"Matt, I really don't think I can make it through this…"

"Dower, please."

"No, Matt. Let me talk. I have things I want to get off my chest and, well, you're the only one here and I need someone to hear it. Call it a final confession if you will."

"Dower…"

"Let me talk. Please. Now where was I? Jess. You have to understand that I love Jess. I mean, I really love Jess. But the thing is, I know I'm not worthy of her. She's young, attractive and smart and I'm… well I'm just some boring old cowardly university lecturer. The thing is, I've been grappling for some time about what the next step is for us. And as far as I can figure, there are only two ways forward for me and her; either we marry or we break up.

"I want with all my heart to marry Jess. But the thing I fear more than anything else is that if I did marry her that I would be keeping her from a better life. What if two years into the marriage she suddenly realised how much younger and more attractive she was? What if she woke up and realised she was spending the best years of her life with me, a silly old man?

"It's why I ran. Back in the forest, I mean. I ran because then, damn it, then I would not have to live with knowing that I would be robbing her of a better life because, damn it, I just can't break up with her.

"But I guess all that doesn't matter anymore. Now that she has found you..."

"Dower, I told you this earlier. Don't talk shit. You ran because you were afraid. Stop over thinking it because there is no shame in it. Men with guns ran before you did and you don't need to make up flimsy excuses for running. And as for me and Jess, that suggestion is even sillier than your reason for running away."

"But I found you together in your room..."

Sanders let out a sigh. "Dower, she only came to me to talk. When you fled and left her in danger like that, it really hurt her. And since she couldn't talk to you about it, and Kenny is as approachable as a piranha with rabies, she came to me. She needed a friend. Someone to listen to her. That's all."

"So, you didn't..."

"No. I don't do the dirty on a mate. Look, Dower, I'm not the best bloke to give relationship advice. I haven't had a relationship with a woman more than a month in my whole life. But let me tell you this. She loves you too. And that crap about not being worthy of her? Well, that's her decision to make."

Dower listened to Sanders' words solemnly. As Sanders talked, Dower unconsciously reached down to the pocket on his pants and checked the small box was still there. It was, and it felt reassuring that it was still with him. He bit his lip, turned around and cursed. He wished he could have had that conversation on the boat with Jess. But now, lost and in the middle of the sea, he knew that conversation would never happen.

A grunt and splash from Sanders drew his mind back to the present. "Are you ok?" Dower asked.

"Yeah. It's just... well, you're an expert on animals and stuff. What do you know about fish that bump into you?"

"Bump into you?"

"Yeah, bump into you. Deliberately swim into you and bump you with their nose."

"Fish don't bump into you. Only..."

"Sharks. Yeah, I know sharks do it. I watched a shark special on television once and this guy was talking about how in the lead up to an attack they often bump their prey first. They make a couple of passes, bump them to see how much fight is in the prey and then, well, then they attack."

"So why did you ask?"

"I just wanted to check if other fish did it. You know, just in case."

Sanders grunted again and there was another splash as he punched at something under the water. Dower's eyes started to widen.

"I… I'm pretty sure it's only sharks that do that. Is one doing that to you now?"

Sanders grunted and again made a move to punch. "One, two… maybe more. Hard to say. It's too dark for me to see. But I definitely think there is more than one. Listen, Dower, it might be a good idea for you to move farther away from me." Sanders' voice was deadpan as he spoke.

"Oh my God," Dower said, suddenly looking around himself fearfully. "How did they find us so quickly?"

Sanders grunted and punched. "I'm bleeding. In the fight with Mohede the gun went off and a bullet scraped my leg. They would have sensed the blood as soon as I hit the water."

"Oh my God," said Dower, frantic now as he started to imagine dark shapes circling below him too. "How can you be so calm about this?"

"Because I have to be," Sanders said, before swivelling sharply and punching something just below the surface.

Dower wished he had Sanders' courage. One time when he and Jess had gone on holiday to Port Lincoln, South Australia, Jess had convinced him to go out on a boat and go diving with great white sharks. It was diving in a cage, of course, and perfectly safe. Yet he remembered distinctly, from the awful sickness he felt when the instructors filled the water around the boat with bloody red clouds to the crippling fear that overcame him the moment the shark was first sighted. Some idiot even piped through the theme music from the movie *Jaws* through the boat's speakers for a laugh, which did not help either. But the thing he could not forget the most was the lines upon lines of crooked, sharp teeth and those dead cold eyes as the monster circled the ship. Jess said it was one of the most amazing experiences of her life. Dower would not know. He did not even dip a toe into the water that day, nor go near a beach for the rest of the trip.

And now, as he stared into the dark water around him, the visions of those cold eyes and jagged teeth came bubbling to the surface of his mind. Dower again felt the crippling fear that had overcome him that day return. Only this time it was different. This time he had no choice, and there was no cage either.

There was a splash not far from Dower's right and he let out an involuntary shriek.

"If one bumps you," Sanders said, "you have to strike out. Try and hit it in the eyes or the gills. Don't let it think you are an easy target."

But I am an easy target, thought Dower. Dower's eyes darted at the water below him, wishing they could penetrate the dark depths. Not knowing or seeing was the worst part. It was the anticipation of the attack that was the most maddening. These killers were silent and hidden and they could strike at any moment and you would not know it until its teeth penetrated your flesh and tore blood and bone. There could be one lining him up right now, or then again, maybe not.

Dower turned and decided to swim a few feet more away from Sanders. It felt like a cold and cowardly thing to do, but Sanders had suggested it. And Sanders was right. If the sharks got into a feeding frenzy over his body, they would lash out and bite anything. Such a frenzy would consume Dower next if he was close enough.

Dower had only swum a few strokes when he stopped at a sight that chilled him to his core. It was the stuff of nightmares for any sea bound swimmer and had been the stuff of nightmares for Dower for weeks after he first watched the movie *Jaws*. It was the sight of the crescent shaped dorsal fin cutting a line through the water directly across the path he was swimming in.

Dower paused, his heart hammering at his ribs like an innocent man banging on his jail cell door after being served the death penalty. For a moment Dower thought he might have a heart attack, such was the maddening speed his heart rate increased. Then he started to hope it would happen. Better that than the hellish wait for the attack that now seemed inevitable.

Suddenly there was a bang and a bright, phosphorescent red star shot up into the sky and bathed the sea around them in a surreal glow. Dower's attention was immediately drawn to look up. He cursed, the glare of it putting spots in his eyes.

"It's a flare," he called, "somebody is out there."

He shifted his gaze downwards, searching for the source of the flare. He squinted, cursing the spots in his eyes, when suddenly he saw it. A small, bright orange object riding the sea waves in the distance.

"Sanders, a boat," he exclaimed, excitement filling his voice. Dower started waving his arms above his head in an effort to be seen. "Hey!" he shouted as loud as he could. "Hey, over here."

Another flare shot up into the night sky. Dower swam to turn about.

"Sanders, help me call out…"

But Dower's voice trailed off as he turned a full three hundred and sixty degrees. There was no sign of Sanders anywhere.

"Sanders?"

***

Setiawan's eyes were ablaze with anger as the young pirate dragged the bleeding body of Darsani into the mess by the arms before dropping the limp arms to the floor. The young pirate had barely taken a step away from the body when Setiawan grabbed a handful of the young pirate's shirt and pushed him up against a wall. Setiawan leaned close, and the fear was evident in the boy's eyes.

"What is the meaning of this?" Setiawan hissed.

"It was Surjanto. We saw this man dumping something over the back of the boat so Surjanto shot him and then sliced open his eye."

Setiawan snorted. "I should have known. But why did you bring him here? He's practically dead already."

"Surj…"

"Bah!" Setiawan interrupted and threw the young boy aside. "Surjanto told you to. I get it. Now go stand over there with the others and keep an eye on these prisoners."

Under the fierce gaze of Setiawan, the young pirate joined the others, careful not to glance back at Setiawan lest he incur more of the pirate leader's wrath. Setiawan began pacing the room when another pirate entered carrying another body over his shoulder. Setiawan was about to launch into another tirade against this pirate when the pirate turned and he spied the long, blond hair hanging from the head. The pirate laid the body on the floor carefully. Setiawan crouched over the body and brushed the long blond hair away to reveal a woman's face with a dark bruise on her forehead.

"Who is she?" he pondered aloud.

"I don't know, but she released the rescue boat just before I got to her."

"Did you see if there was anyone inside?"

"No. I didn't see anything."

Setiawan placed two fingers on the woman's neck and felt her pulse. He nodded, pulled his fingers away and stood up. "I will have to question her when she wakes. She seems a bit out of place here and I'd like to know who or what was on that rescue boat."

As the pirate joined the others, Setiawan dug his fingers deep into his beard, scratching his chin as he studied the group of prisoners before him. None had yet to come forward to identify themselves as either the caller on the phone nor the planner behind this attack. Both must still be hidden somewhere on the boat. Setiawan's brow furrowed. If they were part of this, then why had they not come forward yet?

Just then two pirates who he had sent to re-check the engine room entered the mess.

"It's empty, sir. This is everyone."

The report did not please Setiawan and he turned away from them in dismay. His eyes settled on Darsani, who had now passed out, then they swivelled across to the blond woman. He tilted his head to the side, regarding her curiously as he again scratched his chin through his beard.

A raucous laugh from the corridor outside the mess woke Setiawan from his reverie and he turned in time to see Surjanto enter the mess with a new group of prisoners. Three men in all. Surjanto had a devilish grin on his face which immediately made Setiawan think he was up to something.

"Which one of these men is the captain of this ship?" Setiawan asked.

Surjanto's grin seemed to widen and look even more evil. "He was a bit hot under the collar when we found him and he needed to cool off."

Setiawan's eyes narrowed. "What do you mean 'cool off'?"

Surjanto shrugged. "He went for a swim."

"You mean you threw him overboard?"

"I guess that is another way to put it," Surjanto said mockingly.

"Damn it, Surjanto; I told you no killing. Yet here we are, one man with multiple gunshots and no eye plus the captain thrown overboard. How many others, Surjanto?"

Surjanto cast a quick glance at his men before turning back to Setiawan. "No others."

Setiawan stepped closer and stared deep into Surjanto's eyes. "Are you sure, Surjanto? Are you sure there were no more mishaps or people who needed cooling off?"

"No. No one else."

Setiawan continued to hold his gaze. "My contact hasn't come forward yet. I specifically said no killing because we need this contact to help us with what we came for. Are you telling me the truth here?"

Surjanto swallowed and broke eye contact under the pirate leader's gaze and glanced about him. They stopped on the motionless body of the prize fighter. He pointed at the prostrate body.

"I found him on the poop deck. It looked like he was in a struggle with someone and threw them out to sea."

"And then you shot him?"

Surjanto nodded.

Setiawan turned and looked at Darsani once more. "Let's hope he wakes and can talk to us then."

As Setiawan turned, Surjanto caught his first glimpse of the blonde woman's unconscious form. "Hello, what is it we have here? A plaything for the boys?"

"No one is to touch her until she wakes. She might be the one."

"Her?" Surjanto said and screwed up his face. "No chance."

Setiawan frowned. "We'll see. And if not, then we ransom her. I'm sure whatever government she belongs to would be keen to get her back in one piece." Setiawan watched as Surjanto continued to stare at the blond woman and watched as a malicious smile curled at the edges of Surjanto's mouth. "Did you hear me? I said one piece."

"Sure. One piece. I hear you," Surjanto said without taking his eyes from the woman.

Setiawan pursed his lips and scratched his chin. He glanced at the woman then back to Surjanto before seeming to come to a decision. "In the meantime, we have a job to do. I want you to take some men and start opening those shipping containers. The WMD must be in one of them."

Surjanto reluctantly pulled his eyes from the woman. "Do you know what type of bomb we're looking for?"

"No. It's why we need the contact. When you find it, just be careful with it, okay?"

Surjanto nodded and turned to gather some men to take with him. Setiawan turned away to study the woman once more as he thought back on what he was told. There was something very important on this ship he had come here to steal. Something that had the power to kill many, many people and was of great interest to those who spent a lot of money funding this mission. But he had no idea what he was looking for. It could be a bomb as big as a crate or a deadly virus in a tiny vial. He needed his contact or the man who phoned through the ship's location. His mission depended on it.

14

Another flare flew up into the sky and arced towards Dower as he waved his arms frantically in the flickering pale red glow. It could have been just his imagination, but Dower was certain that the boat was closer.

"Over here!" he yelled at the top of his voice.

Suddenly there was a splash behind him and the sound of someone gasping for air. Dower turned to see Sanders had resurfaced and was breathing heavily.

"Sanders, thank God. I thought they had taken you. Are you bitten badly?"

"I'm not bitten. I went under hoping the flare light would let me see what we are up against."

Dower waited for him to say more, but it was clear Sanders would need a prompt. Something splashed the water on Dower's right. He glanced quickly but missed it. He turned back to Sanders. "And?"

Sanders was staring at the waters about him. Tension was clear on his face, but he was alert and his muscles taut, ready to launch into sudden action like a spring-loaded bar mouse trap. "I couldn't see much. Just shapes in the dark. Big shapes. Four by my best count. Maybe some smaller ones deeper down but I can't be sure."

"Oh God," Dower whimpered. "How long do you think we have?"

"I don't know. But sooner or later one is going to tire of just bumping me and give into the temptation and take a bite."

Dower shivered despite the warmth of the tropical waters. He turned his body to examine the boat once more. It was definitely closer. As the light of the flare began to fade another was launched.

"I think they've seen us," Dower said hopefully.

There was a big splash behind him and Sanders grunted loudly. Dower's head shot around to see Sanders wincing with pain.

"What happened? Did one bite you?"

Sanders grimaced. "No, but one just hit me like a bloody cannon ball. They are definitely getting more aggressive."

Dower bit his lip to stop his teeth chattering and looked away when something brushed his foot below. He shrieked. It was loud and high pitched and not a sound he was proud to make, but it was an accurate representation of how he felt in that moment.

Turning to the boat, Dower raised his arms up frantically. "Hurry up, damn you."

The sound of the boat was audible now and Dower could see it closing. There was a splash to Dower's right and he turned to see the crescent shape of a dorsal fin cutting a lazy arc around him before sliding back under the surface once more. Dower let a low whimper escape his mouth and turned back to the incoming boat.

It was much closer now and Dower could make out more detail in the flickering flare light. It was an oddly shaped boat, somewhat like an orange submarine, and it bounced roughly along the water. A hatch in the side of the boat was open, and he saw a figure leaning out of it as it approached. The figure was pointing at them. Dower waved, and the figure waved back.

"Sanders, they see us," Dower exclaimed and turned to his friend.

Sanders gave a thumbs up and smiled. Just then Dower saw the evil shape of a shark fin pierce the surface behind Sanders and make a sharp turn towards him.

"Sanders, behind you!" he shouted.

Sanders half turned and kicked out of the path of the shark. There was a huge splash as the shark breached the surface and snapped its tooth filled maw at Sanders. The attack narrowly missed and the malicious predator whipped past Sanders and crashed back down below the surface in a storm of white water.

"Holy shit!" Sanders cursed. Dower said nothing but shook with fear as the sight of the mighty beast and its sharp teeth and cold eyes gnawed at the corners of his mind.

A shout from behind shook the thought from his mind and Dower turned to see the boat had closed dramatically. He could see clearly now it was Sianturi leaning out the hatch. Sianturi fired another flare and then shouted instructions inside. The boat slowed as it closed in on Dower's position.

"Hurry," Dower shouted, "there's sharks everywhere."

As if to prove the point, a shark fin broke the surface and cut a path between Dower and the boat.

Sianturi disappeared briefly inside the boat and reappeared with a bright orange ring connected to a rope. The boat pulled close to Dower and Sianturi hurled the lifebuoy out. It landed close to Dower, and it only took a few tired strokes for Dower to grab it. Sianturi immediately started pulling Dower in. Dower was content to let Sianturi reel him in when something again brushed Dower's foot and he started kicking hard to speed up the process.

At the boat, Dower struggled to pull his heavy, water-soaked body out of the water and up inside. Sianturi leant his muscle and Dower staggered inside to collapse onto the floor.

"Hurry. Sanders is surrounded by sharks and could be attacked at any moment," Dower shouted.

The roar of the engine sounded as the driver pushed forward the throttle on the boat. Dower turned to see the driver for the first time and his breath caught in surprise.

"Captain Arwadi?"

Arwadi glanced down briefly at Dower before returning his attention back to the controls. Arwadi's mouth was a thin line and he did not look happy to be here. His clothes were also heavy and water logged.

"Ease up, we're almost on him," Sianturi shouted and Arwadi pulled back on the throttle.

Dower struggled to his feet and edged towards the open hatch. He saw Sianturi lean back and throw the donut to Sanders. It was a near perfect throw, and Sanders only had to reach out to grab it. Just then a shark fin broke the surface and sliced a direct line towards Sanders.

"Sanders, look out!" Dower shouted. But Sanders was tired. He turned lethargically as he reached out for the lifebuoy. The shark closed fast and Sanders' hand slipped off the floating ring. Sanders dove forwards, launching into a freestyle swim to get out of the great predator's path. But the shark adjusted its path too.

"Grab the ring," Dower shouted.

But it was in vain.

There was a mighty splash as the shark kicked hard and reared up out of the water to launch its attack. White teeth gleamed a hellish red in the flare light as it opened its mighty mouth. Sanders was taken somewhere below the hip and as the shark disappeared below the surface. Sanders was taken down with it.

"No!" Dower shouted as the white water caused by the splashing calmed.

Sanders felt teeth piercing his skin either side of his knee as the shark's jaws clamped on him and dragged him down. Sanders responded with punches to the gills and eye. Knowing this was it, life or death right here, he knew there was no room for his peaceful animal loving side. If this beast was going to take him, he would leave it scarred for life in the process. Sanders rammed his hand into the shark's eyes and tried to wrap his fingers around the eyeball and pull it out. He failed, but the shark loosened its grip. Sanders followed with a quick jab to the opposite eye with his other hand and the shark released its grip.

Sanders kicked free and immediately kicked upwards. Pain stung his leg and unbeknownst to him, blood from his leg wounds started clouding the water in his wake. The nearby sharks sensed the increased blood in the water and their heightened senses went immediately on alert.

Sanders was almost at the surface when another shark made a run at him. He failed to see it as the dark shape loomed and the deadly predator opened its mouth. But he sensed it just in time, twisting his body just enough to avoid the snapping jaws that would have taken him at the hip. He gave the shark a quick jab in the gills as it passed. From the corner of his eyes Sanders caught sight of another dark shape in the depths and it was all the impetus he needed to kick harder towards the surface.

Sianturi and Dower scanned the surface for movement as Sianturi pulled the lifebuoy back in. Dower stared, his eyes flicking about wildly as he clutched the side of the hatch with white knuckles. Suddenly Sianturi's hand shot up and pointed.

"There," he cried, and almost instantly Sanders' head broke the surface. Almost instantly Sianturi's arm jerked out as he threw the donut once more. Sanders turned and reached for the lifebuoy immediately. This time he held on and Sianturi and Dower began reeling him in. Hand over hand they worked, pulling Sanders as quick as they could towards the rescue boat. Sanders looked left and right, wary for any further approaches by a hungry shark.

As Sanders reached the boat, he flung the ring aside and gabbed the edge of the boat. Dower offered his hand but Sanders declined the offer.

"I'm a big guy. No offence, but I don't think you'll be able to pull me in."

Dower smiled and pulled back from the breach. As he did so, he saw the distinct shape of a shark fin break the surface. It was running parallel to the boat, but made a quick, sharp turn and accelerated towards Sanders.

"Get in, quick," Dower shouted.

Sanders glanced up and did not bother looking around. The wide eyes of Dower told him all he needed to know. With a final surge of strength, Sanders grit his teeth and pulled his heavy body out of the water and into the boat. The frustrated shark snapped at the empty air where Sanders' legs had just been and retreated below the surface.

As Sanders collapsed on to the bench seat opposite the hatch, Dower gasped as he looked down to see the curved line of puncture wounds that lined Sanders' leg. Each wound was filled with pooled blood.

"Looks like we were just in time," bellowed Arwadi as he opened a compartment and retrieved a first aid kit from it. Sianturi stepped across the boat and took the kit from Arwadi.

"I'll take care of the leg, you keep circling. There could be more of your men out there."

"I doubt it," said Arwadi. "I saw these two go over and that's all. There's no one else out here."

"We can't be sure of that. Keep circling and make sure of it," Sianturi replied, before pulling the kit forcibly from Arwadi's hands. Arwadi scowled, but Sianturi ignored him and turned to Dower. "You look out the door like I did and fire flares for light. Keep your eye out, there could be more men in strife out there like you were." Finally, Sianturi turned to his patient. "Right, get those pants off so I can put these bandages on properly."

"Geez, Sianturi, the least you could do is give me some flowers first," Sanders grumbled.

"I tried, but the florist was closed," Sianturi retorted sharply.

The interior of the rescue boat was quite simple. Each side had a curving bench seat against the hull, broken only on the starboard side by the hatch which opened outwards. At the rear of the ship was a raised deck and the wheel, which was where Arwadi stood. The rear deck was raised to allow the driver a view over the boat's cowl to see where the boat was going. It was deceptively roomy inside the cabin, though the men did have to hunch over a little when standing.

Arwadi engaged the engine and they began a wide, bumpy, searching arc of the area. Arwadi insisted on the arc, pointing out that Sanders and Dower had drifted well off the path the ship had taken. Dower shot flares regularly into the sky and squinted at the endlessly rolling sea around them for any shape or movement that broke the monotony of the waves. But there was little to see beyond the rising and falling waters of the sea.

Sianturi had finished his work and glanced down at the remaining flares. He frowned.

"We'd better made the next one the last one. Just in case we need them to signal a ship or plane. If anyone else is still out there, they are with God now."

Dower nodded and took the last flare from the box before Sianturi tucked it under the seat. Dower studied it carefully before raising an arm and firing it into the sky.

"Do you see anything?" Arwadi called from the helm.

Dower scanned the waters and shook his head.

"No, there doesn't seem to be anyth…. Wait. I think I see something. Yes. Someone is waving," Dower exclaimed.

Arwadi muttered something that resembled a curse. "Where? Which side is he? Portside or starboard side?"

"Um… he's on the right."

"Starboard side," Arwadi corrected, before engaging the throttle. The rescue boat engine roared and the orange capsule that was the boat bounced across the waves towards its target. They were closing when the last light of the flare flickered out of existence leaving just pale moonlight ahead of them.

"Kill the engine," Dower shouted. "We are close; maybe he can swim to us and we won't need another flare."

Arwadi cut the engine off and Dower leaned out to shout.

"Hello, is there someone there?"

"Yes, I can see you. Stay where you are and I will swim to you," came a shout back.

Dower pulled back into his boat and turned to the others. He scratched his head and frowned. "That sounded like Cheong."

There was a thump as Arwadi punched the wheel. Dower looked at him curiously before turning back to the door. This time he could see the swimmer approaching. It was indeed Cheong.

"Need any help? I can throw a life ring to you."

"I'm fine," Cheong grunted as he swam for the boat.

Dower helped him in and stood back as Cheong stepped dripping into the rescue craft. Remarkably, Cheong was still dressed head to foot in his bright purple suit, gold tie and shiny black shoes. But for his wet clothes, and some bruising around his eye, you would not know Cheong had been through any sort of ordeal. Sanders looked up and snorted.

"Wow, Kenny, looking as schmick as always. You didn't even think to take the tie off?"

Cheong straightened his tie and patted down his suit before turning his nose up at Sanders.

"And I see you have regressed further backwards to your caveman origins, Mr Sanders. Abandoning pants now, are we?"

Sianturi stepped between them and directed Cheong to take a seat. Dower pulled closed the hatch and sat himself.

"Okay, Captain," Sianturi said, "what do you suggest we do now?"

At the word captain, Cheong looked up sharply and cast a glance to the rear of the boat to where Arwadi stood at the wheel.

"You," Cheong hissed and pointed a shaking finger up at Arwadi, "you are the reason I'm here. You had me thrown overboard when the pirates took your ship."

"Nonsense," Arwadi spat.

"You lie," Cheong continued. "One of your men came to my cabin and dragged me out and threw me overboard upon your order."

"It was not on my order," Arwadi growled. "It could have been anyone. There were a lot of angry crewmen on my boat when they learned I had taken a job from a *tionghoa*. I'm not the only one who despises your kind, and when those pirates came, they all blamed me. 'See, this is what you get for taking a job from a *tionghoa*' they all said. I'm not surprised one of my crew took matters into his own hands and threw you off. Who was it? I should give the man a pay rise."

Cheong scowled. "A big man in orange overalls. Hits like a sledgehammer."

"That sounds like Darsani," Arwadi mused. "He's a good man."

A growl escaped Cheong's throat when Sianturi interjected.

"Okay, that is enough. We're all in this together now so let's try to get through this peacefully. Captain, do you have any idea where we are?"

"Yes, we are in the South China Sea and we are a long way from civilisation."

"Can we get to land from here?"

"There is only one island near here. It is called Bingwen Island, and it's to the north. But Bingwen Island is uninhabited. If we go there, we become maroons. Nobody ever goes there. We are better staying in this boat and letting the tides drag us west. By dawn tomorrow we may hopefully have drifted far enough to take us close to civilised land or at least within radio contact of it."

Sianturi frowned and shrugged. "Well, it's a plan at least. I guess we had all better get settled in then. It's going to be a long night."

15

Jess O'Mara groaned and rolled slightly to the side. Her head ached and her mouth was dry. She tried opening her eyes but the world around her was too bright. She squinted, letting her eyes adjust, before slowly opening them more and more.

She found herself lying on the mess room floor surrounded by the grim-faced crew of the *Kekal*. It took a few seconds before she recalled those last few moments before the pirate had hit her. She grimaced and forced herself to sit up to get a better view of the men around her. Pain lanced her brain but she forced herself up and looked around. Sianturi was not here. She heaved a sigh of relief. Hopefully he would find Simon and Matt. Then she noticed something else amiss. There was no sign of Cheong or Captain Arwadi either. She was without a friend and alone.

In front of the rows of sitting men stood their armed guards. Dressed mostly in black and carrying AK-47s, the pirates looked eerily like the soldiers Cheong had employed to capture the Horse Serpent. She wondered if they were somehow connected, and that these men had taken the ship to recapture the prize that the others had lost.

She studied the pirates one by one. None of their faces were familiar in any way, but she never took a good look at the soldiers earlier. She noticed one of the pirates seemed to be regarding her thoughtfully. He had a thick beard and scarred arms, and had a habit of scratching his chin when he was thinking.

She studied him, and for a moment their eyes caught on one another's, and she was certain he was looking at her and searching for meaning. The eye contact was broken when another man entered the mess. He had a savage look about him. His hair was wild and he had a grotesque scar on his cheek. His face seemed to carry a permanent sneer, and he walked with an air of arrogance about him.

The scar-faced man spoke quickly and briefly to the bearded man. The bearded man's jaw dropped, and he suddenly burst into a shouting rant. He paced, shouting and gesticulating wildly. Scar face pointed to a man on the floor, who O'Mara had not previously noticed. The man lay in a pool of blood and his eye was a gory mess. She looked away quickly and turned back to watch the exchange.

The bearded man continued to rant. Occasionally scar face would retort with something but was quickly shouted down. Eventually scar face crossed his arms and looked away while his senior continued to speak. The rant soon died off to a grim silence. The crew around

O'Mara glanced at one another and whispered gossip amongst themselves. Occasionally she would catch one giving her a dark glare. O'Mara wished she understood their language as she was certain something was up.

She took her attention away from the crew and back to the pirates. Scar face was staring at her like a wolf. As she met his stare, he smiled hungrily, revealing a shining gold tooth. He licked his lips and blew a kiss at her while grabbing at his crotch. She looked away, resisting the urge to shudder. She made a note she would have to keep away from that one.

She noticed then the bearded man was watching her again. But rather than look upon her with any desire, he seemed rather to be weighing her up. She studied him a moment, deep in thought herself, before raising a hand and beckoning him over.

His eyebrows shot up immediately and his eyes lightened. He glanced quickly at scar face before slowly approaching her. The nearby crew shuffled away as he approached.

"Do you speak English?" she asked as he got close.

"Yes, I do," he responded in a thick accent and kneeled down by her side.

"And you are the leader of this group?"

"Yes, I am." The pirate leader said nothing more but continued to stare at her. He appeared to be waiting for something.

O'Mara coughed and placed a hand to her throat. "My throat is parched. Could I possibly get some water?"

The bearded man turned and shouted an order to one of the other pirates, who disappeared into the galley only to return a moment later with a filled cup. He came forward and offered the cup.

O'Mara took the cup and drank slowly to give herself time to think. The bearded man continued to watch and wait as she did so. She glanced about, realising all the eyes in the room were on her. There was an air of expectancy in the room.

She lowered the cup from her lips and turned back to the bearded man.

"You have been waiting for me to wake," she ventured speculatively.

"Yes, I have," the pirate leader said.

"Because you want to speak with me."

"Of course," the pirate leader said, but questions remained in his eyes.

O'Mara coughed and lifted the cup to take another slow drink. There had to be a reason the pirate leader was waiting on her like this. She lowered the cup.

"Do you know who I am?" she asked.

"Why don't you tell me?" the pirate leader responded.

Jess lay the cup on the floor and held out a hand. "Help me up. I'm still a little groggy from the hit your man gave me."

The pirate leader pursed his lips before standing and helping her to her feet. Jess looked about the room as she started forming a plan in her head. The odds were bad. She was on her own here and would need to have her wits about her if she was to survive. If she slipped, she might find herself at the mercy of that scar faced predator who continually stared at her. She knew what she needed to do. It was going to be risky, and the very thought of what she would need to do chilled her to the bone, but it offered a chance of survival, even if it were only a thin chance at that.

She turned back to the pirate leader. It was time to play her first piece.

"My man is missing," she said casually. "Do your men know what happened to my man, Mohede?"

The pirate leader's eyes widened a little at the mention of Mohede's name. He motioned towards the bullet riddled corpse of Darsani on the floor. "My men think they saw this man throw someone overboard. Could that have been your man Mohede?"

"Can they describe the man he threw over?"

"No, just that he was smaller than this man."

O'Mara studied the man on the floor. It was clear he had lost a lot of blood and his breathing was shallow. It was a good bet he would not awake again and talk. O'Mara took a deep breath before turning to the pirate leader. "It was probably him that was thrown over then. Did he mange to make contact with you?"

The pirate leader gestured to his men. "That is why we are here."

"Of course," she said. Parts of the puzzle were starting to slide into place.

"What is your name?" the pirate leader asked.

"My name is Jess O'Mara."

"Tell me, Miss O'Mara, what it is you were doing when my man found you? He said you launched the rescue boat from the ship and there was someone inside it."

Jess shivered over the interrogating stare of the pirate. "Yes, there was. He was a colleague. I needed to get him off the boat so that he wouldn't know that I was involved with… this." The word 'this' seem to hang in the air, floating between them as the pirate leader evaluated her through narrowed eyes.

"Listen," she said, "I know what you have come for. I can take you to it and help you get it off the boat safely. You won't be able to do it without me. I am the expert on this."

The pirate leader's eyes widened and he leaned back. His mouth broke into a smile, and then a laugh. He turned to his men and exclaimed to them. Some smiled. Scar face scowled.

"We have been waiting for you to reveal yourself," the pirate leader continued in English. "My name is Leo Setiawan and I am at your service. I must say I am relieved to find you. We have no idea where the cargo is. We already searched the shipping containers on deck but they are all empty."

Empty? The word echoed in her mind and she wanted to curse. Sianturi must be behind this. His whole manner from the start was suspicious. He appeared from nowhere to join their voyage. He constantly asked questions about their cargo. And now she thought on it, he seemed pretty keen to get her off the ship. And now this revelation. Empty containers. His whole reason for being here was fake. He was the one who brought the pirates here, and now she would have to continue the bluff that she was him.

"Yes, the containers on deck are just a decoy," she said.

Setiawan rubbed his hands gleefully. "And the real cargo. Do you know where it is?"

"Yes, I was in charge of loading it onto this ship."

A smile broke out on Setiawan's face. "Can we see it?"

O'Mara pursed her lips and nodded. "Yes, of course. I have no doubt you are eager to see it. It's quite the sight."

16

All were quiet in the rescue boat as it bobbed over the waves of the South China Sea bound westward with the tides.

Sanders' head rested against the hull as he nodded as sleep beckoned him. His muscles ached with fatigue and his leg hurt despite the painkilling tablets that Sianturi had given him. He shifted position, trying to find a more comfortable way to rest and drift off. But his leg ached and he turned and turned again.

Across from him, Dower was already soundly asleep and gently snoring. Sanders opened his eyes and glared jealously at the professor. He then noticed Cheong, sitting straight and glaring across the boat. Sanders turned to see what he was staring at and saw the same expression mirrored by Arwadi at the opposite end of the boat.

Pressure in Sanders' bladder forced him to stand up groggily. Pain sensors from his leg want off as he eased weight onto his wounded leg for the first time.

"Where are you going?" Cheong growled.

"I need to piss."

"There is a small deck with handholds aft of the boat you can piss off," Arwadi said.

"Great. Which way is aft?"

"It's out the door at the back," Arwadi said with disdain.

Sanders staggered to the back of the boat. Unlike the ship, this small boat really rode the ups and downs of the waves and Sanders struggled for balance as he made his way to the rear of the boat. At the back he pulled down the lever and swung the hatch door open. As Arwadi had said, there was a thin deck and handholds.

The moon was high in the sky now as Sanders hung onto the boat and peed. The air was thick with the smell of the sea and the only sound to be heard was the gentle lapping of water. It was almost peaceful here and Sanders let his eyes close as he relieved himself. After he finished, Sanders turned to return to the cabin when something caught his eye. For a second he thought he had imagined it, but as he stared a little longer, he was certain he could see it. There was something floating out there on the sea.

"Hey," Sanders shouted into the cabin, "do you think you could fire up the engine and reverse the boat a bit?"

"Whatever for?" Arwadi responded.

"There's something floating out there."

"It's probably some old driftwood or rubbish. We should conserve our petrol for later."

Sanders turned away and studied the dark shape floating on the surface some more before turning back to Arwadi.

"Just reverse it up a bit. We won't use much."

Arwadi rolled his eyes but drew himself up and started the engine.

"What is it?" Sianturi asked.

"I can't say," Sanders said, "but it feels important."

Sianturi joined Sanders on the small aft deck as Arwadi gently reversed the boat. As they drew nearer to the object, Sianturi gasped.

"It's a body," Sianturi said quickly.

As they drew closer, Sanders could see it too. It was a man floating on his back.

"Ease up," Sanders said and leaned out. Arwadi shut off the engine and the boat continued to gently drift towards the body. Sanders reached forwards and grabbed the clothing to pull the body on deck. Arwadi shone a torch onto the face. Sianturi stepped back in shock.

"Who is it?" Cheong asked from inside the boat.

"It's Mohede," Sanders said, and placed two fingers against the man's neck to feel for a pulse.

"Throw him back," Cheong said, before turning to Arwadi and pointing. "He is the real reason the pirates came to your ship. He stole my phone and called them."

"And he was part of your group," Arwadi snarled in response. "You brought him on my ship, so I still blame you for this."

Sanders stood and dragged the body of Mohede into the cabin of the boat.

"What are you doing?" Cheong squealed. "Leave him out there."

"I'm not doing that. He's still alive."

"But...but he called the pirates. He's behind all of this," Cheong pleaded.

"Actually no, he's not. He was just the messenger. There is a bigger villain at play. Whoever cut him free of the ropes in Cheong's room is behind this."

Sanders pulled Mohede in and dumped him down on the floor between them all. Sianturi stepped forward and took his seat overlooking the unconscious form of Mohede.

"So you intend to wait until he wakes to interrogate him?" Sianturi asked.

"Yes, I do," Sanders said as he set about looking in the box drawers under the seats.

"And what good would that do to you now? The ship and cargo is long gone."

Sanders looked up at Sianturi for a moment but said nothing.

"Ah," said Sianturi turning to Arwadi. "He suspects one of us might be behind it."

A snarl formed on Arwadi's lips. "It's like I said before. It's the *tionghoa* who we should blame for this."

Sanders turned to Arwadi with eyes aflame. "I'm starting to tire of your racist rhetoric, Arwadi. Perhaps it's you who we should be scrutinising for this seeing as you are so quick to put the blame on others."

"Ha. Do you honestly think I would give up the *Kekal* so easily? That ship is my livelihood. My everything. You would have to be mad if you think I would leave it in the hands of pirates while I was floating alone in the sea."

"And how did you end up in the sea, Captain?" Sianturi interjected.

Arwadi glared at Sianturi. "I was thrown off. There was one pirate with a big scar on his face. He blew open the door of the bridge with dynamite and then gutted one of my men right before my eyes. A real cruel bastard that one was. It was he who threw me off my own ship and left me to drown."

While Sianturi talked, Dower roused from his sleep and sat up quietly to listen. At the end of Arwadi's story, he turned to Sianturi.

"And what about you? How is it you ended up out here?"

Sianturi turned and there was a hint of anger in his eyes. "It was your girlfriend who did it."

"Jess?" Dower asked in surprise.

"Yes. She saw you two go over the side when that pirate went to shoot you. I was just trying to help her. I guided her to this boat and she was supposed to eject from the ship in it to search for you. But when I got in to check the equipment, she ejected the boat from the ship and here I am."

"You don't suppose she's behind this?" Arwadi suggested.

"Don't be ridiculous," Dower said angrily.

"Oh no? How long have you known her?" Arwadi asked.

"Over twelve years now."

"Then maybe you're in on it too."

"Enough," Sanders shouted and everyone silenced. "This is getting us nowhere. Mohede is the key to this. He can tell us who cut him free and then we'll know who the traitor is."

"What if it's too late by then?" Cheong asked.

"What do you mean?"

"What if Arwadi is lying and we are close enough to land to find somewhere and get help? What if he is behind this and his plan is just to drift while the pirates get away with our precious cargo?"

"Precious cargo?" Arwadi barked with laughter. "You mean your supposedly special racehorse and his medical supplies? Yeah, that sounds like a great haul for a stunt like this."

Sanders stared at Arwadi a moment. There was something in what he just said that tickled the back of his mind with remembrance. He stared at Arwadi, repeating what he had said in his mind before his eyes swivelled to Sianturi. He raised a finger and pointed to Sianturi.

"You," he said and started wagging his finger, "you said your containers were full of supplies. But when I threw Mohede into one, the sound boomed as though the whole thing was empty."

Suddenly everyone turned to Sianturi with accusing eyes.

"Is that so?" drawled Arwadi.

Sianturi turned to Arwadi. "They are the ones lying about their cargo. They don't have a horse and I can prove it."

Sanders shot a quick glance to Dower and then Cheong. They both wore guarded expressions.

"How so?" Arwadi asked.

Sianturi turned to Sanders. "When I asked what breed of horse you had, you told me it was a Java pony, correct?"

Sanders pursed his lips, wondering what Sianturi was trying to prove. "Correct," he said slowly. Dower cursed softly.

"You see," Sianturi declared triumphantly.

"Indeed," Arwadi said thoughtfully.

Sanders looked from Sianturi to Arwadi and back again. "So what if it's a Java pony?"

"Java ponies are only good for making workhorses" Arwadi said. "Any idiot knows they are terrible racers. Sianturi has caught you in a lie. Unless you are indeed as dim-witted as you all seem. So, tell me. Which is it, are you idiots or liars?"

Just then Cheong stood up. "We are wasting time arguing about this. We shouldn't be out here floating and hoping for the best. We should make for that island."

"Sit down, *tionghoa,*" Arwadi barked.

Sanders stood up and clenched his fists. "That's it, Arwadi. I have had enough of this racist crap. I warned you on the ship what would happen if you persisted with it, so put them up."

Sanders raised his first and advanced on Arwadi. Arwadi shook his head and stood up. But instead of raising his fists, he dug one hand into the jacket he was wearing. "Let me remind you," he roared in a voice that boomed over all of them, "that I am still captain here, even without my ship." He pulled his hand from his jacket, revealing a dull metal pistol. He raised the handgun and pointed it at Sanders. "And when I am captain, you address me as such. Now sit down. All of you."

Cheong immediately sat, but Sanders remained standing. "I said sit down," Arwadi repeated. Sanders scowled and lowered himself slowly onto the bench seat.

"Now listen up, because this is what is going to happen," Arwadi barked. "We are going to continue to drift, just like I said. It seems both of you have been lying to me about your cargo so until this man Mohede wakes up and tells me who put him up to calling those pirates, I'm going to assume you are all in on it and are all guilty. So, if you are innocent, you had better start hoping that man Mohede wakes up, because if he doesn't, I'm going to report all of you to the authorities and have you arrested once we are rescued. Understood?"

Arwadi glared at them individually, pointing the pistol menacingly at each of them in turn as he did. Nobody answered the challenge.

17

The moon was high in the sky as the small armed group marched down the centre of the main deck of the container ship *Kekal*. Among the group of fifteen was Leo Setiawan, leader of the pirate expedition that captured this ship. Beside him walked a blond woman, who on the surface marched as though she belonged alongside these criminals but inside, she was turning to water. Behind her marched Setiawan's second in command, the ruthless Amentung Surjanto. And behind him, twelve of their men, leaving just the one man at the helm of the ship and two others to guard the prisoners.

As the group passed the first set of crates, O'Mara could not help but turn her head to the side and gaze into the dark depths. It was as Setiawan had said. These containers were indeed empty. She turned back to see Setiawan was watching her. She swallowed.

"Decoys," she said and smiled.

As she walked, O'Mara's legs began to feel like jelly. She was putting up her best show, but she began to worry that her fear was starting to come through. She tried to focus on the job ahead. Her plan, and the delicate plan she had in mind, was on a razor's edge.

"Tell me," Setiawan said conversationally as they came up onto the second set of empty containers. "What kind of weapon is it? Is it nuclear, chemical, or something else?"

O'Mara turned with eyes wide. "You don't know?"

"They would not tell me. Technically we probably shouldn't even be looking at it, but I am curious."

"But what did they tell you?"

"Only that it's unlike any other weapon we've seen before and it will kill thousands."

O'Mara turned away and looked straight ahead. The Horse Serpent used as a weapon? The idea was almost unfathomable, but somehow believable. She had seen how easily the Horse Serpent had torn through the armed men Cheong had hired. Once it got into a frenzy it killed ten trained and armed men in seconds. What type of carnage would the Horse Serpent unleash if set free in the middle of a busy city? Such a monster would not be easy to take down, certainly not by mere local police, and could inflict a momentous number of casualties once it got the scent for the kill. Blood would flow through the streets like a torrent. It would make the recent mass stabbing attacks carried out by jihadists seem like child's play.

"Well?" Setiawan prompted. "What kind of weapon is it?"

"Biological," O'Mara answered flatly.

"Like a natural virus or something?" Setiawan persisted.

"It's better if you wait and see it for yourself."

Setiawan scratched at his beard thoughtfully but there was a definite glint in his eyes and a smile in the corner of his mouth as he pondered the meagre information she provided.

As they passed by the second set of opened containers O'Mara again took a quick glance inside to confirm what she had been told. These containers were indeed empty as well. As she glanced to the side, she caught a glimpse of Surjanto from the corner of her eye. He seemed to be staring at her so she turned fully to see. He smiled cruelly at her and the gold tooth glinted under his snarling lip. She turned and continued walking forwards while repressing the urge to shudder.

The third set of containers were equally dark and cavernous, with not a hint of cargo in sight. As they passed the fourth set, she did not even bother looking.

With the four crates behind them, the group was no longer protected from the oncoming breeze or the salty spray blown into the air as the bow crashed against the waves as the ship ploughed its way forward through the sea. O'Mara felt a breeze brush across her face filled with cold droplets that tickled her skin like the icy fingers of a dead man. She shivered as she looked ahead and saw nothing but darkness in front of the ship.

As O'Mara slowed to a stop, Setiawan looked at her curiously.

"Well?"

"It's here," O'Mara said, and pointed to the hatch that led down into the foremost hold of the ship. O'Mara held her breath as Setiawan leaned down to open the hatch. With his hand on the handle, he turned up sharply. O'Mara jumped and shifted position.

"You seem nervous," Setiawan said. "Is it safe to go in there?"

"No, it's perfectly safe, it's just…" It's just last time I was down there the Horse Serpent was roaring like a lion, she thought to herself. If he opened the hatch and heard that, the jig was up.

"It's just…?" Setiawan prompted.

"It's just that I am always awed when I come into contact with something as powerful and dangerous as this weapon. To have such destructive power is…"

"Inspiring," Setiawan finished her thought. "I must admit, I feel the same way myself. Come, let us go down and see it. I yearn to see the device that brings such emotions to the fore."

The hatch handle turned with a click. O'Mara found herself again holding her breath as the pirate leader pulled open the hatch. But no sound came from within. Not even a breath.

Setiawan stepped down the first set of stairs and urged O'Mara to follow. She bit her lip as she watched him descend. She cast a quick look at Surjanto and his cronies before stepping down to follow.

The first set of stairs ended with a small platform. It was dark in the hold, and Setiawan felt around for a switch. Finally, he found it and he flicked it on, filling the large expanse below them with a pale-yellow light. Below them the truck and horse trailer were visible. Setiawan examined the scene before turning with one eyebrow raised.

"It's a disguise," O'Mara stammered. "Like the empty containers, we used a horse trailer to cover up the smuggling of the WMD."

Setiawan nodded slowly and turned to the truck and trailer once more.

"Where is it?" he said in almost a whisper.

"In the trailer."

Setiawan nodded and resumed his descent into the hold.

The footfalls of the soldiers on the steel steps echoed loudly in the hold as they noisily stamped down the stairs behind her. O'Mara eyed the trailer nervously, certain at any moment the creature would rouse and make a noise of its own and raise the alarm amongst the group. Suddenly she heard the sound of scraping, like the beast's heavy body sliding along the steel cage floor, but as she glanced around at the others, she realised she was the only one that had heard it. She swallowed nervously and continued down the stairs.

As he reached the bottom of the stairs, Setiawan launched into a march of long, quick strides. O'Mara hurried down the last few steps but he had gotten away from her. She walked as briskly as she could, trying as best she could to not look too hurried and raise suspicion, but fast enough to not let Setiawan get too far ahead and discover the truth and expose her trap before she had the chance to spring it.

But Setiawan slipped out of her sight as he rounded the side of the truck. O'Mara glanced behind to check if any of the soldiers were paying attention to her, only to find that vile pirate Surjanto still had those evil little eyes of his on her. She turned and grimaced, maintaining her current pace and hoping that Setiawan had not already discovered the truth.

As she rounded the truck, she saw Setiawan standing and staring into the opened back of the trailer. She slowed, fearing he may have already learnt the truth, but he did not look at her as she approached. She closed and drew up to his side. She eased out a breath as she realised it was too dark to see into the trailer.

"I must admit," Setiawan said as he stared into the dark depths, "that I too am a little awed."

Soon, Surjanto and the other men arrived at the rear of the trailer. Surjanto took one look at his dumbstruck leader and gave a sneer of contempt. He said something loudly in a brash voice, only to be met by an angry glare from Setiawan. One other pirate snickered and drew a rebuke from his leader. The man went quickly silent. Finally, Setiawan turned to O'Mara.

"Can we bring the weapon out and see it?" he asked.

O'Mara's heart hammered against her ribs. This was the moment she had been waiting for. She dug a shaking hand into her pant pocket and pulled out a keyring and held it out to Setiawan. "The device is held in a cage in the back of the trailer. We did that so nobody could get to it. Here is the key. All you need to do is open the cage and step in to get it."

Setiawan glanced down at the keys and licked his lips nervously. Surjanto made another remark and the same culprit as before laughed again. Setiawan turned and shouted an order. The laughing man stopped and looked around nervously. Surjanto smiled and urged him to approach Setiawan. The pirate half smiled and came forwards. Setiawan took his rifle from him and pointed to the keys and then the trailer as he spoke. The pirate glanced at the keys and then the dark inside of the trailer. As he turned back to take the keys from O'Mara, she could see his confidence had deserted him.

The pirate took a deep breath and pulled himself agilely up into the back of the trailer. He squinted, making out the steel frame of the cage in the minimal light. He looked down at the key in his hand and jingled it lightly. There was a low sound in front of him, as though something in the dark in front of him moved. He glanced nervously behind him, wondering if someone else had heard it, but only saw Setiawan urging him forward. He turned back to the cage, shaking the thought from his mind and stepping closer.

As he reached the cage his nose crinkled. There was a strange, animal smell in the air.

"What are you waiting for?" called a voice from behind.

He half turned to call back his reply. "It smells strange in here. Like an animal or something."

"Of course it smells like animal. It's an old horse trailer. Get on with it."

The pirate turned back to the cage and reached out to grasp the cold steel of the cage. He ran his hands down the bars, feeling the cage's shape and searching for the lock. He found it easily enough. He squinted in the dark as he tried to slot the key into the keyhole. Finally, it slipped in and he turned the key with a click. The door swung outwards slightly, tapping the pirate on the shin.

Suddenly the pirate felt the eerie sensation he was being watched. He slowly looked up into the cage and saw two yellow, baleful slitted eyes staring at him. A low growl emanated from the cage and there was the sound of claws scraping against steel.

The pirate tried to push the cage back closed but he had barely made a move when the beast launched its attack. The cage door crashed into the pirate's head as the Horse Serpent burst through the open cage with a roar.

The unearthly roar echoed through the vast hold, wiping the smiles off the faces of the smirking pirates like a brand-new wonder cleaner. The pirate inside screamed, but the sound was cut off almost immediately by a loud, wet crunch.

Surjanto stared wide eyed at the trailer a second before turning to the blond women. His eyes narrowed.

Just then there was another roar booming throughout the hold. The pirates started looking nervously about. Surjanto yelled for calm, and ordered the men to ready their rifles. Some men complied, slinging their AK-47s from their backs and clipping in their magazines.

O'Mara turned to Setiawan, whose face had dropped with fear. "If you want to live, you'd better start running," she said.

His eyes swivelled from the trailer to meet hers. "What have you done?" he asked.

O'Mara had barely opened her mouth when the Horse Serpent burst from the trailer in a flash of green and landed deftly in front of them. Setiawan stared in wide-eyed horror as the emerald beast stretched its muscular torso and raised its horned head on its long, trunk-like neck high above him. The beast's jaws dripped with bloody saliva as it twisted its neck to look down onto Setiawan.

Of the men in the hold, Surjanto was the quickest to recover from the shock of the monster's dramatic and sudden appearance. He turned to see the slack jawed men looking down their sights as the beast reared up onto two legs in front of their leader with the intent of striking him down.

"Fire, you fools," Surjanto hissed.

The two men glanced quickly to Surjanto before squeezing the triggers on their weapons. The assault rifles barked in their arms and lit their faces up like fireworks, but they were off target and pinged off the floor and harmlessly away.

While failing to injure or scare the Horse Serpent, they had succeeded in drawing the Horse Serpent's attention away from Setiawan. The beast's neck twisted as the Horse Serpent's eyes zeroed in on a new target. Before the two gunmen knew what was happening, the Horse Serpent twisted its body and launched into a charge towards them.

The two rifles flashed as the pirates fired at the incoming monster, but the hot lead did nothing to falter the beast's stride. One pirate lost his courage and broke before the beast arrived. The Horse Serpent immediately was drawn to the movement and altered its trajectory in pursuit. The first pirate kept firing at the beast which flicked its thick tail at him as it neared, smashing him in the chest and hurling him backwards to land with a flop.

The fleeing pirate glanced over his shoulder to see the Horse Serpent in pursuit. He shrieked, throwing his gun aside in blind panic. He ran as fast as his legs could take him, but it was not enough. The beast's long strides easily outpaced him, and the Horse Serpent stretched its long neck forward and clamped its jaws over the pirate's shoulder and hoisted him in the air. For a moment he hung there, legs dangling down as the mighty Horse Serpent lifted him up by the shoulder. Blood dropped down onto the hold floor as the man screamed in agony. The Horse Serpent flicked its head left to right violently, shaking its prey like a puppy with a favourite toy. Flesh tore under the sharp teeth of the monster as the unfortunate pirate was thrown left to right until the violence and the pain of the act made him pass out.

Its prey no longer responsive, the Horse Serpent dropped its victim to the floor with a thud. It then turned to the other pirates in the great hold.

Surjanto had run to the man hit by the beast's tail as it passed. His chest was caved inwards and he coughed blood. Fear filled his eyes as Surjanto drew his curved blade from his belt, but as far as Surjanto saw it, it was a mercy to cut the man's throat.

He looked across to Setiawan, ready to curse the leader for having been drawn into this trap, but Setiawan had turned and was running for the stairs.

"Coward," Surjanto hissed and turned to the ten men who remained. "Weapons out and form a half circle," he roared. "Set your weapons to automatic fire. Let's draw the monster onto us and fill it with lead."

Surjanto sensed hesitancy in the group as they shuffled into formation. "Move!" he roared.

The Horse Serpent watched them with minimal interest as it placed one heavy claw over the fallen pirate's body and placed its jaws over his head. The jaw muscles tightened and the creature pulled and twisted at the head. There was a sickening wet crack followed by a squelch as the Horse Serpent pulled the pirate's head from his body. It then lifted its head high, opening and closing its mouth in a series of loud crunches as it crushed the skull before swallowing it down.

Surjanto walked behind the men, murmuring words of encouragement and slapping them on the back. "There is no way this monster can run into ten AKs. We will tear the life from its body before it reaches us. Keep still and aim well."

Surjanto glanced at the beast as it watched him curiously. He scowled and yelled at it. "Come on," he roared. He pulled a pistol from his belt, stepping between two men to fire at it. In response, the beast roared loud enough to rattle the sheet metal flooring of the hold. Surjanto fired again.

The Horse Serpent charged.

"Fire!" Surjanto bellowed. At once ten AK-47s roared to life, spitting rapid blasts of lead at the charging monster. The bullets thudded into the thick, armour-like scaly covering of the Horse Serpent. Many bullets were deflected harmlessly off the protective scales, but some lodged between them. Small pricklings of pain registered in the Horse Serpent's mind and it roared as it charged.

The first clip of each man was emptied and they moved quickly to reload. The beast altered its charge, drifting to one side to attack the arc from the left. The man on the end looked up, realising the monster's charge was now aimed at him, and fumbled the next magazine and it fell to the floor. He bent down to retrieve it, but the magazine slipped from his grip as he kept an eye on the charging monster.

"It's not stopping," he cried and broke away to run. His flight affected the group, and three more broke away to flee.

"Hold!" Surjanto roared, but it was in vain. The hail of bullets had done very little to slow the beast's charge, and two more men broke to run.

The four men that stood their ground had no chance. The Horse Serpent lowered its head as it closed. The first man was struck below the ribcage and gored by one of the Horse Serpent's horns. The Horse Serpent thrust its head to the side with the force of a speeding train. The horn tore the man's flesh like paper and he was thrown across the hold with his innards spilling from the wound and sloshing across the floor like a rain of gore.

The second man had his gun smashed from his hand as the beast's claws raked at him. As he reached for the pistol on his belt, his hand flopped uselessly, hanging by only a few sinews. The man barely got his scream out before the Horse Serpent swiped a second time, ploughing deep lines across his face and neck, the latter of which spurted and sprayed fountains of blood as his body collapsed to the floor.

No sooner had the second man gone down when the Horse Serpent leaped onto the third. He held out one arm defensively as the huge bulk of the creature bore down on him like a boulder in a landslide. The creature hit hard, and the man's body slapped the floor forcefully, his head smashing against the surface and cracking like an egg.

The last pirate turned to Surjanto, but found that Surjanto too had now fled. He turned back, just as the mighty tail flicked along the floor and swept his legs from under him. Pain seared his brain and he looked down to see his shins bent at unnatural angles. As his mind tried to comprehend his broken legs, a shadow passed over his head. He looked up to see the lines of teeth and dripping red maw of the monster closing around his vision. He screamed.

The scream was cut short by the wet crunch that signalled the end of the fourth pirate, spurring Surjanto into a sprint. He looked up to see that Setiawan was already mounting the stairs leading out of the hold. He cursed Setiawan again for running, but deep inside cursed him more so for making the more sensible decision.

The monster roared again and Surjanto dared a glance over his shoulder to see the beast was in pursuit. Surjanto was close to another pirate and he veered towards him. If Surjanto was to get away, he needed the monster distracted. He closed on the man in front and kicked the man's foot as he ran. The other man immediately stumbled and fell flat on his face. The Horse Serpent leaped as the man tried getting back to his feet. Surjanto looked back to see the beast had stopped and was pulling the man's arm from his body. Surjanto allowed himself a grim smile.

Setiawan reached the top of the stairs and flung the hatch aside. He looked behind him to see only half the men he had brought here still alive. He swore, pulling himself out of the hold and running across the deck. He hoped the last man out would have enough sense to close the hatch and lock it behind him.

Surjanto reached the foot of the stairs at the same moment as two other men. He bustled them aside and began climbing. He looked up to see two men at the first landing and another man taking the next flight. There was no sign of Setiawan.

"You," he ordered, pointing at the two men on the landing. "Fire at that monster and hold it off while we climb."

One man faltered, but refused to obey and started up the next flight of stairs. The second man stopped, swinging his rifle from his back and aiming at the creature. He let off a few quick shots. The Horse Serpent diverted its course away from the men at the foot of the stairs and started charging his position.

"Keep firing, it won't reach you," Surjanto urged.

The man bit his lip and nodded, squeezing off a few more shots as the Horse Serpent approached. It slowed to a walk as it stood under the platform. The pirate unclipped his magazine and reached for a fresh one when the Horse Serpent reared up onto its rear legs. Its long neck snaked upwards as it stretched towards him. The pirate stepped back nervously.

"Keep firing," Surjanto ordered.

Just then, the Horse Serpent's head slipped under the bottom rail of the stairs and clamped onto the pirate's leg above and below the knee. Before he knew what was happening, the pirate was pulled crashing into the railing as the Horse Serpent tried to drag its prey down. His body caught against the railing, and the Horse Serpent shook its head back and forth trying to pull the pirate down. The screams were short-lived but the beast continued wrenching at its victim. The stairs shook with each concussive blow and the air was filled with a loud clang each time the Horse Serpent pulled his body into the rails. Finally, the leg came free in a spray of blood.

Surjanto stepped past the corpse of the man that was twisted and broken against the railing and continued his climb. The two men ahead of him reached the top and set off across the deck without looking back. Surjanto heard a cry from behind and the stairs suddenly shook. He took a quick look behind to see the monster had leaped onto the stairs and was working its way up to the two trailing men. It was all the inspiration he needed to push up to the top.

The cool wind sprinkled with sea spray hit him like an arctic blast after the still confines of the hold-cum-charnel house. He pulled himself out and turned to the rear of the boat. Far ahead he saw Setiawan, followed by the other two pirates who had managed to escape the carnage below.

There was a shout from below and Surjanto turned to see the beast was gaining on the two men as they struggled up the remaining stairs. Surjanto pursed his lips and looked around. He knew he could not let the monster escape the confines of the first hold and turn this ship into its own private hunting ground. He turned back to the men and drew his pistol from his belt and aimed.

The first shot echoed loudly through the hold and hit the lead pirate in the leg. He immediately stumbled and fell into the stairs. The second shot rang almost as loud and the bullet punched the second soldier in the chest and pushed him back. And then the Horse Serpent was upon them, its tail swishing wildly through the air while the blood dripping jaws darted forwards to attack.

Surjanto slammed the hatch door shut, drowning out the screams from the massacre in the hold below. The hatch closed with a click, and Surjanto slumped to the deck, breathing heavily. He had succeeded in closing off the monster from the rest of the ship, but the venture had been costly. Surjanto started counting the losses in his head. Counting himself and Setiawan, only two other men had survived. That meant ten men had died in the carnage below. Ten men dead. For what?

Then Surjanto frowned. There was someone he was forgetting. The blond woman. His eyes narrowed as he looked aft. He saw only Setiawan and the two other survivors who had been quick enough to get out ahead of him. Just where had that blond woman gotten to?

18

Arwadi's assertion of leadership did nothing to ease the tension in the small boat that gently rode the waves of the South China Sea. The passengers all sat in silence as distrustful and suspicious glances were cast amongst each other. At one point, Mohede groaned, drawing everyone's attention like a penalty shot in a World Cup final, but the interest dissipated quickly when the man did not wake.

Dower sat at the very front of the boat, nestled into the crook of the join. His eyes moved from Sianturi to Arwadi and back. Both spent a lot of time looking at Mohede. As he watched he thought about Jess. His situation had improved a lot since he was pulled from the sea. He might live to survive all this, but what of her? He had hundreds of questions he wanted to ask Sianturi. How had she been the last time he saw her? Was she frightened? Do you think she found somewhere safe to hide? Did you see the pirates? What would the pirates do to her?

On and on the questions turned over in his head. But he did not speak up. Lines were drawn in the boat, and Sianturi may well be the reason for the pirate attack. For all intents and purposes, he was an enemy now and he could not trust any answers the man might give anyway.

As the night wore on, Arwadi dimmed the cabin lights to preserve battery.

"Try to sleep. There's nothing else to do out here anyway."

"Maybe next time you should pack a deck of cards on one of these things," Cheong sneered sardonically.

"Not a bad idea," replied Arwadi, "it would help me learn your poker faces and I wouldn't have to rely on this half-drowned scumbag to learn if any of you are lying and are in fact connected to the pirates."

"Or maybe we'd learn you are the one who is corrupt, eh Captain?" Cheong spat derisively.

But rather than rise to the taunt, Arwadi smiled whimsically and shook his head.

With the lights on the craft dimmed, Sanders soon drifted into a snoring sleep. Dower was not surprised. Even with the worries that plagued his own mind, Dower too started succumbing to the exhaustion from the day's events and the gentle rocking of the boat. Before long, his own head was nodding and not long after he drifted to sleep.

But it was not a restful sleep that welcomed Dower. Within an hour or so of first drifting off he awoke, finding his neck in an uncomfortable position. He gave it a rub and opened his eyes. The deck lights were out now and he could hear the soft rhythmic breathing of the others in the boat. There was a little light coming through the open hatch on the side of the boat, and Dower squinted to see if Arwadi too had dared to sleep or if he stayed awake to watch over them. Eventually he gave up, conceding it was too dark to see Arwadi well enough from his position.

Dower leaned back and tried to resume sleeping. Thoughts of Jess again stirred in his heart and mind, swirling around his brain like a maelstrom of fear and apprehension. He shifted and moved again and again, but his head was too busy consumed with worry for her to rest and sleep just would not return to his weary self.

Sometime later he heard someone stirring. He kept his eyes closed, still trying to sleep himself, when he heard the sound of a zipper followed by the low trickle of someone peeing in the water. The moment seemed to stretch uncomfortably long as Dower pretended to sleep while the person peed, but eventually it ended. There was a long pause then, and Dower wondered whether the man who had peed had resumed sleep when he heard the figure moving around once more. Dower was tempted to turned his head and squint through his eyes to see who it was and what they were up to when he heard a soft plop in the water. Dower smiled, amused by the sudden thought of someone holding onto the side of the boat and pooping into the water. It was the thought that lowered his guard against the worry that consumed his mind and allowed sleep to finally take hold.

Dower woke to the sound of his name being called. His brain was still foggy and his head ached, and all he could make out was the sound of Sanders shouting. He opened his eyes to darkness, but Arwadi must have flicked on the cabin lights as he was suddenly blinded by glaring light. As Dower squeezed his eyes shut and waited for them to adjust to the sudden change, he became aware of another sensation. The iron-like smell of blood.

"Dower," Sanders shouted again, "wake up. Someone has murdered Mohede."

Dower squinted enough to allow some light into his eyes as he sat up. As his eyes adjusted, he found them drawn to the large crimson puddle that swung left to right with the swaying of the boat. In the great puddle lay Mohede with a deep, gaping, crimson lined slit across his neck.

"His throat has been cut," Arwadi declared, standing over them sternly. "This proves the man who set him to call the pirates is on this boat. Knowing we would interrogate Mohede as soon as he woke, the traitor knew he would be exposed the moment he spoke and has thus murdered this man to cover his tracks. One of you here are responsible for the taking of my ship."

"It's obvious to all of us who the traitor is," Sanders said, before pointing to Sianturi. "It's Mr empty shipping containers over here."

Arwadi raised an eyebrow. "Is that so? And tell me, did anyone else hear this hollow boom or are we just to take your word for it?"

"Shut up, the lot of you," Arwadi roared. "I am tired of this bickering. As far as I am concerned you are all suspicious to me. Now, one by one, you are all going to empty your pockets. One of you must have the murder weapon."

"No, they won't," Dower said dazedly.

"Eh?" Arwadi barked. "What do you mean by that?"

Dower put his hand to his forehead. "My God," he exclaimed, "I was awake when the murder happened. First, they peed over the side, then they cut Mohede's throat, and then finally they dropped the knife overboard. I was awake the whole time and heard the splash as they threw the weapon away. Oh my God."

Dower shook his head in bemusement before looking up. Everyone stared at him expectantly.

"And the killer is…." Arwadi prompted.

"Oh, I didn't see who it was. I turned away to give the person privacy while they peed."

Arwadi gave the look of a child who had received a lump of coal on Christmas Day. "Well thanks for that brilliant piece of information. It was very enlightening. I guess now it comes back to detective work. So, the murder weapon is gone. No problem. Let's talk about how you all came to be here." Arwadi stepped forward, pointing the pistol at Sianturi. "First you came to me and asked if anybody had been around offering me big dollars to take a quick trip out of the country. Seems to me you knew they would be coming, eh?"

"That's not exactly how it was," Sianturi mumbled and shifted uncomfortably.

"Shut up," Arwadi boomed.

Sianturi looked to the floor and said nothing. Arwadi stared at him a long moment before taking another step forwards and pointing the gun at Cheong.

"Then a mere few hours later this *tionghoa* clown with this other dolled up dolt Westerner came offering that very deal. Now I don't know what you two are. But I do know something. There is something very off about what you are up to. Tell me, what is this cargo of yours that I took onto my ship?"

Cheong scowled and stared in defiance, saying nothing. Sanders glanced his way and looked up at the captain. With every word Arwadi had said, he had moved closer and closer to Sanders. Sanders looked at

Arwadi, then the gun in his hand. If only they could distract him a little longer and get him to edge a little closer. He leaned forward, adjusting his balance ever so slightly.

"It is an animal," Dower said, "but one that is nothing like you have seen before."

"Is that so?" Arwadi asked, turning the gun onto Dower and taking another step forward. "And what type of animal is it then?"

"That's enough," Cheong cut in. "How do we know you are innocent of all this, Captain? Because you have the gun? It seems to me you are at the heart of this. You know we are within reach of an island yet instead of guiding us there you opt to drift at sea and waste time, allowing those pirates to get away with our cargo. It seems to me you knew from the start we had something valuable on board, so you contrived this situation to steal our cargo from the get go."

Arwadi scowled and took another step forward. There was a squelch as he put his foot down on the sticky floor. One more step and he would be standing directly between Sianturi and Sanders.

"And how is it then I am stuck out here with you?" Arwadi asked.

"All part of an elaborate plan. Who would suspect a captain thrown from his own ship? No one. Then when we are rescued and taken back to Indonesia your ship and crew just happens to be waiting for you back in the docks. Wouldn't be the first time you've run a scam like that to steal someone's cargo, would it, Arwadi?"

Arwadi took another step forward. "How dare you."

Suddenly, Sanders snapped into action. He stood rapidly, grabbing Arwadi's gun wielding arm just below the wrist and hitting Arwadi's side with his shoulder. Arwadi had not been ready for the attack, and toppled to the side. Sianturi squirmed out of the way to avoid being crushed as the two men began wrestling for the gun. Arwadi was strong, but Sanders had the advantage and slammed the gun hand repeatedly against the seat. Just then Arwadi's grip faltered, and the gun flew from his hand and clattered across the bloody floor of the boat.

Cheong was quickest to react, dashing forward to retrieve the fallen pistol. He picked it up and turned to aim at the two wrestling combatants. The captain ceased struggling and Sanders eased himself up from the scrap.

"Yes, Kenny," Sanders roared with delight. He stepped forwards towards Cheong with a broad smile on his face.

Cheong turned the gun to point it at Sanders. "Stand back," he ordered.

Sanders paused, the smile giving way to a look of confusion. "Kenny?"

"Stand back I said," Cheong ordered.

Sanders raised his arms in surrender. "What the hell, Kenny?"

"Well, well, well," Arwadi said, pulling himself up from the floor. "It seems I was right all along. You can't trust a *tionghoa*." Arwadi turned to Sanders, a look of mirth on his face. "You worked with the traitor all along and you didn't even know it."

"Shut up," Cheong roared, and turned to Dower who was cowering in the corner at the front of the boat. "You, move out of there. I need to sit in a position where I have all of you in front of me."

Dower raised his arms and eased himself up and walked over to join the others. Cheong sat in the spot he had only just vacated.

"Now, Arwadi, get behind the wheel. You are taking us to Bingwen Island. And this time it's not a suggestion, it's an order. Now get to it. I need to meet those pirates before they start doing something silly like looking into our cargo."

Arwadi stood and slowly walked to the rear of the boat to engage the engine. A mild smile seemed to be playing at the corner of his mouth.

"The rest of you may as well sit and get comfortable," Cheong said. "We're not likely to get there until dawn." Cheong sat and watched as three men slowly sat and Arwadi brought the engine to life and began turning the boat.

Sanders clenched and unclenched his fists as he glowered at Cheong. "Do you plan on telling us what this is all about? Why the big double-cross?"

"You would not understand," Cheong spat.

"Let's start with this then," Arwadi called from the back, "what is in that horse carriage in the front of my ship and why is it so damn special?"

"It's the Sipatahunan Cave Horse Serpent," Sianturi said.

All eyes immediately turned to him in amazement.

"How did you know that?" Cheong snapped.

"Higson didn't trust you, Cheong. He sent me to keep an eye on things and make sure his cargo made it safely to Singapore."

"You're doing a swell job of that," scoffed Arwadi.

"Then why were you asking all those questions if you knew we had it?" Dower asked.

"I'm sorry about that. I am a private eye by occupation and it is habit. Plus, I was testing you. If something did go wrong, I had to know if it was by your mistake or an action of Cheong here. But I guess that is not up for debate anymore."

"Okay, so you are Higson's man. Tell us, what is this all about?" Sanders asked.

"It's about people like him," Cheong said, pointing to Arwadi who stood at the rear of the boat.

"Him?" Sanders said in confusion.

"Yes, him. Racist thugs who target Chinese Indonesians like myself with no cause but blind, racial hatred." Cheong straightened, and with one hand began loosening the tie around his neck. "You know, I hate these clothes. I find neck ties so constricting. And these colours are just so gaudy. But do you want to know why I wear them? To look successful and to be noticed by race hating scum like him. I wear these clothes to rub my success and my wealth in their faces. If they are going to hate me, then the least I can do is show them I am richer and better than them."

Cheong lifted the brightly coloured tie over his head and threw it onto the floor before undoing the top button of his shirt.

"Sanders, you say you stand against racism, but you are a white man who comes from a country led by white people. You can't even begin to understand racism. Blind hatred of Chinese Indonesians exists for one reason. It's because we are successful. We have commercial acumen and we know how to build wealth. We are good at it. Too good apparently, because a president once declared the wealth of Chinese Indonesians was a problem. Can you believe that?"

"But by dressing the way you do to show and flaunt wealth, aren't you only playing to that perception?" Dower asked.

Cheong cast Dower a glance but did not answer the question. "It was during the nineteen nineties that this anti-Chinese sentiment was at its peak. While President Suharto was putting on shows for the media, he was stupidly reinforcing the resentment many felt towards Chinese Indonesian wealth.

"My family was a family of florists. We weren't rich by any stretch of the word. But we lived comfortably in a community of other Chinese Indonesians. I was eleven years old when the protests against us started. I can't say I remember all the news clearly, or why those protesting students were shot, but I remember the violence that followed clearly enough.

"They came into our street with all manner of ramshackle weapons intent on only violence and destruction. My father was a peaceful man. He only wanted to reconcile and negotiate with the men. He was clubbed over the head and stamped to death by the first wave of rioters. In a way, he was lucky. Unlike my mother, who was forced to endure hours of torture at the hands of these men. I know, because they held me down and forced me to watch while they did it. She survived, but the wounds she endured from that day never healed."

Cheong seemed to stare off in the distance for a few moments, before his attention drew back to the men in the boat.

"Many Chinese Indonesians left the country after that. My mother and I couldn't afford to, and thus we were forced to stay in a country where most people hated us.

"The thing is, those riots did not happen by accident. They were organised by a group of extremists who are against the imbalance of wealth of Chinese Indonesians and seek to eliminate our presence from the economic and political landscape of the country. They foster hate, stir minds and are not afraid to spill blood to get what they want.

"These same people reared their ugly heads again recently. When they saw a Chinese Indonesian was going to become governor, they used social media to spread lies and propaganda, and a hundred thousand marched the streets of Jakarta in protest against him. I feared it was going to be nineteen ninety-eight all over again. We were lucky this time, but this can't go on. We cannot live with these age-old hatreds and jealousies that could at any moment turn to ugly violence, like what was committed against my parents and neighbours."

Cheong bit his lip and turned away to wipe tears from his eyes. Sianturi coughed and both Dower and Sanders both turned away to give him a moment. Even Arwadi was notably quiet, using the moment to analyse the instruments on the panel as a distraction. It was Dower who first spoke up next.

"But what does any of that have to do with the Horse Serpent?"

Cheong cleared his throat and turned back to them with a hard look in his eyes. "The Horse Serpent is a weapon. You saw it in the forest. It is a killing machine. These people… they would do anything to get hold of a weapon like that. Something that they could let loose in the middle of the Chinese quarter in Jakarta and the streets would be awash with blood. They view it as a WMD."

"An animal is not a weapon," Sanders said, shaking his head. "You cannot think of one that way. They follow their natural instincts. When it was in the forest, it was defending itself and its habitat from intruders, nothing more. We cannot look upon them as killers or weapons for following their instincts."

"But more than that," added Dower, "I don't see how stealing it from Higson prevents it from getting into their hands. He can't be bought off and it would be safe far away in Australia."

"I didn't steal it from Mr Higson to stop it from getting into their hands," Cheong hissed. "I stole it from him to put it right into their hands. And then, as they all gathered around to see this fantastic beast that I had brought them to carry out their killings, I would open the cage.

Don't you get it? The very lure I am using to get to them is the way I will kill them all. And now, thanks to our racist Captain Arwadi, I won't be there when the pirates take possession of the Horse Serpent and I won't be there when they hand it over to the extremists. So, if you don't mind, Captain, please hurry the damn hell up and get me to Bingwen Island before the Horse Serpent is lost."

"So, all of this is just… what… revenge?" Dower asked.

"No, it's a means to an end. The end of those men who caused the riots that destroyed my family."

Sanders shook his head. "You're nuts, Kenny" he spat. "Spilling more blood will only create more violence."

"Not if I get to the men at the top. And believe me, for something as rare as this, they would be there."

Sanders shook his head and huffed. He tapped his foot impatiently and his mouth contorted shapes. Finally, he turned to Cheong. "I can't let you do it, Kenny. I understand why you want to do it, but I can't let you do it. The Horse Serpent is a unique, amazing creature. It's not a weapon. I can't let you use it to kill and be killed."

Cheong straightened and pointed the gun at Sanders. "And how exactly do you plan to stop me, eh? You dare move an inch closer and I'll put a bullet in your chest. You got that?"

Sanders' eyes narrowed as he stared at Cheong. "I don't know how, but I will stop you from using that beautiful creature as a weapon. That, Kenny, is a promise."

19

Setiawan stood on the bridge looking down across the main deck of the *Kekal* as though he were looking at his own grave. He buried his fingers deep into his thick, knotted beard and scratched at his chin. There was a palpable sense of fear amongst the remaining members of his group. Especially now that the word of what happened in the front hold had spread amongst them.

"Dawn," a voice said from behind.

Setiawan turned, his eyes heavy with worry. "Dawn? That is too long. Can't we get there any faster?"

"The screws are turning as fast as they can go. It's the best we can do in this old ship."

"It's not soon enough," Setiawan grumbled. "Can we call back the chaser boats to rescue us?"

The man behind the wheel was downcast. "No. Surjanto smashed the ship's comms to make the ship go dark not long after coming onto the bridge as per…"

"Operating procedure. I know. If he had not done it, I would have reprimanded him. I just didn't expect us to be the ones needing the radio and now I wish I had it." Setiawan turned to look wearily back down the front of the ship and shook his head. "Then the plan stays the same. We take this ship to Bingwen Island."

"And then what?" asked a voice from behind.

Setiawan turned and saw Surjanto had arrived in the shattered doorway of the bridge.

"On the north side of the islands is a small bay. There are other boats waiting for us there. We were supposed to transfer the WMD onto them but…"

Surjanto walked into the bridge eyeing the pirate leader questioningly. "You're going to leave it here on the ship? Won't there be consequences for failing in the mission?" he asked.

"Perhaps. They can't blame anyone for wanting to run. You said the creature was safely locked down in the hold. If they still want it, they are more than welcome to come and get it themselves."

Surjanto drew up beside Setiawan and stared down the bridge. But unlike his leader, Surjanto did not wear a look of despair. His eyes burned with rage and his mouth was twisted with anger.

"This is your fault, you know," Surjanto said. "You let that woman trick you into thinking she was your contact and she led us into a death-trap."

"If I was tricked it was because you lost us the contact. For all we know, that man you shot and cut the eye from was our contact."

Surjanto scowled and stared at the distant hatch cover for the front hold of the ship. Then his eyes moved slowly across the deck, studying every detail and every shadow for movement like an eagle searching for prey.

"What I wouldn't give to be able to interrogate that blond woman right now. Where do you suppose she went?" Surjanto said slowly.

"Went? She's dead. Just like the rest of the men that went down there."

Surjanto turned and studied the pirate leader. "I'm not so sure. I don't think she would have led us down there without a way out for herself. She meant for that monster to kill us. Of that I have no doubt. But I don't think it was suicide she was planning."

Setiawan turned to meet Surjanto's eyes. "She didn't make it out. I was first and you were last, and she was nowhere in between. She's dead."

Surjanto turned and stared down the deck once more. "I don't buy it. I think she's still down there. Down in the front hold."

Setiawan turned and followed Surjanto's gaze to the hatch. "There is no way of knowing without going in there. And that isn't going to happen. Not while that monster is in there."

"Then I have your permission then?"

Setiawan frowned. "Permission for what?"

"Permission to let it out so I can go down and check the hold for her?"

"Are you insane? You would let that beast loose on this ship just to find that woman?"

Surjanto's gold tooth gleamed as he grinned maliciously. "Oh, I'll do more than find her. I will make her feel every one of those ten deaths she caused down there with her little trick. I will treat her with so much pain and suffering by the end she will beg to die."

Setiawan shook his head. "You can't do it. You can't set that beast loose just to pursue petty revenge. You'd be putting all our lives at risk. I cannot allow it."

There was a long moment of silence as Surjanto nodded while staring at the forward hold hatch. "Okay. Then tell me this. What are you willing to do to stop me?"

"I beg your pardon?"

"You heard me. I am going down there and I am letting that monster out. And when it leaves the hold, I am going in and I'm finding that woman." Surjanto pulled the pistol from his belt and flicked the safety off before pointing it at Setiawan. "Now, I'll ask you again. What are you willing to do to stop me?"

"Damn you," Setiawan hissed. "You set that beast free and you will kill us all."

Surjanto smiled and eased away from the pirate leader and edged towards the door. The gun remained aimed unwaveringly at the scowling face of Setiawan as he backed away. He stepped past the broken door hanging loosely on its hinges from the blast. He glanced down and smirked at it. "I wouldn't suggest staying on the bridge if I were you."

A roar of profanity bubbled up from Setiawan's throat but before he could spill them out, Surjanto was gone.

"Son of a bitch," cursed Setiawan. He ran to the door and turned to find Surjanto had already disappeared down the stairs to the level below. Setiawan bolted down, only to see Surjanto at the far end of the hall. Surjanto turned back, gave a quick smile, before dropping down the next flight of stairs. Setiawan stared down the hall, surveying the floor still streaked with blood from where they dragged the man Surjanto had shot.

"What now?" came a quavering voice from behind.

Setiawan turned. "You aim this ship at Bingwen Island the best you can, then you get the hell out of there. We'll just have to barricade ourselves with the crew in the mess hall and hope for the best."

***

It had all happened very quickly. From the moment the Horse Serpent burst from the back of the trailer and stood over Setiawan, nobody took another glance at O'Mara. All eyes were instead drawn to the great emerald beast, and it was all she had needed to escape their clutches.

O'Mara had already taken a few steps to her left before the creature fully stretched above the pirate leader, and was safely behind the trailer when the shooting started. She crouched down as Setiawan ran past in blind panic, then slid under the horse trailer to hide. There was enough room underneath for her to slide under on her stomach, and in the low light of the hold she was certain she would not be seen.

It was difficult to make out much of the action from where she lay. But one thing she knew for sure was the Horse Serpent was equally as devastating and deadly here as it was in the forest.

She watched as the Horse Serpent chased and picked up one man, only to drop his bloodied and broken corpse a few moments later. She saw the pirates form a firing arc. They were better drilled than the soldiers in the forest, but it made no difference to their fates. Gunfire echoed deafeningly through the hold as the pirates opened fire on the

Horse Serpent, only to fail and be torn apart by ruthless killing efficiency. Blood and bodies hit the floor with alarming quickness and the pirates broke and ran. The air in the hold, already stale from the hours it was locked off from the world, was now warm and thick with the scent of blood.

O'Mara squeezed out of a little nook to watch the fatal flight to the hatch on the stairs. The last two men would have made it if Surjanto had not gunned them down. And then the hatch was slammed shut, closing the beast in the forward hold with her.

Sensing the immediate threat was over, the Horse Serpent calmed. It approached the hatch and nudged it, but finding it did not yield turned back to the bodies of the men it had killed on the stairs. O'Mara had to turn away as the Horse Serpent began tearing the flesh from the dead men and devoured their meat.

Somewhere, another pirate had survived and regained consciousness. He whimpered pitifully and called out. O'Mara could not understand the words, but the wretched sound of his cries, combined with the ripping sound of human flesh from above, made her start to feel ill and she cupped her hands tightly over her ears to block the hellish din out as she hid under the horse trailer. It dimmed the sounds, but did not block them out completely.

To distract herself from the awful scene around her, she thought of Dower. She pictured him in her mind. She pictured him lying beside her, looking upon her with his warm, brown smiling eyes as he used his fingers to gently push her blond locks away from her face. As she thought of him, she bit her lip with worry. For all she knew he was nothing but a floating corpse somewhere out in the South China Sea now. She hoped like crazy that someone would find him before it was too late.

In her mind she played the conversation they should have had on the rear of the ship earlier. She knew Dower was no hero. He was not a manly man like Sanders. He was not the kind of man to mete out justice with his fists should someone insult her honour. But that is not what she wanted from a man anyway. She could stick up for herself and she liked his soft, gentle side. She knew what to expect out of him as a partner in most situations. What she did not expect was that he would run away when her life was in danger.

She sighed and wiped a tear from her eye. She loved him and knew she could find it in her heart to forgive him if only she knew why he did what he did. Now it pained her to admit that she may never know.

After some time, the whimpering man must have passed out or died, and the cries stopped. O'Mara pulled her hands from over her ears and found that the sound of ripping flesh and crunching bones had also ceased. She eased forwards from under the trailer to look up at the balcony to see if the Horse Serpent was sleeping. But the Horse Serpent was no longer there. She glanced about, wary of where the deadly creature may now lurk, but she saw no sign of it. Deciding it was safest to remain hidden, she slid back under the trailer once more.

O'Mara did not notice when the Horse Serpent descended from the stairs back down into the main hold area. She only became aware of its presence when the large, clawed feet came into her narrow field of view. She froze, barely able to breathe as the beast approached the trailer. She heard the wide, round nostrils sucking at the air as it sniffed at the air. The creature padded forward. Its steps were surprisingly light on the floor. She edged back, trying to move as quickly and as quietly out of range of the beast.

The Horse Serpent's nose dropped below the line of the trailer and it sniffed again. From this close, O'Mara could see the dried blood around the beast's mouth and smell the foul stench of human meat on its breath. O'Mara held her breath as the beast pushed against the trailer with its head, causing its suspension to creak as it shifted above her. The beast sniffed again, before pushing once more with its head. O'Mara gasped as the tire opposite her was lifted from the floor.

Suddenly there was a noise from the hatch door of the hold. The Horse Serpent stopped, holding dead still for a moment before pulling back. Someone banged on the hatch door above them. The Horse Serpent drew away from the trailer and slowly approached the stairs leading out of the hold. O'Mara pushed her head out from under the trailer and looked up to see pale moonlight shining through the open hatch.

O'Mara flicked her eyes to the Horse Serpent. It approached the stairs and mounted them with an agile elegance. The stairs creaked, but otherwise made no sound. The Horse Serpent moved quietly up the stairs with the stealth of a seasoned predator. O'Mara marvelled at how naturally the beast moved up this man-made structure. Her eyes then flicked to the open hatch, wondering if a pirate stood just outside, unaware that the Horse Serpent was almost upon him.

The Horse Serpent moved quickly to the open hatch, and an instant later, it was gone. O'Mara waited, expecting to hear further gunfire, screams and violence. But there was no sound forthcoming.

Finally feeling alone, O'Mara slumped back on the ground and relaxed. It had seemed like an age since she had done so, and even lying here on the solid steel floor of the hold felt somehow luxuriant now that the danger was gone.

Just then a shadow blocked the moonlight filtering through the open hatch. O'Mara felt her muscles tense up once more. A human form appeared from the shadow. In the back of her mind she hoped somehow that it would be Dower coming to her rescue and here to get her out. But that only happened in movies and fairy tales, and the thought was quickly dashed as she made out the ugly, muscular shape of Surjanto lowering himself into the hold.

Surjanto stood at the top of the stairs and surveyed the hold below him. O'Mara was sure he could not see her from his vantage point, but she instinctively shrunk back under the trailer regardless. He stood at the top, as motionless as a statue for some time, before slowly drawing a curved knife from his belt. He turned and began his descent into the hold.

O'Mara watched as he slowly and deliberately moved down the staircase. She cringed as he reached the bottom. His face was a cruel mask of hatred and his blade glinted dully in the light as he stepped away from the stairs and began walking towards the truck. O'Mara pressed back, eager to stay out of sight. She watched his boots as he approached the cab of the truck. He swung open the door and climbed up inside.

O'Mara measured the distance between her position and the stairs with her eyes. How far could she get before he became aware of her? Was it enough for her to get up the stairs and away? She stretched her legs and rolled her ankles to get the blood flowing faster into them. But if she made it to the top of the stairs first, what then? The Horse Serpent was now free up on deck, not to mention the other pirates on the ship. How could she make it past such an array of potential dangers? To flee through that would surely be running the gauntlet.

Surjanto's boots thumped the floor as he dropped once more form the cab. O'Mara shifted her eyes back to Surjanto's boots as he walked the length of the truck and peered into the covered rear. She saw him jump to hoist himself up into the rear, and his boots were gone.

O'Mara turned back to the stairs. Again, she measured the distance. She ran regularly, but only to keep fit. This was something else altogether. This was a mad sprint to get away from a lunatic with a knife, only to run into who knew what other danger. But surely, she thought, anything was better than lying here and waiting for Surjanto to find her.

She swivelled her body around so that she lay on her stomach facing the staircase. Surjanto would be in the back of the truck somewhere. If she eased herself out carefully and crept towards the stairs, that might just give her enough of a head start on him.

Suddenly the two boots of Surjanto thumped down on the floor behind her. Contrary to what she thought, he had climbed the outside of the trailer and had now dropped to the ground near her feet. She barely dared to breathe and the moment seemed to stretch for an eternity until two hands grabbed each ankle and pulled.

She reached up desperately, trying to grab onto the undercarriage or the axel or anything that would prevent her from being dragged out of her cover, but she only succeeded in painfully breaking a nail as she was cruelly wrenched out from under the trailer.

"No!" she yelled as she was forcefully dragged out into the open. She scrabbled at the floor, searching desperately for a handhold that just was not there. Once clear, Surjanto released his grip on her ankles and grabbed her shoulder to flip her onto her back. She tried to resist, but the cold sensation of the curved blade against her throat drew away some of her will to fight.

Sitting on her hips, Surjanto grinned foully. O'Mara shivered as she looked up at his cruel features. His scar was dark and bulbous. Whatever caused such a wound surely must have left a mark not just on his face but also his soul. The gold tooth in his mouth glinted as he ran his tongue across his teeth. She noticed then he was eyeing the shape of her body.

Surjanto pulled the knife away from her throat and grabbed at her shirt.

"No!" she cried and attempted to push his hands away from her. He slapped at her arm but she grabbed it with both hands and tried hanging on. But Surjanto was strong, and while she wrestled one arm, he dropped the knife and punched her with the other. The blow hit hard, and her head smashed against the floor causing her to blackout momentarily.

When her senses cleared, she found Surjanto cutting the last of her shirt away. He reached for her bra when she again screamed and grabbed at his hands. "No!" she howled as he attempted to push his elbow down onto her throat. She felt herself weakening, and all she saw above her was the wide, heartless eyes, vile scar and sinister smile as her attacker pushed home his advantage.

Suddenly there was a thump and from the corner of her eye, O'Mara saw a flash of green. Surjanto's smile wavered as he sensed the presence beside him. O'Mara pushed, but he held her firm. Slowly, Surjanto turned his eyes away from her and slowly turned to the source of the sound. He barely had a second to take in the form of the Horse Serpent when the beast's head struck down and its jaws closed over his head, snapping shut like a steel trap. There was a loud crunch and O'Mara's face and chest were sprayed with blood. O'Mara wiped her eyes clear and looked up to see the limp body of Surjanto being lifted into the air above her by the Horse Serpent.

For a moment O'Mara stared up in wonder, but she was quickly brought back to her senses as Surjanto's knife slipped from his fingers to clatter to the floor. She turned, twisting her body back onto her stomach before scrambling back to the trailer. She slid under before swivelling around to see the Horse Serpent.

Blood patted down like rain around the Horse Serpent's feed. There was another savage crunch and the headless corpse of Surjanto fell to the floor. O'Mara blocked her ears as the Horse Serpent crunched on the head, breaking it down to size before swallowing the bone riddled pulp.

The Horse Serpent then leaned down and sniffed at the corpse of Surjanto. Those big, yellow eyes studied the body before the beast turned its head and looked directly at O'Mara. Their eyes caught, and for a long moment the two stared at each other.

Without warning, the Horse Serpent raised its head out of view and then walked towards the trailer O'Mara had slunk under. She pulled back, fearing the beast may try reaching underneath now that it knew where she hid. Her eyes darted to the trailer above, wondering if it even provided safety at all. She had seen enough of the beast in action now she would not be surprised if it could easily flip over to reveal her unprotected.

But the Horse Serpent did nothing of the sort. It stopped next to the trailer and then proceeded to do the oddest thing: it laid down on its side next to the trailer with its back to her. For a moment O'Mara could only stare as the monstrous beast settled onto the floor only a few feet away from her. The trailer above her creaked as the beast nudged it with its back before finally settling still. O'Mara stared at the beast's back in disbelief.

Up close, she could see the thick, heavy scales on the creature's back were heavily marked by the recent battle in the hold. In many places scales had been damaged with great divots taken from them. The beast had not come away as unharmed as it had appeared to.

O'Mara reached a trembling hand forward and gently touched the back of the Horse Serpent. It was only a light touch at first, to see if the great beast would allow it, before she placed her whole hand there. She ran her hand across the Horse Serpent's back, patting it gently, careful to avoid any sore spots. She found the moment even more awe inspiring than the first time she had touched it, because this time it was not caged and tied, this time it was allowing her.

As she felt her way along its back, she heard the Horse Serpent's breathing settle into a steady rhythm of sleep. She pulled her hand away amazed. She turned her body around and looked again at the stairs leading out of the hold. She could quite easily sneak out of here as it slept and close the hold behind her, sealing the Horse Serpent in. She would look quite a sight, clambering out of the hold covered in blood with her shirt torn open. But how she looked would not matter. All that would matter was that she was safe.

O'Mara turned back to the Horse Serpent's scaly green back. She reached out again, touching the surface lightly and feeling oddly comforted by it. Somehow, through all of the pirate attack and subsequent events, she had never felt as safe as she did now as she lay next to the Horse Serpent. She admonished herself for the craziness of the thought, having seen the Horse Serpent in action and knowing how quickly and efficiently it killed, yet here in this moment there was no threat.

O'Mara lay her head down and did not look again at the stairs. She had made her decision to stay where she was.

20

The softening of the dark was barely perceptible at first, but soon the soft glow on the eastern horizon grew in strength before the fiery red sun clawed its way up into the morning sky.

There were many bleary eyes that greeted that first light of the new day. Locked away in accommodation cabins on the *Kekal*, weary pirates with weapons clutched so tightly in the hands it made their knuckles white greeted the dawn with bloodshot eyes as they stared out of their cabin windows. Their eyes flicked about restlessly, searching for signs of the apex predator that they believed was stalking the deck for prey. None of them were more worried than their leader, Setiawan, who despite finding relief that his second in command Surjanto had not returned and was presumably not going to cause him any more headaches, knew that if he somehow survived to get off the *Kekal*, he might not survive the interrogation that followed after his superiors learned of his catastrophic failure here.

Bleary eyes too met the first light of day on the rescue boat that had launched from the main ship some ten hours earlier. Nestled in the crook of the bow and blinking rapidly to keep his eyes moist was Ken Cheong, a man who was trying to keep himself sharp and alert before his enemies. Opposite him were four sets of tired eyes, all beaming hostility and watching him relentlessly for an opening as the rescue boat slowly chugged its way to the same destination as the ship who had once bore it.

It was only in the *Kekal*'s front hold, in the most unlikely of circumstances, was there anyone getting a fitful rest.

O'Mara was not aware she had drifted to sleep, lying beside the monstrous Horse Serpent, until she was shaken awake some two hours after dawn.

The whole ship seemed to shudder around her, shaking and bouncing as though in an earthquake. Overhead, the horse trailer squeaked as it shook and bounced with the shuddering ship. The Horse Serpent leaped to its feet, only to crouch aggressively as it looked wearily about. O'Mara rubbed her eyes before reaching up to hold onto the trailer above as the shuddering became accompanied by a raucous roar. The shaking seemed to last a long time but O'Mara sensed the ferocity of the shaking decrease with each passing moment. Finally, the noise and shaking eased away and the deck listed slightly to one side. O'Mara could still hear the humming of the ship's engine, but the sense of movement was gone.

"We've hit land," O'Mara said. She let go of the trailer above her and allowed herself a smile. "Holy shit, we've hit land," she exclaimed. She turned and saw the Horse Serpent watching her oddly. Slowly, it eased itself out of the crouch and began sniffing at the air. Curiosity must have gotten the better of it then, and it walked around the trailer and to the stairs, before climbing up them. O'Mara pulled herself forwards to watch the Horse Serpent approach the hatch. It paused at the hatch and turned to look at her. A second later, it leaped through the hatch and was gone.

O'Mara stared at the hatch a minute before pulling herself out from under the trailer. Her mouth was dry and her face caked with dried blood. She approached the rear of the truck and climbed in. Amidst the jumble of gear in the back, she found a travel bag she did not recognise. Unzipping it, she found plain men's clothing. She frowned and searched for a tag, but there was nothing to indicate who this might belong to. She shrugged, pulling a t-shirt that looked her size out and continuing her search. In another corner she found a plastic shopping bag filled with water bottles. She greeted the find as though she had just stumbled upon a pile of gold coins, and celebrated by cracking the seal on one bottle and gulping down the contents thirstily.

Discarding the empty bottle aside, O'Mara clambered out of the rear of the truck with the t-shirt and plastic bag clutched in one hand. She made her way around to the cab of the truck and twisted the mirror around to view herself. She gasped at the bloody faced apparition she saw. She pulled off her torn shirt and cracked a second bottle of water open. She wet the shirt and began to clean away Surjanto's dried blood from her face and chest with it.

Just then the hum of the ship's engine cut out. O'Mara paused, listening intently but hearing nothing further but the lapping of waves. A smile crinkled the sides of her mouth. That was the sounds of waves splashing against a shore.

She turned back to the mirror and resumed cleaning herself. There were still some red stains in her hair, but short of a full shower she did the best she could to clean herself of Surjanto's blood. As O'Mara pulled the t-shirt over her head, she surveyed the hold. Bloodied, half devoured bodies lay where they had been discarded by their voracious killer. O'Mara could barely believe she had slept so easily amongst this macabre mess of corpses.

O'Mara took one last look in the mirror before nodding to herself. It was not the best she had looked, of that there was no doubt, but for someone who had only recently been attacked and sprayed with blood, she looked okay.

Before exiting the hold, O'Mara eyed the rifles that lay with the bodies on the floor. She was tempted to pick one up and use it to threaten any pirates that may be waiting for her above deck, but she quickly pushed the thought aside. She did not know how to operate a rifle, and her holding one was more likely to get her shot at than to warn anyone off.

Picking up the last remaining bottle, O'Mara walked to the stairs, ready to finally leave the slaughterhouse that was the front hold of the ship.

As O'Mara climbed the stairs, the sound of lapping waves grew louder. She was convinced now the ship had run aground. But where? She could only wonder.

She stepped through the hatch and out into the morning sun. She turned, shielding her eyes from the bright light, to take her first glimpse of Bingwen Island. Despite being only a moderate size and existing far out at sea, Bingwen Island was rich with wild plant life. Trees stretched high, creating a thick canopy of leaves to shield the dark forest floor from the sun. Dark shapes flitted amongst the thick undergrowth at the base of the trunks of the taller trees, suggesting more life beyond that of plants here. There was a perfumed scent to the air, and O'Mara spied many purple and white flowers blooming around the edges of the undergrowth. The island looked very much like an idyllic paradise getaway; if only it did not have a container ship beached at its shore.

O'Mara was busy taking in the details when she heard a cough behind her. She turned to see Setiawan flanked by three men with rifles aimed at her on either side of him. Their eyes were aflame with hostility.

"So, we meet again Miss O'Mara," he said. "How very unfortunate for you."

O'Mara's eyes flitted about, searching the deck and containers that lay across it.

"If you are looking for your pet beast, it has abandoned you. It jumped off the bow of the ship and disappeared into the trees not long ago. Now tell me, have you seen Surjanto?"

"He's in the hold. What's left of him, that is."

Setiawan's eyes turned to the open hatch before swivelling back to O'Mara. "That was a very dangerous trick you pulled. I knew this ship contained a deadly cargo, but I could never have imagined that. I should have you killed for what you did. Eleven of my men have died here because of you."

O'Mara gave a hesitant smile and raised her hands. "But you won't, will you? You are not like Surjanto."

"No. You are right in that regard."

"Then what are you going to do?"

"Escape," Setiawan said, "and you are coming with us. You have cost us plenty already on this trip, the least we can do is get some of that back in ransoming you."

"You won't," O'Mara said defiantly. When he regarded her sceptically, she elaborated. "My parents both passed away some time back and my partner went overboard during your attack on the ship. God knows if he is even alive anymore."

Setiawan lifted a pistol. "Well regardless, your government will pay for your safe return. Now, we are getting off this ship. Move."

***

The morning light passed through the matrix of carbon crystal, bending and refracting as it struck against the multi-faceted surface of the stone to project the light back outwards. To the naked eye, this effect made the diamond, which sat set upon a delicate yellow gold ring, appear as though it sparkled like a night star.

"It's a beauty," Sanders said almost breathlessly.

"It sure is," replied Dower. "Though God knows if Jess will ever see it."

"You can't think like that," said Sianturi. "For all you know, she could still be aboard the *Kekal*, safe and sound and hidden away from the pirates. When were you going to ask?"

Dower's eyes dropped to the floor. "I... I'm not even sure I was... am... going to."

"But you have bought the ring. Surely that means you have committed to asking for her hand in marriage?"

Dower closed the small box and tucked it back into his pocket. He cleared his throat and scratched his head. "The thing is, I bought this ring over a year ago. I thought it the right thing for us, and it's something I very much want to do. But I guess I have just been too afraid to ask."

"Are you worried she will say no?"

"I've seen the way people look at us. They wonder why an attractive woman like her has settled for an old man like me. She's leagues ahead of me. Everybody knows it. I know it. Sooner or later, she will realise it too. And by fleeing in the forest like I did, I've probably brought that time even closer."

Sianturi cast a glance at Sanders.

"Hey, don't look at me," Sanders said. "I told him he was nuts already. Dower, listen, it doesn't matter what anyone else thinks, this is between you and her. You want to marry her, right?"

Dower nodded.

"And does she?"

"I don't know."

"And how will you find out?"

Dower turned away. "It's not that simple."

"Actually, it is that simple. All you have to do is ask her."

Dower stared out the open hatch to the rolling sea. He was starting to regret showing the ring and raising the discussion with the others. They did not understand his position. Jess was amazing, and he was… plain old him. He did not always feel this way about their relationship. At the start he had been carefree and running with the flow. But the more serious they had become, the more he had become aware just how they looked from the outside.

"What about you, Arwadi?" Sianturi asked and pointed at the gold ring on Arwadi's left hand. "You are married, perhaps you can give a better perspective on things than us."

Arwadi shook his head. "Don't think that because I am married I understand love or women better than you do. Take my wife. I understand her least of all people on the planet. Whenever I come home from a long trip at sea, she tells me how badly she misses me, yet when I stay home all she does is yell at me. 'Get your feet off that table'. 'Stop watching TV all day'. 'When are you going to finish painting the bedroom'. Sometimes I wonder if it's really me she misses, or the opportunity to yell at me."

Dower leaned forward and rubbed his temples. "Listen, guys, I really appreciate the support, but I really think Jess and I just need to sit and talk things through and…" Dower glanced at Sanders who was as alert as a cat on the hunt and staring at a point beyond Dower's shoulder. Cheong!

Sanders noticed the gap in the conversation and his eyes flicked to Dower. He mouthed the words 'keep talking'.

"Uh… yes," Dower stuttered, "Jess and I just need to talk on things and we go from there."

Dower's eyes flicked to Arwadi, and then to Sianturi. Both men had also become very alert and were staring at the same point Sanders had. Dower continued to talk, slowly turning his head as he did so.

"I tried talking to her on the ship. But then the pirates came and that meeting was cut short. Probably for the better. I had no idea what I was going to say anyway."

Dower turned to see Cheong was finally succumbing to fatigue. Cheong was leaning against the side of the boat. His face was slack and his head nodded with the ups and downs of the rolling sea. The pistol rested on his leg in a loose grip.

Sanders eased himself to his feet and stepped lightly around Dower and over Mohede's body towards the prone form of Cheong. As he eased quietly forwards, Dower and everyone else in the ship found themselves holding their breath in anticipation. There was a dreadful creak as Sanders lifted a foot away from the sticky blood on the floor. He stopped, still as a statue, but Cheong did not rouse.

Dower's eyes flicked to the pistol, glinting as it sat on Cheong's leg like a precious jewel ready for the taking. His eyes then danced back to Sanders, who crept forward with delicate precision like a thief creeping upon the jewel in a museum, surrounded by red laser detectors and tripwires that would set off an alarm the instant he made a false step.

Just then the boat dipped and rocked harder as a bigger wave hit. Sanders reached out and placed a hand on the hull to keep balance. All eyes flicked to Cheong, fearing he would suddenly wake to find Sanders almost upon him. But rather than wake, Cheong instead had a long string of saliva fall from his mouth.

Dower let out a breath slowly and watched as Sanders took another step forwards. Another bigger wave hit and Cheong slid forwards before rocking violently back into a sitting position with his eyes snapping open. Seeing Sanders almost on top of him, Cheong's face screwed up with rage as he snapped up the gun. Sanders dashed forward, hoping to slap the gun from his hand and tackle him to the ground.

Sanders lunged, but as he did another wave hit. The boat rocked and Sanders lost balance. The attack could not have gone more wrong. Instead of leaping into Cheong, Sanders tumbled sideways and crashed onto the bench like a child belly-flopping into a swimming pool. Cheong skilfully jumped to his feet and swung the pistol around to aim at Sanders' head. Sanders barely had time to glance up to see the vile grin on Cheong's face before he pulled the trigger.

Sanders pulled his arms up to protect himself in a reflex action. But as the seconds passed without the expected sound or impact, Sanders pulled his arms away and looked up. Cheong was staring dumbfounded at a small flame that emerged from the muzzle of the gun. Sanders stared at the flame a moment before drawing himself back to his feet. Cheong tried to back away, but there was no place to go as he was backed up against the side of the boat. Throwing the useless pistol aside, Cheong clenched his fists and raised them defensively.

The fight was mercilessly short. Sanders caught Cheong's first punch with practised ease, and before Cheong knew what was happening, his arm was twisted behind his back and his face pressed against the side of the boat. Sanders turned to the others with a smile.

"Got rope?" he asked.

When Cheong was safely tied up, Sanders retrieved the pistol from the floor. He turned it over in his hands, looking at it at every angle before pulling the trigger once more to see the small flame shoot from the tip.

"This is a cigarette lighter. What the hell, Arwadi?"

Arwadi shrugged. "Okay, you got me. I'm a smoker."

"But you let him take control of us with it. Why?"

Arwadi gave a cheeky smile. "All part of a ruse. I knew one of you here had to be responsible for Mohede and the pirates. I had also come to the conclusion that the killer would also know where the pirates were going, and would want to get there themselves. And if the killer took control and led us to the pirates, they would also lead me back to my ship. All I want is to get back to my ship. So, to get there, all I had to do was lose the gun and the traitor would reveal themselves."

"Wait a minute. Did you let me get the pistol from you on purpose?"

"Do you really think I would be so foolish as to walk amongst you like that?"

Sanders glanced back down at the lighter and released the trigger to kill the flame. There seemed to be a look of disappointment on his face.

"So, what is the plan now then?" asked Dower.

Arwadi stood, walked back to the helm and began checking the boat's bearings. "We continue to Bingwen Island. If they are making a rendezvous there, then I can guarantee they are switching boats. We might be too late to stop them making off with your Horse Serpent, but I can still get my ship back at least." Arwadi bit his lip and turned to Dower. "And if we're lucky, we get your woman back too," he said in a softer voice.

Dower nodded and unconsciously clutched at the small box containing the engagement ring in his pocket. He could only hope.

21

A rough shove in her back sent O'Mara stumbling forwards. She kept her feet and turned to scowl at the pirate behind her. He responded in turn with a cold, merciless stare.

"Keep moving," Setiawan grumbled.

It had been almost an hour since the small band of pirates had clambered down from the beached ship and began their trek around the edge of the island. The ship had long been lost behind the curve of the coastline, and for all intents and purposes, they were now alone. Though it would have been quicker to cut directly through the middle, the thickly forested interior of the island seemed too dark and foreboding to enter. Particularly now it had a monster predator in the Horse Serpent loose and hidden within its depths.

The pirates were clearly discomforted by it. Even those who were not in the hold had heard what the beast had done and duly feared it. They might have appeared outwardly confident as they strutted along the beach of Bingwen Island, but if one dared take a closer look then you would see sweaty brows over restless eyes that continually darted to the trees on their left every few seconds, and their fingers nervously hovering over the trigger of their weapons.

It was hot on the beach and the going was hard. The sun was already climbing high into the sky and working its debilitating heat over the earth below. Matters were not helped by the thick, soft sands of the beach, which were like walking through quicksand.

O'Mara's stomach growled with hunger and her legs screamed with fatigue as they pushed her relentlessly on. She had no doubt the fatigue was equally draining at them, but they were driven to continue by the fear of what lurked beyond their vision in the trees.

O'Mara felt another rough shove in her back and this time she stumbled and fell to land on her hands and knees. Setiawan pulled the men to a stop as he stared darkly down at her.

"I need a drink and a break," O'Mara said.

Setiawan stared at her a moment with his hands on his hips. He said something in his native tongue, and the men around her dropped their gear and sat in the sand around her.

"We rest for five minutes," Setiawan said in English.

O'Mara nodded and flipped over onto her bottom to sit. Setiawan did not sit, but unscrewed his flask and took a short sip. He studied O'Mara a moment, then offered the flask to her. Despite her hesitations, she took the flask and took three long gulps from it. The water was warm and did not taste perfect, but she would have drunk anything in that moment to sate her thirst.

Setiawan crouched beside her and took back the flask. He took another small sip and tucked it back into the pouch on his belt.

"You mentioned earlier your partner went overboard during the capture of the ship. Was he in the rescue boat you released from the ship just before your capture?"

O'Mara glanced up sharply. "No. That was someone else. I released the rescue boat in the hope that it would somehow find my partner and he would be saved. Though I am not sure I can trust the man inside to have saved Dower."

"Oh? Why is that?"

This time it was O'Mara who studied him. "On the ship, after I regained consciousness, I was watching you. I suspected you were waiting for someone. An inside man, so to speak. That was Sianturi, and he was the man that was inside the rescue boat. It was supposed to be me inside, but he went in to check the gear and your man came. I panicked and released the rescue boat just before getting captured."

Setiawan's eyes seemed to shift and focus on some distant point. His hand disappeared under his beard and he scratched his chin thoughtfully.

"The name Sianturi is not familiar to me. Tell me, what makes you suspect he was our inside man?"

"The containers on the ship," O'Mara said. "They were all his. What kind of man pays for and travels with empty shipping containers between countries? A suspicious one, that's who."

Setiawan continued to stare and scratch for another few moments before pulling a small notebook and pen that had been secreted in his bandolier. He flipped the pad to a blank page and wrote the name 'Sianturi' on it. He closed the notepad and tucked it away before turning back to O'Mara.

"It was good of you to volunteer this information. It saves me from having to torture it out of you later. Tell me, is there anything else I need to know?"

O'Mara's eyes widened a little and she shook her head. "No, nothing else comes to mind."

Setiawan opened his mouth to speak again when he was cut short by a loud cracking sound coming from the forest behind him. The pirates were on their feet in an instant, raising their guns in the direction of the forest. For a minute they all stood, silent and still, watching and waiting. O'Mara strained her ears for another sound, but all that could be heard was the soft breaking of waves against the shore behind her. She recalled how silently the Horse Serpent had moved in the hold. It had crept up the stairs almost soundlessly, and neither she nor Surjanto had heard its return until it was too late. For all she knew the Horse Serpent stood there now, watching them from just a few feet in. Hell, she thought, it could well have followed them the whole way since the boat and they could never have known it.

There was another sharp snapping sound, like that of a twig breaking. O'Mara jumped and one of the pirates fired four rapid shots into the thick undergrowth. Setiawan roared for him to stop, and again quiet settled over the island. All eyes darted back and forth across the thick undergrowth in front of them, searching for any sign of movement or life. Setiawan said something, and the man who had fired the shots turned with a look of horror on his face. Setiawan motioned to the trees and repeated the order. The pirate closed his eyes and gulped hard before turning back to the trees and slowly walking forwards.

At the edge of the tree line, the soldier looked briefly back. Setiawan motioned him on. Looking downcast, the pirate turned back to the trees to step under their cover. Within seconds he had disappeared out of sight under the thick canopy.

On the beach, it was easy to track his progress as he bustled noisily through the undergrowth. The constant snapping of twigs and brushing of leaves was clear and audible to those on the beach. The pirates on the beach remained quiet and eyed their surroundings nervously. Suddenly, the man in the forest called back. Almost immediately the tension amongst the pirates eased as they lowered their weapons and dared to cast smiles amongst one another.

"What happened?" O'Mara asked, confused.

Setiawan turned with a relaxed smile. "He shot and killed a monkey," he laughed.

O'Mara turned to see one of the pirates dancing around and pretending to be a monkey while another ran away from him in mock fear. It lightened the mood considerably and soon others were commenting and laughing.

Suddenly there was a loud roar followed by a dire, blood curdling scream. The scream was barely two seconds long when it was dramatically cut short.

The jovial mood of the pirates died in an instant as the pirates turned their guns back towards the forest. The silence returned, and as O'Mara looked into the forest, she had the eerie sensation she was being watched. She flicked her eyes up into the trees, but there were certainly no monkeys looking on.

"Get up," Setiawan ordered in English. "We have to move."

O'Mara pulled herself to her feet and found herself being hustled forwards as Setiawan ordered the men to move on. Back into a forced march, O'Mara pushed forward through the thick, draining sand with one eye on the thick forest to her left. The pirates around kept their eyes and guns aimed at the forest, and as O'Mara pushed on, she realised it was not just a feeling. She knew they were being watched.

***

There had been a great deal of excitement when Arwadi first declared the island and his ship had come into sight. Excitement for everyone, that is, except for Cheong, who watched with impassive eyes.

Sanders had been the first with the binoculars, hanging out the side hatch and casting them over both the ship and the island. There was little detail to be made out at that range, but he spent a good two minutes studying the scene before passing the glasses on.

As they closed, details became clearer. Many men were gathered on the decks of the ship, many waving to the small craft as it approached. Arwadi took a look through the binoculars and was quick to confirm it was his crew he saw. When asked if he had seen any sign of O'Mara, he only shook his head sadly.

The closer they got to the ship, the more the others let Dower stay with the binoculars and scan all the people on deck, lest O'Mara suddenly appear. But she did not. Sanders found himself wanting to comfort Dower but had no idea what to say. If O'Mara was still alive, she was not here. It was a disturbing thought for them all.

When they were close to the ship, Arwadi gave the wheel to Sianturi before snatching the glasses from Dower. He could see the ship clearly listing to one side and was eager to inspect the damage. But without divers to check underneath the waterline, there was no way of telling how badly the ship's hull was damaged during its beaching. That did not stop Arwadi from releasing a colourful string of adjectives to describe the situation and what he would do to the pirates if he caught one, however.

As the rescue boat pulled up alongside the ship, a rope ladder was thrown down from below. Arwadi was first up, closely followed by Dower. At Sanders' insistence, Sianturi was next up. Sanders watched him go, still not ready to trust him despite his claim that he was Higson's man. When Sianturi was gone, Sanders turned to Cheong.

"You're staying here, Kenny. For your own safety, I think. I don't know what happened on the ship since we were last here, but I'm betting Arwadi isn't the only racist on board who might have a score to settle with the man who brough the pirates to them."

Cheong said nothing and looked away, refusing to meet Sanders' eyes. Sanders stepped forwards, checking the bindings were still tight, before leaving out the rear of the rescue boat and disappearing up the rescue ladder. The moment he was out of sight, Cheong began wriggling at his bonds.

Sanders swung his big frame on deck to find the captain surrounded by a dozen men all babbling at once. He turned away to see Dower staring towards the front of the ship. Sianturi had one hand placed on his shoulder.

"What happened?" Sanders asked.

Sianturi turned with a look of worry written in his eyes. "The crew say O'Mara led a number of pirates to the front of the ship. They don't know what happened next, only that less than half the pirates returned with wild tales about a green monster tearing their ranks apart."

"She led them to the Horse Serpent."

"And set it free it seems. It was a brutal trick that killed many pirates."

"And O'Mara?"

Sianturi looked a little uncomfortable and glanced quickly at Dower before continuing. "They don't know. She never returned with the surviving pirates."

Sanders looked towards the front of the ship where the front hold lay. He took a deep breath before turning back to Sianturi.

"What of the surviving pirates? Where are they now?"

"They left not long after the ship beached on the island. They'd be halfway across it by now you would think."

Sanders nodded, taking the information in.

"We have to check the hold," Dower said. Sianturi and Sanders turned to him. "I have to know if she is there."

"I can do it," Sanders offered. "You don't have to come… just in case."

"No, I will go down. I have to."

The three of them began a slow walk down the centre of the ship towards the front hold. Dower kept his eyes forward and his face a mask. Sanders glanced inside the empty shipping containers as they passed them and shook his head with amusement.

As they closed on the hold, Dower stopped suddenly.

"What is it?" Sanders asked.

"The hatch. It's open."

Sanders glanced up to see that was indeed the case.

"Then the Horse Serpent…"

"Is loose," Sianturi said, finishing Sanders' sentence. "But where?"

But instead of answering, all three men looked up at the thickly forested island in front of them. A smile slowly formed on the lips of Sanders as he surveyed the perfect hunting ground for a forest predator.

"Go, you good thing," he mumbled softly. "Give 'em hell."

22

They had been jogging for thirty minutes when Setiawan called the men to a halt. All of the pirates were covered with a gleaming sheen of sweat, though whether the sweat came from the heat or from fear was debatable.

"It's only a short break to catch our breath," Setiawan explained to O'Mara in English. "Then we get moving again."

"Do you think it is safe to rest?" O'Mara asked.

Setiawan turned away, showing he had no intention of answering the question. He unbuckled the water bottle and unscrewed the cap as he scanned the forest. This time Setiawan did not offer his bottle to O'Mara, but took his own refreshing drink before tucking the bottle back away. The pirates slunk into the sand, sitting and panting. One particular pirate, red faced and a little overweight, was breathing particularly hard as he collapsed into a lying position. O'Mara had to look away to hide the smirk as she stretched her hamstrings to keep the blood flowing through them. Her legs were aching from the heavy work, but she was faring better than some.

As O'Mara stretched, she found herself again restlessly scanning the trees. The feeling of being watched had not left her, so much so that the hairs on her arms stood up with prickling awareness. She wondered if the sensation was indeed from the Horse Serpent, crouching in wait just beyond their eyesight within the dark folds of the forest, or just the monkeys that were native to this island.

At the thought of the monkeys, she glanced up into the higher branches above. If there were monkeys here, they were hidden now. But that beggared the question: who are the monkeys hiding from? From the men, or something far more deadly?

Setiawan did not sit like the others. He watched O'Mara peculiarly as she stretched before turning and beginning to pace back and forth across the hot sand, eyeing his men impatiently. O'Mara watched as he checked his watch four times in a minute. He was eager to move on, and she did not blame him. She wondered if he had the same sensation of being watched.

At last, Setiawan grew impatient of the waiting and ordered an end to the rest. The pirates pulled themselves to their feet and began easing back into a jog along the sand. O'Mara turned and settled back into a rhythm when she heard a shout from behind. Setiawan mumbled something before calling the group back to a halt. O'Mara turned to see the red faced, slightly overweight pirate from earlier walking well behind with the shoelaces on one boot hanging loosely.

Setiawan called to him and he acknowledged with the wave of a hand. He unslung the rifle from his shoulder and placed it in front of him before crouching down to attend the undone shoelace. One of the pirates near O'Mara made a remark, bringing snickers from another. O'Mara herself repressed a smile as she looked back at the final pirate. Then the smile died from her face.

The shoe-tying pirate had stopped, frozen, and his hands were shaking. As O'Mara watched, the pirate slowly turned his head to the trees. O'Mara felt the hairs on her arms stand up with renewed vigour.

Suddenly a flash of emerald green detached from the trees and launched upon the crouched pirate. He raised one arm up in a feeble defence as the Horse Serpent pounced on him. The Horse Serpent caught the pirate's arm in its mouth as its two front paws crashed into his body. The Horse Serpent then wrenched its head back pulling the pirate's arm clean off his torso as it crashed down feet first.

The pirate screamed in agony as the Horse Serpent flung the removed arm aside to bite down on his neck.

O'Mara was mesmerised by the attack when she felt someone grab her fiercely by the arm and pull her forward. The spell broken, she looked up to see Setiawan had grabbed her and was forcing her into a sprint. She staggered a few steps before settling into a pattern and Setiawan released his grip. As she ran, she looked at the faces of the pirates around her. Their eyes were wide with fear. These men knew they were being hunted.

O'Mara turned to look back behind her. Far behind, the dead pirate lay face down on the sand with a growing red stain around him as the blood flowed too quick for the sand to absorb. But the dead pirate was the least of their worries. The Horse Serpent had taken up the chase and was hot on their heels in pursuit.

O'Mara turned and pushed herself to run faster. The thick sand made it difficult and she veered closer to shore where the sand was dense with water and harder packed. She glanced out at the water, wondering if it would be safer out there. Then she discarded the thought. Though she had never seen the Horse Serpent swim, its massive paws could no doubt push it through the water much faster than any of them could move.

O'Mara hastened a look back. The Horse Serpent was closing. Only Setiawan and one other pirate ran in front of her while the other three lagged behind. The one at the very rear began to panic. He called to the others and appeared to be pleading. As O'Mara cast another glance, she saw his eyes were screwed tightly shut and it appeared he was crying.

The lead pirate in the race must have taken pity on his mate, and O'Mara saw him twirl the gun from his shoulder and check it over. Within a second he stopped and turned, raising the rifle to his shoulder to aim. O'Mara had to veer further to her right to avoid not only the line of the gun, but also prevent herself from running straight into the man. Her feet splashed water and she stumbled as she passed the gunman.

O'Mara was barely a few strides past the pirate when the first reports from the gun rang out. Setiawan turned and shouted to his men, no doubt urging them to run, not engage. O'Mara turned too, but the man with the gun stood his ground. The beast was not far from the last pirate now, and as O'Mara watched, the Horse Serpent's neck stretched forwards and the beast opened its mouth wide. The pirate screamed as the jaws of the Horse Serpent clamped on his shoulder and hoisted him off the ground.

The pirate with the rifle found no clear shot as the Horse Serpent continued to run with his mate in its mouth. The man continued to scream in agony as the bouncing motion of the beast's run caused his wounds to jar painfully where the beast held tight.

The gunman bit his lip and begged forgiveness to the wind before plugging two shots into his friend to end his misery. But it did not stop the beast. The gunman turned, trying to sling his rifle back over his shoulder and break back into a run. He looked up to see Setiawan and the others were well ahead of him now.

He pushed into a run, but as he did, he realised he had left it until too late. The beast was behind him and full of charging momentum. The beast was almost on top of him. He called for help but it was too late.

O'Mara turned away as the pirate was trampled under the great weight of the Horse Serpent. The pirates around her were breathing hard, and one started losing his gait when Setiawan called for them to slow down. O'Mara eased to a walk before taking a look back to catch a quick glimpse of the Horse Serpent disappearing back into the trees with the corpses of the two men.

Somehow O'Mara knew that was not the last she would see of the beast.

***

The smell in the hold was almost unbearable. All around corpses lay, some half devoured and others just simply going bad in the tropical heat that permeated the hold. Further, bloated flies with bulbous eyes had already been drawn to the smorgasbord of human meat in their droves and were crawling gleefully over the exposed flesh and blood.

Dower, with one hand holding a cloth over his nose and mouth, was desperately swatting them away from the foul carrion as he tried to identify the bodies. It was a grim task, and so far, thankfully, all of the bodies he had looked at were men.

Pulling back from the most recent grim cadaver, that of a headless man, Dower approached the truck and leaned on it for support. He felt bile at the back of his throat and swallowed it back down. But whether he felt sick from the foul, macabre scenes of death around him, or from fear the next body he looked at would be that of O'Mara, he just could not say.

"Another pirate," Sanders called from not far away. "Only a couple more to go."

No doubt the words had meant to be reassuring, but Dower felt anything but. The sheer brutality of the killings in this hold were well beyond anything he could have imagined. He had seen the Horse Serpent partially in the forest, and it had killed with ferocious precision that day, but he had not seen the corpses of the victims close up like this to understand how ruthless and effective the Horse Serpent was as a killing machine.

Dower glanced across to see Sanders following a trail of intestines across the floor to another body when he turned away. He looked up at the cab of the truck, wondering if there was any water still inside. As he approached the cab, he noticed a pale blue cloth on the ground in front of him. It was torn and covered in spattered blood. Dower bent down, recognising the cloth immediately. It was the shirt O'Mara had worn the last time he saw her.

Dower picked up the cloth from the floor and stared at it for a long moment as he felt the cloth between his fingertips.

"I think that's all of them checked," Sanders said, surprising Dower at his sudden appearance at his side. "They are all pirates. What's that?"

"It's Jess' shirt. The one she was wearing last time I saw her. It was lying right here on the floor."

Dower's eyes started filling with tears and Sanders clapped his arm around his shoulders. "Easy, mate. Finding the shirt but not her is a good thing. She probably took it off and discarded it. She's not here, mate. These bodies are all pirates. There is still hope."

"But the tear and the blood…"

"Are not related," Sanders cut in. He leaned forward and pointed at some of the drops on the shirt. "Look here. This is blood spray. It's on the outside of the cloth. This wasn't caused by a wound on the wearer, this was the wearer getting hit by blood. Don't assume anything. Not until we have found solid evidence."

Dower nodded and wiped his eyes with the back of his hand.

"Come on, let's get out of here. This isn't a healthy place to be."

As they climbed out of the hold, they saw Sianturi approaching with two thick ropes coiled over his shoulder and another thinner one in his hand with a frayed end. As he got closer, Sanders pointed to the frayed end in his hand.

"That one is no good," he said.

"Indeed, it's not," Sianturi agreed. "I have bad news. This was the rope you used to bind Cheong."

"What?" Sanders said sharply as his face reddened.

"Arwadi sent two men to retrieve Cheong from the rescue boat. From what I can gather, there was about to be a little trial and retribution occurring here on deck. But when they got down there, Cheong was gone and the ropes were found like this. Perhaps we should have emptied his pockets. He might not have dropped the knife he killed Mohede with after all."

"Damn it," Sanders cursed and stepped forward to slam his open palm against the nearest shipping container. There was a soft hollow boom from the impact. Sanders paused a moment, then turned to take the ropes from Sianturi.

"What are you planning to do now?" Sianturi asked.

"Well," said Sanders, taking the ropes and slinging them over his own shoulder, "I plan to go onto the island and recapture the Horse Serpent. And if I find that little rat bastard Cheong, I'll bring him back too."

"And the pirates?"

"I don't think I have enough rope for them. They'll have to stay put until I come back with more."

Despite himself, Sianturi found himself smiling and shaking his head in wonderment. "Are you sure you are up to this with that injured leg?"

"I just popped another couple of painkillers. I'll be fine."

"I'm going too," stated Dower.

Sanders and Sianturi turned in surprise.

"Are you sure, mate?" Sanders asked.

Dower was chewing his lip and glancing about nervously. He looked up and met their gazes. "I have to. This…I… I just have to."

"It's okay, mate. I get it. We'll go together and we'll find her. Don't worry about that. What are you going to do, Sianturi?"

"I'm staying here. The captain says the comms on the ship are ruined and we are stranded. But I may just have an ace hidden up my sleeve."

Sanders raised a questioning eyebrow but Sianturi responded with a quick wink before turning away. Sanders shrugged and turned back to Dower.

"Are you ready?"

"As ready as I'll ever be."

"That's the spirit. Righto, let's get moving then."

***

Cheong had long passed the pretence of keeping up appearances. He had discarded the suit jacket with matching pocket square not long after creeping ashore, and now he stopped to roll up the sleeves of his shirt. He would never have looked this untidy publicly, but he had to do what the situation called for, and it was too damn hot to be dressed like that on a tropical island like this.

He tucked the two cufflinks in his pocket. They were solid gold. He may need to use those for currency or bribes later on. He checked his gold watch worked as well before slipping that off too and sliding it in with the cufflinks. He had plenty of money in the bank, but that was no good for buying his way out of here. Because that is what he would have to do now. As far as he saw it, there was only one way of escaping this island and the situation he was now in, and that was fleeing with the pirates.

Thankfully the pirates had left an obvious trail for him to follow. Bingwen Island was devoid of human life, so the footprints in the sand could only have come from one source. He frowned as he followed them. There were far less pirates than he had expected.

Cheong half walked, half jogged as he followed the footprints in the sand, when he found himself slowing to stop at an odd sight. One set of footprints disappeared into the undergrowth and did not return. He looked up, trying to peer between the thick greenery as he wondered what had happened.

Cheong looked back along the beach, then cupped his hands over his mouth and called out. "Hello?"

He waited a few seconds but there was no response. Considering it a moment, Cheong glanced quickly the way he came before diving between the trees.

Almost immediately he felt cooler, shaded under the thick foliage from the sun. There was silence around him as he stepped deeper in. The sand gave way to reedy clumps of grass and the trail of footprints disappeared. Cheong stopped, thinking he may be wasting his time here, when he became aware of a noisome buzzing. He followed the sound, and after a few steps he was assaulted by the thick stench of blood.

A fat fly landed on his face and he brushed it away angrily. The pests seemed to swarm all around him now, and he thought he may be missing something when he turned and caught a glimpse of bright red blood spattered on the leaves of a palm. Stepping forward and pushing the fronds aside, Cheong gasped at the bloody mess before him.

The pirate lay on his back, his blank eyes staring emptily up at the trees above. But for a curled moustache, the man was clean shaven. His body was intact, but the gap between his chin and his collar was a hollow red mess swarming with hungry flies.

Cheong turned away, willing himself not to vomit. He had often been described as a bloodthirsty businessman, but he never had the stomach for real blood.

Taking a deep breath, Cheong turned back to the corpse to search it, carefully avoiding the bloody mess of a neck. In the pirate's bandolier Cheong found a water bottle and a holstered pistol. He took both of these. On the belt he found a handheld radio. Unclipping the radio, Cheong stepped away from the body and returned to the beach. He took a quick swig of the warm liquid from the bottle and scowled with discontent.

"The sooner I get back to civilisation the better," he mumbled and re-capped the bottle. He tucked the pistol in the back of his pants and resumed following the footprints in the sand while studying the handheld radio. He flipped the switch and was greeted by the hiss of static. He held the radio to his face and depressed the button on the side.

"Hello?"

Static. He tried again.

"Hello?"

More static.

"Hello? Is there anyone who can hear me?"

The radio hissed and Cheong looked down at it with disdain. He turned it over, wondering if he needed to change the frequency or find some other switch to make it work when suddenly the static stopped and a gruff voice came through the speaker.

"This is Setiawan speaking. Who the hell is this?"

Cheong licked his lips and smiled. He knew the name. Setiawan was the man who had been organised to lead the raid on the ship. Cheong raised the radio to his face once more as confidence bloomed inside him.

23

The small lagoon was a quiet and relaxing place. Surrounded by tall trees and open to the sea only by a narrow inlet, the waters were calm and protected by the elements. Three boats lay bobbing in the gentle waters of the lagoon. Two were speedboats, much like the chaser boats the pirates had used to hunt their quarry in the South China Sea. The last boat was much larger, with a long front deck allowing it to transport a small shipping container if it needed to. All three boats sat on the far side of the lagoon, much to Setiawan's dismay.

Setiawan eyed the trees surrounding the lagoon with suspicion. The Horse Serpent had ambushed them more than once by secluding itself in the thick undergrowth. He was certain he could not trust the appearance of safety here either.

But the scene was so serene it was hard not to be lulled into a sense of security. All was quiet and still. Suddenly Setiawan's radio crackled to life.

"Hello?" came a voice through the small speaker. Setiawan looked around in alarm, fearing the noise may have attracted an unwanted predator. Well, one in particular. But there was no movement around him except the gentle swaying of leaves and branches in the soft breeze.

"Hello?" the voice came again. Setiawan pulled the radio from his belt and eyed it curiously. As far as he knew, all his men other than the two left with him here now were dead. He glanced up at the boats, wondering if someone had stayed behind to watch them and was waiting for him now.

"Hello? Is there anyone who can hear me?"

There was no movement from the boats. The radio signal was not coming from there. He frowned. Someone had to be playing games with him. He lifted the piece to his face and clicked the button.

"This is Setiawan speaking. Who the hell is this?"

"My name is not important. All you need to know is that I know who you are, why you are here and where you are headed. On the north side of this island there is a small lagoon with boats waiting for you. I know who put them there and I know who you work for. Do I have your attention now?"

"I'm listening."

"Good. I have a situation and I also need to get off this island. I have gold with me now and I can get you more money later if you can help me. You are to wait for me at the boats. Understood?"

Setiawan dug one hand into his beard and scratched at his chin. He studied the boats and turned to his last two men.

"You two," he called them, "I want you to start walking around to those boats. Carefully. That monster might still be hiding here somewhere. Pick the one that looks the fastest and start her up."

"What are you going to do, boss?" one asked.

"I'll wait here with the girl. That inlet looks shallow. You drive the boat to there, and when you pull it up, we will wade across and get in."

The pirate glanced at the radio. It was clear he had overheard the conversation Setiawan had been having.

"Don't worry, I'll arrange it so that you both get a cut if this clown is who he says he is. Now move quickly and quietly. I don't want to stay on this island longer than I have to."

The two pirates moved off, trotting with their rifles ready as they started circumnavigating the sleepy lagoon. Beside him, O'Mara settled down to sit in the sand. The radio burst to life again.

"Are you still there, Setiawan?"

Setiawan scratched his chin and lifted the radio up once more.

"Yeah, I'm here. How much money are we talking to get you off this place?"

"Ten thousand US dollars."

Setiawan watched the two pirates walking at the edge of the lagoon. They seemed to be talking to one another. He hoped they were keeping their voices low. Idiots.

"It's not enough," Setiawan said into the radio.

There was a pause on the other end and Setiawan pulled the notepad he had written on earlier. He flicked to the appropriate page, quickly reading the name again before tucking it back into his pocket.

"Fifteen thousand."

"Come on, don't hold out on me. I need a lot more than that for me and my men. Besides, this mission has been a complete bust up and I know who you are. If you want me to keep quiet on how you screwed this up, you're going to have to give me a lot more than that, Sianturi."

At the sound of the name, O'Mara's head jerked up sharply. Setiawan smirked as he released the button on the radio and reverted to English. "Yeah, that's right, Sianturi. I got your old friend on the radio. It seems he's here on the island too and looking for a way off. I'm just organising your happy reunion now."

Setiawan chuckled and turned away to check the progress of his two men. He frowned as he saw no sign of them. His eyes tracked back to where they had been when he last looked, and he measured the distance to the boats. There was no way they would have covered the distance in that time. In fact, he doubted they would even have come to getting a quarter of the way there.

Part of the sandy beach surrounding the lagoonwas obscured from view from this angle by a low hanging branch, and Setiawan took a few steps forward to get a better view.

"Twenty-five thousand, and that's my final offer," came the voice from the radio.

"Sorry, Sianturi. You're going to have to start speaking six figure sums here before I wait around on this island longer than I need to. I can't justify risking my life for any less than that."

A couple more steps and Setiawan had moved past the leafy obstruction to see the full beach all the way to the tree line. There was no sign of his men anywhere.

"Fine. One hundred thousand it is. But on one condition. Tell me how you know my name."

"The blond bitch told me. Now hurry up, you've got ten minutes to get here or we're gone," Setiawan said and turned the radio off. He eyed the trees warily as he scanned for any sign of his men or the Horse Serpent. He took a couple of slow steps back, distancing himself from the trees as he did. He turned, quickly glancing at the lagoon and began shrugging off his rifle and bandolier.

"Ok, O'Mara, it's like this," he said, turning to where she sat. "We're going to swim across the lagoon to the…" His voice cut off as he realised he was alone. Sometime in the last few distracted minutes she had snuck away from him. He looked down at the sand to see a trail of deep footprints leading back along the beach they had just come from. The prints curved with the coast and disappeared behind the trees.

"Shit," Setiawan swore, turning from the boats to the footprints and back again. He knew after his failure here he needed money to disappear from the men who hired him. Could he trust this Sianturi person? Setiawan shook his head and cursed, before turning away from the boats to pursue O'Mara.

***

Cheong could not believe his luck. Sianturi? It was a perfect cover. All he had to do was maintain that identity and he might even be able to slip away from the pirates without paying and lose them forever. A grin crossed his lips.

"Fine. One hundred thousand it is. But on one condition. Tell me how you know my name."

He waited. If he was to maintain this false identity, he needed to know how he got it.

"The blond bitch told me."

Cheong stared at the radio in disbelief. O'Mara was still alive? The pirate leader must have plans to ransom her, he thought. It made sense. She was attractive and innocent looking. Once her photo got into the media, the press would be all over the government to do something. It was a good strategy but it had one problem for Cheong. She could identify that he was not really Sianturi. He depressed the button to talk again.

"Ok listen, make sure you have her tied and gagged before I get there. When she sees me, she'll go nuts and she can kick like a mule. Got it?"

Cheong waited for a response, but none came. After a minute, he lost patience.

"Setiawan, can you hear me? I want her tied and gagged," Cheong made sure he put a heavy emphasis on the word gagged, "before I get there. Tell me you hear this."

Again, there was nothing but silence. Cheong looked at the radio and cursed. He jogged on, hoping his message got through.

***

It had been easier to slip away from Setiawan than O'Mara had first thought. She had always planned to slip away, but at the moment she realised Setiawan had been speaking with Sianturi on the radio, she knew that the time had come for her to make a break for it. With the big pirate leader distracted by his conversation, O'Mara crawled a few feet to the harder, wet sand before climbing to her feet. Setiawan was busy looking at his men on the other side of the lagoon, so she turned and ran.

O'Mara stretched into a sprint and did not look behind her. The curve of the island soon blocked any direct line of sight between her and Setiawan, so she continued to run on the hard sand by the water's edge. Occasionally she glanced at the thick trees and scrub, but as she ran, she had that same sensation from earlier that made the hairs on her arms stand up and she was certain she was being watched.

A gunshot rang out behind her.

O'Mara ducked her head reflexively before turning to look behind. She saw the bearded pirate leader coming around the curve of the island in pursuit. Setiawan had his pistol raised above his head but when he saw her turn, he pointed it forwards in her direction.

O'Mara cursed to herself. She had hoped Setiawan had chosen to flee over chasing her, but evidently the lure of her ransom was stronger than the quick escape.

O'Mara pushed harder. Her legs ached with fatigue and she was weak from not having eaten any breakfast, but she hoped that if she sustained this sprint for long enough the pirate leader would lose the will to chase and take the chance to escape.

There was a second loud bang and a plume of sand fountained up from the ground a few feet to her right. She cursed. Setiawan was clearly not the giving up easy type. So much for that theory. She glanced quickly over her shoulder to see he had resumed the chase.

Sweat prickled O'Mara's skin and she was desperate for a drink. She was already feeling the early effects of dehydration as she sprinted over the hard sand. Behind her Setiawan yelled and cursed. There was another gunshot and this time the spurt of sand from the beach was closer than before. She hastened another look over her shoulder. But she looked at the wrong moment. The beach in front of her curved left and she found herself ploughing into thick, soft, dry sand. The sudden change in footing sent her stumbling forwards. She battled to keep her feet, but a sudden pain in her ankle sent her crashing forwards onto her hands and knees into the ground.

Setiawan let out a rousing cheer that was suddenly cut short. She looked back, expecting him to be almost upon her, but instead she saw him pulling to a rapid halt. The whites of his eyes were visible as his eyes bulged, staring at something beyond O'Mara.

Suddenly she felt a chill of fear. The hairs on her arms stood tall. She slowly turned to see two great clawed emerald feet in the sand just two feet from her own hands. She followed the line of the beast, up its muscular legs, over the heaving torso, higher still along the long, curved neck to the great horned head of the Horse Serpent. Its two yellow focused on her as the creature emitted a low growl.

24

A long trail of ants had plunged from the covered safety of the dark forest and across the sparkling white sand, drawn to a platter of meat chunks and blood stains close to the water. Dower knelt down as he watched their industrious trail as they ran backwards and forwards in their hundreds, scrounging whatever food they could from this site of slaughter.

Sanders was less interested in the ants, but rather the displaced sand that indicated the comings and goings of people and Horse Serpent alike.

"Here's what I think happened," Sanders said as he returned to stand over Dower. "A few feet back there, the Horse Serpent must have ambushed them. Most ran, but it seems like one must have stayed behind. Probably shooting. This is where the Horse Serpent killed the first, and just over there the second two."

"And the others?" Dower asked.

"The Horse Serpent didn't pursue them. At this stage we can assume they have escaped for now."

Dower bit his lip. "And Jess?"

"I would have to assume she was not one of these two. She wouldn't have been the shooter, and I doubt one would have stopped to shoot if it was her. I'd say the three who died here were friends."

Dower stood and brushed the sand from his knee. He turned and looked at the trail of footprints in the sand, wondering which of them could belong to O'Mara. As odd as it was, he wished he knew which one of the line of prints was really hers. He shook his head. A simple footprint should not mean so much. He should not get so sentimental about a mark in the sand.

"And where are the bodies now?" Dower asked.

Rather than answer, Sanders followed the line of larger prints leading away from the body and over to the trees. He stopped just at the edge as he waited for his eyes to adjust to the shade.

"Have you heard of animals storing food?" Sanders asked.

"Of course. Many animals do it. Particularly those in harsh seasonal climates that know there will be a long time until food is next plentiful."

"Do you think the Horse Serpent would be one that qualifies for that category?"

"No, why?"

Sanders waved the question away. "Okay then, suppose the Horse Serpent did a quick tour of the island and realised food was scarce. Do you think it would then start storing food?"

"That would require quite an advanced intelligence for an animal to make those deductions. What exactly are you getting at, Sanders?"

"That the Horse Serpent took the bodies away for a reason. It's storing them. I bet if I follow this trail through the forest, I'll find a nest or something like it. Back on Java it had its cave. Somewhere here it's made a new home and has taken the meat there."

Dower nodded and glanced north along the beach. "Listen, this is really interesting and I'd love to hypothesise more on this later, but don't you think we ought to get going after Jess?"

Sanders sucked a breath in through his teeth. "Actually, I was thinking we should split up. If I'm going to catch the Horse Serpent again, I'll only do it by setting up an ambush at its nest or whatever it has. I'm only going to find it by following the trail here."

"But Jess…"

"You keep chasing her," Sanders said, then suddenly dived forward into the scrub. Dower watched a moment, confused over whether the decision had been made and enacted when suddenly Sanders remerged from the greenery holding a rifle up like a trophy.

"Here," Sanders said, "take this."

"But I have no idea how to use one," Dower protested.

"Look here. This is the safety. This is how you set it on semi-automatic. That means each pull of the trigger will shoot one shot. And here is how you set it on fully automatic. I'd suggest you don't use that, you'll run through your bullets too quickly."

Dower looked down dumbfounded as Sanders flicked the rife back to safe and placed it in his hands.

"Are… Are you sure about this?" Dower asked.

Sanders looked down and then glanced back at the forest. "I know it's not ideal, but if I don't get ready to catch the Horse Serpent back where it is taking the bodies, I might not catch it at all. The Horse Serpent is hunting them and will take their bodies back to the one location. I have to get there before it runs out of bodies to hunt."

Dower nodded and looked down at the gun.

"Listen, Dower, there is one other thing I wanted to say. All this stuff in your head about you thinking you are not worthy of Jess… you have to end that today. For whatever reason that you ran, it doesn't matter. Self-preservation is a natural instinct. That whole fight-flight thing. So you think running means you aren't worthy of her? Well, listen up. Today you can change all of that. You can prove you are worthy by acting like you are worthy. Don't pass up what today offers you. You have to redeem yourself for running away. It may not mean you two end up getting married, but at least you can hold your head up high and know that you deserve to have her at your side. And if it means anything, Dower, then you should know I think you are worthy of her. Do you understand what I am saying here?"

Dower stared at the gun in his hands. He closed his eyes and took a deep breath before nodding. Sanders slapped him on the shoulder.

"Good. Now, I want to be clear. I'm not asking you to be stupid here and get yourself killed, but if Jess means as much to you as you say, then you fight for her. You got it?"

Dower looked up to meet Sanders' eyes before nodding again.

"Good. Now, we'd both better get going if we are to get on top of things here."

Dower nodded and turned away. He began following the footsteps when he stopped and turned back to Sanders.

"Hey, Matt," he called.

"Yeah?"

"Thanks."

Sanders nodded and watched Dower turn and resume following the footprints. He watched Dower walk a good minute. He wondered whether he had just made a good call or not. It was risky. Dower might just get himself killed. But Sanders did not see any other way around this. He had to act on his instincts now if he was going to recapture the Horse Serpent.

***

The Horse Serpent turned its head to one side, examining O'Mara through one slitted pupil as she cowered on hands and knees before it. The Horse Serpent was so close she could see her own fear-stricken reflection in its eyes and smell the blood in its breath. It opened its mouth slightly, revealing the sharp, bloodied teeth inside its mouth. A mouth so wide her whole head could easily fit inside. The beast lowered itself into a crouch, readying itself into an attacking position.

O'Mara grimaced and accepted her fate. It seemed somehow poetic that the very beast she had set free to kill others would wind up killing her too. It was karma. She only hoped there was an afterlife where she could reunite with Dower once more.

Suddenly the Horse Serpent jumped, leaping over O'Mara and landing with a heavy thump behind her. O'Mara had barely turned when she was flicked with sand as the Horse Serpent kicked into a run. Beyond the Horse Serpent, O'Mara saw Setiawan turn and run.

For a moment O'Mara watched the pursuit. The Horse Serpent gobbled up the distance between them hungrily, and it quickly became apparent that the pirate leader was in deep trouble. O'Mara turned away, not willing to witness the bloody end of Setiawan. Despite who he was, and that he had taken her prisoner, he had not been overly unkind to her and did not deserve the brutal end he was about to receive. That sort of end should be reserved for bastards like Surjanto.

Setiawan's screams were mercifully short. At least it gave him a quick death. Gathering herself, O'Mara looked up. She knew there was no point in running. If the Horse Serpent wanted to kill her, it would. She was tired, weak, dehydrated and hungry. She did not have the energy to run, and it would be pointless anyway. She had seen enough of the Horse Serpent's killing prowess to know this.

Ahead of her the Horse Serpent stood over the inanimate body of Setiawan. She saw its chest heaving as it breathed. It stood tall and was watching her. For a minute the two watched each other, before the Horse Serpent turned back to the corpse of Setiawan. It clamped its jaws around one leg and lifted the body with ease. Setiawan dangled from its jaws like a Christmas decoration for a moment before the Horse Serpent turned and approached the trees. Before disappearing behind the foliage, the Horse Serpent again took one last look at O'Mara. It held her gaze for a good few moments before finally turning and disappearing from view.

O'Mara released the breath she had been holding. She had not realised she had stopped breathing, but felt relieved by the fresh air that she now sucked down to her hungry lungs. The air tasted good as it reminded her that she was still alive.

Slowly O'Mara dragged herself to her feet. It took more effort than she cared to admit, but her internal candle was burning low and she was in desperate need of replenishment.

For a moment she stood, considering which way to go. She was still close to the lagoon, but she had no idea where the other two pirate goons had gone, nor did she have any idea how to operate a boat. In the opposite direction was the ship. It was the longer way, and despite the roaming Horse Serpent, getting back to the ship would somehow feel safer. After all, the crew surely would have radioed for help now they were back in control of the ship.

O'Mara turned, choosing the long walk to the ship over the pirates' boats. She wanted nothing further to do with the pirates or their belongings.

As O'Mara began her slow walk south, her eyes turned out to sea. The waves bounced and glistened as far as she could see. The events of the last twenty-four hours began playing back in her mind. Her vision grew misty as she thought about Dower. Was he still out there somewhere? It was unlikely. He probably did not even survive the night. Dower was a terrible athlete and an even worse swimmer. He would not have lasted long alone at sea.

There was no doubt in her mind that the traitor Sianturi would have left him and Sanders for dead. It seemed utterly unfair that she would never see either of them again. Now she would never know why he had run in the forest and she was at odds as to whether she could ever forgive him for the act. She wanted to scream. Scream at the world for its cruel and unjust ways. Scream at Sianturi and his treachery that led to the pirate attack. Scream at Dower for running away in the forest and then for not running on the ship and instead picking up the gun. And scream at herself for not taking the time to listen to him as they stood alone on the poop deck. That was the last time they would ever be together.

She wiped the errant tears from her cheeks and cursed her emotions. She was dehydrated enough without losing further moisture to tears. She walked on, trying to find something else to think about and distract her mind with. She thought of home, but home only reminded her of Dower and it would never be the same again. She thought of friends, but all her friends were mutual friends with Dower and she could not think about them without thinking about him. She cursed. As hard as she tried, everything she thought about would somehow turn back to Dower. Because Dower was her life, and she could not imagine it any other way than with him. It's why she would have forgiven him, no matter how lame his excuse for running was, if only she knew why.

As O'Mara passed a curve in the island, she saw a figure approaching ahead. Her eyes were too blurry to see, but she saw the figure raise its hand and wave. Hope suddenly surged inside. Someone had bothered to follow her. She suddenly smiled. Someone had cared enough to follow her. She began jogging forward. She knew it was fanciful to believe it was anyone but a member of the ship's crew, but fantasy took over as she ran forward with surging belief in miracles as her heart longed for the perfect end to this nightmare, and for this to be Dower himself walking down the beach to carry her away from this hell.

The distance closed and she wiped her tears away to see her saviour at last. But it was not who she expected to see. She ran forward and hugged him anyway, grateful, at least, not to have run into another enemy.

"Cheong," she exclaimed. "How did you get here?"

Cheong looked mildly uncomfortable from the hug before looking at his clothes in an embarrassed fashion. He began rolling down his sleeves and straightening his shirt.

"I never went anywhere. I hid on the ship where no one could find me and stayed hidden the whole time. I came out before and learned from the crew what had happened. It's very sad what happened to Mr Dower, Mr Sanders and the captain. I tell you, that scoundrel Sianturi is lucky not to be around, because I have some choice words for him. But tell me, Miss O'Mara, how is it you came to escape the pirates?"

O'Mara glanced at the trees. "The Horse Serpent ambushed and killed them one by one. Come, we shouldn't hang around, the Horse Serpent may be stalking us too. We need to return to the ship quickly."

O'Mara grabbed his hand and began to step forwards and pull him along with her.

"No," Cheong shouted, before clearing his throat and repeating it more calmly. "No. We can't go that way. The radio on the ship is broken and the ship is stuck in the sand. The pirates are all dead, you say?"

O'Mara nodded.

"Good. We need to find their boats. They may have a radio onboard and we can call for help. Tell me, before the Horse Serpent attacked, did you see where the pirates were going?"

"Better than that," O'Mara said and smiled, "I saw the boats themselves. There is an inlet to the north and the boats are in a small lagoon."

"Excellent. Do you suppose you could lead me there? It is our way out of this great mess."

"Of course," O'Mara said and turned to lead the way.

Cheong turned to check they were not being followed or spied on before walking after her. She turned to look at him and he smiled and motioned her on. When she turned forwards, he reached around to his back to where he had tucked the pistol into his belt. He pulled it out and quickly checked it before tucking it back away and allowing himself to smile.

25

Sanders looked around with frustration as he ran his fingers through his hair and cursed. He had lost the trail again. This had to have been the fifth time now. Despite the great bulk of the Horse Serpent, it knew how to move through thick undergrowth without leaving an obvious trail behind it.

Sanders had expected it to be easy. He expected a trail of destruction to be left in the Horse Serpent's wake. Broken branches. Bent ferns. Torn foliage. But the Horse Serpent was too lithe for that, despite its great bulk, and it had left Sanders frustrated.

Sanders looked upwards and found himself being watched from above. It was not the first time he had sensed his watchers. The small monkeys had been curious about him and had followed him from the first few moments he had entered the trees. They were white, but had black faces with inquisitive eyes and long tails. He hoped they would do more than watch. Even if they could not point out the direction of the Horse Serpent's nest, at least they could warn him if they sensed it approaching through loud, panicked screeching.

Sanders sighed and looked about. It was hard to get bearings this deep in the island's forest. There was no direct sunlight here, so he was no longer certain which way was north.

Then he spotted it. A splotch of blood on a leaf. He stepped towards the leaf and lifted it gently and dabbed his finger in the liquid. He lifted his stained finger to his nose and sniffed. It was definitely blood.

He pushed past the bush and continued to move forwards in search of the next vital clue when he became aware of a buzzing. He stopped immediately, trying to zero in on the sound. It was not the buzzing of one fly. It was the buzzing of many. He knew suddenly that he was very close.

He looked up into the trees for his monkey spies. He spotted one lazing in a nook of a branch watching him lethargically. He smiled, hoping that if the monkey was relaxed it was a good sign the Horse Serpent was not nearby. Or perhaps the little monkey was confident that even if the Horse Serpent was near, he was not in danger that high up in the tree. The smile died on Sanders' face. He hoped it was the former.

Focusing again on the buzzing, Sanders crept slowly forward through the thick undergrowth when he started to become aware of a smell. It was the smell of blood. Sanders spied a line of ants, just as he had seen on the beach, and began following them. The buzzing grew louder and Sanders pushed aside a great leaf to reveal the macabre sight of four dead bodies swarming with bloated flies and insects. The pirate bodies lay in a disorderly manner. Their limbs were twisted in uncomfortable positions as their dead eyes stared wide in shock. Great rents had been torn in each corpse, revealing what was undoubtedly their death blows. There was no sign that they had been fed on by the Horse Serpent yet, further fuelling Sanders' belief that the Horse Serpent did indeed intend to come back to these at a later point.

Behind the pile of bodies was a large rock, over which a tree had fallen. It provided partial cover, and Sanders was certain this was the start of a nest. The Horse Serpent was used to sleeping under the cover of a cave, and this fallen tree against the rock was the closest thing the beast must have found to its old habitat.

Sanders stared at the small place sadly.

"This isn't your home," he said softly. "This just isn't right. You don't belong here. There isn't the food or shelter that you need. I need to take you off this island for your own sake."

A monkey squawked above and he looked up sharply. But it was only the lazy monkey from before defending his nook from a newcomer who seemed to like the look of his spot. Or it was his sibling. Sanders remembered fighting with his brother over the best seat when he was young too. Sometimes people were not that greatly separated from their animal cousins.

Sanders turned away with a smile and started analysing the surrounding trees. Unhooking the rope from his shoulder and pulling the Bowie knife from his belt, Sanders started preparing for the Horse Serpent's return.

***

Dower had maintained the jogging pace for as long as he could but fatigue got the best of him and he dropped back down to walking pace. He was panting heavily as he reached for his bottle and took a drink. He cursed himself for not being fitter. He should have gone with Jess on her daily jogs, but he had always found an excuse not to. He had papers to mark. He had journals to catch up on. Someone released a paper on a newly discovered cryptid. There was always something. And now that he needed that fitness more than ever, he found all those excuses to be poor and shallow.

He looked down at his podgy belly. Nothing marked his lack of exercise like it. He had always thought bellies like his only belonged to heavy beer drinkers. But he did not like or drink beer. It was simply from his inactive lifestyle. One that he now regretted.

Despite the progress that Dower had made, he could not help but feel a sense of frustration. He had no way of knowing if he was any closer to O'Mara or not. Further, he did not even know if he was pursuing her either. There was one set of prints in the sand that was smaller than the others. They could be hers, but that could also be more hopeful thinking on his behalf than anything else.

The AK-47 felt heavy on his shoulder. He felt uncomfortable carrying it, not only because of the bulk of it, but also for what it meant. Sanders clearly expected there would be trouble ahead, but Dower had not touched a gun in his life before this trip and now he was expected to use one against experienced pirates. This was not some Hollywood film where the nobody picks up a gun for the first time and mows down swathes of enemies. This was real life, and Dower was more likely to shoot himself in the foot than kill a hostile.

Dower looked down at the prints again. Five sets of prints in total. One had to be Cheong. He was somewhere ahead too. If he assumed they still had Jess, then that was three pirates and Cheong. That is if the Horse Serpent had not gotten to them first. That made it four guns to one. Not only was he inexperienced, he was outnumbered and outgunned. He did not like the odds.

But he knew this time he could not back down. Sanders was right. This was his shot at redemption. Even if it meant he would have to die to prove himself worthy of Jess.

The thought of O'Mara spurred him on. Dower eased himself back into a jog, hoping he could close some ground on them.

This section of the coastline was quite curvy, forming S-shapes, giving Dower a large view ahead as he rounded one curve only to have a long walk before more of the beach was revealed. As he rounded one particular curve, he saw a long line of beach open up ahead that ended at the next curve. Rounding the curve far ahead, he saw a figure walking on the sand close to the shoreline. He recognised the figure immediately.

"Jess," he said breathlessly, before raising his voice to a yell. "Jess."

The figure kept walking. Dower called again but the figure disappeared behind the curve of the island. Dower cursed as he scanned the long stretch of sand between them, but his brief glimpse had given him hope, and hope urged him into a run.

Dower ran like he had not run in a long time. He did not know where the energy that filled his legs suddenly had come from, but he was grateful as he passed over the sand with urgency. He had not run like this since… since high school, he thought. Since that day he had to run from Billy Hartigan to avoid being beaten up. That thick headed lug nut bully Hartigan. God, he hated that guy.

The burst of sudden energy that filled Dower died quickly, but he pushed on regardless. He had seen O'Mara, and that was all he needed to drive him onwards.

He approached the curve he had seen her pass behind with surging hope. He was certain the sprint had closed the ground between them significantly. This time if he saw her and shouted, she was certain to hear him.

He rounded the curve, slowing a little to gather his breath. The curve was long, and he found himself impatient for it to end and for him to get a clear view forward. Suddenly, O'Mara came into view again, this time much closer than before.

"Jess," he yelled and broke into a run. "Jess, it's me."

He sprinted forward as O'Mara stopped to turn. She stood motionless, her eyes and her jaw hanging loosely as he ran to her. Tears started to fill his eyes and he wiped them away desperately. He could not take his eyes from her as he ran forward. She looked tired, bedraggled and shocked, but she could not have looked more beautiful to him in this moment. Everything was perfect until a second figure broke into his field of vision. Cheong.

Cheong stepped towards O'Mara and reached for something behind his back. Before Dower or O'Mara knew what was happening, Cheong had his arm around O'Mara's shoulders and a pistol pressed to her temple.

"Stop right there, Dower," Cheong roared.

Dower pulled to a stop, holding his hands in front of him to indicate surrender. "Easy, Cheong. Let's talk this through."

"Throw your gun away first," Cheong ordered.

Dower flicked the strapping off his shoulder and let the rifle fall into the sand at his feet.

"Now step away from the weapon."

Dower stepped forwards, closing the gap between himself and Cheong and O'Mara. Cheong sneered, but Dower noticed his eyes flick from Dower to the forest and back many times in quick succession.

"Where's Sanders? Is he hiding in the bushes or something?" Cheong asked.

"No, it's just me, Cheong. Now please, let's talk this through. There's no need for violence."

"What the hell is going on here?" O'Mara asked.

Dower's eyes turned from Cheong's sneer to O'Mara. She looked at him in a confused and frightened manner. He longed to run forward and hold her.

"Cheong was an imposter. He betrayed Higson and he betrayed us. He was the reason the pirates attacked the ship. He organised it all. He wanted to steal the Horse Serpent and use it as a weapon."

"Cheong was the imposter..." O'Mara repeated.

"Yes, and it wouldn't have had to come to this if you had done the right thing and gone home after catching the damn thing."

"Well, that's the thing about Jess. She cares for all animals that are put into her care. I should have known she'd never walk away." Dower turned back to Cheong. "Listen, Cheong, it doesn't have to go like this. I'm not after you. I just want Jess back. That's all."

Cheong bit his lip and again glanced at the trees. His eyes searched the line for a long moment. Dower took another step closer and Cheong quickly turned back.

"No. I need her. She's my leverage to get out of here, and after you and the others hog tied me in the rescue boat, I'm not taking any chances." Cheong turned to the trees and yelled. "You hear that, Sanders? I'm not handing her over so just stay back."

"Sanders isn't here. It's just me."

"Ha," Cheong yelled.

"It's just me, Cheong. You have my word on it."

"Shut up," Cheong shouted and pointed the gun at Dower.

O'Mara reacted immediately. She quickly lifted her arm and then slammed her elbow into Cheong's stomach. He reeled backwards and she clutched at his arm, pulling it free of her. Dower leaped forwards, stung into action by O'Mara's fight. The gun went off but the bullet flew harmlessly in the air as Cheong reeled from the blow. O'Mara pulled away from Cheong but he twisted his body to aim the gun at her. Dower closed and grabbed Cheong by the arm. A second shot was fired just as Dower crashed into Cheong. O'Mara heard the bullet whistle past her ear as she dove for the ground.

Then Dower and Cheong were grappling. Cheong grunted and cursed in frustration as he tried to turn the gun on Dower. Dower gritted his teeth, pushing against Cheong's arm as the barrel of the gun was forcibly turned towards him. A third shot was fired and Dower felt a sharp pull on his shirt. He braced for pain, but none came. The bullet must only have clipped his clothing.

A victorious smile broke on the face of Cheong as he pushed with renewed strength on the pistol. Dower looked down as the pistol was shakingly forced to turn on him. In desperation, Dower leapt forwards. Cheong was surprised by the move, and fell backwards to land heavily in the sand with Dower on top of him. As they landed, the gun fired a fourth time.

O'Mara screamed.

***

The sudden activity from the monkeys in the trees above him alerted Sanders of the approach. He glanced up to the monkey in the nook. The monkey stood and glanced to the side, before quickly jumping to another tree and disappearing from view. It could only mean one thing. The Horse Serpent was coming.

Sanders looked down at the ropes. It had only been a short time but he had used the minutes industriously. A network of ropes lay across the ground, forming a weblike trap of netting to ensnare the Horse Serpent once it stepped into its clutches. It was a similar trap to the first time he caught the Horse Serpent. He would reveal himself and tempt it into a charge, before using his network of ropes to trip and capture the great beast with his nooses. Sanders nodded, satisfied with his work and the job he had done in keeping it all hidden. He secreted himself behind a tree and waited.

The footfall of the Horse Serpent was incredibly soft for a beast its size, and it was only by the soft brushing of branches against its hide that Sanders was able to track its approach. This was not the first time he had seen it move, but he was again astounded by how light footed and agile it was at moving through the forest. No wonder he had found it hard to track.

When he felt it close enough, Sanders stepped out from his cover and in view. He stood just in front of his trap, with the Horse Serpent's hoarded food not far behind him. He was certain having its nest invaded would see the Horse Serpent charge.

But as he stepped from cover, the Horse Serpent stopped. It carried the dangling corpse of a bearded man in its jaws. Blood dripped down from the dead pirate's wounds as the beast stood and stared at Sanders. After ten seconds the Horse Serpent opened its mouth and dropped the dead pirate into a crumpling heap. Its tongue flicked out of its mouth as it cleaned its muzzle of blood.

Sanders tightened his grip on the rope for comfort as he waited for the moment the beast would charge. But the Horse Serpent remained still, studying him from a distance.

"Hey," Sanders called as he lost patience with the waiting. "I'm right here. What are you waiting for?"

The beast bowed its head and snuffed at the dead pirate before returning its gaze to Sanders. Slowly, it stepped forward towards him. Sanders cursed silently as he watched it pad slowly through the undergrowth, closing on his position. His whole trap had been built around the beast charging him. This was no charge. The Horse Serpent had learned.

As it neared, Sanders started to feel a nagging sense of self-doubt. If he could not trip the beast, it was going to be difficult to tangle it within his web of ropes. He glanced quickly down, revising his plan. He did not like having to revert to improvisation, but the situation required it. He glanced quickly back up to the Horse Serpent. He knew how he could draw it into his trap. He would need to run and draw it into a chase.

The Horse Serpent approached the tree with the first trip rope and stopped. It looked at Sanders a moment before looking down. It scratched at the ground and pulled at the rope, revealing the attempted trap.

Sanders let out a gasp. "Clever girl," he said breathlessly.

He took a step back and pivoted his hips. The Horse Serpent was close enough now. He had to run and draw it into the chase. Still holding the rope, Sanders let out a cry to ensure he had its attention before turning and breaking into a run. Almost immediately he heard a crash of undergrowth being pushed aside and he immediately turned to spring his trap. Only the Horse Serpent was not there.

The crack of a branch beside him alerted him to the Horse Serpent's presence. He had failed to lure it through the clearing, and it was now approaching him from the side.

"Shit!" Sanders cursed, and ducked back through the clearing. The trap had been intended for an approach from the front, but it would still work when approached from the side. He stepped over the network of ropes and turned to again face the Horse Serpent.

But the Horse Serpent had again stopped. It stood just beyond the trap, watching Sanders curiously. He looked into its big, yellow slitted eyes and admonished himself for not recognising the high intelligence it had earlier. He looked down at his trap with a sudden feeling creeping over him that it was completely useless. He glanced up to see the Horse Serpent again circling around to get to him.

Sanders watched the Horse Serpent and slowly backed across his ropes. He needed to try to keep it between himself and the beast. He stepped past the trap and his feet hit something behind him. The sudden flurry of buzzing flies told him he had backed up against the pile of corpses. He glanced down, seeing a discarded AK-47 lying not far from his foot. He regarded the weapon a moment. If he got it and fired it, there was a good chance it would enrage the beast into the charge he wanted. He could lure it into the trap.

He glanced back up at the beast and wondered. What if he could not catch it? What if it was too smart to be drawn into his trap? What then? It knew he could not continue this dance with the beast forever. Perhaps he would be drawn into the worse possible scenario here. Perhaps he would have to kill it.

He looked at the hard scales across the beast's hide. It had been marked by conflict but bore no signs of any serious injury. The AK-47s had only scratched the beast, but perhaps it was because they shot in panic. He looked up at the big yellow eye. Perhaps a targeted blow to a weak spot would be more effective.

Just then the Horse Serpent lowered into a crouch as if preparing to leap. Sanders put the thought of the AK-47 aside and adjusted his grip on the rope. This was it. This was the moment.

The Horse Serpent launched forwards, building momentum with every step. Sanders watched the beast approach, its thick muscles bulging with each powerful stride while the large head, perfectly balanced on the long neck, glanced down this predatory hunger and the mouth opened wide.

The Horse Serpent was almost on the net when Sanders pulled the rope. But the Horse Serpent had bluffed him. The beast turned at the last moment, its great feet skidding across the turf at the sudden turn as the beast pivoted sideways. Sanders looked on as his ropes grasped at clean air before falling back into the dirt uselessly.

But the beast was not done. The beast turned again, adjusting its position to run parallel to where Sanders stood. Sanders dropped the rope and glanced quickly about. His main trap had failed but there were trip ropes still in place. Perhaps he could still get it down and mount it as he had the first time.

Sanders turned to run to a new position when the Horse Serpent's tail flicked out and clipped his ankles. Swept from his feet, Sanders tumbled forwards and into a roll. He tried to use the momentum of the roll to leap back up into a run when the Horse Serpent's tail swept through again. This time Sanders was not able to twist into a roll and staggered sideways to fall.

Sanders grunted as he hit the dirt. He tried to pick himself up but found himself nudged in the side and forced to roll onto his back. The Horse Serpent placed a great paw on his chest and held him to the ground. Sanders looked up just in time to see the great maw of the beast coming down onto his head.

26

The gunshot still echoing in her ears, O'Mara ran forwards towards the two men on the ground. Dower had gone limp but his back still heaved as he gasped for breath.

"No!" O'Mara cried as she clutched Dower by the shoulder and rolled him off Cheong. Blood stained his shirt and he was breathing heavily.

"No," O'Mara repeated as tears clouded her eyes. "This can't be happening. Not when you just came back."

Dower reached up and cupped her face with his hand. He stroked her temple where the gun had been held gently with his thumb. "It's okay," he said, "I'm not shot."

O'Mara sniffed and wiped away the tears to look down. Dower's shirt was indeed stained with blood, but it was not his blood. She turned to see Cheong with his hands clutched to his stomach. Fresh blood leaked from between his fingers and he coughed weakly. The pistol was on the ground near his side and O'Mara snapped it up quickly and threw it aside.

Dower pulled himself up and leaned forward to hug her. She grasped him tight, almost squeezing all of the air out of him.

"Oh my God," O'Mara sobbed, "I thought I had lost you."

"Me too," gasped Dower as he held her tight.

They held each other for a long hug before O'Mara pulled away. She turned to Cheong and raised her fist aggressively. "And you," she roared.

Dower reached out and held her fist. "Don't."

O'Mara stared at him incredulously. "But after everything he did."

"No, Jess. You can't condemn him without knowing his story." Dower turned to Cheong and looked at him sadly. "I don't agree with what you did, or what you tried to do, but I understand. I only came for Jess. You are free to go on your way and make your escape."

Cheong looked up and coughed. Blood spattered his lips. "That's awfully generous of you, Mr Dower, but I'm afraid I won't make it."

Dower looked down on Cheong's quickly paling skin and knew it was true. The blood was leaking too quickly from the wound in Cheong's side and was pooling in the sand. Cheong coughed and more blood appeared on his lips. He smiled weakly. "I suppose you think I got what I deserved in the end, eh, Dower?"

"No, Cheong, I don't think that at all. Actually, I think quite the opposite. You deserved better than what you got in life. A lot better."

Dower placed his hand on Cheong's arm and gave it a reassuring squeeze. Cheong bit his bottom lip and looked up.

"You are too kind, Mr Dower. Too kind. Thank you for saying it."

Cheong coughed and shook violently. The process lasted only a few seconds as the life faded from Cheong's eyes. Dower pulled his hand back from Cheong as the blood flow slowed despite Cheong's hands falling limply away from the wound. Dower reached forward and closed Cheong's eyes.

"Hopefully now he finds peace," Dower said softly.

O'Mara stood up and looked at the trees. Dower stared at Cheong a moment longer before hauling himself to his feet and turning to Jess. He reached out and took her hand.

"Listen, Jess. There is something I have to say. I am so incredibly sorry for running away in the forest back in Indonesia. That whole incident has been running through my head day and night ever since and I…"

O'Mara placed her finger on his lips to stop him talking.

"Just tell me why you ran," she said softly.

"I ran because I'm a coward. But it wasn't the Horse Serpent I was afraid of. It was my future with you."

Jess snorted with laughter, but tears were prickling the corners of her eyes. "What do you mean scared of a future with me? Is the thought of spending the rest of your life with me so terrible? Or have you found another even younger former student you want to hook up with instead?"

"God no, Jess, it's not that at all. I am scared you will one day wake up and realise you can do better. I mean, do you really want to spend the rest of your life with an old man like me?"

"God, Simon, is that what this is all about? Do you think I'd be somehow better with someone else?"

Dower blinked away tears and glanced about. "Jess, I've seen how other people look at us. I know what they think. And they are so right. So, tell the truth Jess, would you really want to spend the rest of your life with someone like me?"

O'Mara glanced at her hands as she fidgeted with her nails. She sighed. "No, Simon" she said at last. "Not someone like you. Just… you."

For a long moment Dower stared at Jess as his brain tried to comprehend the words she had just said. A smile began twitching at the edge of his mouth. "Wait, did you just say you would like to be with me the rest of your life?"

"Yes, Simon."

"Wait," Simon said suddenly and plunged a hand in his pocket. He looked up, joy suddenly filling his eyes. "We need to do this properly."

Dower pulled his hand from his pocket and dropped to one knee. He fiddled with something in his hand before turning back to O'Mara and raising a diamond studded gold ring towards her.

"Jessica O'Mara, will you marry me?"

O'Mara gasped and brought her hands to her mouth. She stared at the ring then glanced to Cheong's body. "Did you have to do this right next to a corpse?"

Dower shrugged. "I went with the moment. What do you say, Jess? Will you marry me?"

She pulled her hands from her face and offered her left hand forward. "Yes, Simon. Yes, I will."

Dower slid the ring on her finger and stood up to kiss her deeply. When they finished, he felt like laughing as he stared deeply into her eyes.

"Don't you think you had better call Sanders from his hiding spot in the trees now?" O'Mara asked.

"Sanders isn't here."

"Are you serious?" she said. Her eyes widened. "You came to rescue me on your own?"

He nodded.

"My God, you are just full of surprises today. So, tell me then, where is Sanders? He did make it too, right?"

"Yes, he did. We split up a while back. He went to catch the Horse Serpent."

"On his own?"

"Yes."

Just then a huge roar echoed across the island. A group of birds took to the air in a flutter of wings and beat their way out to sea. Dower and O'Mara turned to the trees fearfully.

"I hope he's okay," O'Mara said.

***

Sanders screwed his eyes shut and waited for the killing blow. He did not feel sadness or regret in the moment. A ranger like him, who surrounded his life with dangerous animals all the time, knows there is always a risk. Animals can be habitual and predictable, but even with the greatest of planning and diligence, when you are dealing with dangerous animals you are always taking your life into your hands.

He had taken his life into his hands the day he leapt from his boat to rescue Ravager. The water around was murky. There was no way of knowing whether or not there was a crocodile in the dark water around him. But damn he loved that dog, and there was no way he was leaving Ravager to be croc food.

He had risked Higson's life that day too. Even if Higson had been able to work the boat, they were so deep into Kakadu looking for bunyips he could have travelled for weeks and not found a way out. Would it have made a difference to Sanders' decision if he had known Higson was a mining billionaire? Probably not. Sanders was never one to value possessions too highly. Certainly not more than a loyal and loving dog like Ravager.

Animals were amazing creatures. Take Ravager as an example. He had never met a person in his life that gave the same level of love and loyalty but expected nothing but food and a good scratch behind the ears in return. With men, you could not even buy loyalty.

Cheong had proven that. Higson could have given him anything. Cheong had a job and, judging from the clothing and accessories he wore, he was paid plenty for it. But did that buy Cheong's loyalty? No, not in the slightest. At the first opportunity, Cheong tried to steal from him. You never got that sort of betrayal from animals. They behaved as they should. Predictable, and defined by natural instincts. Just like the Horse Serpent, who was just about to kill him. He felt no qualm with the Horse Serpent for killing him. It was only following its natural instincts.

Sanders stirred. Seconds had passed since he had screwed his eyes shut. Was he dead already? He had not felt a thing.

Slowly Sanders opened his eyes. The Horse Serpent still lay its great paw on his chest and stood over him. It peered down at him with one great yellow eye. Its mouth was closed and it was watching him closely. Sanders looked at the paw on his chest, which now felt more like it was resting and less like pressing, before looking back up into the great eye.

"What's going on?" Sanders asked.

The Horse Serpent roared. It was an enormous roar that sent birds flapping and monkeys screeching through the forest. Sanders' ear drums pounded under the assault and he felt the sound thunder through him and shake his blood. And then it stopped.

The Horse Serpent lifted its foot off his chest and strolled back to the discarded body of the bearded man. Sanders put his hand where the Horse Serpent's paw had been and slowly sat up. He reached forward and rubbed his ankles. They were sore, but not badly damaged. He rubbed them ponderously. He had seen the Horse Serpent snap a man's neck in the forest with a whip of its tail yet here was Sanders, slapped across the ankles, with only a case of mild bruising?

Sanders hauled himself to his feet and turned. The Horse Serpent was watching him.

"Okay, I got your message. You're warning me off. Fine. I'll leave you be."

Sanders turned and walked gingerly away from the nest. His ankles were sore and the bite on his leg began to ache again. His heart hammered at his chest as he pushed through the thick scrub. He could barely believe the beast was letting him go free. He heard a monkey squeak from a tree above and glanced up at it. The Horse Serpent could not stay here. That much was true. There was no sustainable food supply here. It would devour this small colony of monkeys in no time. And then what? It would be a shame to leave the Horse Serpent here to die a slow, starving death. He would have to come back for it, but better prepared next time.

The noise of a branch snapping close behind drew Sanders' attention sharply. He turned to see the Horse Serpent standing right behind him. It stopped just as he did, and looked at him as though it was waiting. Sanders glanced up at the face, trying to glean meaning, before turning and resuming walking. This time Sanders paid attention to the sounds behind him and sure enough, just as he had thought, the Horse Serpent was following him.

Ahead, Sanders saw the bright sunshine of the edge of the tress and beyond it, the endless stretch of blue sea. He pushed forwards towards the beach, finding the presence of tress all around and the following Horse Serpent suddenly suffocating.

He stepped out onto the beach and shielded his eyes from the glare when a voice caught his attention.

"Sanders? Oh my God, Sanders?"

He turned to see two shapes running towards him along the beach. He squinted to get a better look at them as they closed the distance.

"Dower? O'Mara? Holy shit, Dower, you did it," Sanders exclaimed and stepped forwards to greet them. Just then the swish of leaves and the crack of a branch snapping came from behind Sanders as the Horse Serpent emerged from the trees.

Dower thrust his arm out and stood in front of O'Mara protectively. The Horse Serpent stopped and turned its head to look at them.

"You don't need to do that, Simon," O'Mara said.

"I do, O'Mara. I need to protect you. I'm not running away from the fact ever again."

"I appreciate the sudden turn of bravery, Simon, but you don't need to protect me from Sanders or the Horse Serpent."

"What do you mean?"

She pushed his arm down and stepped forwards towards the Horse Serpent. She raised her open hands outwards towards it to show she meant no harm.

"It's weird, but since the Horse Serpent was freed, I've felt like… like it's been protecting me."

Dower looked at the closing distance between O'Mara and the Horse Serpent. His mouth twisted in worry. "Are you sure about this, Jess?"

She stopped, turned and nodded. Dower held his breath as he watched her walk within range of the beast's long neck and sharp teeth. It watched her curiously as she approached with her hands stretched forward. Dower held his breath as she stepped up right next to it and laid her hand on its flank and ran her hand along its great, scaly body.

The Horse Serpent turned away and looked down the beach.

Sanders watched in wonder and turned to the gaping Dower. "Just how intelligent did you predict this beast might be?"

Dower turned his eyes slowly to Sanders. "As smart as any other reptile out there. But without proper tests, who can say?"

"I can say. She's very intelligent. Perhaps even mildly tamed."

"Why would you say that?"

"Back in the trees she got past my traps. She learned from the last time I caught her and worked her way around it. That's fast learning. Second, she has the ability for self-control and restraint. She could have killed me with ease back there, but she chose not to. She just wanted to show me she could beat me after I caught her the first time. And thirdly, she seems to have an ability to recognise friend from foe. I was thinking as I was walking here and she was following about just how close she lived to that village. Tell me, how could people live so closely to a savage killer? They couldn't. Not unless there was a mutual understanding between the two. But look now. It killed men yet it's not the least bit concerned by us."

"He's right, Simon. I saw the Horse Serpent eat human flesh yet it doesn't look at all of us as meat. It might be she only ate men because there was nothing else. She truly is a unique creature."

Simon glanced from O'Mara to Sanders and back before glancing up at the Horse Serpent looking serenely about it. "I might have to adjust my report for Higson," he muttered.

Just then he turned, becoming aware of a distant sound. A small speck appeared in the sky and slowly grew larger. The whirring sound grew steadily louder as the helicopter closed with dramatic speed and thundered over them as it passed.

"What was that?" Dower asked.

"I don't know, but I think we had better go find out."

As they walked, Dower explained what had happened earlier. Sanders gave Dower a hearty slap on the back at the news of the engagement before giving O'Mara a far gentler kiss on the cheek. He seemed genuinely happy for them and could not resist giving Dower an 'I told you so' look as they walked. But as Dower shared the news of Cheong's death, Sanders' mood turned.

"I'm sorry to hear that," he said sombrely. He looked down at his feet as he walked. "Poor Mr Cheong, he didn't deserve to go like that."

Dower frowned and turned to Sanders. "You just called him Mr Cheong instead of Kenny."

Sanders nodded. "Yeah, I did. After hearing his story and knowing what he has been through, he deserves that respect."

The helicopter had landed on a large patch of sand not far from where the *Kekal* had beached on the island. Its blades rotated slowly as the crew of the *Kekal* gathered around it, chattering and gesturing wildly. Amongst the group was Captain Arwadi, who seemed to be shouting the loudest and calling for order amongst the group.

As Sanders, Dower and O'Mara approached with the Horse Serpent in tow, the men from the ship slowly began to turn and quieten. Some began to melt away back to the safety of the ship as they approached, and soon the man from the centre of the group pushed his way forward to meet the newcomers. The man was none other than Conrad Higson himself.

Higson stepped forwards to greet them before his eyes turned to the Horse Serpent. Instead of fearing it, Higson stepped forward in wonderment.

"Connie," Sanders called and jogged forward to clasp Higson's hand. Higson took his hand and smiled warmly.

"Matt, so good to see you." He turned to view O'Mara and Dower. "So good to see all of you alive and well. When Sianturi radioed me with the news, I was dreadfully worried for you all. And where is Kenny? I have some words for him."

"Mr Cheong's dead," Sanders said plainly.

Higson bit his lip and nodded. "That's a shame. I've never had someone as resourceful and efficient as him work for me before. It's just so sad he could never get away from his demons."

Arwadi, who had been within earshot and heard what had been said, reddened and turned away guiltily.

Higson released his grasp on Sanders' hand and turned to get a better view of the Horse Serpent.

"It's magnificent. Even more amazing than I could have imagined. Tell me though, is it safe for us for it to be free like that?"

"Yes, unless it feels threatened of course."

Higson stared at the beast in wonderment and shook his head. "Remarkable. Simply remarkable. I have help coming. Another container ship and some tugboats. We will set Captain Arwadi's boat to rights and take it back to Jakarta for repairs. In the meantime, do you think you can get the Horse Serpent back into a cage and onto my ship?"

Sanders sighed and looked away.

"Listen, Connie, about that. The Horse Serpent is a remarkable creature. More remarkable than you can imagine. I've been thinking about this a lot and... I don't think it's right to take it from its natural environment."

"What are you saying, Matt?"

"I think we should take it back to where it belongs. Back to the Sipatahunan Cave."

"No," said Higson, "that's not what you are saying at all. You are saying you don't trust me."

"Excuse me?"

"That's right. You don't trust me to take this creature and treat it right. Sanders, I promise you that I have all the right intentions for taking this creature out of Indonesia. I want to take it back to Australia and provide a safe and welcome habitat for it to be studied in. You said it yourself, this is a remarkable creature and one that shouldn't be hidden from the world."

Sanders wavered, and looked back to Dower and O'Mara. O'Mara stepped forwards.

"If you don't mind me cutting in here," she said as she approached. "We have been through a lot here, and somehow the Horse Serpent has come to a position where it trusts us. We have a responsibility to ensure that the right thing is done by it."

Higson smiled. "Of course, that's why I offered you all jobs at my zoo."

"Jobs?"

"Yes. Didn't Cheong tell you about the jobs?"

"No, he never mentioned it. A bit like the pirates, I suppose..."

"I have roles for each of you at the zoo. I didn't just send you out to catch an animal, I sent you out to learn and help me with the animal. I always intended to have each of you to look after the animal beyond its capture. I would not have it any other way. Now tell me, can I have your trust that you will be in charge of the Horse Serpent, its habitat, health and diet in my zoo?"

Sanders and O'Mara shared a glance and nodded.

"Deal," they said in unison.

EPILOGUE

Slow music played as lights skipped across the floor, highlighting the small number of couples as they danced in unison to the sappy old love song. There was a murmur about the room as people who were not dancing clustered in groups sharing stories and laughs. It was a warm night, and spirits in the room were high.

Amidst this joyous company, Sanders stood alone by the bar with one half emptied glass of beer in his hand as he shuffled through the white cards before him. His hands shook and he had a sweaty sheen on his forehead.

"You look nervous," a voice said.

"I am," Sanders replied without looking up. "I've never made a best man's speech before and I hate public speaking."

"Are you telling me that the one man who survived a shark attack, climbed over the back of a speeding truck while being shot at and who singlehandedly captured the Horse Serpent is afraid of standing up and talking in front of people?"

Sanders looked up from his cards to see a warmly smiling Higson.

"Connie, mate, those things are nothing. I'd take swimming with sharks over speaking in public any day of the week. I can't stand it. All those eyes looking at me like that. It's just… scary."

Higson smiled and turned to the dancefloor. "It was a lovely ceremony, was it not?"

"It was," Sanders agreed. "Both Simon and Jess looked amazing."

"Indeed, they did."

The conversation slipped to a lull and Sanders turned from Higson and again began glancing over the cards in front of him and mouthing the words on them.

"I see you are busy, perhaps after your speech we could catch up for a quick chat?"

Sanders looked up with apology in his eyes. "Look, if this is about Ravager running around in the Horse Serpent's enclosure, I'm sorry about that. I didn't realise the zoo had opened and they were just playing. I didn't have the heart to separate them and you have to admit, the visitors did get quite a show."

"No," Higson chuckled, "it's not that. Although I'd rather it didn't happen too often or people will start showing up and demanding for the Horse Serpent and dog show. I actually wanted to talk to you about…

well… a zoo with one animal isn't that much of an attraction, if you catch my drift."

Sanders stared at Higson a moment before Higson smiled and excused himself. Sanders watched him go before turning back to the cards in front of him. He had trouble focusing on the words in front of him with the quote from Higson ringing in his head.

The music stopped and the dancers resumed their seats. Sanders looked up, realising it was his cue to return to his seat. He forcibly pushed what Higson said out of his mind as he shuffled the cards back into the correct order. He knew what Higson meant. Higson wanted to capture another cryptid. Possibly another dangerous one. Well Sanders could not afford to think of that now. He had something far more frightening to deal with.

He had to deliver a public speech.

THE END

CHECK OUT OTHER GREAT DEEP SEA THRILLERS

THE BREACH
by Edward J. McFadden III

A Category 4 hurricane punched a quarter mile hole in Fire Island, exposing the Great South Bay to the ferocity of the Atlantic Ocean, and the current pulled something terrible through the new breach. A monstrosity of the past mixed with the present has been disturbed and it's found its way into the sheltered waters of Long Island's southern sea.

Nate Tanner lives in Stones Throw, Long Island. A disgraced SCPD detective lieutenant put out to pasture in the marine division because of his Navy background and experience with aquatic crime scenes, Tanner is assigned to hunt the creeper in the bay. But he and his team soon discover they're the ones being hunted.

INFESTATION
by William Meikle

It was supposed to be a simple mission. A suspected Russian spy boat is in trouble in Canadian waters. Investigate and report are the orders.

But when Captain John Banks and his squad arrive, it is to find an empty vessel, and a scene of bloody mayhem.

Soon they are in a fight for their lives, for there are things in the icy seas off Baffin Island, scuttling, hungry things with a taste for human flesh.

They are swarming. And they are growing.

"Scotland's best Horror writer" - Ginger Nuts of Horror

"The premier storyteller of our time." - Famous Monsters of Filmland

CHECK OUT OTHER GREAT DEEP SEA THRILLERS

SHARK: INFESTED WATERS
by P.K. Hawkins

For Simon, the trip was supposed to be a once in a lifetime gift: a journey to the Amazon River Basin, the land that he had dreamed about visiting since he was a child. His enthusiasm for the trip may be tempered by the poor conditions of the boat and their captain leading the tour, but most of the tourists think they can look the other way on it. Except things go wrong quickly. After a horrific accident, Simon and the other tourists find themselves trapped on a tiny island in the middle of the river. It's the rainy season, and the river is rising. The island is surrounded by hungry bull sharks that won't let them swim away. And worst of all, the sharks might not be the only blood-thirsty killers among them. It was supposed to be the trip of a lifetime. Instead, they'll be lucky if they make it out with their lives at all.

DARK WATERS
by Lucas Pederson

Jörmungandr is an ancient Norse sea monster. Thought to be purely a myth until a battleship is torn a part by one.

With his brother on that ship, former Navy Seal and deep-sea diver, Miles Raine, sets out on a personal vendetta against the creature and hopefully save his brother. Bringing with him his old Seal team, the Dagger Points, they embark on a mission that might very well be their last.

But what happens when the hunters become the hunted and the dark waters reveal more than a monster?

CHECK OUT OTHER GREAT DEEP SEA THRILLERS

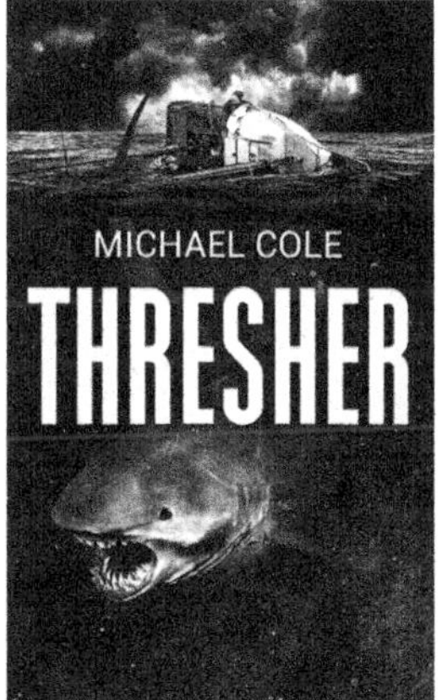

THRESHER
by Michael Cole

In the aftermath of a hurricane, a series of strange events plague the coastal waters off Florida. People go into the water and never return. Corpses of killer whales drift ashore, ravaged from enormous bite marks. A fishing trawler is found adrift, with a mysterious gash in its hull.

Transferred to the coastal town of Merit, police officer Leonard Riker uncovers the horrible reality of an enormous Thresher shark lurking off the coast. Forty feet in length, it has taken a territorial claim to the waters near the town harbor. Armed with three-inch teeth, a scythe-like caudal fin, and unmatched aggression, the beast seeks to kill anything sharing the waters.

THE GUILLOTINE
by Lucas Pederson

1,000 feet under the surface, Prehistoric Anthropologist, Ash Barrington, and his team are in the midst of a great archeological dig at the bottom of Lake Superior where they find a treasure trove of bones. Bones of dinosaurs that aren't supposed to be in this particular region. In their underwater facility, Infinity Moon, Ash and his team soon discover a series of underground tunnels. Upon exploring, they accidentally open an ice pocket, thawing the prehistoric creature trapped inside. Soon they are being attacked, the facility falling apart around them, by what Ash knows is a dunkleosteus and all those bones were from its prey. Now...Ash and his team are the prey and the creature will stop at nothing to get to them.

Made in the USA
Middletown, DE
01 July 2022

68226025R00129